BOOK TWO OF
THE DARKWOLF SAGA

THE
IRON
CITADEL

MITCH REINHARDT

THE IRON CITADEL

DEDICATIONS

For Mom

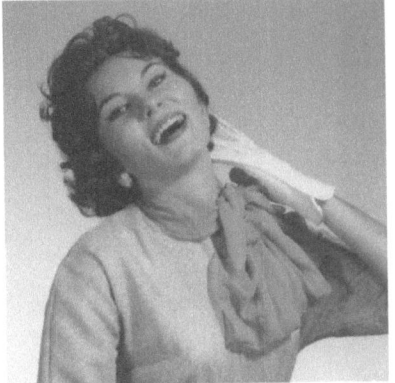

Thanks for everything. Especially the cheese toasties.

In loving memory of Murphy

My best friend and loyal companion who gave so much
unconditional love each day.

Acknowledgements

Developmental Editor – Charlotte Rains-Dixon
Copy Editor – Valerie Williamson
Supplemental Editor – Alison Owens
Cover Design – James Egan at Bookfly Design
Interior Design – Jason Anderson at Polgarus Studio
Beta Readers – Sue Call, Stacey Call, and Alison Owens
Proofreader – Danny Hay

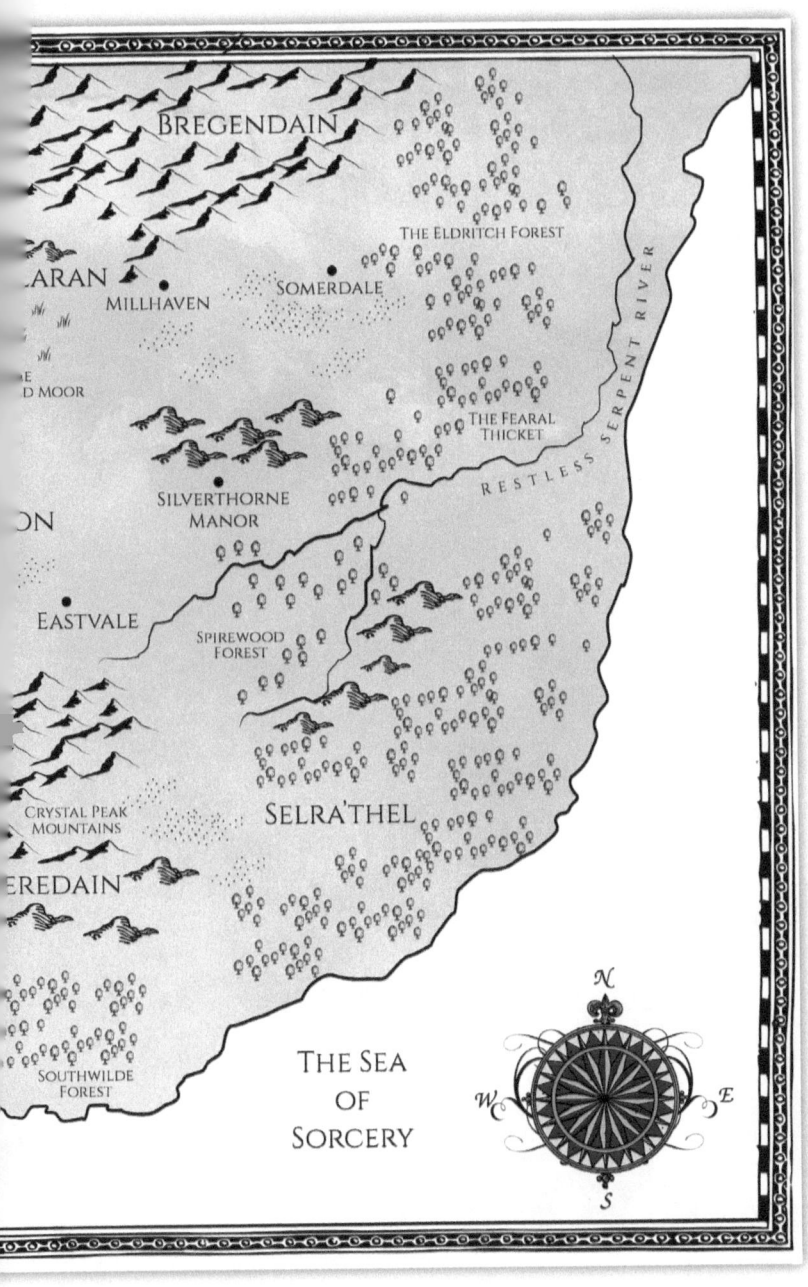

BREGENDAIN

...ARAN

MILLHAVEN

SOMERDALE

THE ELDRITCH FOREST

...E
...D MOOR

THE FEARAL
THICKET

RESTLESS SERPENT RIVER

...ON

SILVERTHORNE
MANOR

EASTVALE

SPIREWOOD
FOREST

CRYSTAL PEAK
MOUNTAINS

SELRA'THEL

...EREDAIN

SOUTHWILDE
FOREST

THE SEA
OF
SORCERY

N

W   E

S

CHAPTER ONE
AN UNINVITED GUEST

Geoffrey Vincent had spent the last two hours studying world history in his book-filled room on the first floor of the spacious house. Glancing at the digital clock that rested on his nightstand, he decided it was time for a break. He yawned as he closed the large book and slid it across his desk, then stood and stretched his slim arms out while he arched his back. Geez, his left arm still ached. Pushing up his sleeve, he felt the large purple and blue bruise that had formed on his bicep and winced in pain when he pressed it. Another present from Sawyer's bullies at school earlier that day.

It wasn't that long ago that he, Sawyer, and Jane had had the adventure of a lifetime. Geoff had hoped that the life and death experiences they shared in Alluria would have changed Sawyer and that he would leave Geoff alone, but no such luck. Geoff was only alone when he didn't want to be. Yes, home alone again. Nothing new there. Looking out the window, he saw it was dark already. The trees and bushes swayed as a stiff breeze blew through them.

Thump.

What was that? Did it come from upstairs? He remained silent for another minute, but heard nothing else. Must've been a tree limb hitting the roof. It certainly wouldn't be the first time a branch had fallen on the house when it was gusting outside, but it didn't happen often.

"Aw, man," he said, snapping his fingers. He'd forgotten he had to take out the trash and empty the dishwasher before he went to bed or his stepmother would be angry. She had never struck him, but the look in her eyes when she scolded him was enough. He'd been grounded and had his television privileges taken away, but Geoff was convinced he would've been beaten if she'd had her way.

Geoff decided that he'd better get a move on before she returned home. He shoved his history book into his backpack and took off down the hall to the kitchen. Hanging the pack on a chair, he opened the dishwasher and began grabbing dishes as fast as he could. Life had more or less returned to normal for Geoff. He was still picked on at school by Sawyer's friends, or 'posse', as Sawyer called them. He noticed on a few occasions, however, that Sawyer seemed to deliberately steer his tormentors away by calling their attention to something else—usually a good-looking girl walking by or an expensive sports car in the parking lot.

Jane, however, was different. She always smiled and said hi when she passed him in the halls. Every now and then she would even stop and ask him how he was and if he'd been staying out of trouble.

The trouble was a secret they shared. She meant if he'd kept an eye on the wizard's key, a white alabaster key that had transported them to Alluria. His father had stored it on his workbench, along with the rest of the contents of a box from the Carpathian Mountains. His father, a respected archeologist, seemed perplexed by the key, and said more research was needed.

Geoff also thought it was curious that his father never mentioned the large stone archway in the back of the study. On more than one occasion, Geoff considered asking him about the blackened, damaged archway, but he realized that by doing so his intrusions into his father's study would be revealed, too.

Geoff smiled as he sorted the silverware into the kitchen drawer. Their trip to Alluria had been the best adventure ever. Especially with Ishara. He really liked her. She had seemed to take him seriously and even like him a little.

Thump.

There it was again. Geoff stopped sorting the knives and forks and stood still. Did another tree limb hit the house? After listening for another moment, Geoff shook his head and finished with the silverware and dishes, then pulled the large black trash bag out of the kitchen trash bin. He tied the pull strings into a knot, opened the screen door to the back porch, and stepped outside.

Setting the trash bag down, Geoff looked up at the tiny points of light that sparkled in the night sky. He'd always liked stargazing; it made him feel less alone. He took a deep breath and slowly exhaled before picking up the trash bag and making his way to the garbage bin. The breeze tussled his blond hair as he walked.

Suddenly a light flashed behind him. Geoff stopped, looked around, and peered up at the sky again. What was that light? Did someone just take a picture, or was it lightning?

It wasn't lightning; there wasn't a cloud in the sky. He looked back toward their two-story Tudor house and shuddered. Something made his skin crawl. Geoff remained motionless for a couple of minutes, biting his lower lip and watching the house. Then he decided he was scaring himself and tossed the trash bag in the large plastic bin.

As soon as he turned back to his house he saw the flash of light again. It came from an upstairs window. His father's study. It reminded Geoff of a strobe light or an electrical short – or the archway that had drawn him, Sawyer, and Jane into Alluria. A surge of adrenaline ran through him, and without another thought, he dashed back to the house.

It had been two months since their unplanned adventure, but seeing that light again excited him. It had to be Ariel, who was now the high druid. She had helped them return home. She had an archway in her grove; it had to be her. Maybe Ishara was with her.

"Ariel!" he called as he ran into the house and up the steps to the second floor study. She'd never been here before, so she'd be confused by the strange surroundings, he thought, his heart racing. He reached behind the potted plant sitting on the table by the door and grabbed the small key to the study that his father had hidden.

"Hang on! I'm here!" Geoff yelled as he approached the study. But he skidded to a stop as the door shattered and fell away in front of him. Geoff gasped as the air left his lungs. Framed in the doorway, a black-cloaked figure in rotting black leather armor and a ragged black farmer's hat raised its head, revealing a grinning, skeletal face. The stench surrounding the intruder made Geoff gag as he stood, unable to move.

A dull green fire glowed in its eye sockets, and it reeked of decay. From beneath its robe, the invader produced a pair of short swords as it stepped forward. Geoff screamed and ducked a swift swipe that would've decapitated him. His vision was blurred as he turned and ran downstairs, taking the steps two and three at a time as terror tangled his feet. Landing in a heap at the bottom of the stairs, the sound of approaching footsteps pounded in his ears. He ran into the kitchen and frantically looked for a place to hide.

Running out of time, he slid under the kitchen table and maneuvered his body against the wall. The intruder would have to bend over to see him. Geoff held his breath and cupped a hand over his mouth as the black leather boots came into view. He watched them as the attacker strode back and forth.

First, the intruder opened the door to the pantry, then it walked to the kitchen sink and opened the lower cabinets with a sword point. There were only so many places for his attacker to search. Geoff's mind raced. What was he going to do? He tracked the intruder's movement as the black boots walked to the kitchen table and stopped. Geoff's chest hurt, his heart was pounding and his lungs ached for air.

He heard the sound of whirling blades and then *thwack*, the blades penetrated the top of the kitchen table and missed him by a few inches. He stared cross-eyed at the point of the gray blade and shivered, then screamed when the table was tipped over as the swords were pulled loose. He scrambled to his feet and dashed toward the backdoor. A wild glance over his shoulder revealed that the skeletal figure was smashing and kicking the table aside. Nearly crashing through the backdoor, Geoff searched frantically for a place to hide outside.

He heard the door slam shut behind him. The next instant he heard a crash and the sound of glass breaking, followed by footsteps behind him again. The skeletal figure was in pursuit.

"Help! Help!" Geoff yelled.

He raced across a few of the twelve acres that made up his backyard, thinking desperately of where he could hide. He ran past the beige-colored toolshed and ducked behind it. Pressing his back against the wall of the shed, Geoff scanned the rest of the backyard. To his right was his mother's old greenhouse, which had several places for him to hide. Then, without warning, the skeletal figure suddenly appeared from around the corner of the shed, swinging a sword at Geoff's neck.

Geoff screamed and ducked as the blade just missed him and became embedded in the wooden wall of the shed. Running toward the greenhouse, he slid feet first into the door, hoping he might lose his attacker inside. He opened the door and quickly ducked under a low wooden bench that held a row of ferns. Their stalks had grown all the way to the floor, and the large fronds provided excellent cover.

For weeks after they had returned from Alluria, Jane had come to the greenhouse and practiced her plant growth spell. Geoff hoped the jumble of flora Jane had produced would shield him now.

Pulling himself into a tight curl in the darkness, he took a deep breath. A dusty, earthy smell filled his nostrils, and he tried to calm himself so his breathing wouldn't give his position away. There was a scraping sound as the intruder crossed the threshold. Geoff's eyes adjusted to the darkness just enough so that he could see movement as the boots slowly moved past.

He listened as the invader walked around the greenhouse, stopping once in a while to search an area. Geoff stiffened, and his thoughts whirled. Could he sneak out? Was the thing far enough away? Should he try to escape, maybe sneak out while the intruder searched the far side of the greenhouse? Trembling, Geoff was about to slide out from under the ferns when he heard footsteps again.

The black boots appeared, moving past him toward the open door. Then they stopped close by. Too close. A feeling of dread came over Geoff and he shivered. Behind him, he heard a soft rustling of the fronds. He was about to glance in that direction when a hand clasped his ankle and squeezed. Geoff screamed as he was roughly pulled out from beneath the ferns, scraping his knees and elbows on the concrete floor. He was flipped over before he could cry out again. A gloved hand grabbed him by the throat and lifted him off the floor.

Geoff found himself staring into the dull green fires that burned in the skeleton's eye sockets. His feet dangled in midair, and he felt the hand around his neck tighten its grip. As he struggled to breathe and pull himself loose, he could feel his eyes bulge and throb. He tried to call for help, but only made a gurgling sound. The skeletal figure raised a sword with its other hand as Geoff desperately kicked and punched.

Choking, he clawed at his attacker's wrist while darkness crept into the corners of his vision. Then Geoff heard a whipping sound as something lashed itself around the figure's sword hand. As it turned to look, Geoff saw several fern fronds wrap themselves around its neck. Without warning, it dropped Geoff, and he landed hard on his backside. Another fern lashed out with its fronds and wrapped itself around Geoff's attacker, then another and another until he could barely see the dull green glow of its eyes under the entangling foliage.

The entwined figure stood between him and the door, which was the only way out. Geoff scrambled away, his fingers fumbling through the dirt, searching for something—anything—to break the glass walls. Before he was able to find something, though, his attacker sliced and slashed through the entangling ferns. Instead of attacking Geoff, however, it spun around and faced the door. Someone or something had attacked it with blinding speed.

In the dark, all Geoff saw was a flurry of movement as the two combatants whirled and slashed at one another. The clang of blades striking rang out as sparks briefly flew about the greenhouse. The figure in black suddenly staggered backward after receiving several blows in rapid succession. Geoff watched in horror as the skeletal monster was impaled by two curved blades. Without a sound, it sank to its knees and burst into green flames, leaving nothing but ashes.

Geoff gasped and blinked several times. What just happened? As he tried to process what he had witnessed, he heard a familiar voice coming from the silhouette in the doorway.

"Geoff? Are you unharmed?"

He blinked again. He tried to answer, but couldn't. Trembling, he leaned against the wall.

"Geoff?"

The figure stepped forward, sheathed her weapons, and pulled something from a pouch.

"*Iluminara*," she said, and a green glow flooded the area

around Geoff. Through the brightness, he saw a beautiful woman with pointed ears holding a gem in the palm of her hand. He recognized the gem. It was a mage stone. As he stared at it, the elf's sparkling emerald green eyes caught his attention.

"Ariel!" Geoff shouted, flinging his arms around her and squeezing. Her arms then wrapped around him and she laughed. To him, her laughter sounded like that of an angel.

"It is good to see you again," Ariel said.

Geoff released her. "I'd be dead now if you hadn't saved me. Thank you," he said as he hugged her again.

"You are quite welcome," Ariel said. There was something different about her voice, Geoff thought as he maintained his hug. He couldn't say exactly what it was, but she sounded sad or troubled.

"Ariel?" he said with a slight tremor in his voice.

"Yes?"

"What was that thing and why did it try to kill me?"

Ariel sighed and released him. He stepped back. Now that he was closer to her, he could see her attractive features had taken on a slightly gaunt appearance and her eyes had become a bit sunken. She looked exhausted.

"Ariel, what's wrong?"

Geoff watched as the smile faded from her face.

"Ariel?"

"Geoff, you and your friends are not safe here any longer. I am sorry. I wish it were not so because you deserve to live your lives in peace."

"But why are you here? How did you get here? I don't understand." Geoff's mind raced. Never in a million years would he have guessed that Ariel would show up at his house.

"The skeletal assassin that attacked you was summoned by the Shadowlord," Ariel said in a quiet tone. "It was an undead creature whose sole purpose was to kill you, Sawyer, and Jane."

Geoff blinked a few times as he thought about what he had just heard.

"But…why? It doesn't make sense," he said. "We're back home now. There's no reason to—"

"I believe there is reason for the Shadowlord to want your deaths," Ariel interrupted. "At least he believes there is reason, and that places the three of you in danger."

Geoff frowned and shook his head.

"This can't be," he said. "Why is the Shadowlord trying to kill us? We haven't done anything to him."

Ariel placed a hand on Geoff's shoulder.

"It's what you *may* do that concerns him. Word has reached him of your abilities, as well as those of Sawyer and Jane. I believe he sees you and your friends as a threat, no matter where you are."

Suddenly a terrible thought occurred to Geoff and he grabbed Ariel's arm.

"Ishara, is she—"

"She is fine," Ariel said. "She sends her warmest greetings and she wants you to know she misses you."

Geoff exhaled loudly.

"I miss her, too."

"She is very brave, Geoff. She has fought like a lioness against our enemies. You would be proud of her."

Geoff nodded and smiled. "She never misses, does she?" he asked.

Ariel shook her head. "Never with a bow and arrow. Only with her heart."

Geoff blushed. Seeing Ariel again made him miss Ishara more than ever.

"Oh!" Geoff said with a sudden jolt. "Sawyer and Jane! We have to warn them! What if they're being attacked right now? I gotta call them."

Geoff tried to push past Ariel and exit the greenhouse when she stopped him.

"Wait," she said. "The skeletal assassin that tried to kill you was the only one to make it through the portal into your world. The other two have already been destroyed."

Geoff breathed another sigh of relief.

"Thanks again for saving me," Geoff said. "I'm sure Sawyer and Jane would like to see you again. Come inside and I'll call them."

"Yes," said Ariel with a solemn tone. "Please bring them here as quickly as you can."

Chapter Two
Decisions

Back inside the house, Geoff wasted no time in grabbing his cell phone and calling Jane. As he listened to it ring, he watched Ariel wander about examining various appliances. She found the fruit bowl on the counter and held up a shiny red apple. Geoff motioned for her to help herself.

"Thank you," Ariel said as she took two large bites. She looked thin, Geoff thought as she devoured the apple and reached for another. How long had it been since her last meal?

"Take whatever you want," Geoff said. He was about to say there was more food in the pantry when Jane answered.

"Hello?" she said.

"Jane, it's Geoff. Can you come over now? Something's happened."

There was a pause before Jane replied. "What happened, Geoff?"

"It's Ariel. She's *here*. She wants to see you. Can you come over right now? And bring Sawyer with you."

There was another pause, this one longer than the first.

"Geoff, your voice sounds strange. What happened?"

"I'm not sure, Jane. I was attacked but—"

"Attacked?" Jane interrupted. "Who attacked you?"

"I don't know. It was some kind of skeletal assassin."

"Geoff," Jane said, sounding suspicious. "Did you take a nap and have a bad dream or something? There's no such thing."

"Yeah, there was a skeleton with swords," Geoff said. "And Ariel showed up just in time. She saved me. She wants to talk with all of us—you, me, and Sawyer."

Geoff waited, but there was no reply from Jane.

"Hello? Jane?"

"I'll call Sawyer. We'll be there as soon as we can."

Before Geoff could acknowledge her or say thanks she hung up.

"Well, they're on their way," Geoff said. "They should be here soon."

"Your home," Ariel said as she ran her fingers along the polished granite countertop, "is remarkable. I have never seen such finery."

Geoff watched Ariel marvel at the conveniences he had come to take for granted, such as hot and cold running water. She was thoroughly impressed with the pantry and refrigerator, too.

"Humans did all this?" she asked. "Such magic does not exist in Alluria."

"Yep, just us humans," said Geoff. "Like we said when we were in your world; we don't have werewolves or orcs or unicorns. But I guess you can call our brand of magic technology. And, as you know by now, we're kinda lost without it."

"And the device you used to...what did you say? *Call* Jane? Can you call others, too?"

"Oh, yes," Geoff said, looking at the phone. "So long as someone has the same type of device, I can call them no matter where they are in the world; distance doesn't matter."

"Amazing," Ariel said. "I have heard dwarves mention the word technology before, but they have no such devices."

Geoff smiled. He never thought he would ever have an opportunity to impress Ariel. He was going to enjoy demonstrating his creature comforts while they waited for Jane and Sawyer.

<hr />

Jane pulled her family's sedan into the circular driveway in front of Geoff's house. She looked over at Sawyer, who was sitting in silence beside her. He was brooding. It hadn't been easy getting him to agree to come, and he'd been quiet all the way to Geoff's house. Without a word, they got out of the car and rang the doorbell. Geoff opened the door and relief flooded his face.

"Hey, guys," he said. "I'm really glad you're here. Come in. Ariel's in the kitchen."

"Geoff," Jane said, "this better be for real. We want to know exactly what's going on."

"Seriously," Sawyer said, glaring at Geoff. "I *will* beat you down if this is a joke."

They walked down the long hall, their footsteps echoing throughout the house. When they entered the kitchen, there was Ariel standing among the splintered remains of Geoff's kitchen table.

"Ariel! Oh my! What happened?" Jane exclaimed as she rushed to give her a hug. "It's good to see you again! How are you? Are you okay?"

As they embraced, Jane noticed Ariel held her tightly.

"It is good to see you again, Jane," she said with a smile. "I am fine. I trust you are as well."

"Oh, yes," Jane said.

"Rough night, huh Geoff?" Sawyer said as he nudged a piece of the kitchen table with his foot. "Your dad's not gonna be happy when he sees this."

Jane stepped back and Ariel looked at Sawyer.

"Hello, Sawyer Stormlord. It is good to see you as well."

Sawyer winced at being called Stormlord, but he managed a smile and said, "Hi, Ariel. Good to see ya again."

"Ariel, why are you here?" Jane asked. "To be honest, I never thought we'd see you again. When Geoff called and said he'd been attacked and you saved him, I didn't believe it."

"It's true," Geoff said. "I was attacked by a skeleton dressed in black. Ariel showed up and killed it."

Jane straightened a chair and sat in it, surveying the damaged kitchen.

"So why would someone try to kill Geoff? We're home now," Jane said, brushing a dark brown lock of hair over her ear.

"I believe the skeletal assassins were sent by the Shadowlord," Ariel said, "to make sure none of you ever return to Alluria."

Sawyer's dimples showed as he frowned and leaned against the refrigerator, crossing his tan, muscular arms.

"Yeah," Geoff said. "We're in danger again. Seems that the Shadowlord is worried we might do something or get in his way."

"Wait," Jane said, shaking her head. "You said *assassins*. How many attacked Geoff?"

"Only one," said Geoff, nodding at Ariel.

"Three skeletal assassins had been summoned, one for

each of you," Ariel said. "I managed to dispatch two of them, but the third made it through the portal and came here to kill Geoff. If it had been successful, it would have hunted you and Sawyer as well."

"So they had a key, too?" Geoff asked.

"Yes," Ariel said, holding up a dull gray skeleton key. "I took this off one of the first two."

"How did they get a key?" Geoff asked with a frown. "I thought only wizards could use those keys."

"Other powerful spell casters can use them too," Ariel said. "Sorcerers and necromancers, for example."

"Okay," Jane said. "Let me get this straight, even though we're back home, and have *been* home for a while now, we're still in danger?"

"Yes," Ariel said. Then she looked at Geoff. "I do not know how they came by a wizard's key."

"But we didn't do anything!" Jane protested. "It was all an accident. All we wanted to do was get home; we didn't bother anyone."

"I am sorry," Ariel said, "but for some reason the Shadowlord has taken an interest in the three of you."

Sawyer ran his fingers through his thick brown hair and grunted.

"Oh," Geoff said. "How's it going with the war? Yeah, that's it, you're beating him and his army so badly all he can do is send assassins after us, right?"

Jane looked at Ariel, expecting to see her smile and agree with Geoff, but now she noticed her cheekbones were more pronounced and she looked like she had lost weight. Ariel wasn't smiling.

"No, we are losing the war."

There was a moment of silence in the kitchen. Jane couldn't believe what she had just heard. Ariel had been more than capable of overcoming any enemy they faced in Alluria. She couldn't lose. No way.

"I don't believe it," Jane said. "Ariel, you can fight and cast spells. You're awesome! What happened?"

"Yeah," Geoff said. "You're the best ever. You can whip the Shadowlord and I bet his army would disband and go away, wouldn't they?"

"I do not believe that is the case," Ariel said. "He is a formidable opponent and not so easily defeated."

"Okay," Jane said. "So how is he winning? I don't get it. You have all those other kingdoms, right? Dwarves and elves and what was that city you mentioned while we were in Alluria? Chalon? Don't they have a big army?"

"That's right," Geoff said. "And when I was a prisoner of those bandits, they mentioned a place called Cala...something."

"Caladar," Ariel said.

"Yeah, the bandits said the knights of Caladar had never lost a battle," Geoff said.

"We sent envoys to Caladar," Ariel said, "but none have returned and we have had no word. It is possible they will not involve themselves in this war."

"Well, that doesn't seem chivalrous," Jane said. "Maybe the messengers didn't get to them."

"Perhaps not," Ariel said. "We need help if we are to defeat the Shadowlord."

Jane thought for a moment. What could be done? Ariel's world was at war and the evil guys were winning. She glanced at Ariel. She looked sad, or perhaps she was worried about them.

"I am truly glad to see each of you and know that you are well," Ariel said. "What I must now ask of you is difficult. Each of you has unique gifts that can help us. Will you come back with me and save Alluria?"

Jane blinked. Ariel was asking for their help. She never thought that would happen.

"I'll go," Jane said. "We stick together, right? It's what friends do."

"Me too," Geoff said, rubbing his knuckles. His voice was a higher pitch than usual; he seemed excited about the opportunity to return to Alluria.

They looked at Sawyer. His silence during their entire conversation was telling, as was the frown on his face.

"Sawyer?" Jane prompted him.

Sawyer took a deep breath and rubbed his face up and down with both hands. He took a step forward, but didn't make eye contact with any of them.

"Sorry," he said. "I'm out. I can't go back there."

Jane and Geoff looked at each other in disbelief.

"Why not, Sawyer?" Jane demanded. "Ariel needs our help."

"Yeah, I heard," he said. "She wants us to go back and fight a war against the Shadowlord, who happens to be an unstoppable evil badass. No thanks."

"But Sawyer," Geoff said, "Ariel helped us get back home. It's the least we can do."

"I know what she did. I was there, remember? You two go back with her. Go save fantasy land. I'm not going."

"Sawyer, what's with you?" Jane asked. "Why are you acting like this?"

Sawyer turned his attention to Ariel. "Look, no

disrespect. I'm glad to see you again. I really am. And you did save us when we were lost in your world; I realize that. But I gave the sword back. You can go find another Stormlord. There has to be someone else who can use it and help win the war for you. I'm sorry, but I'm not the one. I'm not a hero."

Sawyer turned, and as he was about to walk out of the kitchen, Geoff chimed in.

"Sawyer, come on. We stick together, remem—"

"Shut up, you little nerd," Sawyer snapped as he flashed Geoff an angry look.

"Sawyer!" Jane shouted, standing up. Numerous curse words whirled about in her head, but before she could open her mouth and give Sawyer a piece of her mind, she felt Ariel touch her arm.

"I understand," Ariel said, addressing Sawyer. "It is your choice, and I will not try to sway you. But you must know that the Shadowlord will not stop trying to end your lives. I assure you he will send other more powerful assassins and I will not be here to protect you."

"That's okay," he said bitterly. "I know where my dad keeps his nine millimeter. No boogeyman is gonna get past that. I'm outta here. Good luck, guys."

"Sawyer!" Jane called as she heard Sawyer walk down the hall and open the front door. She ran after him, leaving Geoff and Ariel in the kitchen.

"Sawyer! Wait!" she yelled as she exited the house. Sawyer was already walking down the driveway when he finally stopped and turned around. Jane ran to him, and as she got closer he crossed his arms and clenched his jaw.

"Sawyer," she demanded. "What's wrong with you?"

He shook his head, "I'm not going back."

"Why not? What's the prob—"

"Jane! Are you listening?" His eyes flashed. "Not just no, but *hell* no!"

He turned to walk away again, but Jane grabbed his arm.

"Sawyer, talk to me. Ariel needs our help."

Sawyer pulled his arm away from Jane and sighed. He looked at her and then the ground.

"Jane, when we were running around lost in the forest, you kept saying how much you wanted to get home. You said it wasn't our fight and we didn't belong there. You were right. We don't belong there. That place isn't for us. We're home now and there aren't any orcs trying to bash our heads in or werewolves hunting us. We're back. We're home. And you want to risk your life? For what?"

Jane pulled her lips tight and considered every word Sawyer had said. He had a good point, she thought. It was nuts to go back; they had barely escaped with their lives on numerous occasions.

"Yeah, I know," Jane said. "We don't belong there. But Sawyer, if they can send assassins here to kill us, what choice do we have? You've seen the monsters in Ariel's world. Do you really think your dad's gun will stop them?"

Jane looked into Sawyer's brown eyes.

"If Ariel needs our help," Jane said, "shouldn't we at least try?"

"It's just…" Sawyer let his arms drop as he kicked a loose stone from the driveway into the grass. "I'm afraid," he said quietly, as though he might be overheard. "Jane, I'm afraid. I'm not used to that. Alluria is wild, dangerous, full of monsters, and not for us."

Jane grabbed his hand.

"I'm afraid too," she said. "I think we owe it to Ariel to try. Don't worry. I'll protect you."

"Yeah?" Sawyer said with a grin. "Who's gonna protect you?"

"I don't need protecting," Jane said with a smirk.

"Yeah?" Sawyer sighed and nodded.

"Okay," he said. "We do owe Ariel."

They walked back to Geoff's house, still holding hands.

"Oh," Jane said in a terse tone, "and you owe Geoff an apology."

Sawyer looked at her.

"For what?"

"For being an ass," Jane said. "And for being a bully at school, too."

"Aww, c'mon," he said. "Everyone does it. Why do I have to apologize?"

Jane dropped Sawyer's hand.

"Because I want you to," she said. "And because it's the right thing to do."

Sawyer contemplated what she had said for a moment and sighed again. "Yeah, okay."

They went inside and joined Geoff and Ariel.

"All right," Sawyer said, throwing up his hands. "I'm in. Let's do this thing. When do we start?"

"After you tell Geoff you're sorry," Jane said.

"Oh yeah. Sorry for what I said earlier, Geoff. And sorry for, you know, all the stuff at school."

Sawyer gave Geoff a fist bump.

"We're cool now, right?"

"Yeah, I guess so," Geoff said.

"Thank you. Each of you," Ariel said. "The sight of the Stormblade in your hands, Sawyer, will give us all hope. And to answer your question, we start now."

Chapter Three
Return to Alluria

Geoff scratched his head. Something had just occurred to him.

"Hey, Ariel, you came through the portal upstairs, right?"

"Yes," she said. "When I arrived, I heard your calls for help and hurried to you as fast as I could. I am glad I was not too late."

"Yeah, me too," Geoff said. "But one thing bothers me. If only wizards, sorcerers, and necromancers can use the key and the portal, how did you get here?"

Ariel smiled. "Being the high druid has some advantages. While I cannot use a wizard's key, I can cast the spell of travel and activate the portal in the Eldritch Forest."

"Really?" Jane asked, amazed.

"That's so cool," Geoff said. "So we don't need the key this time?"

"I believe it is best if you bring it with you," Ariel said. "If we become separated, you will still have a way home."

"Okay, good thinking," Geoff said.

"Take as much food as you can carry," Ariel said. "We will have to travel a long way."

"I forgot about those long hikes through the woods," Sawyer said. "Good thing I have sneakers on."

"Same here," Jane said, lifting her tennis shoe-clad foot. "What else should we take?"

"Geoff, can I borrow a suit of armor?" Sawyer asked as he eyed one of the four suits in the foyer.

"Those won't fit you," Geoff said. "You have to be measured for a suit of armor."

"Perhaps we will find something you can wear in Alluria," Ariel said.

"I'm not wearing another corset again," Jane said defiantly. "That was horrible. I could barely breathe."

"Yeah, and you looked funny, too," Geoff said. He stepped into the pantry to scrounge for more food. He turned back around and saw Jane had narrowed her eyes and was glaring at him. Geoff wrinkled his nose at her.

"Have you been visited by others from Alluria?" Ariel asked.

Everyone stopped and looked at her. Ariel was standing in the middle of the kitchen gazing toward the ceiling.

"Um…no," Geoff said as he followed Ariel's stare. "Why do you ask?"

Ariel walked into the hallway and stopped at the bottom of the stairs. Geoff followed her, as did Sawyer and Jane.

"Ariel," Geoff said quietly. "What is it? Is it another assassin?"

Ariel shook her head. "I am not sure."

"Okay. That's it," Sawyer said as he ducked into the living room and grabbed a sword off the wall. "I'm not getting assassinated without a fight."

"Ariel?" Jane said with a slight quiver in her voice.

They stood at the bottom of the stairs and looked at the remnants of the door to the upstairs study. Some of it remained on the frame, but most of the door had been splintered.

"Geoff, your dad is gonna kill you," Sawyer said, looking at the wreckage.

After a moment Ariel shook her head.

"It is gone. For a moment I sensed—"

"What?" Jane asked. "What did you sense?"

"Something ancient and sinister has been here," Ariel said. "Perhaps I sensed the assassin's presence earlier. It is gone now. Come. Gather what you need. We must leave."

"Are you sure that's what you felt?" Geoff asked. His heart had started to beat faster. Ariel looked at him for a few seconds.

"No," she said.

"Great," Jane said. "Now Geoff's house is haunted."

Geoff swallowed. He tried to think if anything strange had occurred recently. Had he heard a noise in the night or perhaps caught a glimpse of some unknown shape or movement? No, not until the skeletal assassin attacked him.

"I haven't noticed anything out of the ordinary," he said. "What else could it be?"

"I do not know," Ariel said. Geoff thought the expression on her face indicated she had other suspicions, but he decided not to question her further. He wasn't sure he'd like Ariel's answers; that is, if she answered him at all. They collected supplies for another twenty minutes before Ariel spoke.

"Very well," she said. "What you have will be fine."

"Okay," Sawyer said. "Here, Geoff. This is yours."

He tossed a small sack of fruits and vegetables to Geoff and followed Ariel toward the steps. Jane was a few steps behind him.

"Hey, Ariel," Jane said excitedly, "will you teach me some new spells?"

"Oh," Sawyer said, "and teach me more sword fighting stuff?"

Sawyer had changed his mind fast. Geoff wasn't sure why he was so gung-ho all of a sudden.

"Of course," Ariel said. "Though I hope you will not have much need for what I teach you."

"What do we do if we run into the Shadowlord?" Geoff asked.

"We run," Ariel said.

"But we chased that werewolf off," Geoff said in protest.

"Yeah, we did," Sawyer said, raising a fist in the air.

Ariel turned and faced them. She shook her head.

"What you did before was outstanding," she began, "but know this; that werewolf was a terrifying foe, and had you not been trapped in the town barracks, you should have run."

"But we won," Jane said. "It limped off."

"Yes, you did prevail and it was an impressive victory," Ariel said. "But I think perhaps luck played a role as well. I want each of you to promise me that if you should encounter that werewolf again, you will flee as fast as you can. Your lives may depend on that. Do not be foolish enough to stand and face either the werewolf or the Shadowlord. Just run."

"But we did really well," Geoff said. "You should've seen us."

"I know. Ishara told me more of your battle after you left.

Truly, you were amazing," Ariel said with a slight smile. "You fought as one and survived, and that is why I ask that you not become overly confident."

"Okay," Sawyer said. "But I doubt we can outrun that werewolf."

"You must try," Ariel said quickly. "I know you will think of a way to escape. Promise me this."

One by one Jane, Sawyer, and Geoff nodded in agreement. As they walked upstairs and slipped past the shattered door to the study, a thought occurred to Geoff. "So what are we supposed to do when we get to Alluria? I'm not sure what we can do about a war."

"There is much you can do," Ariel said. "We shall discover that together."

They walked into the study and Geoff retrieved the wizard's key from the box on the workbench. He found a small chain and put the key on it before slipping it over his head. The others had gone to the archway and were standing in front of it. Ariel examined it closely.

"This damage," she said, "was caused by mage fire. Perhaps a fireball."

Everyone looked at Geoff.

"I didn't do it," he said.

Ariel smiled. "No," she said. "I believe this was done at the end of the last great war. The Soverign War. It was the last time men, elves, and dwarves united to fight against evil. During the last desperate battle for the fate of Alluria, a human wizard named Maelord cast a most destructive spell. A white-hot ball of fire. The explosion was so great that it leveled most of a castle and melted stone. This archway was thought to have been destroyed."

"Hang on," Sawyer said as he pointed at the archway. "So what're you saying? An ancient evil from your world has set up shop in Geoff's house?"

"What I don't get," Jane said, "is why Geoff? And why hasn't he been attacked before now?"

"Yeah," Geoff said. "I'm not even sure how long this archway has been here."

"I do not know," Ariel said. "Perhaps until now the three of you have not been regarded as a threat."

"Soooo," Sawyer said. "Looks like we gotta kill that shadow guy before he kills us."

"But we're here, not in Alluria," Jane said. "Why not leave us be?"

"Why not indeed. I believe that mistake may very well save us all," Ariel said. "It seems your destinies are entwined with that of Alluria."

"Aw, hell," Sawyer said.

Geoff looked at Jane and Sawyer. A shiver ran down his back. The color had drained from their faces and their expressions were somber. Ariel opened her mouth to say something else, but seemed to decide against it.

"Geoff, will you return us to Alluria? You do remember what I told you, right?"

"I think so," he said, stepping forward and pulling the key from around his neck. "You said for me to concentrate on where I want to go."

"Yes," Ariel said. "Think of the Eldritch Forest and we shall find ourselves there."

Geoff looked at Jane and Sawyer again. "Ready?" he asked as he stepped closer to the archway. The key started to pulse with energy.

Jane and Sawyer nodded.

Geoff placed the key in the hole and a tingling settled over his body, a surge of adrenaline meeting it. He began to think about the sacred druid grove in the Eldritch Forest, which was where they had said good-bye to Ariel and Ishara before returning home. The interior of the archway clouded, and as before, began to swirl with green and gray mists.

Ariel placed a hand on Geoff's shoulder. "Well done," she said and disappeared into the archway.

"I can't believe we're doing this again," Jane said.

"I know, right?" Sawyer said.

"Geoff, you better hold onto that key this time," Jane said, pointing a finger at him.

First Sawyer then Jane stepped into the archway. Geoff was alone. He took a deep breath and followed them, keeping a tight grip on the white alabaster key. He found himself caught up in the swirling mists again, spinning around and around until there was a bright flash. Geoff closed his eyes, and when he opened them again he was standing exactly where he pictured—Ariel's sunlit grove in the Eldritch Forest. Ariel, Sawyer, and Jane were standing a few feet away, watching him.

"Geoff!" called a feminine voice from behind him. He turned around just in time to see Ishara as she wrapped her arms around him and gave him a hug.

"I have missed you," she said in his ear. Her breath made his neck tingle and her hair smelled like a bouquet of flowers. Geoff returned her hug. She had lost weight too, just like Ariel.

"Hi," he said. "Good to see you again."

Ishara released him and smiled. Geoff couldn't help but

smile back. Even with her weight loss she was beautiful. The highlights in her dark blond hair sparkled in the sun, giving her a radiance. As he looked at her, he remembered their battle with the bandits, how she had almost single-handedly taken them all out with her bow.

"We shall stay the night here and begin our journey to Chalon tomorrow," Ariel said.

Geoff tried to look away, but maintained eye contact with Ishara and continued to smile at her.

"You look well, sneak thief," Ishara said. "Are you ready for more adventures?"

She raised an eyebrow and turned her head slightly while the corners of her mouth curved up. Geoff gulped and nodded. "Yeah, sure."

They walked over to the others, who were standing beside an enormous oak tree. That tree wasn't there before, Geoff thought. He looked around, trying to get his bearings, then he noticed a light green glow around the tree.

"Oh, wow! Is that the small tree you planted?" he exclaimed.

Jane and Sawyer looked at him, and he saw the confusion in their eyes. Suddenly Jane's face lit up.

"It is, Geoff! Oh my! Look how big it is now," she said. "How could it grow so fast?"

Geoff and Jane looked at Ariel, who smiled and nodded at them. Sawyer looked at the huge tree and rubbed his chin.

"Really, Sawyer?" Jane said as she rolled her eyes. "Do you need to think about it? It's magic!"

"Yes," Ariel said. "The same druid magic that heals and maintains life. The magic of the woodlands."

"It's not like you've never seen it before, Sawyer," Jane

said, putting her hands on her hips.

"Oh, yeah," Sawyer said as a spark of recognition flickered in his eyes. "It was smaller when we were last here, right? But I thought you could only make flowers and grass grow and stuff."

"Any living thing can be healed and revitalized," Ariel said. "The spell that enabled this tree to grow so large and so fast was a powerful one. This tree is now the shepherd of the forest. It will help nourish and protect the other trees and even the animals who reside here."

"Do you think I could learn how to cast a spell like that?" Jane asked, looking up to the top of the shimmering green tree.

"Of course," Ariel said. "When you are stronger. When that day comes I do not think there will be anything you cannot do."

Geoff felt Ishara squeeze his hand. He glanced at her and then at Ariel.

"That goes for each of you," Ariel said, looking at Geoff and Sawyer. "But there is much to learn before that time."

Ariel placed her hand on the trunk and closed her eyes. Geoff heard the sound of wood splintering. He stepped back and looked up, expecting to see a branch crashing down toward them. Jane and Sawyer also stepped back. The trunk where Ariel had laid her hand slowly split open. A green glow poured forth from within the tree, and then it faded.

Resting in the center of the trunk was the Stormblade. The longsword was still in its scabbard, and the large blue sapphire in the pommel revealed the sword's identity. It couldn't be mistaken for any other sword.

"Wow!" Geoff said. "That was the coolest thing ever."

"Good hiding place," Jane said with a giggle and a clap of her hands.

"I kept it safe for you, Stormlord," Ariel said as she handed the sword to Sawyer, "as promised."

A smile crept over Sawyer's face. He took the sword and unsheathed it. Almost immediately small bolts of lightning hummed back and forth along the length of the blade, casting a white hue over their surroundings.

"It appears you were also missed," Ariel said. "It recognizes its master."

"Master," Sawyer repeated as he beamed and stared at the sword.

"We shall continue your training in the morning," Ariel said. She walked to a carved marble stone and sat on it. "As well as your training, Jane."

"Oh, that's awesome," Jane said as she went over to Ariel. "Thank you."

Geoff glanced at Ariel. She was now regarding him with her emerald green eyes.

"Do not worry, Geoff," she said. "We travel to the capital city of Chalon, the city of marvels. A great wizard resides there. If you truly possess the gift of wizardry, he will know."

"Okay," Geoff said. "What's his name?"

"Maelord," answered Ariel.

"Maelord? The same one who blew up a castle a while ago?" Jane asked.

"Yes," Ariel said.

Sawyer sheathed his sword and sat beside Ariel. "Okay, so let me get this straight. We go to the big city, find Geoff a wizard tutor, and then go defeat the Shadowlord and save the world, right?"

"That's not much of a plan," Jane said. "What if Geoff really isn't a wizard?"

"I believe he is," Ariel said. "Just as I believe you and Sawyer have the makings of a druid and a warrior."

Geoff felt Ishara nudge him with her elbow, and he watched as she unslung her bow.

"We shall have a quick look at Somerdale," Ishara said as she tugged him away from the others. "Perhaps scout around a bit."

"Be careful," Ariel said as they left the grove.

Hand in hand, Geoff and Ishara ran through the woods. The forest reminded him of the one they landed in when he, Sawyer, and Jane first arrived—the Spirewood Forest. The trees here were not as tall, however, and he didn't see any signs of the swamp that had once been here, either. The sounds of birds chirping and the earthy smell of fresh grass surrounded them.

It occurred to him that Ishara had a firm grip on his hand. This was new, he thought. He'd never held a girl's hand this long before. He gripped her hand tighter as she led him along. Soon they came to a lush, tree-topped hill overlooking the village of Somerdale.

Geoff could see the entire village, and he zeroed in on the barracks in the center of town. He looked up at the sun, which had begun to set, and swallowed as he remembered the werewolf ripping away pieces of the wall to get to him. Ishara dropped his hand and took a dozen more steps. She dropped to one knee and scanned the empty village.

"So the townsfolk haven't returned yet," Geoff said, taking a knee beside Ishara. "Why not?"

Ishara shook her head. "They do not yet think it is safe."

"Is it the werewolf?"

"Yes," Ishara said. "And there have been reports of the Shadowlord's soldiers approaching from the north."

"Wonderful. So we've landed right in the middle of it."

Ishara sat down facing Geoff and crossed her legs.

"Geoff," she said, looking him over. "Why did you return?"

He blinked a couple of times as he thought about Ishara's sudden and serious question.

"Ariel asked us," he said. "She said she needed our help and that you were losing the war."

Ishara nodded, but said nothing. Geoff continued. "An assassin tried to kill me and Ariel saved me. I guess I owe her."

"And she said nothing to you of the prophecy?"

Geoff looked at Ishara. "What prophecy? Oh! Now I remember. You and Ariel said something about a prophecy as I stepped through the archway and went home."

Ishara smiled. "You have a good memory."

This time Geoff remained silent, waiting for an explanation.

"In the year of three travelers," she began, "outlanders from—"

Ishara was interrupted by the sight of a lone figure going from house to house, scrounging. It was a man wearing tattered animal skins.

CHAPTER FOUR
SURPRISES

"Hey, that's the wild man who helped us with the bandits," Geoff said. "Let's—"

"Geoff, go back to the others," Ishara interrupted. "Now."

Geoff had just cupped his hands around his mouth and was about to shout and get the man's attention, but Ishara's words stopped him. She had an arrow nocked and was aiming in the direction of the tattered man.

"Ishara, what's—" Geoff began, but was interrupted again when Ishara let her arrow fly.

Horrified, Geoff spun toward the man in tattered skins. Behind the man, another figure wearing black skins and leather armor had just rounded the corner of the cottage with an axe raised over his head. The arrow struck the newcomer in the chest before he could swing his axe.

The sudden sound of the arrow's impact and the man's scream startled the tattered man, who had been cramming goods into a rough burlap sack. As Geoff watched, he whirled and faced three more attackers, each armed with a sword and an axe. The man ducked a blow by the first attacker and knocked him unconscious with a left hook to the jaw. The second attacker tried to run him through with his sword, but the tattered man grabbed his arm and threw him against the cottage wall.

The third attacker was felled by another arrow from Ishara. After this last shot, Geoff saw the tattered man look up in their direction. He wanted to wave at the man, but several more attackers appeared and surrounded him.

"Geoff!" Ishara said, pulling another arrow from her quiver. "This is a scouting party for the Shadowlord's army. Go and warn the others. Now!"

Geoff turned and sprinted back toward the center of the Eldritch Forest. He stumbled as he zigzagged through the trees, and could hear Ishara fire off two more arrows as he raced away, his heart pounding in his chest.

By the time he reached the sacred glade, Geoff was exhausted. He dropped to his knees, gasping for air and beckoning to Sawyer, Jane, and Ariel.

Jane was the first to notice that he had returned. "Geoff!" she called as she rushed to him, with Ariel and Sawyer close behind.

"What happened? Are you okay?" Jane asked. "Where's Ishara?"

Geoff looked up and saw Ariel scanning the forest behind him.

"C'mon, Geoff," Sawyer said. "Tell us what happened."

"The wild man dressed in skins," began Geoff with a cough. "He's in Somerdale. He was attacked by scouts from the Shadowlord. Ishara stayed behind to help him."

"Sawyer, Jane," Ariel said, "gather your belongings. We leave for Chalon."

"But what about Ishara?" Jane said.

"I will find her," Ariel said. "Hurry. If there is a scouting party in Somerdale, then the Shadowlord's army is close. Too close."

Ariel disappeared into the forest, following the path Geoff and Ishara had taken.

"Great," Sawyer said with a scowl. "Here we go again, running for our lives." Sawyer frowned as he went back and picked up their sacks and grabbed his sword.

"Geoff, can you walk?" Jane asked. She placed her hands under his arms and helped him to his feet.

"Now do you see why I didn't want to come back?" Sawyer demanded.

Geoff felt Jane stiffen, and she exhaled loudly. She glared at Sawyer and her nostrils flared. She pointed at the archway in the glade.

"Fine. You can go home anytime," she said. "Geoff has the key and there is your way home. Bye."

Sawyer dropped the sacks he carried. He held his arms out and turned around.

"Jane, look around! This is real! It's not a fairy tale. What if someone dies? What if we all die? Did you ever think about that? How would our families find out? Who's gonna tell 'em?"

"We just got here," Jane said, "but if you're too scared then maybe you should go home."

Geoff's eyes bounced back and forth between Sawyer and Jane. Now it was Sawyer's turn to glare at Jane. They stood still, their eyes locked on each other. Finally Sawyer rolled his eyes, bent over, and retrieved the sacks he had dropped.

"Whatever," he said as he marched past Jane and stopped

by the edge of the glade to wait for Ariel and Ishara.

With Sawyer a good distance away, Geoff felt it was safe to say something to Jane.

"I think he's got a point," Geoff said. "If something happens to us, no one back home will ever know."

Her eyes were still fixed on Sawyer. After a few seconds she exhaled and relaxed.

"I know, Geoff," she said. "I know. I just don't think Ariel will let anything happen to us, do you?"

"No," Geoff said. "Should we follow Ariel? She and Ishara might need help. "That wild man can fight, but he was outnumbered."

"No, we better wait here," Jane said, scanning the tree line as she spoke, "because when Ariel and Ishara return I bet we'll be running for our lives, like Sawyer said."

Geoff smiled. At least Sawyer and Jane had agreed on that. Actually, they agreed on most things. Maybe they just liked to argue with each other.

Sawyer was moping beneath a large oak tree with his back against the trunk. He picked at the grass nearby, avoiding eye contact with them.

"Maybe you shouldn't have been that hard on Sawyer," Geoff said to Jane.

"Oh, he'll be fine," she said. "It's hard for him to think about someone other than himself."

"Did you mean it when you told him to go?"

Jane answered after a few moments.

"No."

"Then why…" Geoff let the words trail off.

Jane plopped down in the grass a few feet away from him.

"I was calling his bluff," Jane said.

Geoff sat beside her and scanned the woods for Ariel and Ishara.

"I hope they come back soon," he said, trying to break the tension in the air.

His remark was met with silence as Jane lay back in the grass and closed her eyes. After several quiet minutes, Geoff saw two shapes burst from the forest. It was Ariel and Ishara, and they were running.

"Here they come," Geoff said, standing up. "I don't see the wild man."

As they entered the glade, Geoff noticed serious looks on their faces. He glanced back in the direction of Somerdale.

"Where is he? Is he…," Geoff asked.

"No," Ishara said with a quick shake of her head. "It would take more than a scouting party to kill him. He is fine. He escaped."

Ariel picked up a sack and slung it over her shoulder. She pointed southwest.

"We must hurry to Chalon," she said. "Lionel should know the Shadowlord plans to attack with a greater number than we realized."

Geoff and the others collected their things and fell in line behind Ariel. He leaned closer to Ishara and whispered, "Who's Lionel?"

"Lionel Naram," Ishara replied in a hushed tone as she flashed a glance at Ariel's back. "He is the lord magistrate of Chalon."

"Oh," Geoff said. "So he's a good guy."

"He is a fool," said Ariel without looking back. "He should never have been named lord magistrate. He will ruin the great city of Chalon."

Geoff was surprised that Ariel heard his conversation with Ishara, but the acidic tone in her voice was more surprising-and a bit alarming. He looked at Ishara. She shook her head and made a small chopping motion with her hand to indicate this was a subject better left alone. Geoff decided to heed Ishara's unspoken advice and keep his questions to himself.

They followed Ariel's brisk pace as she led them south. Their path ran along the edge of the Eldritch Forest, and they remained concealed within the trees as they traveled. Sawyer and Jane ignored each other as they walked.

Ishara touched Geoff on the arm and pointed to the north. Plumes of black and gray smoke rose in the distance and cast a haze around them, and Geoff could smell burning wood and pitch.

"All that smoke," Geoff said. "Looks like giant tentacles."

"The Shadowlord's army," Ishara said, tucking a strand of hair behind her ear. "Barbarians from beyond the Dragonscale Mountains. They will attack Chalon and burn it to the ground."

"I thought the Shadowlord—What's his real name? Zorn?—was a hero. What happened to him?" Geoff asked, remembering the bandits' conversation while he and Ishara were their captives during his last visit to Alluria.

"He was," Ishara said with a quick nod. "Many tales have been told about his deeds. No one knows what changed him. He disappeared for a time, and when he returned he attacked several villages, killing nearly everyone."

"Wait a minute," Geoff said as he remembered a conversation he and Ishara had during their last visit to Alluria. "Ariel, you know him, don't you? You two were friends, right?"

Ariel stopped and turned. "Yes," she said, meeting Geoff's gaze. "We were good friends. He was one of the bravest humans I have ever met."

"Whoa, whoa, whoa!" Sawyer said, holding up a hand. "You *know* the Shadowlord?"

Ariel looked at Sawyer. Geoff thought he detected a hint of annoyance in her green eyes.

"If you're friends, can't you go talk some sense into him? Make peace. Stop the war," Jane said. "He'll listen to you, won't he?"

"Hardly," Ariel said dryly. "I said we *were* good friends, but that time has long since passed."

Ariel turned back around and resumed her quick pace. "In fact," she said over her shoulder, "I suspect he would try to kill me if we ever met again."

"So much for friendship," Sawyer muttered, raising his eyebrows.

The sun was dipping below a range of mountains to the west when they stopped for the night. The sky had a pinkish-gray hue as clouds rolled by. Geoff and Sawyer gathered firewood while the others set up camp. Sawyer hadn't said much the whole day, which worried Geoff a bit. He wasn't sure how, or even if, he should start a conversation with him as darkness began to fall. It was Sawyer who spoke first, however.

"I'm still having second thoughts," Sawyer said bitterly. "No assassin tried to kill me, and I doubt that one ever would have, either."

"If you really feel that way," Geoff said, "why didn't you go home when Jane told you to?"

"I don't know," Sawyer said with a long sigh. "I should've

gone home, I guess. I'm not a hero. None of us are."

Geoff considered Sawyer's point for a minute. "You may be right," Geoff said quietly, "but just like in our world, aren't some things worth fighting for?"

"Yeah. Whatever." Sawyer shook his head as he pushed past Geoff with his armload of firewood. Not wanting to be alone in the darkening woods, Geoff hurried after Sawyer.

The mood in camp was somber. Ariel was deep in thought as she prepared their meal, and Ishara was inspecting an arrow she had crafted.

"I noticed we're heading toward some hills and mountains," Jane said. "We won't be in the forest anymore. Will we be safe?"

"Yes," Ariel said as she handed Jane a bowl of hot stew. "Chalon is no more than two days' travel. We will be in the open grasslands, but I do not believe the Shadowlord's army is ready to venture so close to Chalon."

"Shadowlord," Sawyer repeated. "Why does everyone call him *Shadowlord*? Seriously, what kind of title is that, anyway? Is it supposed to scare the peasants? Woo, watch out! The Shadowlord is coming!"

Everyone was looking at Sawyer, who didn't seem to mind being stared at as he continued.

"Shadowlord. Lord of shadows? Yeah, so what's he gonna do, make evil shadow puppets with his hands?"

"Sawyer!" Jane said. "What's—"

"I don't care," Sawyer interrupted, placing his bowl on the ground next to him and standing. "Look, whatever. Just send me home, okay? I didn't want to come back here in the first place."

Sawyer picked up his sword and walked away, disappearing

into the dark forest. No one made a sound for a while. Ishara looked at Ariel and raised her eyebrows while Jane exhaled loudly and went after Sawyer.

"He is rash," Ishara said, "and moody. Are you certain the Stormblade chose him? He does not have the disposition one expects from a hero."

"And what disposition would you expect the Stormlord to have?" Ariel asked.

Jane's eyes hadn't fully adjusted to the dark after leaving camp, but she could see Sawyer's back as he stomped away.

"Sawyer!" Jane called as she stumbled on a rock. "Sawyer, wait!"

Sawyer stopped and faced her. Jane noticed he was frowning as she took a deep breath and tried to think of the right words.

"Sawyer, I'm sorry," Jane said, holding her arms out in frustration.

"I shouldn't have told you to go home. That was mean of me. I don't want you to go. Neither does Geoff. We need you here."

She wasn't sure he'd accept her apology. She looked at him as she stepped closer. Even in the dark she could imagine his brown eyes drilling into her. Was he going to stay mad at her? She said she was sorry. What more could she do? Sawyer placed his hands on his hips.

"I didn't mean to hurt you," Jane said. "I—"

Sawyer had reached out and pulled her close. His mouth was on hers and Jane's heart was beating a path to her throat. His arm wrapped around her. Was this really happening?

Were they really doing this? Oh no! Breathe! And then there was only Sawyer and the dark. Everywhere he touched her she quivered.

And then he was gone from her. Jane blinked and tried to reorient herself, but everything was topsy-turvy. Sawyer was frowning at something over her shoulder. Then Jane heard it, too. Someone, or something was moving in the woods behind them.

CHAPTER FIVE
THE FARMER'S FAMILY

"Sawyer," Jane whispered as she grasped his arm. "Who's out there?"

Sawyer maneuvered her so she was behind him and drew his sword. "I don't know," he whispered back.

"Is it Ariel?" she asked, her heart pounding. Maybe she's getting more firewood."

"It can't be her," Sawyer said in a hushed tone. "She doesn't make any noise. And neither does Ishara."

"Geoff?"

Sawyer shook his head. "He wouldn't be out here in the dark by himself."

Jane crouched and examined the ground until she found a tree limb sizeable enough to use as a club. Her eyes darted back and forth, but she didn't see any movement. She watched as Sawyer scanned the dimly lit forest in front of him. Jane put her hand on his shoulder to let him know she was still behind him. His muscles were taut, and he had assumed a defensive stance with both hands on his sword.

A minute later she heard whispering nearby in the

darkness. She squeezed Sawyer's shoulder and readied her improvised club.

"Whoever is out there, you better show yourself!" Sawyer called in a voice much deeper than normal. "I mean it! We're armed!"

Jane heard more whispers. Sawyer must have heard them too, because he turned and took a step in that direction.

"Get out here where we can see you!" Sawyer called again.

This time Jane heard a low cough, followed by the sound of footsteps crunching leaves and twigs. Four figures emerged from the gloom of the dusk-shrouded trees. Standing before them was a thin, middle-aged man carrying a small boy in his arms. Behind him stood an equally unkempt woman and a little girl. They were shaking and dirty, and their clothes needed mending in places.

The man's head turned back and forth. He appeared to be frantically looking around for something. Holding the child in his arms closer, he seemed to settle his gaze on Sawyer.

"Please, sir…can you help us? My family an' I are tired an' we need food."

Sawyer lowered his sword a little and softened his tone. "Who are you? Why are you out here in the woods?"

The man gulped. "I'm Willelm. That's my wife, Josephine. My boy here is Derek. Our daughter's name is Elayne. Please, my lord, we've been runnin' for the better part of two days. Will you help us?"

The sight of the small boy folded in his father's arms and the trembling little girl made Jane's heart sink. She was saddened by the pitiful state of the family of newcomers. She stepped from behind Sawyer.

"Yes," she said, forcing a welcoming smile. "Of course we'll help you."

Sawyer turned his gaze on her. Jane knew he wasn't so trusting, but she didn't care. These people needed help, and if she could alleviate their suffering even a little, then she was going to do it.

"What happened to you?" Jane asked. Her eyes fell upon the little girl, who gripped her mother's hand. Her hair was tangled and her simple dress was torn in several places. She dipped her head when she thought Jane was looking at her.

"We were attacked by the Shadowlord," he said slowly. "He was ridin' a great black winged beast. We lost our eldest son...Edward." Jane saw him wipe away tears as he spoke. "We're just simple farmers. All we have is gone..." The man's voice trailed off as he was unable to choke back his tears, and he started sobbing.

Jane wasn't about to turn these people away, and she wasn't going to let Sawyer or anyone else turn them away, either. She looked at Sawyer. His eyes were fixed on the small boy huddled into the farmer's chest. Sawyer nodded, but didn't say anything.

"Come back to camp with us," Jane said. "We'll help you."

Josephine began crying and reached out with her free hand. "Bless you, dear. Bless you both. You saved us." Jane took her hand and smiled. As she did, the young daughter disappeared behind her mother.

"Come on," Jane said. For a moment, she thought she sounded too much like Ariel giving commands. She looked back at the little girl peeking from behind her mother and smiled.

When they arrived at camp, Ariel and Ishara were already standing and looking in their direction, hands near their weapons. Geoff jumped to his feet at the sight of the family in tow behind Sawyer and Jane.

"Ariel," Jane began, "we ran into this family in the forest. They need our help."

Jane stopped when she noticed Ariel's stoic expression and looked back over her shoulder. The family had stopped short of entering the camp. They stood staring at Ariel and Ishara with a look of disbelief on their faces, and neither Ariel nor Ishara made a welcoming gesture toward the family.

"What?" Jane asked. "What's wrong?"

"They're...they're elves," Willelm said as he took a step back.

"Yeah, so?" Jane said, not fully understanding what was happening.

"Elves...they aren't to be trusted. They help the Shadowlord," Josephine said.

Ariel's jaw was tightly clenched, which probably meant she was offended by Josephine's accusation. Uh-oh, Jane thought. She had to do something to keep this situation from becoming worse.

"Ariel," Jane said with a quiet voice, "they need help. Look at them. They've been through a lot."

Ariel never took her eyes off the family. She did, however, soften her expression and beckon for them to enter the camp. Ishara laid her bow down as well. Jane turned back to the family. "You can trust them," she said. "They're our friends. They won't hurt you. It's okay. Really."

Willelm and Josephine looked at each other, but didn't

move. Jane heard a slight scraping sound behind her. It was Geoff spooning some stew into a small bowl. He walked up to Josephine and smiled as he handed her the bowl.

"Welcome," he said. "Don't be afraid. We won't hurt you." He tilted his head to the camp. "Come sit by the fire."

Jane's mouth fell open. She was surprised by Geoff's initiative, and even more surprised that the family listened to him and cautiously entered their camp. Willelm sat by the fire, continuing to hold Derek, while Josephine sat next to him with Elayne in the middle. Jane hurried and filled another bowl with stew and held it out to Elayne, who promptly shrank away. She grasped her mother's arm tightly with both hands.

"Go on," urged her mother. "Take the bowl, dear. Eat." Jane smiled at the little girl, who couldn't be much older than ten.

Elayne looked at Jane and then at her mother. She carefully reached out and took the bowl from Jane with dirty little hands. Without looking up, she began to hastily shovel the stew into her mouth with her spoon.

"We thought we'd starve before we found help. Thank you," Josephine said.

A quiet cough came from the boy in Willem's arms and Jane realized he hadn't moved or opened his eyes. He appeared to be sleeping.

"The child in your arms," Ariel said. "He is ill and requires a healer."

Willelm clutched the boy closer and stared at Ariel.

"Aye. He was sick before our farm was attacked," Willelm began, licking his lips nervously. "We've been movin' most of the day just tryin' to stay ahead of the Shadowlord's army."

"The Shadowlord's army attacked your farm?" Ishara asked. "Where is your farm?"

Willelm looked at Ishara, then at Jane. "Our farm was a day's ride north of Somerdale. We didn' see his army. We were attacked by the Shadowlord himself."

Ariel kept her eyes on the boy as she walked over and knelt beside Willelm. The farmer leaned back and gave his wife a nervous look. Josephine responded with a nod. Ariel placed her hand on the boy's forehead and then his cheek.

"He is feverish," she said. "Sawyer, bring a blanket." Ariel moved the boy's hair from his eyes. "What is his name?"

"Derek," Willelm said. "He's seven years old."

Sawyer brought a blanket over and unfolded it beside the farmer.

"Lay him here," Ariel said. Then she turned and signaled for Jane to come closer.

Jane knelt beside Ariel. The boy looked pale, and he was soaked with sweat. Ariel took Jane's hands and placed one on the boy's head and the other on his chest.

"I told you I would teach you more spells. Do you still wish to learn?"

Jane bit her lower lip. "Yes."

Ariel smiled. "Concentrate and repeat these words exactly as I say them. *Ehlia sa maros.*"

Jane closed her eyes. "Ehlia…sa…"

"Maros." Ariel said.

"Maros."

"Again. This time speak the words and remember to concentrate."

Jane took a deep breath. "*Ehlia sa maros.*"

Immediately she felt a warm, calming feeling inside her.

It flowed through her arms, into her hands, and out of her fingers, surging into the boy. What flowed from her and into the sick boy was more than a feeling. It was tangible and real, like an object she had shared with him. Her body tingled with excitement.

"Da?" came a soft voice beneath Jane's hands. She opened her eyes. Derek had awakened with a rosy color in his cheeks.

Astonished, Jane glanced at a grinning Ariel, who rested a hand on her shoulder. "Well done."

Willelm's mouth had dropped open. "Derek? Son?" He looked at Jane and then scooped Derek up in his arms. As he hugged his son, the farmer looked at Ariel and Jane.

"Bless you," he said. "Bless you both. How lucky we are to find druids this night. Thank you." They were joined in a family hug by Josephine and Elayne.

Ariel and Jane stood, watching their embrace.

"How do you feel?" Ariel asked.

"Great," Jane said. "I feel great."

"She can heal with such ease. Her druidic powers grow," an amazed Ishara said, looking at Geoff. "No human has ever been able to cast druidic spells."

"I told you," Geoff said with a smile. "She can also make plants grow. You should see my greenhouse."

"Good job, Jane," Sawyer said as he walked up to Jane and hugged her. "Way to go."

Sawyer's hug flattered her, but Jane felt a little uncomfortable in front of the others. Everyone was watching.

"I am glad you are in better spirits," Ariel said to Sawyer. "Your training will begin again tomorrow morning before we set off for Chalon." She looked at Jane. "I told you I would teach you more spells. I will honor my word. Each day I will show you a new spell. You must do your best to remember them."

"I will. I promise," Jane said.

"Pardon me," Willelm said, still holding young Derek, "if you're goin' to Chalon, may we come with you?"

Jane and the others looked at Ariel. Her usual stoic expression had returned. "I am sorry," she said. "We must hurry to Chalon and you will slow us. Eat and rest tonight. I will stand watch."

Willelm looked at his wife, then nodded. He held his children close.

"Wait," Sawyer said. "Tell ya what. I can help carry the boy. I'll put him on my back. It'll be okay."

"That will not be enough," Ariel said. "We cannot outrun the Shadowlord's army traveling with children."

"But we can't just leave them," Jane said. "They won't survive on their own."

"Yeah," Geoff agreed. "We can help. We can all help."

All eyes were on Ariel as the camp fell silent. She stood motionless, studying the farmer and his family for several moments. The longer she took to decide, Jane thought, the more likely her answer would remain no. Jane glanced at Sawyer. He gave her a little smile – just enough so that his dimples showed.

"My…my lady," Willelm began, but he had to stop and clear his throat. "We won't be a burden to you. We'll run fast an' keep up. We will. If you would help us find safety, we'd be grateful."

"Please, mistress," Josephine said. "Don't let our children die. Take them to Chalon. They're so young."

Ariel looked at Josephine and Willelm. She walked over and crouched down in front of Derek and Elayne. She brushed Elayne's long bangs away from her face. The farm girl leaned closer to her mother, but she managed a small smile for Ariel. Another moment passed then Ariel stood.

"Very well. We will take you with us."

Jane felt a wave of relief wash over her and the mood in the camp lightened noticeably.

"Thank...thank you," Willelm said. "We won't slow you down. I promise."

"She's fast," Jane said, looking at Willelm, "and she never gets tired. She can run all day."

"That's true," Geoff said. "She never needs rest. I think it's a druid thing."

"Or maybe it's an elf thing," Jane added with a smirk.

"Yeah," Geoff said.

"Or both?" Sawyer suggested.

Ariel regarded the three of them with a single raised eyebrow. "You should all rest. Tomorrow will be a long day."

Jane quickly grabbed her blanket and unrolled it by the fire. As she was straightening it, another blanket plopped down beside hers. She looked up and there was Sawyer, all smiles and dimples. He winked and began unrolling his blanket, too. Wonder what he has in mind, Jane thought, rolling her eyes.

She was too excited to sleep. She had been floating on air since Sawyer had kissed her, and with Ariel agreeing to help the family of farmers, she was filled with nervous energy. Plus, she had learned a new spell. This was the one she really wanted to learn – to help others recover from sickness. A grin spread across her face. Now all she needed to do was make sure Sawyer kept his hands to himself during the night.

⸻

Ariel watched as their companions and the stray family fell asleep around the fire. Humans needed their rest, she thought. The family would indeed slow them down. She had calculated their arrival at Chalon by sundown the next day, but now that was impossible.

Ishara stood, then walked over to Ariel and sat on a large mossy rock beside her.

"I have made more arrows," Ishara said. "My quiver is full."

Ariel nodded. "I hope we will not need them tomorrow, but it is likely we will."

"I know," Ishara said. She glanced at the family huddled together in their slumber. "I am surprised you agreed to take them with us."

"As am I," Ariel said. "I have come to realize in these times that everyone needs help."

There was a moment of silence and then Ishara spoke again. "I had hoped we would go further south to Selra'thel and help defend our homeland."

"I believe Selra'thel will be fine," Ariel said as crickets began their nightly chorus. Their rhythmic chirps and the smell of smoke from the fire helped relax her. "It is the humans we must help," she added. "They are not prepared for what comes."

"But Chalon must be aware," Ishara said. "Their scouting parties have seen what the Shadowlord's armies are capable of doing."

"Aye, they are aware," Ariel said as she stood and walked a few paces toward the edge of the camp. Ishara followed her. "But they do nothing to prepare," Ariel added. "They believe they will be safe behind their walls."

"Surely the lord magistrate has—"

"Done nothing," Ariel interrupted. "He has done nothing and a dark horde approaches."

Ishara frowned. Ariel knew she was thinking of a reason for his inaction.

"Why does he not act to save his people and his kingdom?"

"Because he has always been an idiot. He has no head for strategy or war."

Ishara remained quiet.

"Oh, I know he is considered a hero among humans," Ariel continued, "and perhaps he has earned that title. But it will not be enough to save him—or the people of Chalon."

"Will we be enough?" Ishara asked.

"No."

Ishara was about to say something, but a familiar chilling howl of a wolf far to the north stopped her.

Ariel looked north. "The beast comes," she said. Ishara took a step back and reached for an arrow.

"Tonight the werewolf is not our concern," Ariel said, "but I think perhaps it is for the Shadowlord."

"His men cannot stop the beast," Ishara said, shaking her head. "They are no match for it."

"None of us are," Ariel said.

Ishara motioned to the sleeping forms of Sawyer, Geoff, and Jane. "They were."

"No," Ariel said, "They were brave, but they were

fortunate. I believe fate has something else in mind for them."

Another howl permeated the night. The beast had begun to hunt.

CHAPTER SIX
JOURNEY TO CHALON

Geoff was awakened by the sound of someone chopping wood. He opened his eyes and saw the small orange glow of the campfire, over which hung a simmering metal pot. Geoff grunted and sat up on his blanket and stretched, glancing at the others. Nearby, Jane was still curled up in her blanket, while Willelm and his family slept in their blankets on the other side of camp.

The wood-chopping noises came from beyond a thicket of trees just outside the camp. Geoff yawned. From the looks of the light gray sky, he knew dawn was approaching. He looked at his blanket and sighed. Yep, more sleep would be nice, but he got to his feet and followed the curious sounds.

He passed through some trees and underbrush, emerging into a small clearing. There were Sawyer and Ariel, swinging makeshift wooden swords at each other. Sawyer appeared to be doing well; he managed to block or dodge most of Ariel's strikes while keeping his balance.

"Good morning."

Geoff recognized the soft, angelic voice. It belonged to Ishara, who crouched on a boulder overlooking the training session. She smiled at him. She had her dark blond hair pulled back and tied into a ponytail. Her skin was the same golden color as Ariel's.

"Oh," he said. "Hey there. Good morning."

Ishara raised her chin toward Sawyer and Ariel. "He is improving," she said. "He is strong and fast for a human, but he has no balance. Nor does he have the capacity to anticipate Ariel's next attack."

"Hey!" Sawyer called indignantly to Ishara, taking his eyes off Ariel for a second. This resulted in his promptly having his feet swept out from under him and receiving a solid smack on the shoulder while he was in the grass.

Geoff snickered and looked at Ishara as he leaned against the boulder. She gave him a wink and a smile.

"And he needs to work on his concentration," added Geoff in a hushed tone. Sawyer got up, brushed himself off, and again crossed swords with Ariel. A few strikes later he received a blow to his stomach, which doubled him over, and then another blow to his rear.

Even though Sawyer growled in frustration, Geoff couldn't help but notice that Ariel was taking it easy with him. She seemed to be slow with her attacks, for one thing. When they were attacked by carrion mites, Ariel had been an amazing blur of whirling blades in the catacombs of Silverthorne Manor.

Sawyer, for his part, appeared to genuinely be trying to become more proficient a sword. He listened to Ariel's instructions and did his best to apply her lessons – usually with some degree of limited success.

"Mmm, good morning!" Jane said. She had come to watch Sawyer's training. Her brown hair was tousled and she wore her blanket draped over her shoulders. She sat on the ground beside Geoff and crossed her legs.

"Good morning," Geoff said.

"How's he doing?" Jane asked.

Geoff glanced up at Ishara, who smiled at him. "Well, he's doing better."

At that moment they heard a loud *crack* followed by Sawyer jumping up and down while he shook his hand.

"Ow! Oh crap, that hurts!" He put his red and swollen knuckle in his mouth.

"Sawyer!" Jane said as she unsuccessfully tried to hold back her laughter by covering her mouth with her hands.

"Jane, she's killin' me here," Sawyer said, still shaking his hand. "I'm going to need some healing. I've got bruises all over."

"Yeah?" Jane said with a playful smile. "What's in it for me if I heal you?"

"Whaddya want?" Sawyer replied as he picked up his wooden sword.

"Surprise me."

"Okay, I'll think of something." Sawyer said with a sly smile as he readied his weapon again. Ariel attacked first with a high strike, followed by a low strike and a spinning slash aimed at Sawyer's stomach. This time he blocked every blow. Ariel stepped back and nodded her approval.

"Woo! Sawyer!" Jane called as she clapped enthusiastically.

"He is better when you are watching him," Ishara said to Jane. "Perhaps he will progress faster with you near."

Geoff again looked up at Ishara. She saw it, too. Sawyer and Jane liked each other. When did that happen? Yesterday they were arguing and now they were flirting with each other. Geoff shook his head. It was confusing, but he was glad for the change. It would certainly lighten the mood in camp.

"Geoff," Ishara said as she hopped down from her perch atop the boulder. "Come help me prepare breakfast. We should make sure our guests are safe, too."

"Okay," Geoff said. He hurried to Ishara's side. "See ya back at camp, Jane!"

Jane waved, but she never took her eyes off Sawyer.

<hr />

Sawyer looked like a hero, Jane thought. She pulled her blanket snuggly up around herself and watched him spar with Ariel. His defined arms glistened with sweat and his tunic did little to conceal his rounded chest. His sudden kiss yesterday was the most romantic thing she had ever experienced. Last night would've been wonderful if the farmer family hadn't shown up.

She'd been disappointed to find herself all alone when she woke up; she'd hoped that Sawyer would kiss her to waken her. Jane closed her eyes and sighed. How wonderful that would've been. She began thinking about how she could find herself alone with Sawyer again. Perhaps she would help him gather firewood instead of Geoff, or maybe they could fall way behind the others as they walked.

Then Jane heard a loud *whack*, followed by Sawyer howling in pain again. "Ow! Ow! Ow!"

Jane opened her eyes to see him sitting on the ground holding his right knee. Jane chuckled; she couldn't help herself. Sawyer, the star quarterback, the big man on campus, was being soundly humiliated by a girl.

"That really hurts!" Sawyer said.

"Attacking low when your enemy least expects it may quickly end the battle," Ariel said as she helped him to his feet. "Can you walk?"

Sawyer tried to put his weight on his right leg, but winced and shifted to his left leg. "Ow, no. I think it's broken or something."

Jane threw off her blanket and hurried over to Sawyer and Ariel. He raised his injured leg while Ariel knelt and examined it with her hands.

"It is not broken," she said. "Only bruised. Here is the knot."

"Ow! Yeah," Sawyer said. "Feels like it's broken to me."

Jane stood beside Sawyer and put her arm around his waist to steady him. "Is he going to be all right?"

"No, he isn't," Sawyer said. "Gimme some healing, baby."

Jane smiled. She knew then he was going to be fine.

"That," Ariel said, "is an excellent idea."

She stood and looked at Jane. "Here is the chance to learn another spell."

Ariel placed a hand on Sawyer's shoulder, taking over the task of steadying him. She motioned for Jane to examine Sawyer's lower leg.

"Do you feel the knot just below his knee?"

Jane ran her hands along both sides of Sawyer's leg until she felt a rather large bump on the outside of his leg.

"There," she said, pushing on it with her thumbs.

"Ouch! Yeah. There it is," Sawyer said, wincing again.

Jane looked up at Ariel, who had a slight smile on her face.

"*N'tara*," Ariel said and nodded.

Jane put her hand over the hard bump.

"*N'tara*."

Just like the night before, Jane felt a warm, gentle sensation from deep inside her well up and pass through her fingers into Sawyer's leg.

"Heeey," Sawyer said. "*That*'s awesome. My leg feels a lot better." He put his weight on it and lifted up on his toes a few times. "I don't feel any pain. Now that's a handy spell, Jane. You better remember that one."

Jane laughed and stood up. Sawyer hopped around, putting pressure on his right leg.

"I thought my football career was over," he said. "Thanks, Jane."

"Don't thank me," she said, pointing toward Ariel with a tilt of her head. "Thank Ariel."

"Yeah, thanks Ariel. You rock," Sawyer said.

"You are welcome. You have progressed much this day-both of you. Well done." Ariel turned and headed back to camp.

Jane watched as Ariel walked away. Then Jane turned to Sawyer and wrapped her arms around his neck. "Well done." She hugged him as he placed his hands around her waist. He was still warm from his morning lesson. Jane let her hands slide down to his broad shoulders and then his arms. She felt his firm muscles shift beneath his tunic. He squeezed her waist and she tilted her head back, just an inch or two away from his face and looked into his dark brown eyes.

"Well done to *you*," he said, displaying that movie star smile of his. "I was wondering when we'd do this again."

Jane raised an eyebrow, doing her best Ariel imitation.

"Me too." She pressed her lips against his, giving him first a long kiss, then a short, gentle peck. She felt Sawyer pull her even closer and hold her tighter, his arms enveloping her body as he lifted her off the ground. Jane was surprised by her forward behavior, but she found Sawyer irresistible at the moment. She grabbed the sides of his head with both hands, tangled her fingers in his thick locks, and squeezed, never letting her lips part from his.

Sawyer set her down and she took a deep breath while she fanned herself with her hand.

"Wow," Jane said.

"You got that right. To be continued."

Jane smiled.

Sawyer took a playful swipe at Jane with his wooden sword. She feigned a scream and jumped out of the way, laughing.

"By the way, you're getting really good," she said. "I think that's the first time Ariel ever said anything good about any of us, isn't it?"

Sawyer laughed. "Probably. I know she likes beating me up. I've got bruises on bruises."

"Hmmm. Maybe I'll have to give you some more healing." She flashed a flirty look at Sawyer.

"Fine with me," he said. "I hurt all over. I mean *all* over."

Jane rolled her eyes. "Watch it," she said. "I'll get Ariel to teach me how to turn you into a bug or something."

"She can't turn people into bugs," Sawyer said. "Can she?"

Jane didn't answer. It was best to keep him wondering. After breakfast, they began their journey west, leaving the forest and entering the open, rolling grasslands for the first time. Ariel led the way, followed by Jane and Sawyer, then the family of farmers, with Geoff and Ishara bringing up the rear.

A refreshing gust of wind blew past, carrying the scent of grass and flowers. Jane closed her eyes and held her arms out, letting her hair flow in the breeze. The open plains were beautiful. They were walking in a sea of grass. Here and there, hills of various sizes and shapes dotted the landscape. To the south, a small mountain range climbed skyward. Its green peaks were sprinkled with gray rock formations, which increased in number closer to the top.

Jane looked over her shoulder. Willelm, Josephine, and their kids were keeping up, as promised. Behind them, Ishara scanned the countryside to the north for enemies. Geoff walked with her, chatting and seemingly unaware of what she was doing. Ariel gradually changed direction and turned southwest, toward the mountains.

They walked until the sun was high overhead and then stopped for lunch. Ariel and Ishara maintained their vigilance while everyone ate.

Geoff had taken a seat in the grass beside Jane.

"Hey, Sawyer," he said. "I think you have a fan."

"Hmmm? What's that?" Sawyer asked, not fully understanding what Geoff was talking about. Geoff pointed toward Derek. The little boy was unable to take his eyes off Sawyer's sword.

"Oh," Sawyer said as he picked up the Stormblade and beckoned to the boy. Jane couldn't help but smile as Derek walked to Sawyer. The little boy seemed to regard Sawyer as a celebrity.

"Are you a knight?" Derek asked.

"Me? A knight? Oh no, 'fraid not."

Sawyer pulled the sword from its scabbard so Derek could have a better look.

"Here, you can hold it. But be careful, okay?"

Derek took the Stormblade from Sawyer with both hands and was nearly pulled over by its weight. Sawyer caught the boy and steadied him. Derek had to exert himself to raise the blade from the ground.

"Oh, my!" Willelm's voice came from a dozen feet away. "That's the...Stormblade!" He looked at Sawyer. "Then you must be the Stormlord, aren't you?"

Sawyer opened his mouth to say something, then closed it. He glanced at Jane and let out a sigh. "Yeah, I guess so."

"You guess so?" Jane demanded. She decided to put Sawyer on the spot. She looked at Willelm. "He had to kill a river troll for that sword," she told the farmer.

"A river troll?" Willelm asked, again looking admiringly at Sawyer.

"Wait a minute," Sawyer said. "I got lucky. That's all."

"He's just being modest," Jane said. "I saw the troll. It was huge."

"I saw it too," Geoff said.

"You see, dearest," Willelm said, putting his arm around Josephine. "We *are* safe. We travel with the Stormlord."

Sawyer rolled his eyes at Jane. She responded by sticking her tongue out at him.

After lunch and a brief rest, they continued toward the mountain range. Jane hurried beside Ariel. "Why're we going toward those mountains?" she asked. "Didn't you say Chalon was to the west?"

"It is," Ariel said. "Perhaps we will not be as exposed as

we are now if we travel along the base of the mountains. And we may find shelter for the night."

"Oh, okay." Jane dropped back and walked beside Sawyer.

"What'd you ask her?" Sawyer said.

"I was just wondering why we're—"

Jane stopped. So did Sawyer and the others. Ariel motioned for everyone to get down and she drew her scimitars. She lowered her stance and readied her weapons. A column of smoke began to rise over the next hill.

Chapter Seven
Oncoming Danger

Geoff turned to Ishara. He was going to ask her about the smoke when he saw her nock an arrow and draw her bow.

"Geoff," Ishara whispered. "Get down!"

He crouched in the grass beside her.

"What is it?" he asked.

"Up ahead," Ishara said, looking intently in Ariel's direction.

Ariel had readied herself for combat. Sawyer drew his sword and motioned for Jane to stay next to him. Willelm and his family crouched and huddled together.

"What's burning?" Geoff asked. Ishara didn't answer. She was motionless. Ariel lay down in the grass and looked over her shoulder at Ishara. A quick wave of her scimitar beckoned Ishara to join her.

"You should stay here," Ishara said, crouching low and moving past Geoff. "We do not yet know what danger awaits us."

Geoff gulped and watched Ishara silently slip past everyone until she was beside Ariel. They whispered to each other and then Ishara quietly continued on to investigate. Geoff flattened out on his stomach and low-crawled to Sawyer and Jane.

"Guys, any idea what's happening?" he asked.

"No," Jane said.

"No idea," Sawyer said, "but I'm getting a bad vibe here." He nodded to his sword, which had begun to emit a white-blue glow.

A chill ran down Geoff's back. "Werewolf?"

"Uh-uh. Something else."

Sawyer hadn't fallen into a trance, as he had when the sword had warned him of danger on previous occasions. Besides, it was too early in the day for werewolves.

"Well? What do we do?" Jane asked in a hushed tone. "We can't just sit here—"

She was interrupted by Ariel, who signaled for them to come to her. Ariel also motioned for Willelm and his family to stay put. Geoff, Sawyer, and Jane crawled to Ariel's position. She was peering over the top of the hill, keeping an eye on Ishara. Geoff raised his head so he could see Ishara, too. She was perhaps thirty yards ahead of them and was observing something unfolding below.

"Ariel," Sawyer said, pointing to his sword, "it's letting me know danger is near."

Ariel glanced at the Stormblade in Sawyer's hand.

"Keep your weapon out of sight," she said. "At least until we know what sort of enemy is near."

Sawyer nodded and sheathed his sword.

"Follow me and be *very* quiet," Ariel added.

She then slid on her stomach through the grass to Ishara. Geoff was next, followed by Jane and Sawyer. When they reached Ishara, she didn't say anything. She only pointed to a collection of thatched homes and a few small barns below. Some of the homes were burning. Geoff kept his head low and his eyes on Ariel.

"What have you seen?" Ariel asked, peering down at the small hamlet.

"Barbarians," Ishara said. "Another scouting party."

Geoff peeked over the swaying grass and saw several large men who looked similar to the ones who had attacked the man wearing tattered animal skins. They were armed with swords and battle-axes. Some of them wore animal skins and carried shields. Something white and brown lying on the ground caught Geoff's eye. It was the body of a farmer. His white shirt had a few dark red stains on it. Geoff ducked back down, his breathing fast and shallow.

"Oh, no. They killed the farmers," he said. "They're all dead."

"Keep down," Ariel said. "We must slip away before we are noticed."

"Hey, is that Darth Vader?" Sawyer asked, looking at the scene below.

"Where?" Geoff's head shot up over the tall grass. He clearly saw a tall knight dressed all in black plate mail armor and carrying a black sword with glowing red runes on the blade. The knight's cloak was strange. It didn't move or flow with the wind. Instead, it seemed to writhe and undulate, like it had tentacles.

Geoff felt a strong tug on his arm and he found himself pulled back to the ground by Ariel. Her alarmed expression signaled they were in serious trouble.

"*Get down!*" she hissed. She regarded Geoff and Sawyer,

who had also been yanked to the ground. "Have you lost your minds? I do not know of whom you speak, but *that* is Lord Zorn himself. The Shadowlord."

"He's *here*?" Jane asked. "Why is he here? I thought he was with his army to the north."

"I do not know, but we must leave." Ariel pointed back the way they had come, and they crawled back to Willelm and his family. They were still huddled together, and the children were sobbing as Josephine attempted to comfort them.

"Thank the powers," Willelm said. "We thought something terrible had happened."

"Something terrible did happen," Ishara said, looking back at the rising smoke.

"We…we have friends there…they could give us shelter and food."

"I am sorry," Ariel said, looking at Willelm and Josephine. "Your friends are dead. The Shadowlord has seen to that."

"But…but there were children…some the same age as Elayne and Derek…" The farmer's words trailed off. The look of confusion on his face changed to sadness. Willelm wiped the tears from his weathered face.

"The children," Willelm said. "Why would the Shadowlord want to kill them? They were no danger…"

"Who knows why evil seeks to cause harm?" Ishara hissed. "There will be a reckoning. This will not be allowed to continue, nor will it be forgiven."

The tone in Ishara's voice was new to Geoff. As he watched her gather her things it seemed to him that she had seen this sort of occurrence before.

"We turn directly south," Ariel said. "We remain quiet and we travel fast. Once we reach the base of the mountains we stand a better chance of remaining hidden."

Ariel pointed to the south and moved away, still crouching.

Jane knelt beside Elayne and Derek. She took their hands in hers. "It's all right," she said. "It'll be okay." She gave Josephine a reassuring smile. Sawyer pointed in the direction in which Ariel had gone and motioned for them to follow her. The family did so, with Jane beside them. Sawyer trailed behind.

Geoff looked at Ishara. She gazed in the direction of the burning village with a grim countenance.

"Are you okay?" He asked.

Ishara shot him a quick glance, then looked to the columns of smoke. "For a moment, I wanted to place an arrow in Zorn's heart. Had I been alone, I would have done so."

Geoff bit his lower lip. The bitterness in her voice made him nervous.

"Go, Geoff," Ishara said, pointing after the others. "I will not be far behind."

"Are you sure? I can—"

"Go." Ishara's interruption was an order. "I must be sure we are not spotted by the enemy."

Geoff obeyed and followed the others, staying low to the ground and trying to stay quiet as he moved through the tall grass. In front of him, Geoff saw Willelm and his family. They weren't crouching as low as the rest of the party. In fact, Geoff thought they were in danger of being spotted. He stopped and looked back the way he had come. There was no sign of Ishara.

He frowned. He felt safer when she was near. He had seen her fight and knew she could take care of herself in a battle. The Shadowlord was near, however, and Ariel didn't want to risk a confrontation with him.

"Geoff!"

He looked in the direction of the harsh whisper. It was Sawyer. He waved for Geoff to catch up with the others. Geoff hurried along and as he passed Sawyer he heard him whisper, "Are you crazy? What the hell's wrong with you, stopping like that?"

Geoff didn't answer. He crept through the grass, following the others. Hearing Sawyer close behind him, Geoff quickened his pace. The smell of smoke still lingered in the air. They caught up with Jane and the family of farmers after another minute. They had stopped and appeared to be waiting.

"Jane, is everything all right?" Geoff asked, coming to a stop beside her.

"I'm not sure," Jane said. "Ariel's doing something up ahead. She told us to stay here."

"I better go see what's going on," Sawyer said. He tried to slip past Jane, but she grabbed his tunic.

"No, Sawyer," Jane said. "Whatever it is, Ariel can handle it. If she wanted company she would've let us go with her."

"Relax. I'll be right back. Stay here with them," Sawyer said, nodding to Willelm and his family, who were sitting nearby. "I'll take Geoff with me. C'mon Geoff." Sawyer quickly crawled away.

Geoff looked at Jane. She let out a long sigh.

"Go on," she said. "Try and keep him out of trouble."

Geoff crawled after Sawyer, who was moving fast through the grass. They had gone another fifty yards when

Geoff thought he heard the clang of swords followed by yelling. He stopped and listened. Someone was fighting just ahead. Geoff followed Sawyer's trail until he came to the crest of a hill and looked down.

In the distance, Ariel was fighting three leather-clad barbarians who looked similar to those who had burned the village. Two other barbarians were lying on the ground, having already been dispatched by Ariel. Geoff noticed movement to his left. Sawyer was hopping and sliding down the steep hill toward Ariel with his sword drawn.

Ariel, however, finished her enemies before he could reach her. Ariel's spinning attacks were followed by a final move in which she leapt into the air and slashed the last barbarian no fewer than three times before she landed.

"That…that was the best move I've ever seen," Sawyer said.

"Sawyer!" Ariel hissed as she glared at him. "Why are you here? You should be with the others. We have been discovered."

Geoff, not wanting to be alone any longer, stumbled down the hill toward Ariel and Sawyer. As he reached the bottom of the hill, a shadow fell over him. He spun around and saw another barbarian. This one was so large he blocked out the sun. His face was scarred, and he had a wild look in his eyes. Geoff screamed and fell back, landing hard on the ground as the barbarian lifted a wicked-looking battle-axe over his head. Geoff tried to make himself roll away or get up, but he was too terrified to move.

"*Tae'nalara!*"

Geoff felt something invisible rush past him and knock the giant barbarian off his feet, sending him flying backward at least thirty feet. He landed with a heavy thud and remained motionless.

"Are you unharmed, Geoff?" Ariel asked.

She stood over him with a concerned expression on her face.

Geoff exhaled. "Yeah. Yeah, I'm okay. Just thought that was it for me."

Ariel helped him to his feet. He was about to say thanks, but he heard screams coming from nearby. Without a word, Ariel sprinted up the slope toward Jane and the others.

"C'mon, Geoff!" Sawyer shouted as he followed Ariel, sword in hand. Geoff hurried after them, trying to scramble up the hill, sometimes having to use his hands to help pull himself along. He heard Jane calling for help, along with the members of Willelm's family.

As Geoff made it to the top of the hill, he heard the sounds of more fighting. He ran through the tall grass toward the ringing sounds of sword on sword, arriving in time to see Ariel finish off two more barbarians. Sawyer and Ishara had taken a defensive position in front of Jane and the family, weapons at the ready.

"Jane, are you okay? Is anyone hurt?" Sawyer asked, glancing about for more enemies.

Jane's eyes darted around in obvious fear. She seemed unable to focus her attention. The left side of her face was red and began to swell. A little bit of blood trickled from the corner of her mouth toward her chin.

"Jane?" Sawyer asked. This time he turned around. "What happened to you?"

"They came from all sides," Willelm said, exhibiting a nasty bump on his forehead. "We were surrounded.

When…when they showed up, we tried to fend them off."

Ariel walked over to Jane and took her head in her hands. She looked over Jane's bruise. "You are brave," she said quietly. She looked at Willelm. "You both are."

"Ishara, make sure there are no more enemies near," Ariel said. "Stay alert."

Ishara nodded and disappeared into the grass, her dark blond hair dancing from side to side. Geoff watched her go, hoping she would be safe out there all alone. He wanted to go with her, but he knew Ariel wouldn't let him.

"Ouch," Jane said, recoiling as Ariel wiped away the blood from her mouth and chin.

"That ugly one," Jane said. "He punched me." Her voice had an indignant tone. "They're animals," she continued. "Just…animals."

"*N'tara*," Ariel said as she caressed Jane's swollen cheek. The puffy redness subsided, and Jane's face returned to its normal state.

She looked at Ariel. "Thanks."

Ariel nodded and smiled at Jane and then she cast the same healing spell on Willelm. The large lump on his forehead disappeared. He blinked in disbelief and rubbed his forehead.

"I…I…don't feel any more pain," he said. "It don't hurt." He smiled at Josephine and then he bowed his head to Ariel.

"Thank you," he said.

"Ariel!" Ishara called as she reappeared. She pointed behind her. "The Shadowlord approaches!"

CHAPTER EIGHT
THE SHADOWLORD

A wave of despair rushed over Jane as she processed Ishara's words. The Shadowlord was coming for them! She looked at Ariel, as did everyone else.

"Run to the mountains! I'll join you as soon as I can," Ariel said with urgency, pointing south to the cluster of mountains with a scimitar.

"Hurry!" Ishara cried as she whirled around and led the way.

Geoff shot up and dashed through the grass after her, along with Willelm and his family. Jane found herself standing in place, watching Ariel turn to face the Shadowlord.

"Ariel," Jane said, "come with us. We need you…" Her words tapered off just before Sawyer grabbed her wrist and pulled her away. Jane was sure Ariel had heard her. She kept looking over her shoulder, trying to keep an eye on Ariel for as long as possible. Ariel looked in her direction as they ran away.

"Sawyer, we can't leave her!" Jane said, struggling to free her captive wrist. "We have to go back and help."

"Help her?" Sawyer interrupted. "Help Ariel? She can take care of herself, Jane. You know that. If we try to help her then she has to worry about keeping us safe, too." He tugged her along. When they had run for almost half a mile in the tall grass, Jane looked over her shoulder again.

Ariel was no longer alone. A fearsome figure dressed in black plate mail armor had emerged and stood before her. The black knight held a long black sword with glowing red markings on the blade. Jane blinked and looked again. She wasn't sure if the frantic motion of running played tricks on her eyes as she attempted to watch the confrontation. The Shadowlord's cape moved strangely. It didn't move as if blowing in a breeze. It looked to Jane like it was alive.

<hr />

Ariel faced the Shadowlord as a strong breeze whistled by, causing the high grass around them to sway. Overhead, several large clouds blocked the sun. The surrounding landscape took on a surreal appearance, as if trying to decide between light and dark. A hissing sound came from the searing red runes carved into the Shadowlord's blade.

"You have changed your armor, Zorn," Ariel finally said. "And your new sword is…unique."

The Shadowlord didn't answer. Ariel raised her chin defiantly. "I know why you are here," she said. "You cannot have them."

There was still no answer from the dark figure in front of her. Ariel looked into the black visor. A pair of burning red eyes met her gaze. Ariel realized the owner of that hateful stare had been consumed by evil. The hero that had been Zorn no longer existed. Her old friend was gone. She narrowed her eyes and steeled herself.

Ariel remembered how Jane, Sawyer, and Geoff had saved the unicorn in Spirewood Forest, how Jane wasn't afraid to speak her mind or stand up to anyone. She regretted not teaching Jane more spells. Most of all, she regretted not sharing her feelings with Jane and the others. They were humans, but they were worth fighting for, and they were worth dying for. She liked humans better than she realized, and perhaps it was time to forgive them for the death of her parents. If she fell here, in battle with the Shadowlord, it would be a good death.

Ariel pressed her lips together. "So be it." She leapt at the black knight, scimitars slashing and spinning. Her sudden attack must have taken the Shadowlord by surprise, because her first two slashes landed before he reacted. One slash landed across the left thigh and the other across his chest, cutting into his breastplate. The Shadowlord staggered back a few steps, but Ariel pressed her advantage. She continued whirling and slashing as fast as she could.

Ariel landed another strike on his arm, causing him to grunt in pain. She ducked a swing aimed at her neck, then spun and slashed down at the Shadowlord, her weapon biting deep into his shoulder. He growled and swung his sword at her legs. This attack was much faster than his previous one, but Ariel's reflexes enabled her to leap up and evade it. As she did so, she brought both scimitars down on his upper chest, knocking him back.

Something was wrong, Ariel realized. Zorn was much faster and stronger than she remembered. Such an onslaught from her would've finished him before, but he stood there, examining his wounds. Her strikes were precise and lethal;

no man could have survived them. The bleeding from his wounds had stopped, however. How could that be?

"You're formidable," came a deep, metallic voice from beneath the spiked black helm. "You always were." Zorn turned and started to circle her. Ariel matched his every step and kept her scimitars ready.

"I wonder—How difficult was it to kill your beloved friend and teacher? Hmmm? Did you cry?" Zorn glanced down for a second. "No, I don't think I've ever seen you cry. My guess is you slaughtered Bhael and had a nice dinner before going to sleep. Pity. Now *he* was a true druid."

"He was a beloved friend of the forest and my teacher," Ariel said through clenched teeth. "Until you changed him into something as dark and evil as yourself. You will pay for all the suffering you have caused, I promise."

"I did nothing," Zorn said. He pointed his sword at Ariel. "You killed him."

"Aye," Ariel agreed. "I killed him. I had no choice. It was my calling."

"Calling?" Zorn scoffed. "What sort of calling compels you to kill your friend and mentor?"

"Do not speak to me of killing," Ariel hissed. "How many innocent folk have you killed?" She waved a scimitar in the direction of the smoldering farm. "What did they do that warranted death?"

The Shadowlord peered at the columns of smoke wafting away in the breeze. "Some die in war," he said. "You of all people should know that." He turned back to face her. "High druid or no, you cannot defeat me."

"We shall see," Ariel said as she again leapt to attack the Shadowlord. His mocking angered her, but she knew better than to allow that anger to distract her. This time her first blows were blocked by Zorn's black blade. She saw a mailed fist coming straight at her nose. She turned her head in time to avoid the punch, and heard a *whoosh* as the blow just missed her. Had it landed it would've knocked her unconscious, or worse.

Ariel stepped back. Now the Shadowlord's movements were more predatory as he approached her. His guard was up and each step was deliberate. He was stalking her. She had to overcome his dark magic. Her enchanted scimitars worked well enough, but the Shadowlord had yet to show his full might. She had to be cautious. His speed nearly matched hers, which was impossible for a human, yet it was his strength that concerned her. Ariel's elven strength made her a match for any human warrior, but this time was different.

Zorn lunged at her and swung his sword in a cleaving motion. Ariel crossed her scimitars overhead and blocked his blow. The force of the attack almost drove her down. She bent her knees and exerted herself. A low growl emanated from the Shadowlord as she pushed up and away with her scimitars. Then she felt the heavy weight of his strength push back, trying to push her down.

Ariel kicked his midsection, sending him back a few steps. She charged and slashed at him from various directions, again spinning around him like a dervish. Most of her attacks landed, which resulted in grunts and growls of pain from Zorn. He had to fall soon, she thought. No one could live with so many wounds. He thrust his sword at her. Ariel leapt over the clumsy attack and landed beside him.

She slashed his lower back with both scimitars. Zorn

groaned and dropped to his knees. Ariel's next attack was aimed at his neck, but as she slashed at him, the Shadowlord suddenly turned and grabbed her throat, immediately stopping her. She had been baited and she fell for it. No human was that fast. She had underestimated his increased speed and strength. She struggled to breathe and free herself as Zorn lifted her off the ground. She dropped her weapons and tried to pry his hand from her neck.

His grip tightened and the corners of her vision began to blur. Her lungs ached for fresh air.

"Now you die," Zorn said as he lifted her higher. Ariel shut her eyes tightly. In her mind she pictured the tall, green grass nearby wrapping around the Shadowlord. She felt a surge of energy from deep inside. She was the high druid; she was one with nature and its power sprang forth.

She felt Zorn's grip loosen and let go, and she opened her eyes to see him attempting to free himself from a thick, grassy prison. She had willed the grass and plants to fully envelop and trap him. His sword was the only part of him that wasn't entangled. Soon, however, the runes began to sizzle as they grew hotter. Ariel heard a ripping, tearing sound from the green mummy that was the Shadowlord. He was breaking free.

Her concentration, however, never wavered. Layer after layer of constricting, snaking grass and plants enveloped Zorn until he remained motionless. Ariel took a step toward him to examine him and heard a low rustling. Something was wrong.

She noticed what looked like black smoke seeping through the tiny cracks and crevices of the Shadowlord's grassy prison. The smoke began to squirm and writhe as it continued to drift from the inert figure. His cloak, she realized. It must be his cloak. It was a cloak of darkness and evil.

Ariel's thoughts were interrupted by a violent explosion in front of her. She shielded her eyes as debris and bits of vegetation flew past. Before her stood the Shadowlord in all his dark splendor. The next instant he swung his black sword at her. Ariel dove to the ground as the blade whooshed over her head.

Grasping her scimitars and attacking in one fluid motion, her weapons struck the outside of Zorn's thigh. He dropped to a knee. Ariel sprang to her feet and swung at the back of Zorn's neck, intending to decapitate him. Something stopped her in midswing, however. To her surprise, the Shadowlord's cloak had wrapped a black tentacle around her wrist. Ariel slashed it with her other scimitar and freed herself.

It was like slicing through smoke. What sort of dark magic had she encountered? Ariel stepped back. The black, writhing cloak had taken on the appearance of a sinister, multi-appendaged creature. Its tentacles swiped at Ariel, keeping her away from the Shadowlord. As Ariel retreated, she slashed at the black arms that whipped about her. Each time she struck one it fell to the ground, turned into black wisps, and flowed back into the cloak.

As Ariel sliced at the tendrils that struck at her, Zorn got to his feet. He appeared to be unharmed, which was impossible. Ariel knew her low attack to his leg should have incapacitated him. No, she thought. He was much more than an evil man now.

"Zorn," she said quietly. The attacking tendrils ceased as

the Shadowlord stepped forward. "What happened to you? Why do you bring war upon the world?"

Zorn stopped. "I am destined to bring a new age to Alluria," he said in a dark tone. "Many will die before this war ends, but is it not always so in war?"

"And how many warriors did you lose to the dark wolf last night? They will never return to their homes in the mountains."

"Aye," he said with a nod. "Too many. The beast was particularly vicious. I will deal with him myself."

"Do not be a fool," Ariel said. "Even with your new powers and weapons you are no match for it."

"Perhaps not," Zorn said, "but I do not hunt the beast. I hunt the man."

Ariel's jaw dropped. Of course. The Shadowlord was hunting the man who became the beast at night. He was hunting Alex, not them.

"He saved you many times over," Ariel said. "You know this. Once we all fought together. Once we were friends. For the sake of that friendship and all that is good, stop this madness. No one else needs to die."

Ariel lowered her scimitars as a signal of her willingness to end the battle. Zorn also lowered his weapon and looked down. He appeared to be considering her plea. She continued, "Let me help you rid yourself of the darkness inside."

The Shadowlord raised his head and looked at her, and she tightened her grip on her weapons.

"You will fail, Ariel," he said. "You cannot stop what must happen."

"I must try," Ariel said. "End this."

"No!" He shouted as the cloak on his back expanded violently toward Ariel and enveloped her surroundings. Not even her elf sight revealed anything; she was in complete darkness. She heard Zorn's footsteps as he moved, and raised her scimitars to defend herself. He was now circling her.

"I see you," came a low voice from the darkness. "I know of two who need to die. You and Alex."

The voice was behind her and it was close. Ariel turned and slashed with both weapons, but struck nothing. Suddenly she felt a sharp, piercing pain in her upper arm and screamed as the smell of burning flesh assailed her senses. The Shadowlord had stabbed her left arm, and the blade's burning touch had cauterized the wound.

"Did you ever think you would die alone in the dark?" he asked, his voice full of scorn.

Ariel heard his footsteps again. She moved away from his voice, remembering how quick he was with his earlier attacks. She had to find a way out of this darkness before he cut her to pieces. Another hot, stabbing pain shot through her right thigh. Ariel screamed again and dropped to her knees.

She felt the cool, moist soil and grass beneath her hands. From the surrounding darkness she heard the Shadowlord's mocking laughter. She dug her fingers into the ground and waited till she felt it. A vibration. She felt every step he took and she knew exactly where he was. She felt something else. Warm energy flowed from the ground into her fingers, then hands, then to her wounds. She felt her skin harden and her form began to change.

Nature's awesome power flowed through her as she grew in height and strength. A beautiful pair of antlers sprouted from her head and her skin took on the appearance of bark from the ironwood tree. Ariel stood. She had grown to over seven feet tall and now she felt all living things around her. Their life forces permeated the darkness and saturated her, strengthened her. She saw the Shadowlord not ten feet away to her right. He was a black shape among an ocean teeming with life. He stood motionless, watching her transformation.

The power of life and nature coursed through her body and rippled inside, aching to be unleashed. Sensing she was able to see him in her new form, Zorn attacked. With a wave of her hand, Ariel commanded the winds to blow about her enemy, and a great gust of wind stopped him. The winds swirled with such force that bits of earth were ripped from the ground and circled the Shadowlord.

The darkness that had engulfed Ariel retreated and now resumed its wicked, wriggling form as his cloak. The Shadowlord yelled with rage and lunged at her. His blade struck her torso. Ariel felt a burning pain, but her bark-like skin protected her, for the most part. She crossed her arms and looked at Zorn.

"It is you who will fail," she said.

She flung her arms out in front of her, sending a great eruption of wind at him. The Shadowlord was blown off his feet and sent sailing far away though the air. Ariel watched his black shape disappear in the distance. Such a flight would kill any living man, but, she feared, not Zorn.

CHAPTER NINE
EVENING CONTEMPLATIONS

"Shouldn't we at least try to help Ariel?" Jane posed the question to Ishara and Sawyer. "If what we hear about this Shadowlord is true, won't she need help?"

"Ariel instructed us to find a safe place here at the foot of the mountains," Ishara said. "And then we will wait for her. She is elven-kind; more than a match for any human warrior."

Ishara's bravado seemed forced to Jane, who noticed Ishara furrowed her brow and bit her lower lip.

Sawyer raised his eyebrows and glanced back in Ariel's direction. Jane sighed and wrung her hands as she watched for any sign of Ariel's return.

"She'll be okay," Geoff said. "You'll see; she can take care of herself. After all, she's the high druid, right?"

"Indeed," Ishara nodded. "And a powerful one at that."

"Whoa! Did you see that?" Sawyer jumped to his feet, pointing back the way they had come. "Look!"

Jane also stood, as did Geoff, Ishara, and Willelm.

"What...what is that?" Willelm asked as a localized windstorm swirled violently over the green hills. No one answered; they only watched in amazement as the winds moved as if they were sentient. They were too far away to see what was happening at the center of the gusts.

"Is that Ariel?" Geoff asked, looking at Ishara.

She was watching intently, but she answered him with a quick nod.

"Look!" Sawyer pointed again. A black shape was hurled away from the squall with alarming velocity and disappeared in the distance.

"What *was* that?" Jane wasn't sure. Had she just seen someone launched like a rocket? She grabbed Sawyer's arm.

"It was him, wasn't it?" Geoff looked at Ishara. "It was the Shadowlord, right?"

"Yes," Ishara said. "It was."

"Then...then it's over?" Jane asked. "There's no way he could survive that, right?"

"One can only hope," Ishara said as she stepped forward and scanned the green hills.

"That was awesome!" Sawyer shouted. "She owned him!"

Jane smiled and clapped. It wasn't so bad here this time, she thought. With the Shadowlord dead, the war wouldn't continue. His armies would retreat back to the north and that would be the end of it.

"I do not understand. *Owned* him?" Ishara asked. Jane laughed, because Ishara was giving Sawyer a look like she thought he was crazy.

Sawyer laughed, too, and sheathed his sword. "Yeah. She won. She beat him up. She defeated him!"

Jane and Geoff laughed. Sawyer smiled at Jane and winked. He had that familiar mischievous smirk on his face.

"What? Oh yeah, you guys don't have video games here,

either," Sawyer said lightly. "You never played Halo or Battlefield or—"

"Oh, Sawyer, shut up," Jane interrupted, playfully putting her hand over his mouth as he feigned speaking and mumbled.

"Don't listen to him," Jane told Ishara as she pressed her hand firmly against Sawyer's mouth to stifle him. "He's nuts."

Ishara smiled.

"So what happens now?" Geoff asked.

Jane looked at Sawyer and then Ishara before answering.

"We go home," Jane said. "Right?"

Jane's heartbeat sped up at the thought of the Shadowlord's defeat. Could they really be going home soon? Her eyes became moist and she gulped back a sob as she realized how frightened she had been. They had survived an encounter with death. Normal things like the junior prom and kissing Sawyer again seemed like a million miles away.

"Even if Lord Zorn is dead," Ishara said, "it is best if we continue to the capital city of Chalon. News such as this must not be kept secret, and they will be safe there." Ishara indicated Willelm and his family as she finished speaking.

"Aye. Thank you," Willelm said as he wrapped an arm around his wife. "Thank you all."

Suddenly a troubling thought came to Jane. Where was Ariel? What if Ariel was injured? What if she needed help?

"We should go find Ariel," Jane said. "What if she's hurt?"

"She isn't," Geoff said. "Look!"

Jane and the others turned and saw Ariel trotting over a hill, coming their way. Jane let out a sigh of relief. She felt

Sawyer put his arm around her shoulders. She wrapped her arm around his waist and squeezed.

"It's all good now," Sawyer said. "No more bad guys in black."

"Yep, all good," Jane said.

As they watched Ariel come closer, Jane noticed she was holding her side as she ran. Was she out of breath? No, not Ariel. It seemed she could run for days without resting.

"Something's wrong," Jane said, her smile melting away. She let go of Sawyer and dashed toward Ariel, with the others close behind. Jane hoped she wasn't too badly injured. She and Sawyer were the first to reach Ariel, who had stopped and was bent over slightly, pressing her hand to a bleeding wound in her side.

"Are you okay?" Jane called. "Let me heal—"

"It will not heal," Ariel said, almost out of breath. "But I am, as you say, okay."

"I don't understand," Jane said. "I can try the healing spells you taught me. Oh...you're hurt in several places!" Jane placed her hand on Ariel's shoulder.

"If we don't do something," Sawyer said as Ishara and Geoff arrived with Willelm and his family, "you'll bleed to death."

"Let us help you," Ishara said with a slight bow of her head.

"I should have said they cannot be healed quickly by magic," Ariel replied. "However, they will heal with time."

Jane frowned. Ariel must've just been through a terrible battle and she obviously had a high threshold for pain. She examined Ariel's wounds more closely. Jane wasn't a doctor, but they didn't appear to be major wounds. The problem was how to stop the bleeding.

"Perhaps you and Ishara will help me bind these wounds?" Ariel asked.

"Yes, of course," Jane smiled reassuringly. "We'll take care of you."

Sawyer offered Ariel a shoulder to lean on as they walked back to the mountains. Jane took the other side, and she felt Ariel place most of her weight on the two of them.

"So that was the Shadowlord?" Sawyer asked. "You sent him flying miles away. He's gotta be dead when he lands."

"Aye, it was him," Ariel said. "Unfortunately, he is protected by the darkest magic. I believe we will see him again."

"Seriously? He can't survive that," Sawyer protested.

No one answered, and Jane's heart sank. She hoped Ariel was wrong, but deep down she knew that was unlikely.

They made camp under an outcropping of rocks at the base of the mountains and kept only a small fire burning so they wouldn't be noticed. Jane, Ishara, and Josephine all pitched in to bind Ariel's wounds with strips of cloth torn from Josephine's skirt and an extra cloak from Ishara's pack. Jane was surprised at Josephine's skill with cleaning and bandaging wounds. She was not the only one to notice.

"You are skilled at this," Ariel said from her spot by the fire.

Josephine smiled and nodded over her shoulder toward Willelm. "I've had plenty of practice. In his younger days he was a good fighter himself, but he always managed to return with a wound or two."

"Thank you," Ariel said.

"I don't get it," Geoff interjected, pointing at Ariel's arm and leg. "How is it your magic won't heal your wounds?

We've seen you heal worse than those before."

"You musta tried to heal yourself," Sawyer added. "Let Jane give it a shot, maybe she can heal you."

"I can at least try," Jane said hopefully.

"Very well. Please try." Ariel rubbed her injured side, indicating Jane should start with that wound. Jane placed her hand over the cut. She felt Ariel's warm body under her fingers and closed her eyes, then took a deep breath and concentrated as she spoke. "*Ehlia sa maros.*" She felt the same warm energy as before well up from deep inside and travel down her arms and fingers toward Ariel, but as the healing energy reached Ariel's wound, something prevented it from flowing into her. In Jane's mind, she saw a black patch over Ariel's wound that repulsed Jane's healing attempt like a wall. Jane gasped and opened her eyes, quickly removing her hands.

"Something's there," she said. "Something dark is covering your wounds. I can't get through."

Ariel nodded as if she expected that result.

"Wait," Sawyer said. "Don't you know another healing spell? The first one Ariel taught you. Isn't that spell a stronger one?"

Jane turned back to Ariel feeling a little more hopeful. Ariel smiled. Jane opened the pouch Ariel had given her and poured some crushed leaves over the wound. Again Jane placed her hand over the wound, and this time she uttered the words *Ilinara tae ullnara taethos.*

A larger surge of energy moved down Jane's arms and rebounded as soon as it reached Ariel's wound. This time Jane felt a malevolence. Something sinister had touched Ariel and left its mark.

"Oh!" Jane again removed her hands and looked at Ariel in astonishment. "The dark spot, it's evil. I think it *wants* you to suffer. I can feel it. Is it alive?"

Ariel shook her head. "I have been wounded by evil; this is true. But what you feel that prevents your healing is a residue, a small bit of the evil left by the Shadowlord's sword as it struck me."

"You aren't going to die, are you?" Geoff asked.

Ariel looked at Geoff and smiled. "No. Not tonight. My wounds simply need time to heal."

"Then you should rest," Ishara urged as she picked up her bow. "I will keep watch tonight."

"I'll stay close by in case you need something," Jane said as she put her hand on Ariel's.

"Aye, we both will. You rest now," Josephine said with a quick glance at Jane for approval.

Jane nodded and Ariel closed her eyes. It occurred to her this was the first time she had ever seen Ariel injured – or for that matter, seen her sleep. Jane turned to Sawyer and motioned for him to follow her. She walked beyond the other side of their camp, just far enough away for privacy.

She sat on a cold rock. Sawyer sat beside her, placing his sword on his other side. She took his hand and looked at him.

"Sawyer, I'm worried," she began. "Ariel is the best fighter we've ever seen. There isn't anyone she can't beat. But she barely survived her battle with the Shadowlord. What if next time she isn't so lucky?"

Sawyer looked down and thought for a moment.

"Yeah," he said. "I'd never be able to last more than a few seconds against Ariel in a fight, and if this Shadowlord guy almost killed her…" He let his words trail off and he sighed. "We've heard all along that he was a great warrior, right? If he can go toe to toe with Ariel, then I don't want to mess with him."

"Me either," Jane admitted. "When I tried to heal her and I said there was something evil keeping her from being healed…I've never felt anything like that. It was awful."

"There isn't much in Alluria that's familiar to me either," Sawyer said.

"No," Jane said, squeezing his arm to get his attention. "I mean it. I *felt* evil. Can you imagine what that's like? There was nothing good—no hope, only hate. It's as if something wanted her to bleed to death. It's hard to explain."

"Hey, you tried," Sawyer said. "Ariel is tough. She'll be all right. Besides, she won, didn't she? Sure, she's hurt, but wow! Did you see what she did to him? I bet he's still flying over Alluria."

Jane smiled, then as she thought about it she began to giggle. "He should've booked a flight on a different airline, huh?"

"Oh yeah. She took it to him."

"Badass," she said, laughing a little louder. "That's what Geoff called her; a badass."

Sawyer threw his head back and laughed. "No doubt."

Jane rested her head on his shoulder and sighed. "She owned him."

She looked out over the grass-covered hills that lay in front of them. She was comfortable. She felt safe. Whatever happens tomorrow, she was safe right now with Sawyer. She ran her hand up and down his arm.

"Sawyer," Jane whispered. "Do you still think we made a mistake coming back? I don't know what I was thinking."

"You were thinking about helping others," he said as he looked into her eyes. "It's what you do."

Jane tilted her head back.

"No. It's what *we* do." Sawyer leaned closer and then she felt his soft, warm lips on hers. She caressed the side of his face and neck as he wrapped an arm around her waist and pulled her close. Jane's heart was pounding. Whenever he pulled her close, her skin tingled. She ran her fingers through his thick, dark hair then grabbed a handful and pulled him back. She kept her lips on his and leaned on him.

Sawyer grabbed her hair and gave it a gentle tug. The next instant they slipped off the back of the rock and she let out a yelp as they landed in the grass with her on top of him. They looked at each other and laughed.

"Jane? Sawyer? Are you guys okay?" Geoff called from back at camp. "I heard something."

They remained motionless, looking at each other and trying not to giggle.

"Yeah, Geoff," Jane said. "We're fine. Sawyer just slipped on a rock." Her eyes gleamed and she smiled as Sawyer glared at her.

"He's clumsy like that," she added.

Suddenly she felt Sawyer's fingers aggressively tickling her sides. She opened her mouth and giggled as she squirmed and tried to fight off Sawyer's tickle attack.

"Okay," Geoff called back. "Ishara said to stay close."

"He's worse than a little brother," Sawyer whispered, still groping for Jane's side. Jane had managed to grab his wrists and twist them away, but she knew Sawyer was letting her handle him. She felt his strength as she struggled, and that was exciting, too.

"We'll be there in a minute," she answered. "I'm helping Sawyer up."

Her last sentence barely escaped her mouth before Sawyer placed both hands on her head and pulled her lips down to his. Oh wow, she thought. She let out a low moan as Sawyer placed his hands on the small of her back and held her tight. She felt his chest rise and fall with every breath he took. She ran her hands over his chest and lightly dug her nails into him. He responded with a flex.

"Mmm," she said. "Flex the pecs."

As she kissed him again, he alternated flexing the left side of his chest then the right in rapid succession.

She giggled. "How do you do that?"

Sawyer smiled. "Dunno. I just do it. Left, right, left, right, left, right."

She slapped his chest then pretended to play the bongos on him as he continued to flex. Sawyer's skin was warm.

"Hey," he said. "Shouldn't we be getting back?"

"Nope."

Jane was surprised at her immediate answer. She didn't want to seem too eager, but she didn't want this moment to end.

"Okay," he said. "Come 'ere." He wrapped his arms around her and pulled her to him again. She liked it when he took charge and kissed her. Something suddenly occurred to her. She lifted her head and looked into his eyes.

"Hey," she said, propping her head on her elbow, which rested on his chest. "What's the deal with you and Kylie? I haven't seen you with her lately. Are you two still dating? Because if you are..."

Sawyer shook his head. "No, she dumped me a week ago.

She said she just wasn't getting what she needed from our relationship."

"Oh? And what was missing for her?"

"Dunno," Sawyer said, putting his hands up in the air. "I'm not mature enough for her is the way she put it."

"Hmmm. Go figure," Jane said.

"I know, right?"

"So what did you do – or what *didn't* you do?" Jane asked, suddenly suspicious.

Sawyer wrinkled his nose and rolled his eyes.

"I kinda forgot her birthday," he said.

"Sawyer!" Jane punched his chest. "How could you do that to her?"

"Yeah, I know. I messed up big time."

"I bet she was hurt," Jane said.

"She was. I told her I was sorry and wanted to make it up to her, but she told me she was done. It was the last straw."

"Last straw? What else did you do?"

"She didn't like the way I treated Geoff and the other nerds. She said I was a childish bully."

Jane rolled off him and sat up. "Well, she has that right. You and your jock buddies need to leave Geoff alone."

"Hey, what's wrong? I thought we were doing so well…"

"Sawyer, sometimes you're so irresponsible. You can't just do what you want and not think there will be consequences. Geoff matters. So did Kylie."

Sawyer rolled onto his side in the grass.

"Are you really upset?"

"You can be such a jerk, you know that?" Jane said in digust.

"I don't mean anything when I mess with Geoff. It's just

too easy. He's a good target, I guess."

"He's a person, just like you. Leave him alone from now on. In fact, stop picking on anyone at school."

"Hey, what did I do? I just answered your question and you get all mad at me," Sawyer protested.

He was right. She had ruined their romantic moment. She didn't want to be 'Sawyer's next girl,' however, and she wanted to be sure he and Kylie weren't still dating.

"I'm sorry," she said. "Just promise me you'll stop picking on Geoff and his friends."

"I don't think he has any friends."

"Sawyer!"

"Hey, I'm not trying to be mean. But I never see him hanging out with anyone, do you?"

Jane tried to remember the last time she had seen Geoff doing something with other kids, but she wasn't able to recall.

"No."

Jane felt Sawyer place a hand on her back and start to rub her shoulders. She closed her eyes. Whatever stress she felt moments ago was rubbed away by his magic fingers. Jane lowered her head so he could rub the back of her neck, too. Not only did he rub her neck, but he also rubbed her temples. She could really get into this. Suddenly Sawyer stopped, jumped to his feet, and pointed to the north.

"Hey! What the hell is that?"

CHAPTER TEN
THE PROPHECY

Jane's eyes followed Sawyer's finger. There, in the distance, a long, intermittent trail of orange lights snaked its way toward the west. She squinted in an effort to figure out what she was seeing.

"What is that, Sawyer?"

"Dunno," he said. "C'mon. We better tell the others." They hurried back to camp and found Geoff sitting beside Ariel, who was resting, while Ishara scanned the forest. Willelm, Josephine, Elayne, and Derek had settled in for the night by the fire.

"Hey," Sawyer said. "There's a bunch of lights out there. That way." He pointed to the west.

"We don't know what they are—" Jane was interrupted by Ishara.

"Refugees," Ishara said. "Families and survivors walking to Chalon in hopes of finding safety."

"Wait. How do you know?" Jane asked.

Ishara nodded in the direction Sawyer had pointed. "Elves have exceptional night vision. I saw them some time ago."

"Oh yeah," Jane said, remembering Ariel's uncanny sight in the dark as they had fled from the werewolf.

"Should we join them?" Geoff asked. "Safety in numbers, right?"

"Not tonight," Ishara said. "Ariel needs rest. Perhaps we will catch up with them tomorrow."

Geoff glanced at Ariel. "Yeah. She does need rest."

"Pardon me," Willelm said as he sat up. "If those folks are like us, they'll have heard the same stories, won't they? They'll have heard elves are in league with the Shadowlord and helped start this war."

"So do we avoid them?" Jane asked. "We're going to Chalon, too. Isn't that a big city filled with humans?"

"They won't try to hurt you and Ariel, will they?" Sawyer asked, looking at Ishara.

"I do not know," Ishara said. "The people you see walking through the darkness, they have lost their homes and perhaps their loved ones. Who knows what they will do if they see an elf?"

"But your people are fighting the Shadowlord," Jane protested. "You aren't helping him."

"True enough. We fight for our lives," Ishara said, looking at Willelm, "just as you."

"Do you think the elves will come and fight with humans again? Like the old days?" Willelm asked.

"I do not know," Ishara said. "There is so much distrust."

"Yes," Ariel said. Everyone turned to her and listened. "Elves and humans must stand together or all is lost. I am sure I can help convince the elves to renew their alliance with humans, but I am not sure humans wish such an alliance."

"Then we have to tell them," Jane said. "We have to

make them understand. We have to tell them what we've seen."

"That," Ishara said, "is not an easy task. Humans can be so…" Her voice tapered off.

"Irrational," Ariel said. "Chalon is filled with humans. It is the largest city in the realm and the center of trade."

"Aye," Willelm said. "I've been there. Once, when I was younger. A great walled city where goods from everywhere can be bought an' sold."

"So this Lionel guy." Jane cleared her throat. "What is he again? The lord of Chalon?"

"Lord Magistrate," Ariel said.

"Okay, so we go to Chalon and convince him and anyone else to join the elves and we fight the Shadowlord."

"A good plan," Ariel said. "That is my intention when we arrive at Chalon."

"But didn't you say Lionel can be a butthead?" Sawyer's question drew several strange looks from the others. "Oh, right. Sorry. I mean, isn't he hard to get along with?"

"He is, but I hope our dire situation will make him more reasonable," Ariel replied.

"So what do we do if you can't convince him to join with the elves?" Geoff asked.

"And," Sawyer added, "aren't the elves still under siege or something? They're fighting the Shadowlord in their own backyard, right? So how do we get the elves and humans together even if Lionel *does* agree to an alliance?"

"There are more than a few elves," Ishara said, "who would resist such an alliance. Our people do not trust humans. There is a long history of betrayal and war associated with men. Animosity exists on both sides."

"Oh great," Sawyer said. "Sounds like even if we did get elves and humans together they're gonna fight each other instead of the Shadowlord."

"Dwarves," Geoff said. "What about the dwarves? They'll fight, won't they?"

"Yeah!" Jane said, looking at Ishara and Ariel hopefully. "That's a good idea."

"An alliance already exists between elves and humans," Ariel said as she shifted her weight to her uninjured side, "but it has been ignored for hundreds of years by both sides. Elves had honored the pact in the past, but the kings and leaders of men have not. And when they chose to do so, they demanded payment."

Jane frowned as she thought about what Ariel had said. With years of fighting and distrust, there didn't seem to be any way to bring men and elves together.

Jane looked at Ariel. It looked like she'd drifted off to sleep. "Baldon," Ishara said. "Baldon Stonemaster. He is the key to the dwarves."

"Baldon? Who's Baldon?" Sawyer asked.

"He is the king of Keredain," she said, pointing with her bow to the south. "And he is a friend of the lawful ruler of Chalon."

"Lionel," Sawyer said.

"No," Ishara said. "You have already fought him."

"Wait," Geoff said. "Is that—"

"The man in tattered animal skins? Yes," Ishara said. "His name is Alex, and he is the crown prince of Chalon. He has also been hunting us."

Another silence fell over the camp. Geoff cleared his throat. "But he *helped* us get away from those bandits. I saw it. He may be weird, but he's a good guy. Why would he hunt us?"

"It is the werewolf that hunts you," Ariel said quietly. "The beast is drawn to you as darkness is drawn to light. The man seeks to protect you."

"Okay," Jane said. "*Why* is it hunting us? We've been asking ourselves that ever since we first arrived. What makes us a tastier meal than anyone else?"

"Your auras," Ishara said. She walked over to Jane and Geoff and knelt, setting her bow down beside her.

"As Ariel said, darkness is drawn to light. Your auras shine and are visible to those who can see such things—elves, orcs, dwarves, and a few other races, for example. Magical and unnatural creatures can see it, as can darker, evil creatures."

"Like werewolves? So what is an aura anyway?" Sawyer asked.

"It is who you are and who you have the potential to become. When I look at the three of you I see a bright shimmer around you. That is your aura."

"And what do you see when you look at Ariel?" Jane asked.

"I see a similar glow. Her aura shifts between gold and white."

"Because she is the high druid," Jane said.

"Because she is elven-kind."

"When you saw the Shadowlord, what did his aura look like? I bet it was solid black," Sawyer said.

"Yes," Ishara said.

"And Alex?" Jane asked. "What did you see when you looked at him?"

Ishara hesitated. Her eyes darted back and forth as she chose her words before she spoke.

"Within him is a struggle between light and dark. I saw this when we met him. I see black and white. Such a contradiction of auras indicates a tortured soul. However, I saw more of a black aura when I looked at him."

"So he's evil, too. Just like the Shadowlord," Sawyer said.

"I do not know," Ishara said with a quick shake of her head. "He is torn inside; that much is true. I think it is a mark left on him by his curse. Perhaps his rage darkens his aura. I am only surmising."

"But getting back to Jane's question," Geoff said. "I remember you started to tell me something when we saw the wild man in animal skins—Alex. Remember? Back at Somerdale? It had to do with a prophecy. What was it?"

"What're you talking about, Geoff?" Sawyer asked.

"Do you remember when we went home the last time we were here?" Geoff looked at Sawyer and then Jane. "I told you I heard Ariel and Ishara talking about it being foretold that we would come, or something like that, I think."

"The three travelers," Willelm said quietly from behind Geoff. "The Outlanders."

They turned and looked at him. Jane noticed that his mouth had dropped open. What had surprised him like that?

"Yeah," Geoff said. "That was it."

He turned back to Ishara. "Wasn't it? You began to tell me, but then the wild man, Alex, was attacked."

Ishara took a breath and looked at them.

"Many years ago, the oracle of Khorthos, an island far to the south, foresaw many things. She was dying, but she prophesied the coming of these dark times, when Alluria faced a great evil and would fall into chaos. Because she was on her deathbed, many dismissed her ramblings as a fit of delirium. It had become more of a myth or children's fable until recently."

There was another moment of silence, then Sawyer spoke. "Let's hear it."

Ishara closed her eyes. "In the year of three travelers, outlanders from far away, the white warrior will fall and a time of darkness begins. The lands shall be torn asunder and their people splintered. In the mountain kingdom, storms and love prevail. Only a knightly sacrifice may bring an end to chaos, for there will only be peace when the dark wolf and the scarlet dragon embrace."

"Yeah, right," Sawyer said. "So what does all that mean? We're the three travelers?"

"That is what Ariel believes," Ishara said. She looked at Geoff. "It is what I believe as well."

"So the three of us show up and war breaks out? Seems like we should've stayed home," Sawyer said.

"I guess Lord Zorn is the white warrior," Jane said, licking her lips. "That makes Alex the dark wolf, but I have no clue about the scarlet dragon."

"I don't know about you," Sawyer said with a shake of his head, "but after seeing that werewolf up close twice now, I'm pulling for the scarlet dragon to win, 'cause I don't see that thing hugging a dragon."

"Um, guys," Geoff began, looking at Jane and Sawyer, "that prophecy didn't say anything about the three travelers surviving and going home."

"He's right," Jane said. "Is that all of the prophecy? What happens to us?"

"I do not know," Ishara replied. "But I also believe in happy endings." She smiled at Jane.

"And," Geoff continued, "the prophecy doesn't say who wins, the good guys or the bad guys. 'There will only be peace when the dark wolf and the scarlet dragon embrace.' Neither one sounds like a something to cheer for."

"Geez, Geoff," Sawyer said, picking up a pebble and tossing it at him. "Did you already memorize it? You can stay up all night analyzing what that mumbo jumbo means, but I'm getting some sleep." He turned to Ishara. "Unless you want me to take a shift at watch?"

Ishara shook her head as Jane glared at Sawyer. Jane couldn't believe what she had just seen, and punched Sawyer in the arm.

"Ow! What?" His confused gaze indicated he had no idea why she punched him.

Jane leaned close and whispered through her clenched teeth, "You said you would stop picking on Geoff, remember?"

"Oh…yeah…right," Sawyer said. "Sorry about throwing a rock at you, Geoff." He turned to Jane. "Happy?"

"Not really," she said.

Sawyer let out a loud sigh. "Okay, I'll work on it."

"Work hard," Jane demanded. She noticed little Derek, who was sitting beside his father and staring at Sawyer. She nudged Sawyer and motioned toward the small farm boy. Sawyer glanced at him and then looked down. He seemed genuinely ashamed of his behavior. Sawyer beckoned Derek over and let him hold the Stormblade again.

The boy's eyes lit up, and he smiled as he grasped the sword. Sawyer showed Derek how to properly hold it in his small hands, and the boy's eyes brightened. His reverence for

Sawyer was nothing short of hero worship. Jane realized that to everyone else in Alluria, Sawyer was a hero, whether or not he agreed with that assessment. Sawyer and Derek played for a little while before Josephine made Derek return the sword to Sawyer and get to bed.

"Not bad, hero," Jane whispered in his ear. "Not bad at all."

Sawyer grunted. "I'm no hero," He nodded at Ariel. "She's the hero."

"That's true," Jane said. "But I think we can have more than one hero, don't you?"

"Nope," Sawyer said flatly. "She can have the honors all to herself. I'm just a sidekick, like the rest of us."

"Sawyer," she said, "you carry that sword and that makes you the Stormlord. To these people that means you're some kind of legendary hero. They look up to you."

"Yeah?" he said, smiling. "Guess I better watch my language, huh?"

"I don't get it," Jane said. "Back in our world you have no problem being Mr. Popularity and a star quarterback. But here, you're just kind of going through the motions."

Sawyer stopped preparing his blanket for sleep and thought. Jane didn't want to guilt him or make him feel bad. She put a hand on his arm.

"Hey," she said. "Don't worry about it. I know if the time ever came, you'd rise to the occasion. You always do."

Sawyer nodded. He may not let on as much, she thought, but he enjoyed playing the part of the hero.

That night as they slept, she snuggled into his back and wrapped her arm over him. She didn't see another line of torch-bearing refugees pass by in the distance, nor did she hear them. Jane tossed and turned, dreaming of a dark castle high in the mountains. She was flying toward it, but she didn't want to go. She was trapped. As she flitted in and out of sleep, she thought she heard someone walking around. In another part of the camp, two small, shadowy figures tiptoed away into the night.

CHAPTER ELEVEN
TRAIL OF REFUGEES

"Ishara," Geoff said between breaths as they ran away from camp, "where're we going?"

Running through the cool night air with Ishara was an adventure. They traveled west, into the grasslands and toward the trail of burning torches in the distance. Geoff knew Ishara wouldn't have nudged him awake if she didn't have a good reason. He didn't care what the reason was as long as he was with her.

They stopped on a grassy slope. The moonlight accentuated Ishara's features, especially her green eyes, which became luminescent in the dark.

"I wish to have a closer look at these people," Ishara said. "Ariel needs rest, so that makes you the next quietest member of our group."

"Okay, but why do you want a closer look?" Geoff asked. "Will everyone be all right back at camp? What if those barbarians attack while we're away? Worse yet, what if we bump into the Shadowlord?"

"It is only for a moment, sneak thief," Ishara answered. The others will be fine. If we see the Shadowlord, we run."

"But why do you want me to come with you?" Geoff asked. You're much quieter and faster without me tagging along."

"I am not sure," Ishara said. "Perhaps it is because I enjoy sneaking with you."

"Me too," he said with a quick smile. "So what's the plan?"

"There," Ishara pointed to a grouping of five or six people trudging along with torches.

"I hear voices," Geoff said, "but we're too far away. If we can get close enough to hear, why don't we just go up to them and start a conversation?"

"Because," Ishara said, "I am an elf. Do you not remember what Willelm and Josephine said? Humans blame elves for this war. So…"

"Oh. Yeah, that's right." Geoff swallowed. He was glad it was dark, because he felt his face suddenly become warm. He felt like he was sneaking into his father's study again.

A quick nod and tilt of her head indicated they were to resume their sneaking. A rush of adrenaline invigorated him as they continued toward the long line of orange dots against the dark landscape. They kept to the lower dips between hills. Slowing as they approached their target group, Ishara held up a finger for quiet. Geoff stopped and listened. He heard several voices over the sounds of carts and horses. With her keen hearing, he was sure Ishara heard them long before he did.

"How much further to Chalon?" asked an elderly male voice with a cough. He was answered by a teenaged boy. "Not far now, Father. We'll be there by midmorning. Then we'll be safe."

"Elves," spat another man. Geoff could hear the loathing

in his voice. "I hate 'em. What'd we ever do to 'em? We should kill them high an' mighty tree lovers. All of 'em."

Geoff looked at Ishara. He tapped her on the shoulder and whispered into her ear, "Elves aren't attacking them. It's the barbarians and the Shadowlord. Can't they see that?"

Ishara shook her head. "I do not think so. Rumors and conspiracies have a way of revealing the darkest undercurrents in people. No, I believe all who have seen the barbarians are either dead or captured. It is human nature to label everyone and everything. Those who are different are often shunned and persecuted."

"Yeah," Geoff said. "That's pretty much right, even in my world. I usually get persecuted every day at school."

Ishara turned to him with a puzzled look. "You? Persecuted? Are you not accepted by others?"

"Not really," Geoff said, smiling to hide his embarrassment. "I'm not like most teenagers." Ishara stared intently at him as he swallowed and continued. "I'm shorter and weaker than the others, so I get picked on."

"Do you not have friends who will stand with you and protect you?"

Ishara's question caught him off guard. "No," he said.

"And Jane and Sawyer? Are they not your friends?"

Geoff fidgeted in the grass. He hadn't prepared himself for this line of questioning, and he was worried Ishara wouldn't like him anymore because he was weak.

"Well, yeah. I don't know. Jane is nice to me."

"And Sawyer Stormlord?"

Geoff didn't say anything, but he knew his silence was a clear answer for Ishara. She clenched her jaw and turned back to the refugees. For the next ten minutes they heard more of the same. Elves were blamed for everyone's misfortune. Some passing refugees mentioned dwarves as well.

"We should return to the others," Ishara said.

They stayed low as they made their way back. Before they entered camp Ishara stopped and looked at him.

"You should know that I am fond of you, Geoff. I wish you could see what I see when I look at you."

Geoff's eyes opened wide and this time he swallowed loudly. He had no idea what to say.

"Know this; I will not allow you to be harmed or mistreated."

"Thanks," he said.

Ishara kissed him on the cheek.

"Now get some rest, sneak thief. We travel to Chalon tomorrow." Ishara's smile had returned.

Geoff surveyed the camp as he entered. Nothing had changed, except Jane and Sawyer were snuggled in each other's arms. They really do like each other, he thought as he prepared for sleep. He looked at Ishara, who had resumed her watch. She returned his look and winked.

Geoff smiled and pulled his blanket over his shoulders. He took a deep breath and closed his eyes. A peaceful feeling washed over him.

Hours later, the smell of smoke and the sound of something sizzling woke him.

"There he is," Jane said with a bright, cheery voice. "Wake up, sleepyhead."

Geoff sat up and let his blanket fall away as he stretched. He yawned and looked around. Jane, Josephine, and Ishara were huddled around the campfire preparing breakfast. Derek and Elayne danced about and played as they ate from their small plates. Willelm laughed watching them as he also ate. Ariel had also awakened and was on the far side of camp testing her wounds. Sawyer was snoring. His arms were wrapped around Jane's blanket.

"Why's everyone so happy?" Geoff asked.

Josephine and Jane exchanged glances and smiled.

"Because," Ishara said as she walked over and presented him with a plate of breakfast that consisted of bread, cheese, some warm and tasty-smelling sausage, and an apple, "we will be in Chalon soon."

"And we will be safe," Josephine piped up. "Safe and sound."

"Aye," Willelm said, popping a piece of bread into his mouth. "I should be able to find work sure enough. An' I'll wager we won't have any problem finding a place to settle for the evenings until the war is over. Then we go home an' rebuild."

Geoff thought Willelm sounded way too upbeat, considering what he and Ishara had seen last night, not to mention the burned village the day before. He quietly ate his breakfast, which was delicious. When he was done, he stood and stretched again as the morning sun warmed his face. He closed his eyes and stood still, soaking in the sun's rays.

"Get up, Sawyer!" Jane said. She had prepared his plate and knelt beside him, shaking his shoulder. "Time to eat. Let's go, lazy man."

Sawyer sat up with a snort and looked around.

"Wha? Where am I?"

The surprised look on his face and the disheveled state of his hair made Jane laugh as she handed him a plate.

"Here," she said. "Eat up. We gotta get going."

"Thanks, babe," he said to Jane, not realizing he had uttered a term of affection. Geoff caught it, and judging from the sidelong glances and smiles between Josephine and Ishara, he wasn't the only one.

Sawyer finished his breakfast even faster than Geoff, and soon thereafter they set out for Chalon. Ariel limped noticeably, which worried Geoff. He shot Ishara an inquisitive glance, and she reassured him with a nod. As the dirt road came into view, more refugees were seen on their way to Chalon. Ariel stopped and pulled the hood of her cloak over her head. Ishara did the same.

"Why are you pulling up your hoods?" Jane asked.

"It is as Willelm said," Ariel answered. "Most humans blame elves for their troubles these days. I would rather we not have anything unfortunate happen on our journey."

"Aye," Willelm said. "Don't worry. You saved us. We'll tell them the truth. We'll tell them all."

"Aye, indeed," Josephine said. "They must know elves aren't to blame."

"I thank you," Ariel said from under her hood, "but for the time being, let this be our secret."

She tossed a blanket to Ishara. "Your bow," she said. "It is elven and must be concealed."

Ishara wrapped her bow, tied it with a couple of pieces of leather, and tucked it under her arm.

"Sawyer," Ariel said as she pointed at his sword, "perhaps you should conceal the Stormblade as well. It is easily recognizable."

Sawyer did as he was told and they joined the refugees on the small dirt road. Geoff thought it looked more like a worn path in the grasslands. There were several wagons and carts filled with personal belongings, and some carried people who were too young or too old to walk. Some carts carried wounded people, too. He was about to ask Jane if she thought it would be a good idea to help them with a healing spell when she walked past him. She went to the back of a cart in which a young mother was caring for her daughter.

The girl couldn't have been more than five or six years old.

"Jane," Ariel said.

The tone in her voice was stern and carried an implicit warning. From the look in her eyes, Geoff was sure she didn't think it was a good idea to cast spells here. Jane turned around.

"I can help them," she insisted. "Both of us can."

"Jane, come here," Ariel said.

Jane hesitated. She looked back at the sick girl and her mother, and then went to Ariel.

"What?" Jane asked, holding her arms out from her sides.

"Do you remember our earlier lesson when we discussed how you can weaken yourself? Casting too many spells will take a toll on you."

"I remember," she said. "But what good is being able to heal people if I can't do it? Look at them, Ariel. They need us."

"Yes," Ariel said. "They *all* need us to heal them in some fashion. Look at how many people are before us. You are compassionate and strong. I admire that in you. But you are not strong enough to heal them all."

Jane looked around. "*We* can."

"Jane, what do you think will happen if they discover you have healing powers? If *we* have healing powers? We will be overrun with people begging for help." Ariel pointed to her hood. "And if they find out what I am…"

Jane sighed. "I understand. You don't have to help me. I'll help as many as I can, and when I start to get tired I'll stop. I promise. But I have to try. It's the right thing to do."

Ariel studied Jane for a moment. Geoff saw her green eyes move from Jane to the refugees and then she nodded.

"Very well," Ariel said quietly. "Here, take this with you. It contains more materials for your spells." She handed Jane another leather pouch.

"Thank you. I'll be careful." Jane whirled around and dashed back to the cart with the girl and her mother. Geoff kept his eyes on Ariel. She watched Jane with an approving expression, but something occurred to Geoff and he walked over to Ariel.

"Ariel, if you gave Jane your spell components, how will you help heal these people?"

Ariel leaned closer to Geoff and whispered, "You are very observant, Geoff. I will tell you. I no longer need such materials to cast spells."

"Oh, okay," he said. "It's a high druid thing."

"It is," Ariel said. "I am, however, still learning about humans. The three of you have taught me so much. Perhaps I was wrong to think so poorly of them. You are amazing, Geoff. You all are."

Geoff smiled. Ariel had just shared some of her feelings with him, and he found that comforting.

"Thanks. We think you're amazing, too."

Ariel placed her arm around Geoff's shoulder.

"You may not realize this yet," she said, "but ever since you returned to Alluria, good things have begun to happen."

Geoff looked down and thought about what Ariel had said. What was she referring to? They hadn't done anything except run for their lives, like before.

"I don't understand," he said. "We're just following you. We're just kids."

Ariel stopped and leaned close again. "Kids? I think you are giants." She pointed to Jane in the back of the cart. "Look."

Geoff and Ariel looked on as Jane healed the feverous girl. Her mother immediately burst into tears as she hugged and kissed Jane, thanking her profusely. Sawyer was following the cart, watching Jane and giving her a thumbs up.

"See?" Ariel said. "Amazing."

Geoff smiled. "So you like humans better now?"

"Some, yes." Ariel said. "There are only a handful of humans of which I am fond; three in particular."

A wide grin fell across Geoff's face.

Other refugees heard the commotion and came to see what had happened. Once they discovered Jane was a healer, she was surrounded. Just as Ariel had predicted, they begged her to help their sons, daughters, wives, husbands, and even their elderly parents. Sawyer stepped in and put an arm around her while he waved them off.

"Wait! Hold up! Get in line!" he shouted. "We'll be along as soon as we can, okay?"

Most of the refugees, mainly farmers and laborers, followed Sawyer's directions. A handful were so desperate for Jane's help they wouldn't leave her. Jane went from one injured or ailing person to another, healing and comforting them. She didn't hesitate; she was determined to help as many as she could before her strength gave out.

"Come," Ariel said as she tapped Geoff on the arm. "Get me to that wagon. I see some men who are gravely injured."

Geoff helped Ariel to a wagon that was pulled by two oxen. Inside lay four men with recent battle wounds. The amount of blood made Geoff feel a bit queasy, and he looked away as he helped Ariel into the wagon. Ishara caught his eye. Where did she come from? She had been behind him the whole time. She was smiling at him.

A loud cough from the wagon brought his attention back to Ariel. She chanted and gently ran her fingers over the men's wounds, and one by one, they opened their eyes. Geoff was overcome by a sense of happiness. He watched as they examined their fully healed wounds and stared at each other.

Geoff and Ishara helped Ariel off the wagon as the men thanked her. Ariel acknowledged them with a wave of her hand and a quick bow of her head.

"See?" Geoff said to Ariel with a big smile. "Amazing."

Ariel raised an eyebrow. Word quickly spread among the refugees that they had not one but two healers traveling with them. Jane and Ariel each worked tirelessly to restore the health of any refugees in need as the column moved along. Geoff was relieved no one tried to pull Ariel's hood back and reveal her elven features. Would they still be grateful for her help if they knew she was an elf?

The four men Ariel had healed were members of the local militia and showed their appreciation by helping keep Jane and Ariel from being mobbed by the other refugees. They assumed the role of bodyguards, keeping an eye out for their safety.

Willelm and Josephine were elated to find some old friends to travel with and thanked Ariel and the others for all they had done. Ariel gave Willelm a small pouch of gold coins and bade him find safe lodging for his family as soon as they arrived in Chalon. Derek let it slip to some other kids that Sawyer was the Stormlord. Thankfully, no one believed him, and Sawyer was left alone.

The sun was high when Geoff felt a tap on his shoulder. He turned to find Ishara pointing ahead of them, at something in the distance

"Look there," she said. "Chalon."

Chapter Twelve
Chalon

Geoff stopped and his mouth fell open. Sunlight danced and sparkled off tiled roofs and glinted from battlements along the ramparts and towers of the large walled city before them. It was roughly rectangular, with two outer walls completely surrounding it. The outer curtain supported no fewer than two dozen massive round towers, while the inner curtain boasted at least twenty towers along its higher wall structure.

Within the walls, Geoff saw roofs of smaller buildings, some with plumes of gray smoke rising from their chimneys. The stream of refugees led right to the front gates, which were gigantic thirty-foot ironbound wooden doors behind an equally impressive portcullis.

"Beautiful," Geoff said with amazement. "It's beautiful."

Ishara laughed. "Not bad," she said, "for humans."

A large crowd of people had gathered at the portcullis, which Geoff realized had been lowered to prevent anyone from entering the magnificent city. Makeshift tents and shelters had sprung up just outside the giant gates.

"Why is the gate closed?" he asked.

"Because," Ishara said, "it is a human city ruled by greedy humans. We should not expect better treatment."

"But these people need help," Geoff said. "They need protection and shelter. They need food."

"Their needs are of no concern for the nobles," Ishara said. "Especially to the lord magistrate, who uses his office to line his pockets with gold."

Geoff frowned. How could this happen? It didn't seem right that so many were left to suffer.

"Stay close," Ariel said as she moved past.

She still had her hood pulled over her head, and with her slight limp she blended in perfectly with the crowd of refugees. Sawyer and Jane were behind her, and seemed to be marveling at the great walled city as well.

"This is so cool," Geoff said. He wondered what life was like in such a city, but Ishara gripped his collar and pulled him after the others.

"You are *not* staying close," she said. They fell back in line, and as they neared the walls, Geoff saw the city's defenses bristled with all sorts of medieval weapons of war, such as ballistae and catapults.

"It looks like the castles I toured in Italy with my family a few years ago," Jane said. "You should've seen them, Sawyer. They were wonderful."

Jane was smiling and had a bounce in her step. She grabbed Sawyer's wrist and pulled him along. Geoff smiled. Jane and Sawyer were having fun, and since he was being dragged down the dirt road to Chalon as well, he may as well enjoy the situation, and learn something about medieval life.

As they passed more and more of those who had been exiled from their homes, Geoff took notice of two girls with dirty faces and unkempt hair riding in the back of another ox-drawn cart. They must be sisters, Geoff thought, because they look so similar, but the vacant look of their red and swollen eyes was what affected him the most. His smile faded, and a wave of sadness descended on him. Jane had stopped skipping and also took notice of the homeless people around them.

"I wish I could do something for these people," Geoff said. He felt a gentle squeeze from Ishara as she grabbed his hand.

"You are doing something," she said. "We all are. It is, however, unfortunate that those who are the most innocent suffer the most in war."

Geoff had read enough about war in history class to know Ishara was right. Still, being this close to war made him tremble a little.

"I hope Ariel killed Zorn," Geoff said.

"As do I," Ishara said quietly. "As do I."

Once in a while Jane would stop and cast a healing spell on a sick or injured person, but after a while, she became visibly weaker and began to have difficulty maintaining her balance as she walked. Sawyer wrapped an arm around her waist and steadied her.

"I think that's enough healing for a while," Sawyer said. "You need to take it easy."

Jane didn't respond. She leaned heavily against Sawyer and let him guide her to the great walled city.

"As I suspected," Ariel said, "her compassion for others is remarkable. She would help them all at the cost of her own well-being."

Jane had always had a soft spot for those in need,

especially animals. She had a good heart; Geoff didn't need to see her aura to know that.

As they drew nearer to the gates of Chalon, Geoff noticed hundreds of refugees had set up camp along the road and next to the walled city. The smell of cooking fires lit by dung made him choke, and he covered his nose and mouth with his shirt. The unsanitary conditions surrounding them were appalling.

Sounds of moaning came from all around as Geoff realized many more people required medical attention. Some exhibited gaping wounds and cuts that appeared to have been the result of battle, while others were pale and vomited from illness.

"Why doesn't someone help them?" Geoff asked.

"Lionel," Ariel said grimly. "Only a pompous, callous fool would do nothing to ease their suffering."

Sobs and wailing from the destitute folk at the foot of the gate went unanswered as guards standing high atop the walls looked down at them with indifferent expressions.

"Sawyer," Ariel said, "come with me. Let Geoff and Ishara take care of Jane."

Sawyer nodded as Geoff hurried to Jane's side. She seemed to be getting weaker. Ishara positioned herself on the other side of her. Between the two of them, they gave her enough support so that she could continue walking.

Ariel gave Sawyer instructions as they walked to the large gate. "We must convince them to let these people inside. If it should become necessary, reveal the Stormblade to the guards above."

"Wait," Sawyer held up a hand. "Didn't you tell me it would be dangerous to show the sword to people? Won't they try to kill me for it?"

"Sawyer," Ariel said. "These people are suffering and need something to believe in; they need hope. If they see the Stormblade being wielded by the Stormlord…well, that should be enough for now. And I doubt the gates will remain closed."

The lamentations and noises from the surrounding crowd made it impossible for Geoff to hear Ariel and Sawyer as they stood before the gates. He noticed that Ishara's attention was focused on them, however.

"What're they going to do?" Geoff asked.

Ishara shook her head. "I am not sure."

Geoff opened his mouth to ask another question, but before he uttered a single word Ariel's voice rose above the clamor all about them.

"You there! Guard! Open these gates!"

A lone guard standing above on the wall flung the remaining swill from his cup down at Ariel.

"Be gone, wench! Off with ya!"

"I am no wench. Open them, I say!"

"Ya deaf? Be gone, I say!"

"These people need help. Are you blind? Let them in and give them shelter."

The guard's tone became a taunt. "The gates'll stay closed by order of the king!" he said.

"King? What king?" Ariel demanded.

"Ya been hidin' in a forest? What's the matter with ya? I mean his majesty, King Lionel the First, high king of Chalon and lord of Alluria."

Ariel didn't respond. Their conversation had drawn the attention of many nearby refugees. Then Ariel removed the hood which concealed her elven features. There were gasps, and then silence fell over the area. Sawyer glanced around. His eyes were wide.

"I am Ariel Windsong of Selra'thel, high druid of Alluria, lady of the House of Windsong, designated representative of the elven kingdoms, sacred protector of the Eldritch Forest, holder of nature's gift and I demand you open these gates now!"

"Oh, wow," Jane said.

Geoff's jaw dropped. The incredulous look in Jane's eyes showed her to be as impressed by Ariel's credentials as he was. Ishara only smiled. Now he began to understand why Ishara had always deferred to Ariel. She's elven nobility. He always thought she looked regal, but Geoff had no idea she was all those things. Her commanding tone drew the attention of more guards as they gathered to gawk at the elven beauty below ordering them to open the gates.

"Wicked fairy!" came a female voice from the nearby crowd.

"Treacherous elf!" called a rough male voice as a bit of cabbage was hurled at Ariel, striking her in the back.

"Uh-oh. What do we do?" Geoff asked. Ariel was pelted with all manner of rotten fruits and vegetables. Sawyer was also struck by a few errant projectiles meant for Ariel.

Ishara pulled her bow out and quickly nocked an arrow.

"Ariel!" Geoff shouted as he ran toward her and Sawyer. He stopped for a moment, however. Something caught his eye. To his left, in the crowd, he saw a figure wearing a dark gray cloak spin and run away. There was too much commotion to see much more, but it quickly disappeared. There was something familiar about the way it moved, gracefully maneuvering through the crowd. Suddenly he was bumped by a surge from the crowd of refugees and fell to the muddy ground. He heard Jane's voice over the jeers and insults aimed at Ariel. She was calling his name.

Geoff continued to be bumped and trampled as he rolled around, trying to get to his feet. He managed to get to his knees when he felt someone grab his arm and help him up. It was Ishara.

"Are you unharmed?" she asked, looking him over.

"Yeah, I'm okay," he said, brushing some of the filth off when he noticed the smell. "Ugh. Gross! This isn't mud! At least, not all of it."

"No, it is not," Ishara said as she took a step back. Ariel and Sawyer were completely surrounded by the refugees, who had become more hostile. They hurled racial slurs and accusations at Ariel, blaming her for all their misery.

"Hey! Hey! Stop it! She didn't do anything! She's on your side! She's here to help! Leave her alone!" Sawyer shouted, holding up his hands in an attempt to calm them.

"Sawyer, show them the Stormblade," Ariel said as they were jostled about.

Sawyer quickly removed his sword and held it overhead. At that moment the sun caught the large blue sapphire, and a brilliant blue flash emanated from it.

More gasps and then loud murmurs rose from the astonished crowd. They were no longer concerned with Ariel. Their eyes were fixed on Sawyer and the Stormblade. Geoff wondered what would happen next.

"The Stormblade! The sword of heroes!" someone shouted.

"The Stormlord is here! He's come to save us!"

Sawyer looked at Ariel. "What do I do now?" he whispered.

"Tell them to open the gates."

Sawyer looked up at the guards, who were every bit as shocked as the crowd that surrounded him and Ariel.

"Open up in the name of the Stormlord!" Sawyer looked at Ariel, who gave him a quick nod.

Geoff couldn't help but notice the slight quiver in his voice. Sawyer seemed unsure of what to do. From atop the wall, Geoff heard the command given to open the gates. Ariel beckoned to Geoff and the others to join her and Sawyer. Jane was still a little weak, so Ishara and Geoff steadied her as she walked. As soon as she was close to Sawyer, he wrapped his free arm around her waist, keeping the Stormblade raised overhead. There was a loud *clank* followed by a deep grinding sound as the massive doors slowly swung open.

Guards stood aside as they walked through. They had the same stunned looks on their faces as the crowd of refugees, who followed them into Chalon. Geoff felt as if he had walked into a picture of an old medieval castle in one of his father's books. The streets were cobbled and narrow. Various artisan shops flanked them as they made their way to a large walled castle within the city.

"It's wonderful," Jane said.

It would be so cool to live here, Geoff thought, his heart beating faster. Walking through a large medieval city for the first time was exciting, as though they had entered another era. He saw real blacksmiths hammering away at their forges, and the ringing noise their hammers made as they struck hot metal seemed like music.

He smelled fresh-baked bread, as well as meat roasting over a fire. He also smelled hay, cows, goats, and pigs. Guards, peasants, and nobles mingled and walked by; everything was as Geoff expected. This was medieval civilization, and it was astounding.

"Ariel," Sawyer said, "how long should I keep holding this sword up?"

Ariel glanced over her shoulder at the crowd of refugees who had finally been allowed to enter the city.

"I would say you can put it away. Thanks to you, we have helped many people."

Sawyer quickly lowered his sword and covered it. He looked a little embarrassed.

"Don't be bashful, Sawyer," Jane said. "You did your good deed for the day."

"I feel like I'm leading a parade," he said.

"Ariel," Jane said, "where are we going?"

"There," she said, pointing at the tall, formidable structure that rose before them on a hill within the city. It was a castle surrounded by thick walls no less than forty feet high. At each corner of the wall stood a huge rounded tower. It was the top of the towers that caught Geoff's attention. They had thatched roofs, but there were large, twenty foot openings as well. It didn't make sense to Geoff. Why would they build towers like that?

He was about to look away when he saw movement from the top of one of the towers. He blinked and opened his eyes wide to reassure himself of what he saw.

Three great winged creatures had appeared in an opening of one of the towers and taken flight, each one carrying an armored rider. The creatures also looked like something he had seen before in books, but Geoff was too shocked to remember where.

"Wow! They're awesome," he said. "What are they?"

"They are sentinels," Ishara said. "Gryphon riders. Warriors of the skies."

"That is so cool," Geoff said as he watched the three figures bank, turn northward, then disappear beyond the walls. "I gotta ride one of those!"

"It usually takes years of training to master gryphon riding," Ariel said, "but you may have a chance to ride a gryphon when this war is over."

The crowd of refugees behind them had, for the most part, gone their own way after being allowed to enter Chalon. Some still followed them, however. They were talking among themselves about the Stormblade and they regarded Sawyer with a certain reverence. Shopkeepers and patrons stopped and stared at Ariel. She hadn't raised her hood, so her elvish beauty was on display for all to see.

Some people shouted for Ariel to go back to her trees, but as long as Ariel walked beside Sawyer, she seemed to be safe. They walked through the streets until they came to the gates of the castle within the city, which were a smaller version of the main gates.

These gates were open, however. Several guards stood aside as they passed. Geoff thought this was odd behavior until he realized they recognized Ariel. The crowd of people who followed them were not allowed entry into the castle grounds.

"Ariel, have you been in the castle before?" Jane asked.

"Yes. Many times."

Ariel's voice had a bit of an edge to it. They walked into the massive castle and the sheer opulence of the interior was overwhelming. Gold embroidered tapestries hung on the walls, while the floors were a white polished stone. The beautiful furniture was oak and adorned with plush, comfortable-looking pillows. Hand-painted vases and fixtures decorated every room and every table. The guards here wore chainmail armor and deep purple surcoats emblazoned with a golden gryphon rearing up on its hind legs.

They were finally greeted by a small, waspish-looking man. He wore a long, extravagant maroon robe and carried a bouquet of roses, which he offered to Ariel. He had oily jet-black hair that was combed over in such a way as to hide his baldness, and he was heavily perfumed.

"Ah, Lady Ariel," he said with a bow. "You grace us once again with your beauty and elegance."

"Take us to Lionel, Anslo." Ariel said, ignoring the roses he held out to her.

"Of course! Of course!" Anslo bowed again and led them up a wide flight of steps made from the same white polished stone.

"My Lady Ariel," he said with a quick glance over his shoulder. "Much has changed since your last visit. He is now King Lionel the First. Please be aware of that."

Ariel said nothing. They walked down a long hall that was flanked with heavily armed guards on both sides and came to a set of thick wooden double doors inlaid with golden images of gryphons. Two large guards moved aside as Anslo waved them off and opened the doors. He entered the great hall and bowed low.

"Your majesty, may I present—"

Ariel pushed past Anslo, almost knocking him down. She still had a slight limp, but her eyes flashed with anger as she walked into the room with her hands on the pommels of her weapons.

"Usurper! Betrayer!"

Chapter Thirteen
Lionel the First

"How dare you claim to be king! Chalon is not yours to rule, and who are *you* to turn away your own people?"

Ariel's voice echoed throughout the luxurious chamber. The entire room was lined with white stone columns, and a large mosaic of a gryphon inlaid with gold stretched across the floor. Jane grasped Sawyer's hand as they cautiously followed Ariel inside, with Geoff and Ishara behind them. Three men stood facing them on the far side of a long wooden table, apparently discussing a map laid out before them, while a beautiful elven female with light brown hair and lavender eyes sat to the side in a plush high-back chair.

The man in the middle of the three wore a golden crown and dark purple robes, while the other two wore gray plate mail armor. They looked at Ariel as she stormed into the room. A scowl formed on the face of the man wearing the crown, while the two armored men showed no expression.

"Ariel," the man wearing the crown said, his voice laced with disdain, "have you run out of trees to save?"

The man speaking had to be Lionel.

"*Hal'inari*, Ariel Windsong. It is an honor to see you again." The female elf stood, bowed slightly, and placed her hand over her heart.

"*Hal'inari*, Seqwil Ferncliff. I am glad to see you here in these dark times." Ariel bowed her head.

"Yes, yes. Hal'inari, hal'inari, hal'inari. Why do you invade my throne room? I'm busy. I have a war to plan." Lionel waved his arms in a mock salute to Ariel.

"Please, King Lionel," Seqwil said, "Ariel is now high druid over the realm and a true leader of the elven kingdoms. I ask that you show her the respect that she has earned many times over."

Jane kept her eyes on Seqwil Ferncliff. Who was she? She had a commanding presence about her. Compared to Lionel, Seqwil was both regal and sophisticated. Her lavender eyes sparkled with intelligence, and every move she made was so graceful. Jane liked Seqwil right away.

"I'm well aware of her status among the elves," Lionel said, "but that matters little here." He motioned to Seqwil as he spoke to Ariel. "I have the duly designated elven ambassador from Selra'thel here. Why should I listen to a druid?"

Ariel took a step toward Lionel. "Careful. I do not require your respect."

"Good, because you don't have it. Now, if you'll be kind enough to leave with your brood of street urchins, I have pressing matters that require my attention."

Brood? Street urchins? What an ass, Jane thought as her nostrils flared and her face became flushed. She clenched her teeth and glared at Lionel. She hoped Ariel would slap his face.

"A dark army approaches," Ariel said. "I am here to warn you of what we have seen."

"Oh? And what have you seen?" Lionel asked. "Do you think us blind? I already know about the army approaching from the north."

Jane couldn't stand by and listen any longer. The pompous way in which King Lionel spoke to Ariel was infuriating. She let go of Sawyer's hand and stepped forward.

"You should listen to her," Jane said. "Ariel fought the Shadowlord and saved us."

Jane felt the cold gaze of the king fall upon her. He looked at her like she was nothing more than an annoyance.

"Silence, girl. You'll mind your tone with me or I'll have you in chains."

"I will not allow any harm to come to her or any of the others you see before you."

Ariel's voice again took on a commanding tone as she locked gazes with King Lionel. For a moment they glared at each other in a silent test of wills. The two armored men flanking the king had moved their hands closer to the swords at their sides.

"Your Majesty," Seqwil said, "perhaps a brief respite is needed? You have been poring over your battle plans as well as other matters of the kingdom for some time."

Ariel and Lionel stared at each other for another several seconds, then Lionel turned his attention to Seqwil.

"Yes. Quite right," he said. "You are as wise as you are beautiful, my lady."

Seqwil bowed her head.

Jane exhaled. She didn't realize she had been holding her breath, but the tense situation unnerved her. Sawyer leaned close and whispered in her ear, "Holy crap, Jane. That was awesome. Just don't get us killed, okay?"

Seqwil placed herself between Ariel and Lionel. "Ariel, may I have a word?" she asked.

Ariel nodded. Seqwil took Ariel's arm and walked several steps away with her. Jane took a few discreet steps in their direction and strained to hear their conversation.

"Please be aware," Seqwil said in a hushed tone, "the situation is grim. An army from the Iron Citadel to the north has gathered and threatens Chalon. Lionel has been devising a way to stop the Shadowlord's hordes."

"Lionel is incapable of devising anything. However, the situation is worse than that," Ariel said. "Another army approaches from the east. This one is commanded by the Shadowlord himself."

"Then we are caught between two armies," Seqwil said. "Chalon cannot stand against two armies from the Iron Citadel, and if the humans fall, so shall the rest of the free peoples of Alluria."

"Agreed," Ariel said. "What of the dwarves of Keredain and Bregendain?"

Seqwil shook her head. "I have heard nothing of the dwarves."

Jane stepped closer and dragged Sawyer with her as she continued to eavesdrop.

"King Baldon of Keredain is a mighty warrior, as are his people," Ariel said. "Any foe able to defeat dwarves in their mountain strongholds must indeed be terrible, one not to be trifled with under any circumstances."

"What are we to do?" Seqwil asked.

Ariel returned her gaze for a moment and then glanced

back at Lionel, who was busy drinking wine from his golden goblet.

"I do not know," Ariel said.

Jane swallowed and squeezed Sawyer's hand. If Ariel didn't know how to defeat the enemy and make things right then what could anyone do?

"Ouch!" Sawyer said. "Hey, you're digging your nails in deep, aren't you?"

He held up the hand she was squeezing. Red gouges lined his palm.

"I'm sorry, Sawyer," Jane said, letting go of his hand.

"I didn't say let go," he said. "What's wrong, Jane?"

She shook her head. She didn't want to answer him at the moment because she knew Ariel would hear. Jane felt a shiver run down her back. Everyone in the city of Chalon was in trouble.

"I'll tell you later," Jane said.

"So, grandest of druids and highborn among the elves; what sort of sacred tree do you have that will save us?" Lionel's voice was loud and mocking. Jane opened her mouth to tell him to shut up, but decided that wouldn't be wise. To her surprise, Ariel maintained her composure as she approached Lionel and looked at the map on the table.

"I have no such solution," Ariel said. "However, I bring counsel, so—"

"Stop right there," Lionel interrupted her as he pointed a finger at Geoff, Jane, Ishara, and Sawyer. "Why are those filthy children still in my throne room? This is no place for their like."

"You would turn away heroes in such dire times?" Ariel asked as she walked over to them.

"Heroes? Them?" Lionel scoffed. The two warriors beside him laughed.

"You would turn away the Stormlord?"

The laughter stopped and Lionel put down his goblet. Ariel turned to Sawyer and nodded. Without a word he removed the sword from under his cloak and held it aloft for all to see.

"Then it *is* true," Seqwil said. "I had heard rumors, but I never thought they were real."

Lionel took a big gulp of wine, wiping the excess from his lips and chin on a sleeve. He sat his goblet down and walked around the table. He looked Sawyer over for a minute, clearly sizing him up.

"So *you* are the Stormlord? Where did you find that sword, boy?"

Jane frowned and bit her lip. Lionel was really getting on her nerves with his attitude. Fortunately, Ariel answered.

"He found it in the lair of a river troll. He slew the troll, and so the Stormblade is his by rite of combat." Lionel regarded Sawyer again. Jane mentally braced herself for another insult aimed at Sawyer, but none came.

"Indeed? A river troll?" Lionel said with a nod. "No small feat. Your fighting skills must extend way beyond your years. What's your name, boy?"

"Sawyer Collins," Sawyer said.

"His skills with the sword are excellent. I am training him myself," Ariel said. There was a hint of pride in her voice as she spoke.

"There isn't a warrior in the realm who would pass at the chance to learn from Ariel," Lionel said. "Heed her advice and learn well, boy."

"Sawyer," Jane said. "He just told you his name is Sawyer."

Again Lionel turned a cold gaze to Jane. She was determined to not back down and returned his stare. A few choice words right now would be okay, she thought, but Sawyer gave her a quick nudge with his elbow and she let the words slip away.

"Perhaps you should teach your human children some manners as well," Lionel said. "I'll be glad to help with that."

"I have already told you that you will not harm them," Ariel said. "And their manners are fine."

"We are all thankful for the arrival of the Stormlord," Seqwil said, "but there are many preparations to make. Our enemy approaches from the north and the east. Perhaps we should attend to the matter at hand?"

Lionel returned to his map. It was clear from his expression they were not welcome. Then a fidgety guard entered the room, bowed, and approached Lionel. Jane and the others looked on as Lionel leaned in close, allowing the guard to whisper into his ear. Lionel kept his eyes on Ariel while listening to the nervous guard. Jane frowned. This wasn't good.

A nod from Lionel sent the guard scurrying from the throne room. Lionel lifted his chin and regarded Ariel again.

"According to my scouts," he said, "it appears the Shadowlord's eastern army will be at our gates in two days."

Lionel went to the map on the table and moved a couple of black pieces closer to the center.

"What of Caladar?" Seqwil asked. "Surely they will come to our aid. They have a pact with the kingdom of Chalon."

"Where are they?" Lionel stretched out his hands and looked about the room in mock bewilderment. "Our enemies surround us while our friends forsake us."

"Did you aid Selra'thel?" Ariel asked flatly.

Lionel glared at her. "No. I sent emissaries and their bodies were returned filled with these." He picked up an arrow that had been lying on the table and tossed it to Ariel. "And," he continued, "I sent emissaries to Caladar, Uln, Eastvale, Aelshore, and Keredain. Only Eastvale and Aelshore have sent troops and supplies. The others…"

Ariel looked the arrow over as Lionel's voice trailed off and then handed it to Ishara, who took it and studied it intently.

"So," Lionel said, "if elves are our allies then why are they killing our emissaries? I have reports of elven warriors attacking caravans as well. Do you need further proof?"

Lionel walked to his throne, picked up something that had been lying beside it, and tossed it to Ariel. It was an elven longsword.

"That was found with the bodies of several of my envoys on their way to Selra'thel. Can you explain why?"

Seqwil cleared her throat. "Your Majesty," she said, "as ambassador, I wish to inform you that elves are not capable of such treachery. We have al—"

"Spare me your excuses," Lionel interrupted, never taking his eyes from Ariel. "Well?"

Ishara turned the arrow over and over in her hands, looking for any clue that might prove useful. When she had completed her examination, she looked at Ariel with a grim expression and nodded.

"I do not know how these elven weapons came to be found among the bodies of your envoys."

"Oh, I know," Lionel said. "You wish to create a gulf

between us and our real allies. You wish for Chalon to stand alone so we'll fall to the Shadowlord. In fact, you wish for all human kingdoms to stand by themselves. Easier to conquer that way, eh?"

"Regardless of where these weapons were found," Seqwil said, "elves did not do this. I can assure you of that."

"Then who did? Hmmm? What sort of conspiracy can you offer that will explain this? Why are elves killing my soldiers?"

"Your accusations are misdirected," Seqwil said, stepping between Ariel and Lionel. "Ask yourself this—who would benefit most from elves and men not trusting one another?"

Lady Seqwil was the voice of reason, which seemed to be in short supply at the moment. Jane thought Seqwil was the perfect ambassador. If anyone could make this jerk of a king listen to reason, it would be her.

"Do not think I haven't noticed you brought an elven archer with you as well," Lionel continued. "What a coincidence."

Ishara stepped forward, lowered her hood, and bowed her head slightly. "I am Ishara of Selra'thel."

"Ishara has saved our lives more than once," Ariel said. "You will find her to be a remarkable ally in battle."

"I have no doubt," Lionel said. "Or I will find her to be a remarkable enemy who has found her way into my throne room with the help of her friend."

"She is not your enemy," Ariel said. "Nor am I. Nor the elves. We are here to—"

"To what?" Lionel interrupted, flashing a distrusting gaze at Ariel and Ishara. "I've never truly considered you or any elf to be a friend or ally."

Ariel walked to the table and planted herself directly in front of Lionel. "If you continue to interrupt me," she said through clenched teeth, "I will give you reason to not consider me a friend."

Jane smiled. She was glad to see Ariel stand up to the king. Lionel looked at Ariel for a moment and then turned away.

"Let's say for a moment I believe you," he said. "Let's pretend the elves aren't behind this war and aren't allies of the Shadowlord. What happens next? Do you expect me to take you into my confidence? Perhaps I should take you into my bedchamber instead."

The two armored warriors flanking Lionel chuckled and smiled. Jane gritted her teeth.

"You have always been a fool," Ariel said. "I see this was a waste of time. I hoped I could reason with you and that for the sake of your people you would be willing to act. I was wrong. Perhaps the wizard Maelord may be willing to listen."

Ariel whirled and walked past Jane and the others, giving a quick tilt of her head indicating that it was time to leave.

"Yes," Lionel called after them. "Perhaps he would be willing to listen…had he not disappeared."

CHAPTER FOURTEEN

MYSTERIES

Ariel spun around. "What do you mean he disappeared?"

"I mean he is gone," Lionel held his arms out. "Does your keen elvish sight see him here?"

"He would not leave Chalon," Ariel said. "This is his home."

"Nevertheless," Lionel said, "he is gone."

Ariel's mind raced. Something was wrong. In addition to being a good and honorable man, Maelord was also a powerful wizard.

"Oh," Lionel continued, "we did search for him. We went to his tower and found this." He tossed a knife toward Ariel. It slid across the white marble floor and came to a stop a few inches from her foot. It was a blood-stained elven dagger.

"The place was a mess and there was blood on the rugs," Lionel said. "There aren't many who can sneak up on a wizard in his own house. Who is stealthy enough to do so *and* overpower a wizard like Maelord? Hmmm. A druid, perhaps?"

"Maelord is my friend," Ariel said.

"Yes, I know," Lionel said. "He *was* your friend. So was Eben Silverthorne. So were Alex…and Zorn. Your friends are dying. Or worse."

Ariel stopped. She remembered them all, and it was as if the ghosts of her friends crowded her for a moment. Sadness, regret, and loss moved across her beautiful face and then were gone. She had lost so much.

"When did Maelord disappear?" Ariel asked, returning her attention to Lionel. He pursed his lips and scratched the stubble on his chin.

"A few days ago," he said. "We looked high and low for his body, but found nothing."

"I would like to search his tower," Ariel said. "Perhaps I may be able to assist in locating him."

Lionel nodded, and as Ariel turned to leave the throne room he added, "He was a good man. I hope you find him. I invite you and your friends to stay here. I will have rooms prepared for you. When you've settled in perhaps you'll return and help us plan the defense of Chalon."

Ariel stopped. It must have taken much for Lionel to be that kind to her. His invitation was the closest he would ever come to asking for her help.

"Given the current state of things," Ariel said, turning back to Lionel, "perhaps I should stay? I can settle in with the others later."

Lionel nodded again and beckoned her to join him at the table. Ariel turned to Ishara and the others.

"Go," Ariel said. "I will come when we are done here."

Ishara led Sawyer, Jane, and Geoff to Anslo, who had been waiting by the large doors. He bowed his head and led them from the throne room. Ariel turned and walked back to the table. Lionel picked up his goblet and a decanter of wine and motioned toward the balcony. Ariel, Seqwil, and the two warriors followed him as he opened the double doors and stepped outside.

"Chalon cannot defeat the two approaching armies," Ariel said, "and since we have not heard from Caladar or the other human kingdoms, we must assume they either cannot or will not join us."

"So what would you have us do? Surrender?" Lionel asked.

"How long before the Shadowlord's northern army arrives at your gates?" Ariel asked.

"Perhaps two weeks," the armored warrior to the right of Lionel said. "The terrain is rocky and hard and they dare not cross the Shattered Moor."

"Since the eastern army is much closer," Ariel said, "we must ride out to meet them before they join with the northern army."

"Ride out and leave Chalon defenseless? You're daft," Lionel said. "We need every available man here behind our walls to defend our people."

"If you cared for your people," Ariel said, "you would have let them inside your walls and given them shelter."

Lionel pointed at Ariel. "How dare you speak to me like I was a petty tyrant, you tree-loving—"

"This bickering," Seqwil said, holding up a hand, "does nothing but play into our enemy's hands. If we cannot agree to work together we cannot hope to prevail. Your Majesty, Ariel's strategy is sound. Fighting one army at a time is much better than facing two armies, even from behind your high walls."

"I will not leave Chalon undefended," Lionel said.

"Perhaps you will not have to," Seqwil said. "I am sure King Andurys of Selra'thel will send whatever aid he can."

"Elves have not forsaken humans," Ariel said. "They will join you."

"Truly?" Lionel said. "Twice I have sent emissaries and received no reply. Where are they? Where are the elves?"

Ariel looked at Seqwil. "King Andurys knows of this and has done nothing?"

"He commanded me to confer with King Lionel," Seqwil said, "while he considers the request for aid. We have taken heavy losses in our battles with the Shadowlord." Seqwil nodded to Lionel. "Like you, he is hesitant to leave his kingdom unguarded."

Lionel looked at Ariel. She ignored his smugness. How odd, she thought. King Andurys had long held that humans—while dirty and vile—were an essential ally. The elves would not leave them to their fate in these dark times.

"However," Seqwil continued, "I believe the elves will come."

"Admirable," Lionel said, refilling his goblet, "but I do not share your confidence in the matter." He turned and looked at Ariel as he took a long drink. "Chalon stands alone."

"Your Majesty, you now have the Stormlord in your midst. The power he wields can turn the tide of any battle," Seqwil said. "He is more than an adequate replacement for a wizard."

"Is that true?" Lionel asked Ariel. "Is that boy an adequate replacement for Maelord? Is he *that good* a warrior?"

"Not yet," Ariel said, "but he has potential. He is learning."

"Potential?" Lionel scoffed. "We have the Stormlord and he has potential. I'm sure that will make us all sleep better tonight knowing he has potential. How grand!"

"He improves each day. He will be a fine warrior," Ariel said.

"Will he be a fine warrior in a few weeks?" Lionel asked. "What of the other two? Will they be fine warriors as well?"

"The girl…has druidic abilities," Ariel said. "The boy I believe to be a—"

"A druid? A *human* druid?" Lionel laughed. "You cannot be serious."

"She can cast the same spells as myself. I assure you she has the makings of a druid."

"A human?" Seqwil repeated. "I…I do not doubt you, Ariel, but a human with the power to command nature is dangerous, and she is so young."

Ariel turned to Seqwil. "Yes, she is young."

"They all are," Lionel said with a wave of his hand. "They're mere children, and thus they are of no help. And of no consequence."

Ariel didn't respond to Lionel. It was a waste of time to try to convince him of their worth. Besides, it might be best for the time being if as few people as possible knew of their extraordinary abilities. Sawyer might be safer as well if he was considered to be only a novice swordsman. But that could also work against him, Ariel thought. He could be seen by others as weak and unworthy of wielding the Stormblade. His training would need to be accelerated.

"So," Ariel said, "is your plan to wait here while the enemy gathers his strength?"

"It is. We have plenty of food and water – so long as you

stop admitting peasants and farmers into my city. We can outlast them. I'm certain of it."

"No," she said. "You cannot."

Another moment of silence followed as Lionel and Ariel looked at one another, considering what each other had said.

"We shall see," Lionel said as he took another drink from his goblet.

"No army can breach our walls," the armored warrior on the right of Lionel said as he glared at Ariel.

"Nevertheless, the Shadowlord approaches," Ariel said. "He would not march two major armies so far without a plan to overcome your walls. What size is the northern army?"

Lionel hesitated. "Thousands," he said.

"When they join with the army to the east," Ariel said, "they will number well over ten thousand strong."

"We will outlast them," Lionel said.

"Our enemy also wields magic, the darkest of magic," Ariel said. "The Shadowlord was the most dangerous foe I have ever faced."

"But you *did* meet him in battle." Lionel pointed at her. "And you must've defeated him or you wouldn't be here. So we've lost our resident wizard, but we've gained the services of the high druid."

"We fought," Ariel said, "but I did not defeat him. Our battle ended with no clear victor."

"I noticed your limp," Lionel said, rubbing his chin. "Your healing magic was ineffective?"

Ariel nodded. "The wounds from his sword do not heal well with magic."

"How could such a weapon exist?" Seqwil asked. "Surely

a healing spell from nature's own guardian is more powerful than dark magic."

"I can heal my wounds a little with my magic," Ariel said, "but not completely."

Lionel leaned on the railing. "Do you require a physician?"

"Perhaps a night's rest will be helpful," Ariel suggested. "We have been through much."

"Agreed," Lionel said. "We can discuss strategies further tomorrow."

As Ariel turned and walked through the throne room, she heard Seqwil speak to Lionel.

"Your Majesty. Until tomorrow."

Her footsteps echoed throughout the chamber as she hurried to catch up to Ariel. Whispers among Lionel and his guards also echoed.

"My King, she disrespects you. She leaves without even a bow," the first warrior whispered.

"Your Majesty, she should be thrown into the dungeons for her insults," the other warrior said.

"She is Ariel, high druid of Alluria," Lionel said. "The dungeon that can hold her hasn't been built."

Ariel and Seqwil exited the throne room, paying no heed to the watchful gazes of the guards. When they were far enough away, Seqwil spoke. "Ariel, is there any way to slow the eastern army's approach?"

"Perhaps, but it will be difficult," Ariel said. She turned to Seqwil. "How long have you been here?"

"Only a month," Seqwil said. "I, too, have found Lionel to be stubborn."

"He trusts no one," Ariel said. "Especially elves. I am curious as to the origin of these false rumors which blame our people for this war."

"As am I," Seqwil said. "But let me ask you about something else. The human boy who carries the Stormblade, is he truly the Stormlord?"

"He is."

Ariel saw a slight frown on Seqwil's face.

"He is so young. Can he fight?"

"He can," Ariel said. "He did slay a river troll by himself."

"No help at all?" Seqwil looked surprised. "Impressive for such a young human, would you agree?"

"Yes."

"May I ask," Seqwil said, "who are the other human children you travel with? His companions?"

"Yes, they are his friends."

"Their auras are bright." Seqwil said as they continued walking away from the throne room. Ariel didn't answer. She was thinking about how she might convince Lionel to attack the eastern army before it arrived at the gates of Chalon. Ariel and Seqwil turned the corner and walked to the end of the hall. Another hall continued to the left and right. Seqwil turned to the left.

"My quarters are down this hall," she said. "Should you require my services please do not hesitate to come see me."

"Of course," Ariel said. "It is comforting to have you here. We should talk more."

"I agree."

Seqwil bowed her head, as did Ariel, and they parted. Ariel turned right and went to the guest rooms near the end of the sconce-filled hall. Much was the same as she remembered. The plush carpet beneath her feet was new, however. So were the gold and silver embroidered tapestries that hung from the walls.

She glanced over her shoulder, but saw no one. Ariel opened the door to the first guest room and found the others. Sawyer, Jane, and Geoff were looking out the window. Geoff was pointing to some interesting structure in the distance, while Sawyer and Jane playfully elbowed each other. Ishara was sitting on the floor restringing her bow. They looked up at Ariel when she entered the room. She closed the door behind her and returned their gaze.

"Be on your guard," Ariel said. "Our lives are in great peril."

CHAPTER FIFTEEN
SPIES

"Oh you've got to be kidding," Jane said. "We're already in danger? We just arrived."

She had pinned her hopes on dinner, a hot bath, and a good night's sleep, but after Ariel's announcement, that wasn't about to happen.

"What is it, Ariel? What do you know?" Geoff asked.

"The wizard," she said. "His disappearance is troubling. The enemy has crept into Chalon and can strike anyone."

"I thought you said this Maelord was the most powerful wizard around," Jane said.

Ariel glanced at Geoff. "One of the most powerful, yes."

"Forgive me," Ishara said as she stood up, "but if a wizard of such power can be attacked and killed, then how do we protect ourselves?"

"And who do we protect ourselves from?" Sawyer asked. "And other than someone like you," he added, nodding at Ariel, "who can kill a wizard?"

Ariel considered Sawyer's question, and Jane thought she looked worried. Jane noticed all the others were frowning, too.

"I do not know," Ariel said, "but it takes magic to defeat magic."

"You mean another wizard killed Maelord?" Geoff asked.

"Wizard, sorcerer, witch, druid, necromancer," Ariel said. "All are possibilities. Our adversary must have impressive skills."

"Maybe he was tricked," Jane said. Everyone looked at her. "What I mean is; what if it was someone he knew and trusted? Wouldn't they be able to surprise him?"

"Perhaps," Ariel said. "That is an interesting thought, Jane."

"You think a spy got him?" Geoff asked. "Then it could be anyone."

"Yes," Ariel said.

"Earlier, when we were outside the gates," Geoff began, "I thought I saw someone who kind of looked out of place."

All eyes turned to Geoff. He lowered his head and swallowed. Maybe he needed some coaxing, Jane thought.

"What was it, Geoff?" she asked. "What exactly did you see?"

Geoff rubbed his forehead. "I'm not sure. But just before the crowd became angry and started throwing stuff, someone yelled something that started the commotion. I thought I saw someone in a gray cloak running away."

"Why didn't you say anything earlier?" Sawyer asked. "We got pelted with rotten fruit and veggies. Thanks, Geoff."

"Sorry. I didn't think it was important."

"So what do we do?" Jane said.

"Stay together as much as you can," Ariel said, pointing at Geoff, Jane, and Ishara. "Sawyer, we must continue your training with haste. We begin in the morning."

"Wait," Jane said. "Shouldn't we all go? Wouldn't it be safer if we stayed together?"

"Yes," Ariel said, "but people now know Sawyer carries the Stormblade. That sword is coveted by many, and some may seek to challenge him. And he will be considered a threat by agents of the Shadowlord. It is best if he continues his training."

"Oh great," Sawyer moaned. "I knew it was a bad idea to walk around holding it up for everyone to see. Now I have to look over my shoulder."

"Perhaps we can use that to our advantage," Ishara said. "If he is viewed as a threat by the enemy, can we not set a trap?"

"Indeed we can," Ariel said. "While Sawyer and I train, the rest of you can investigate Maelord's disappearance."

"Don't you mean murder?" Jane asked.

"Lionel never said Maelord was murdered," Ariel replied. "Only that he was missing."

"Yeah, but he also mentioned there had been a fight and blood," Sawyer said. "That Maelord guy is probably dead."

"I do not deny that likelihood," Ariel said, "but we must know what happened to him. If he is still alive then he will need our help."

"I want to watch you train tomorrow," Jane said, moving closer to Sawyer.

Ariel thought for a moment. "Very well," she said. "We will continue your training, too."

Jane's heart leapt. She and Sawyer smiled at each other.

"However, both of you must realize your training will now be intense. I must ask more of you. Our lives may depend on how much you learn from me."

"I understand," Jane said.

Ariel turned her attention to Geoff. His eyes were wide.

"Do not worry, Geoff," Ariel said as she placed a hand on his shoulder. "I have no doubt that you and Ishara will help unravel this mystery for us."

"Will they be safe?" Jane asked with an anxious tone. "Just the two of them alone in the city?"

Ariel kept her eyes on Geoff and smiled. "Yes, I believe so," she said. "They are both small and stealthy, so they may escape notice. Sometimes the smallest ones can succeed where others cannot."

"Geoff, you and Ishara be careful," Jane said. "And stay out of trouble."

"Okay," Geoff said.

There was a knock at the door. Everyone fell silent as Ariel opened it. Standing in the hall was a castle servant. She wore a light blue dress with an apron. She smiled and curtsied. "My Lady, His Majesty King Lionel wishes to invite you and your companions to dine with him this evening."

Ariel glanced over her shoulder and then replied, "We will be happy to join Lionel for dinner tonight."

The servant blinked a couple of times, curtsied again, and scurried off.

"You're never gonna call him King Lionel, are you?" Jane asked.

Ariel closed the door and turned back to face them. "No," she said flatly. "He is no king."

"Okay," Sawyer said, raising a hand. "If he isn't the king, then how come he wears the crown and orders everyone around? He looks like the king to me."

"He has no claim to the throne of Chalon," Ariel said. "He was only charged to maintain the safety and welfare of the citizens of Chalon."

"So where *is* the king, then?" Sawyer asked.

"The king died several years ago," Ariel said. "The crown should be resting on the head of another, but he is exiled."

"Then let's go find him," Jane said. "Let's get the real king in here and save Chalon."

"We do not know where he is at the moment," Ishara said as she glanced at Ariel.

"Someone must know where he is," Jane said. "Is he alive?"

"Yes," Ishara said. "But he is not able to help us."

"Why not? Oh that's right," Jane said, snapping her fingers. "He's a werewolf and eats people."

"Ishara is right," Ariel said. "Besides, we have more urgent matters to deal with, such as your training and the two armies that approach."

"Wait a minute, you don't expect us to actually fight, do you?" Jane stared at Ariel, trying to read her facial expression, but Ariel was as stoic as ever.

"No. I hope you never have to fight, but I expect you to do whatever you must to survive if you are attacked."

Jane looked at the others.

"Tonight, however, we eat and rest," Ariel said.

"Finally," Sawyer said. "I could use a good night's sleep."

Jane snickered. Sawyer's ability to lighten the mood was one of his endearing qualities. She gave him a bump with her hip.

Another knock at the door caused Geoff to start. His face reddened as he looked around to make sure no one noticed.

Ariel opened the door again to find another servant, dressed similarly to the one who just visited. This one was younger, however, perhaps the age of Jane and Sawyer.

She also curtsied. "If you please, My Lady," she said. "We have your baths ready."

"Oooh! A hot bath." Jane thought she was dreaming. "I'm so ready."

"Yeah, you are," Sawyer said. "And especially you, Geoff. That isn't mud on your clothes."

"We are ready," Ariel said. "Yes, please. Lead the way."

They followed the servant to another hall and separated, with the women going into one room and Geoff and Sawyer into another. After they had bathed, they put on the new sets of clothes that had been laid out for them. Geoff's tunic, trousers, and shoes were too big for him; the sleeves extended way past his hands, and his feet made flopping sounds when he walked. Even Ariel seemed to be amused, and she showed it with a wide grin.

Jane, however, felt like a princess in her deep blue gown and silver tiara. She didn't like the long flared sleeves, though, because at dinner she kept dragging them through her food when she reached for something. The meal consisted of dry, overcooked turkey, roasted pig, boiled potatoes, bread, several cheeses, and an assortment of fruit. Wine was served as well, but Jane found it too harsh for her taste, so she drank water instead. Sawyer, however, had no trouble drinking the dark red wine. In fact, he drank too much, and Jane found his hands trying to roam where they shouldn't. On more than one occasion she slapped them off her leg.

"Sawyer," she whispered, "I'm going to smack you if you don't behave."

"You should consider yourself fortunate," said a feminine voice from behind her. Jane turned and looked. It was

Seqwil. She was dressed in a beautiful white gown with gold trim.

"There are many eyes on the Stormlord this evening," Seqwil said. "Such a handsome hero can surely have his choice of companions tonight."

Jane glanced around the great hall. Seqwil was right. Several serving girls were checking Sawyer out and whispering to each other. She leaned over to Sawyer and placed her hand on his arm.

"I think you've had enough wine, Sawyer. Remember, you're a hero and you need to set an example for everyone."

"Hero? Me?" Sawyer's voice was louder than Jane would've preferred. She squeezed his hand.

"Keep your voice down," she said.

"Okay. Hey, I think those girls are looking at me, see?" He waved at one serving girl who smiled and waved back. Jane squeezed his hand again, this time much harder.

"Ow! Hey! What're you doing?"

"I'm trying to keep you from making an ass of yourself." Jane glared at him.

"I'm okay. I'm not drunk...yet. Really. Hey, if I do get drunk can you cast a spell to make me undrunk?"

"No," Jane said. "And you better not get any drunker."

"No worries," Sawyer said. "It's cool."

Jane felt a hand on her shoulder and she glanced up from her chair. Ariel leaned over between her and Sawyer.

"As I said, training for both of you starts in earnest tomorrow. Sawyer, Jane is right. You should not have any more wine. Jane, can I trust you to see that he does not continue to drink?"

"I'm trying," she said. "He's becoming hard to control.

He wants a spell to make him sober."

"Yeah! Can you do that? Hook me up."

Ariel raised an eyebrow. She leaned closer to Sawyer, who wrapped an arm around her waist.

"You should know that if you continue this behavior, I will turn you into a bullfrog."

"More like a horny toad," Jane said.

Sawyer swallowed. He wasn't sure if Ariel was joking. Ariel straightened, and as she turned Jane caught a quick wink from her. When she had gone Sawyer grabbed Jane's knee and squeezed. "Holy crap," he said. "I thought you were kidding. She *can* turn us into frogs and bugs and stuff?"

Sensing Sawyer's worry, Jane pressed the advantage. "I told you. You've seen what she can do. I think she might feed your froggy self to a snake, too."

"Ha!" Sawyer said. "She can't do that to me. I'm the Stormlord guy."

Jane looked him in the eye. "Do you *really* want to find out?"

Sawyer thought for a few seconds, then his manner became serious and he gulped down some water.

"Okay, okay. I better eat some more before I—"

"Make an ass of yourself?" Jane interrupted.

"Yeah, something like that. I better chill."

He shoveled some potatoes and turkey in his mouth. As he chewed he leaned over and whispered to Jane. "Hey, who's that tall, skinny guy beside Lionel? The one dressed in green and yellow?"

Jane looked across the room and saw the man Sawyer had pointed out. He looked to be middle-aged and he was lean. His long, curly hair was a golden hue, and his cheeks were red with rouge. He may have been a fop, but he wasn't bad looking. He and Lionel were whispering to each other and having a heated discussion.

"I don't know," she said. "We'll have to ask Ariel. He looks important."

"His name is Count Vilmar, and he comes from the island kingdom of Khorthos."

Jane and Sawyer turned around and saw Seqwil standing behind them again. She smiled. "He brings a message from the oracle. It would seem that King Lionel disagrees with that message."

"What's an oracle?" Sawyer asked, taking another sip of water from his goblet.

Seqwil leaned over between them. Jane thought she smelled like lilacs.

"An oracle is a soothsayer, or a seer. The oracle of Khorthos is said to be able to see the future."

Count Vilmar and Lionel shooed away any servant that came close and continued their hushed debate.

"That Vilmar guy looks mad," Sawyer said. "Wonder what they're talking about."

"You," Seqwil said.

Jane and Sawyer looked at Seqwil again. Seqwil kept her eyes on the conversation between Lionel and Vilmar.

"They disagree on your importance. Lionel believes you to be nothing more than a boy who found the Stormblade in the weeds somewhere. Vilmar thinks otherwise."

Seqwil turned her attention to Sawyer. "It appears you may soon have to prove yourself."

"Prove myself? How do I do that?" Sawyer asked.

"By combat, of course," Seqwil said. "After all, if you

defeated a river troll you should have no problem fighting any man."

"Uh-oh," Jane said. "Who do they want Sawyer to fight?"

"It is King Lionel who is unsure of your ability with the sword," Seqwil said. "Count Vilmar believes Ariel and admires your bravery."

"Yeah. Great," Sawyer said with a lackluster tone. "So who does Lionel want me to fight?"

Seqwil gently turned his head with a hand under his chin until he was looking at a behemoth of a man. His face looked like it had been chewed up and set on fire. His stringy, patchy hair was black and dangled over his eyes as he tore into a fresh piece of mutton.

"Oh, hell no," Sawyer said, trying to push himself away from the table.

Seqwil placed a hand on his shoulder, stopping him from leaving. "He is called Kruelon, and as you can see, he is a veteran of many battles."

"I'm not fighting that guy," Sawyer said. "He's a monster. He'd probably eat me when he's done with me. Not gonna happen. Lionel can kiss my—"

"Sawyer!" Jane interrupted in a hushed tone. "Shush! If he hears you..."

Sawyer looked at Lionel and Vilmar.

"They better change the topic of their conversation," he said, "'cause I'm not doing any of that trial by combat crap. That guy's arms are as big as my legs."

"It is only a test," Seqwil said, "and you do not have to fight him."

"Look," Sawyer whispered to Seqwil. "I did kill that troll, but it was an accident. It lunged at me and I held the sword up. That troll stuck itself through the eye."

Seqwil ran a slender finger through his thick hair. "Then it is better to be lucky than good. Do you agree?"

Sawyer nodded. Jane looked at Lionel. He must be nuts to think Sawyer could win against a giant like Kruelon. Then something occurred to her. What if he *wanted* Sawyer to lose? Ariel had said more than once the Stormblade was Sawyer's by rite of combat. What if Lionel wanted the Stormblade for himself – or at least in the hands of one of his warriors?

"I have learned," Seqwil said in a hushed tone, "that size does not matter so much in battle. In fact, an opponent as large as Kruelon has many weaknesses."

Jane and Sawyer looked at her.

"He cannot see well with his left eye. Should you find yourself facing him, do not forget that."

Jane watched the big warrior as he ate. She noticed among the many scars on his animal-like face he had a particularly nasty scar running from the left side of his forehead midway down his face. The scar passed over the corner of his eye and the eyelid was indeed damaged.

"Sawyer," Jane said. "She's right. Look at his left eye."

"I don't care," Sawyer said, shaking his head. "I'm not fighting that big bas—"

"Look," Jane said. "Count Vilmar is leaving."

The brightly clad diplomat bowed to Lionel, turned, and left the great hall with three armed bodyguards.

Jane felt Sawyer grab her hand. "Jane, we gotta get outta here before the king sics that giant on me. Let's get Geoff and Ishara and go."

"Calm down," Jane said. "You know Ariel won't let anything bad happen to us."

"Hey, where is she, anyway?" Sawyer asked, turning around in his seat and peering about.

Jane raised up in her chair and surveyed the room. Ariel was gone. It wasn't like her to leave them alone in a room full of strangers. Something wasn't right. She searched the room for Geoff and Ishara. They were a couple of seats away enjoying their dinner and talking to each other.

"I don't know, but Geoff is over there with Ishara." Jane pointed at them for Sawyer.

Seeing familiar faces made Jane feel better; she and Sawyer weren't alone. Jane continued to scour the room for Ariel, but she was nowhere to be found.

She waved at Geoff to get his attention and beckoned them over. "We're heading back to the room."

"Okay," Geoff said. "Where's Ariel?"

"We don't know," Jane said. "She isn't here. Ishara, do you know where she is?"

"No, but I am sure she cannot be far."

"She'll just have to meet us back at the room," Jane said.

The four of them left the noisy great hall just as a few minstrels started playing their lutes. Jane looked behind them. She wanted to be sure no one was following before she spoke.

"Hey, guys, Seqwil said King Lionel wants to have Sawyer fight a big, scar-faced warrior. Some sort of test or trial by combat."

"Why?" Geoff asked.

"Because," Jane said, "he doesn't believe Sawyer is the Stormlord. He wants Sawyer to prove himself or he wants the Stormblade for himself."

"Whatever, I don't care," Sawyer said, looking over his

shoulder as they turned a corner. "I'm not fighting him."

"Sawyer!" Jane cried out. She covered her mouth and clutched his arm.

Chapter Sixteen
The Lost Sword

Count Vilmar and his bodyguards were lying in the middle of the hall.

"Stand back," Ishara said as she walked to the bodies and examined them.

"But he just left the banquet," Jane said, wringing her hands.

"Are they dead?" Sawyer asked.

"Yes," Ishara replied.

"They look like they just fell over," Geoff said. "They didn't even draw their weapons."

"There was no fight. They died as they walked," Ishara said.

None of that made sense to Jane. Count Vilmar may have been a fop, wearing bright colors and being overly dramatic with big gestures, but his bodyguards were well armed and seemed capable of protecting him.

"Were they poisoned?" Geoff asked, looking around.

Ishara didn't answer. She was carefully inspecting the bodies for clues.

"Wait," Jane said. "If they were poisoned, then we could've been poisoned, too."

"Yeah," Sawyer said. "We ate the same meal as they did. We could—"

"They were not poisoned," Ishara announced. "Their necks are broken. We should leave."

"Leave?" Jane said. "Are you nuts? We need to tell someone about this. We can't just leave."

Ishara stood. "Yes, we have to go now. If we are seen, they will think we did this."

"But we didn't," Jane protested. "We're innocent. We just found them this way."

"They can't prove we did it," Geoff said. "We don't have anything to worry about."

"Yes, we do," Ishara said urgently. "I doubt Lionel is the type to believe three children and an elf."

"So what do we do? Where—"

"Shh. I hear someone approaching," Ishara said, interrupting Sawyer. A second later, Jane heard voices behind her. Ishara had a point. What if they were blamed for killing Count Vilmar and his guards? Lionel would definitely throw them in a dungeon, so this was not a good place for them to be at the moment.

Ishara grabbed Geoff's hand and pulled him down the hall and around the corner. Jane took Sawyer's arm and did likewise. The four of them dashed toward their room. Behind her, Jane heard a woman scream and a male voice shouting for the castle guards.

Jane was the last to enter their room, and Ishara closed the door behind her.

"Oh no!" Jane cried. "Someone tore the room apart." Beds, chairs, and tables were overturned, with their clothes tossed over the furniture. Rugs had been moved and their bags had been emptied.

"What the hell?" Sawyer said. "Who ransacked the room?"

"My guess is the same one who killed those four men," Ishara said as she picked up her broken bow. It had been smashed into several pieces.

Sawyer hurried over to his bed. The mattress had been tossed aside and his clothes were strewn across the floor. His white and black tennis shoes had been flung to opposite ends of the room. He kept shaking his head as he searched through the untidy clutter.

"Sawyer," Jane said. "What is it? What's wrong?"

"It's gone," he replied as he stopped and looked at her. "My sword is gone. Someone took it."

"Why did you not keep it with you?" Ishara asked.

"What? Take it to dinner? Have every guy who can hold a sword try to kill me for it? No thanks," Sawyer said.

"A hero does not hide from a fight," Ishara said.

"Look, I'm not a hero," Sawyer snapped. "I said that before, but no one listened to me. The sword is gone. I can't do anything about it now."

The frown on his face indicated to Jane that he felt differently from how he let on.

"Sawyer," Jane said. "I think—"

"No, I'm good. It's okay," Sawyer waved her off as he picked up his clothes.

"You are not good," Ishara said. "The Stormlord without his sword is vulnerable. And while you are relieved it is gone, a great many people will be disheartened. Not everything revolves around you, but we must find the Stormblade."

"Okay, I hate that it's gone," Sawyer admitted, "but where do we start looking?"

"Hey," Geoff said. "What about those four dead guys in

the hall? What're we going to do?"

"Geoff's right," Jane said. "It looks like someone meant to frame us for those murders."

"That," Ishara said, "is exactly what I believe happened. It is no coincidence the Stormblade was stolen and Count Vilmar was assassinated this evening, the very evening of our arrival."

Jane ran her hands through her hair, pulling the dark locks back into a ponytail. Ishara was right; someone had wasted no time trying to set them up. Their enemy could be anyone. Who could they trust outside of this room?

"Ariel will know what to do," Geoff said. "Where is she anyway?"

Sawyer just shook his head while he reassembled his bed. Ishara had begun straightening up the room as well.

"I don't know, Geoff," Jane said. "She just disappeared from the feast. I never saw her leave."

"But if we tell King Lionel what we saw then he won't think we did it, will he?" Geoff asked, looking around for agreement.

"I doubt he will be understanding," Ishara said. "He is not the type."

"He's a jerk," Jane said. "I want to slap him."

"As do I," Ishara agreed.

Jane nodded. She was glad someone else felt the same way about Lionel as she did.

"I actually thought Ariel was going to slap him when she first saw him," Sawyer said. "She's gonna beat him down someday."

"Good," Jane said. "I hope I'm there to see it."

"And to answer your question, Geoff," Sawyer said, "no one saw us, so we're safe."

Jane hoped that was the case, but she had an uneasy feeling about their situation.

"Hey, guys," she said. "What if there was more than one person doing this? I mean, those four men were killed and Sawyer's sword was stolen at about the same time, right?"

No one said anything. Jane searched their faces and realized she had mentioned something that troubled them as well. Sawyer brooded as he stopped straightening up. He returned her gaze.

"So how many bad guys are we talking about here?" he asked. "Do we have any idea?"

"Who knows?" Ishara answered. "But what Jane said makes sense. Do not assume we have only one enemy here."

"Aww hell," Sawyer said, throwing a pillow against the wall. "What's going on? We just got here."

Ishara whirled around and looked at the door. It was closed. Jane was about to ask Ishara what was wrong when she heard the heavy footsteps of several men clomping down the hall. The footsteps stopped at their door, and Jane edged toward Sawyer.

A thunderous banging rattled the door. It was so strong that Jane thought it would fly off its hinges.

The door flew open, and standing in the hallway were three men in plate mail armor, swords drawn. Their facial expressions were grim. Jane slipped an arm around Sawyer's.

"Where is the druid?" the man in front demanded. He was bald, and had a thin, brownish beard streaked with gray. Everyone remained silent.

"Answer!"

"We don't know," Sawyer said. "We haven't seen her since the feast."

"You four will come with us now."

"Why?" Ishara asked.

The thin-bearded man stepped into the room and glared at Ishara.

"Because the king commands it," he said. "And because I say so. Move it, elf."

Ishara's eyes narrowed. Jane squeezed Sawyer's arm. Was she going to start a fight? If she did, they were in trouble. Sawyer didn't have his sword any longer and Ishara's bow was smashed. Ishara did as she was told and walked toward the door.

"Move," the guard said as he gave her a nudge in the back.

After Ishara had left the room he turned his attention to Jane, Sawyer, and Geoff.

"Let's go!" He gestured angrily at them.

They were taken to a chamber beside the throne room. Jane's heart was pounding and her palms were moist with sweat. She had seen this kind of room before when she was vacationing in Italy and France. The guide had called it an antechamber, and nobles used it as a waiting room before visitors were admitted into the throne room.

The well-lit room was as opulent as the throne room, with cushioned chairs and sofas along the walls. The entire floor was covered by thick rugs and three ornate oak tables were in the center of the room. Each had an assortment of colorful flowers in the middle.

Sitting at the far table was Lionel, gold crown perched atop his head while the ring-encrusted fingers of his hands tapped the arms of his chair. They stood in front of him for what seemed like an eternity to Jane.

The silence made her nervous. She wasn't sure what was

going to happen next. She chanced a quick look around the room. At least a dozen guards stood staring at them.

"Well?" Lionel finally said, holding his hands up in a questioning gesture.

No one answered. Jane could hear Geoff breathing heavily beside her. He's about to tell Lionel everything, she thought. They'll be thrown into the dungeons for sure.

"Four mutes," Lionel said as he stood. "Where is Ariel?"

Again no answer.

Lionel walked to Sawyer and grabbed him roughly about the collar.

"Hey! Take it easy," Sawyer said. "We don't know where she is. We were just talking about that when your guards pounded on the door."

"Oh yes, *Stormlord*?" Lionel sneered and pulled Sawyer so close their noses nearly touched. "I seriously doubt a boy can wield the Stormblade, especially one as unremarkable as you. I should have you placed in the stockades for lying."

"He's not lying," Jane said. "He's telling you the truth."

Lionel let go of Sawyer's tunic and stood in front of Jane. She raised her chin and met his glare. She was glad to be wearing a long dress, no one could see her knees shake.

"And who are you, girl?" Lionel asked. "Another one of Ariel's pets? Why would Ariel let you travel with her? She has no love for humans, let alone helpless human children."

Jane clenched her fists.

"We're friends of hers," she said. "We met in the forest."

"And how do three human children come to be in a forest? Did you get lost?" Lionel said.

Jane opened her mouth to speak, but Ishara answered.

"Yes," Ishara said. "Ariel took pity on them and we

escorted them here for their safety."

Lionel looked at Ishara, then Jane and Sawyer. He walked over and stood before Geoff, who was fidgeting and shifting his weight from one foot to another.

"And who are you, boy?" Lionel asked.

"Geoff Vincent…Your Majesty," he said.

Lionel bent over and studied Geoff's face. He squinted and stood.

"You do not appear to be related to one another," he said, "so I will ask again—how is it you found yourselves in a forest and why would Ariel bring you here?"

"Your Majesty," Ishara said, "in these dangerous times Ariel could not leave these children to whatever fate would befall them in the wilds of Alluria. She hoped you would offer them sanctuary in your city."

"Ha!" Lionel scoffed. "Ariel has done much worse. I've seen it with my own eyes. And now she is the high druid? A murderess with the power of nature in her hands. Tell me, does that frighten you?"

Jane wondered what he was ranting about. Ariel would never murder anyone. Maybe she had to kill someone in battle, but never murder.

"No?" Lionel continued. "I see from the looks on your faces that you find it hard to believe. I assure you; Ariel is a killer, and the very evening she arrives, one of my closest allies is slain. Curious, is it not? What is even more curious is her friends have no idea where she is – which leads me to think perhaps they, too, are involved."

Jane's eyebrows shot up. He couldn't be serious. We were at dinner the whole time, she thought. He must've seen us. Geoff cleared his throat. "Your Majesty, with respect, but how can three children and an elf overpower and kill four grown men?"

Lionel shot Geoff a cold stare then took a deep breath. He walked in a circle around them, scratching his chin.

"How indeed?" he asked. "But the question still remains unanswered; where is Ariel? I have no doubt she is responsible for this attack."

"But why would she want to kill Count Vilmar?" Jane asked. "Why would any of us want to kill him?"

"A good point, girl," Lionel said. Jane bristled at the way he called her girl. "If you were agents of the elves," he said, motioning to Ishara, "then you wouldn't want him to deliver my message to the ruler of Khorthos, would you? Especially since it contained a tacit agreement to forge an alliance against the Shadowlord."

Jane remained silent and shook her head a little. Lionel looked them over for another moment, then waved a hand. "Get them out of here," he said. "Keep guards posted outside their room. They are not to wander the halls at night."

Jane and Sawyer exchanged relieved glances. She was starting to imagine horrible tortures waiting for them in the dungeons. They were escorted out of the antechamber by the same guards who had come for them. Once inside their room, Jane heard the unmistakable *click* of the door locking behind them. She turned to the others and flung her arms out wide. "So what do we do now?" she said. "We're prisoners here and the king suspects we murdered an ambassador."

"Yeah," Sawyer said. "We're kinda up the creek..."

"I thought he was going to throw us in the dungeon," Geoff said, "or maybe have us thrown out of the city."

"I wish he had thrown us out of this city," Ishara said.

She turned to Geoff. "I thought you were brave the way you stood up to the king."

Jane thought Geoff's face turned a nice shade of pink. It would be cute if we weren't in so much trouble, Jane thought.

"I assume the penalty for murder is death," Jane said as she plopped down on a bed, "right?"

"Yes," Ishara said. "Death by beheading."

"Gross," Jane said. "That's an awful way to die."

"So we gotta get the hell outta here," Sawyer said. "I'm not waiting around to get my head chopped off."

"Yeah," Geoff said. "We should leave."

"Where would we go?" Jane asked. "And where *is* Ariel? We really need her right now."

She looked at Ishara for an answer, but she only shook her head.

"She must have had a good reason for leaving," Ishara said. "But it is not like her to depart without a word."

Sawyer walked over to one of the windows and tried to open it.

"If we try to escape," Ishara said, "then we would appear to be guilty. King Lionel will be quick to pronounce sentence and have our heads. Our best chance to stay alive is to do nothing that would draw attention to ourselves."

"C'mon, we were minding our own business tonight and look what happened," Sawyer said with a grunt as he kept trying to force the window open.

"True," Ishara said, "but now we know what our adversary is attempting and we can try to counter their plan."

"I'm for countering it by leaving," Sawyer said. "It's crazy to stay here."

"I think Ishara's right," Jane said. She looked at Sawyer,

who had succeeded in opening the window. He looked out as a cool evening breeze blew into the room.

"If we run," Jane said, "we'll look guilty. Let's try to get some sleep."

"We're four floors up at least, so we aren't jumping out the window, and who the hell can sleep?" Sawyer asked. He left the window slightly cracked and walked back to his bed.

Later that night as they slept, a small, greenish mist drifted through the cracked window. It silently swirled about and took the form of a ghostly eye. It surveyed the room and its occupants and then changed form into a small, sickly green spider before crawling under Geoff's bed.

CHAPTER SEVENTEEN
NATURE'S WRATH

The great obsidian hawk soared higher and higher, bathing in the light of the rising moon. The night breeze was refreshing. Only a smattering of clouds lingered above the trees, giving the great bird an excellent view of the ground far below. As she flew, a pain cramped Ariel's heart. It was the pain of loss.

Ariel flew east as fast as the wind could carry her. Behind her, the city of Chalon faded away in the darkness. She regretted leaving so abruptly; it would have been better to tell someone she was leaving.

League after league passed by beneath her. The grasslands of the east were dotted with deserted hamlets. She used the wind currents as much as possible to glide so she could conserve her strength.

For the past several weeks she had felt something growing inside. An ancient and powerful energy coursed through her body, an energy that was both exhilarating and breathtaking. Her shape-changing ability came much easier to her now. She could assume the form of almost anything she wished.

The glow from thousands of torches appeared on the

horizon. The barbarian horde marched to Chalon, compelled by the Shadowlord to speed their journey. Their progress was surprising. At their current rate of travel, they would be at the city's gates much sooner than she had expected. She sensed the source of her pain was behind the army, however.

They had camped at the outskirts of a small fledgling forest and cut down nearly every tree for firewood. Only stumps and trampled saplings remained. Charred areas sprinkled the once lush green landscape. The forest had been flourishing and expanding, but now it was dead.

Anger rushed over Ariel as she circled her way to a grassy meadow in front of the barbarians. She didn't see the Shadowlord among them. She landed and returned to her elven form. Holding her arms out at her sides, she faced the horde and began to chant over and over, *Natura olara termin na'rel.*

The sounds of yells and muttering arose as some of the barbarians noticed Ariel standing in their path. Soon a strong wind began to blow, whipping her dark blond locks about her face. A low rumbling overhead was accompanied by intermittent flashes of lightning. The tall grass swayed with the wind. A warmth flowed into Ariel, nourishing her, invigorating and strengthening her. She grew in height as her skin hardened and became as strong as ironwood bark. Her senses heightened exponentially. Antlers sprouted from her head as she once again became nature's avatar.

In the distance, she saw the orange glow from torches as the barbarians came into view. Their flames whipped about in the violent wind. Clouds formed and churned overhead as she chanted, darkening the entire terrain.

Ariel looked up. In accordance with her desire, an arc of lightning flashed in the clouds. Then another. She took a deep breath. As she exhaled, the winds picked up and swirled around the barbarians and a torrential rain began to fall. Ariel heard several surprised shouts as they struggled to maintain their balance against the gale force gusts that pushed against them. A large group at the front pressed forward, slogging through the wet grass that clung to their legs and ankles.

The next flash of lightning revealed Ariel's menacing silhouette, and the barbarians at the front of the army charged. Ariel called down numerous lightning strikes. Pillars of blinding white light struck the barbarian ranks with such force that their bodies were hurled through the air. Others fell, screaming and clutching horrible wounds as the white light seared their skin. Still some continued their charge. Barbarians were known to hate and fear magic, and they distrusted anyone who cast spells. Normally, such a display of magical power would send them running.

Ariel unsheathed her scimitars and rushed to meet them head on. Her movement was not hindered by the grass or the winds. She crashed into their ranks with tremendous fury and began spinning and slashing at them. Their screams, mixed with the pounding thunder and swirling winds, creating a chilling symphony. In her avatar form, Ariel was too powerful, for rarely did a barbarian axe or sword blade come close to her. She was able to either dodge or deflect the blows.

The first ranks fell quickly. Their bodies lay scattered in the grass and rain. Ariel stood before the rest of the barbarian horde; a great, dark silhouette in the storm directing forks of lightning from an angry sky. Each strike hit with devastating effect, creating a ghastly white chain as they arced from one barbarian to the next. Those who were not electrocuted and burned by lightning strikes, or cut down by Ariel, stopped. Their wide eyes and uncertain looks showed their fear.

A chaotic volley of arrows flew at Ariel, but the swirling winds blew them away. Two more volleys followed, with the same result. Ariel walked toward the rest of the barbarians, arms stretched out wide. A small contingent of a dozen frenzied barbarians, angered and frothing at the mouth, rushed her, but Ariel's slashing scimitars made short work of them. This time, the rest of the barbarians broke and scattered as bolts of lightning struck all around, hurling more bodies through the air. Ariel watched the dark shapes run away in the night. They would be back. If Zorn had been here, she would have had to face him again. Her actions this night gave the city of Chalon more time to prepare for battle. Nothing more. The enemy must now realize there are some who will stand and fight, however. Somewhere in the direction in which the barbarians fled, a chilling howl rang out. It was a howl she had heard before. It was him.

"Even as a monster you defend your people," Ariel said. "You do not deserve to bear such a hideous curse." She assumed the form of a large black hawk again and took to the air. Her powers had indeed become great, but she would rather not face the werewolf. This werewolf in particular would keep coming no matter what. But she had done what she set out to do. Now she winged her way through the clearing night sky back to Chalon.

She arrived at the landing on top of the castle. Her feet touched the cold stones of the landing, and she resumed her elven form again. She was immediately surrounded by guards, however, their weapons drawn.

"Lady Ariel," the guard captain said, "by order of King Lionel the First, I place you under arrest. You are to come with me."

The corner of her mouth curved upward as she looked at the captain. Lionel the First, she thought. She should have expected this sort of treachery from him. He was never one she could trust.

"Why do you arrest me? What of my friends?" she demanded.

"The king wishes it. That's all you need to know."

"My friends," she insisted, looking him in the eye.

"They're fine," he said. "Now give up your weapons and come with us."

Ariel considered his order. If she refused, a battle would ensue, and since she was not sure of the well-being of her companions, she obeyed. She pulled her scimitars from their scabbards and handed them to the captain.

"Blood." The guard held the blade up. "I think we have our assassin," he said. "Take her to the king, and don't let her cast any spells. She will turn you all into swine and feast on you as sure as the sun rises."

A guard roughly pushed her shoulder. "Get going, elf."

Ariel clenched her jaw as she tolerated the rough treatment and descended from the landing with her captors. Half a dozen armed men led her toward the throne room. The captain of the guard had called her an assassin. Someone must have been killed. More guards surrounded her as the doors to the throne room opened.

Lionel was sitting on his throne, crown on his head and

goblet in his hand. When he saw her he took a long drink and wiped his mouth. He was wearing the same rich purple robes he wore at dinner.

"I never thought you'd be foolish enough to return," he said, "but here you are. What have you to say for yourself?"

The entire upper balcony of the throne room was ringed with crossbowmen, and their weapons were aimed at her. The captain walked to King Lionel and bowed as he presented Ariel's scimitars and whispered something in Lionel's ear. Lionel glared at Ariel.

"How dare you—" she started to say before she was interrupted by Lionel, who threw his goblet at her.

"How dare *you*!" he shouted as he stood. "How dare you come here and threaten *me*! I am the king! You come uninvited and pretend to offer help, but as soon as our backs are turned you strike!"

"What are you talking about?" Ariel said.

Lionel looked at her. "At first, I wondered why you would kill Count Vilmar," he said, "but it all makes perfect sense. Somehow you knew I had given Count Vilmar a royal parchment proposing an alliance between Chalon, Khorthos, Caladar, Eastvale, and Riverview. You killed him before he could deliver it. You killed him in *my* castle! If it costs my life and the lives of a hundred men, you will pay for your murderous deeds."

"I did not kill Count Vilmar," Ariel said. "What reason would I have to do so?"

"To kill us!" Lionel said. "To prevent men from forming an alliance that would change the balance of power in Alluria. A strong alliance would challenge the power of elves. You use the Shadowlord to frighten us, and then you see to it that no alliance will be made among free men."

Ariel said nothing. His words were a bit slurred, and his eyes were red from both anger and wine.

"Oh, but I assure you," he continued, pointing one of her blood-stained scimitars at her, "you will not succeed. The free folk of Alluria will unite."

"As well they should," Ariel said.

"Well said, Lady Ariel," said a masculine voice behind her. She turned to see Trelane Cormyth standing in the doorway.

Trelane was the commander of Selra'thel's armies. He was a handsome elf, tall and golden-haired, and his shining silver and gold trimmed armor bore the marks of battle. He smiled at Ariel as he entered the throne room. The rarity of his leaving the elven kingdom to visit Chalon was surprising to her.

"We have been waiting for such news," Trelane said, "and it would be best if you do not let me see you throw your goblet at Lady Ariel again, King Lionel."

He placed a hand over his heart and bowed his head as he walked past Ariel, then he stopped and handed a scroll to Lionel.

"King Andurys sends his greetings and wishes to renew the alliance between men and elves."

Lionel blinked, opened his mouth, and closed it again. He walked back to his throne and sat heavily. He was taken aback by Trelane's words. Ariel, however, wasn't sure Lionel was in any condition to discuss an alliance or much else, for that matter.

"King Lionel," Trelane continued, "what say you? The elves stand ready to aid Chalon."

"Elves…," Lionel said.

"We have much to plan," Trelane said. "Selra'thel was attacked by dark minions and foul magic, but we fought and prevailed. The precious blood of many valiant elven warriors stains the ground at Selra'thel, but now we know we can defeat the Shadowlord."

"And how do I know this is not another elven trick?" Lionel asked. He nodded at Ariel. "We have already been victimized by elven treachery this night. How can I trust your king?"

Trelane's expression became grave. "Do not allow our petty differences to doom us," he said. He turned to Ariel and bowed his head again.

"*Hal'inari*, Lady Ariel."

She placed a hand over her heart and bowed her head as well. "*Hal'inari*, Trelane, lord commander of Selra'thel."

Trelane turned back to Lionel. "And what, King Lionel, do you accuse the high druid of Alluria of doing?"

"Murder," Lionel said as he opened the scroll Trelane had given him and began to read.

"You have lost your mind," Ariel said. "I am not a murderer."

Lionel continued reading the scroll. When he finished, he stood up. "Elves have never been the most trustworthy kind of folk," he said. "This one, Ariel, has freely admitted she dislikes humans. Today she arrives unannounced in my throne room with her usual disagreeable attitude, and tonight, after my feast, she ambushed and killed Count Vilmar, the ambassador of Khorthos, and his guards. Only one item was missing from Count Vilmar's possessions, the sealed scroll I gave him which contained my alliance proposal."

"Did anyone see me kill these men?" Ariel asked.

Lionel shook his head and gestured for another goblet of wine. "We know how lethal you are. You can kill four men in seconds and then turn into a mouse and scurry off to hide, which is what I believe happened."

"Ridiculous," Ariel said as she stepped forward and balled her fists. The absurdity of his remarks were infuriating. "How dare you accuse me of such a crime!"

Lionel sneered at her, but he remained silent.

"You have known Lady Ariel for a long time," Trelane said. "You know her druidic powers and her fighting skills. If she had wanted to kill us, I assure you, we would be dead now."

Lionel sat in his throne, leaning forward and moving his goblet in a circular fashion. He rubbed his forehead and closed his red eyes.

"Do you think us humans so incompetent that we can't catch a single female elf?"

"Take heed, Lionel," Ariel said. "I will endure no more insults from you. By accusing me of murder you risk war with Selra'thel, and that is a war you will not win."

Lionel slowly opened his eyes and looked at Ariel.

"Release her," he said. "We'll get to the bottom of this damnable mess soon enough."

The guards put down their swords while the crossbowmen above stood down.

"The events of this night swim around you," he said. "No one else in this castle could assassinate Count Vilmar and escape unnoticed. For now you are free to go, but you will be watched for as long as you remain here."

Ariel said nothing. She merely took her weapons back

and left the throne room. Trelane followed her. Once in the hall and away from the guards, Trelane spoke.

"Lady Ariel, my army is camped north of Eastvale. If we can convince King Lionel to strike the Shadowlord's army from the west, we will attack from the south. With our combined might we would crush the enemy."

"Agreed," she said, "if he stays sober long enough to see the wisdom in your strategy. Earlier I had asked him to ride out and attack the Shadowlord's eastern army."

"And his answer?"

"He will not leave Chalon undefended. The Shadowlord's eastern army has been turned away…for now."

"How so?" Trelane said with a quick tilt of his head.

"I turned them away with wind and lightning," Ariel said, "but they will return."

"I understand," he said. "I will try to convince Lionel to meet our enemy away from here."

"Selra'thel," Ariel said. "How are our people?"

Trelane looked up and down the hall before answering. "We suffered heavy losses," he said. "However, with our warriors and wizardry, we were victorious. The Shadowlord seeks to isolate Selra'thel now."

"Forgive me for not aiding you. I was too far away and I travel with three human children."

"You were missed," Trelane said, "but you must have had your reasons. These human children you speak of, are they friends?"

Ariel met his gaze. "Yes. I believe they are the outlanders of prophecy."

Trelane regarded Ariel for a moment. He appeared to be searching for any sign of doubt.

"Then they are my friends, too. Will they stand with us in battle?"

"They are not yet ready," Ariel said, "but each day I see their powers growing. Our fate depends on them."

They failed to notice a tapestry they had passed at the other end of the hall ruffle ever so slightly as they spoke. A slim, gray-cloaked figure with a hood pulled over its head slipped silently from behind the tapestry and disappeared around the corner without a sound.

Chapter Eighteen
Training Day

Jane opened her eyes. The sun's bright rays filtered through the window Sawyer had left slightly ajar. Birds were chirping from somewhere outside. The tantalizing smell of freshly baked bread seeped into their room, and Jane took a deep breath. She tried to inhale as much of the wonderful aroma as she could. It was going to be a great day, Jane thought as she snuggled closer to Sawyer. He had crept into her bed during the night. She felt a light nudge on her shoulder.

"Wake up, Jane," Ariel said. Jane snapped awake at the sound of Ariel's voice. She sat up in bed and brushed her messy hair from her eyes.

"Ariel!" she said. "Where have you been? Oh, and the king thinks you—"

Ariel held her hand up to quiet Jane. "Shh. I know; I know," she said. "Ishara told me everything while you slept."

Sawyer shot up in bed with a loud snort. "Ariel!" he said. "So much crap happened last night. Where—"

"I had to leave for a while," Ariel said. "Forgive me. I should have told you."

"Someone broke in and stole my sword," Sawyer said. "They ransacked the room."

"Have you no idea who could have done this?" Ariel asked.

"Yeah, that jerk Lionel," Sawyer said, rolling out of bed. "I bet he sent someone to steal it."

"Lionel may be a fool and a drunkard," Ariel said, "but I doubt he would have your sword stolen. Come, both of you. We must continue your training."

"Why?" Sawyer said. "I don't have a sword anymore."

"Then we must find it," Ariel said. "Get dressed."

Jane tried to straighten her hair with her hands, but it was no use. She climbed out of bed and went to the dresser with a hand mirror and a brush sitting on it. Picking up the mirror, she grimaced at the reflection that greeted her as she began to brush through the tangles in her hair.

"Please hurry, Jane," Ariel said.

"Okay, okay. Just a minute," Jane said.

"Oh! Ariel!" Geoff exclaimed, sitting up in bed. "Where have you been?"

"I will tell you later," Ariel said. "Up. Get up. We have much to do."

They hurried and got themselves ready and Ariel led them out of the castle. As they walked, Ariel reached into a sack she had been carrying and handed them small loaves of freshly baked bread. Jane took her loaf and eagerly tore off a chunk.

"So where exactly are we going?" she asked, putting the piece of bread into her mouth.

"You and Sawyer will come with me," Ariel said, glancing about. "I do not trust this place – nor should you after last night. It would be better if we leave the city and train in secret."

"And what about me?" Geoff asked. "I want to come, too."

"Geoff," Ariel said, leaning close to him, "As we have discussed, I need you and Ishara to discover what happened to Maelord. Try and find Sawyer's sword, too."

The color left Geoff's face. He stood in place, apparently wondering how he would complete Ariel's request. Jane looked at Geoff. Judging by his facial expression, he obviously had no idea where to begin his search for either the wizard or Sawyer's sword.

"Not to worry," Ishara said, standing beside him. "I have been in Chalon before and have an idea where to start."

"Are you sure they'll be all right?" Sawyer asked.

Ariel looked at Geoff and Ishara. "Yes," she said with a smile. "We will draw too much attention to ourselves, but two small, sneaky types are just what we need at the moment."

Jane touched Geoff on the shoulder. "You and Ishara be careful. Don't trust anyone."

Geoff swallowed. "Okay," he said.

"Our enemy has made the first move," Ariel said. "We must be careful. The city can be as dangerous as any wilderness."

"I doubt that," Sawyer said. "That werewolf was as dangerous as they come. You don't see that thing running around in the city."

"I was hoping to see more of this city," Jane said. "Will we be able to explore some?"

"Of course," Ariel said. "We will explore it together. I am sure Ishara and Geoff will know it well soon enough."

Ariel smiled at Geoff while she and Ishara pulled their hoods over their heads.

"So how am I going to train without a sword?" Sawyer asked. "Are we going to use sticks again?"

"I will find something," Ariel said.

She turned to Ishara and Geoff. "Off you go. We will return before nightfall."

Ishara grabbed Geoff's arm and pulled him toward the city just beyond the castle gates. Jane thought they looked like a pair of kids going to play as Ishara's hooded figure bounced along beside Geoff. Geoff's head swiveled about as he tried to take in the sights, sounds, and smells of Chalon.

"Ishara doesn't have her bow," Jane said. "Can she protect Geoff without it?"

"She is proficient in other weapons and fighting techniques," Ariel said, watching the two of them walk away. "She will not let any harm come to him."

With that, Ariel led Jane and Sawyer out of Chalon through a smaller, well-fortified side gate manned by six guards. Jane was surprised when they stood aside and let them pass. They did, however, watch Ariel intently.

Jane took Sawyer's hand in hers. He looked at her and winked. She realized he wasn't just another dumb bully; for all his jockishness, he had good qualities, too. He had a good heart somewhere deep inside, but like most guys, he didn't seem to open up easily, although Jane felt more at ease showing affection toward him around the others. After all, everyone knew they were in a relationship now. Wait, *were* they in a relationship?

Jane hoped the answer was yes. She squeezed his hand without looking at him, and he squeezed hers back. Jane couldn't help but smile. That was a good sign.

Outside Chalon, Sawyer looked over his shoulder. "I

don't see anyone following us," he said. "No spies or guards watching."

"None that we can see," Ariel said as she kept looking forward, "but we are being watched."

Jane turned her head to look back at the castle, but she didn't see anyone following them or spying from the castle walls either.

They walked for a while until they reached an outlying farm. The doors and windows of the farmhouse were closed, the crops hadn't been tended to for a while and were starting to wither in the fields. Jane didn't see anyone around here, either; all she saw was a small dirt road, untended fields, and rolling hills topped with green grass.

"Looks like we're all alone," she said.

"Good. Then we will not be disturbed," Ariel said, opening a door to the barn. "We have much to do."

They entered the barn, where the smell of hay and manure mixed with dirt lingered in the air. There were a few empty stalls at the far end, and beside the stalls rested a large pile of hay.

"This place stinks," Sawyer said. "Why don't we train outside in the fresh air?"

"Secrecy is necessary," Ariel said. "We must accelerate your training if you are to fight like me."

Jane and Sawyer exchanged surprised looks.

"Elves have a way of fighting with sword and fist," Ariel said, "which no human has ever learned until now."

Ariel looked at Sawyer. "You have natural talent. More than any human I have seen before. But talent will not be enough. You must learn what I will teach you. Your life and the lives of your friends may depend upon it."

Sawyer nodded.

"Shall we begin?" Ariel asked, producing a longsword hidden beneath her cloak and tossing it to Sawyer.

He caught it by the pommel and grimaced. "This is heavy," he said. "A lot heavier than the Stormblade."

"All arcane weapons and armor tend to be lighter," Ariel explained. "The same is true of elven arms and armor."

Sawyer took a few practice swings with his sword, struggling to maintain his grip on the heavier weapon.

"Should I keep a safe distance?" Jane asked, watching Sawyer's attempt at swordplay.

Ariel smiled. "That is an excellent idea."

Jane sat down in the pile of hay and watched as Ariel and Sawyer sparred. Ariel was so graceful; she looked like a dancer when she fought. Compared to her, Sawyer appeared to be a slow, lumbering buffoon.

Sawyer did seem to be improving, however. Ariel was hard on him, but she had a good reason to push him. Whether he wanted it or not, he was the Stormlord, a hero of the people.

During one of their breaks, Ariel gave Jane a small tan leather-bound journal so she could record the spells she knew. This kept Jane occupied, since she also went over their pronunciations and entered notes for each spell.

Sawyer's training went on for the rest of the morning and well into the afternoon, stopping only for brief breaks every few hours. Ariel concentrated on Sawyer's balance and footwork, which meant Sawyer had to pick himself up off the ground many times. Once in a while, however, something clicked and Sawyer managed to get it right. When this happened he looked a lot like Ariel, but slower.

Sawyer hit the ground again, landing hard on his backside. "Ow," he said. "That really hurt."

He stood up and rubbed his sore rear. "How did you do that?" he asked. "You just flipped me like I was nothing."

"In battle," Ariel said, "you must use every advantage. I promise you that your opponent will."

"Yeah," Sawyer said. "But I thought we were concentrating on sword fighting today."

Ariel reached into her pack and gave Sawyer a flask of water. "We are training," Ariel said. "I see we need to work on your hand-to-hand combat skills. Your balance still leaves something to be desired. Rest and take some water. You have done much."

"You're getting better," Jane said, hoping to cheer Sawyer up a bit from his day-long beating.

He took a big gulp of water. "Thanks," he said.

"Jane is right," Ariel said. "You are improving. Remember what you learn and it will serve you well."

"Ariel," Jane said with a frown. "Are we going to have to fight? I mean *really* fight? For our lives?"

Ariel pursed her lips as she considered her answer, then she looked at them.

"I hope not," she said. "But if you must fight to save your lives, then you should be well prepared."

"So when are you going to teach me how to fight?" Jane asked. "I don't have a sword."

"Very soon," Ariel said. "I must consider the best weapon for you. But first, we teach you more spells."

Jane felt a sudden rush of adrenaline. She had waited all day for her turn to train with Ariel.

"Okay," Jane said as she closed her spell journal and stood in front of Ariel. "I'm ready."

Ariel regarded her for a moment. Jane wasn't sure if she had said or done something wrong, but a smile crept across Ariel's face.

"You have the heart of a warrior, Jane," Ariel said, "and the compassion of a healer—a potent combination."

"Hey!" Sawyer said. "What about me? I've got a warrior's heart too, right?"

Jane glanced at him and then back at Ariel. "Of course," she said playfully. "You're the Stormlord."

Ariel nodded and smiled. There was an unspoken communication between them. At times, she and Ariel seemed to know what the other was thinking. It was hard for Jane to describe; it was a connection of sorts. Jane chalked it up to intuition.

"So what do we learn today?" she asked.

"Today," Ariel said, "we learn a remedy for any disease and all natural poisons."

"Oh, that's cool," Sawyer said from his resting place in the hay. "I wish I could cast spells."

"Oh no you don't," Jane said. "You just keep swinging your sword – when we find it. Leave the spell casting to us."

"Yeah, yeah," he said as he took another drink from the water flask. "Ariel, that's a big castle inside a big city. How're we gonna find my sword?"

"Ishara and Geoff," Ariel said. "My guess is they will locate your sword."

"I bet Geoff is about to crap his pants being in a real medieval city," Sawyer said. "He probably studied some stone sculpture all day."

"Sawyer," Jane said. "Be nice."

Ariel produced a small vial from a pouch on her belt and

held it up for Jane to see. Inside was a hideous looking milky-white stinger with a red barbed tip at the end. Jane leaned forward for a closer look. The stinger gyrated and writhed with random spasms.

"Gross," Jane said. "Where did you get that? Is it still alive?"

"This is the stinger from a gholaranian swamp scorpion," Ariel explained, "a dangerous creature whose venom causes paralysis and death."

"It's ugly," Jane said, wrinkling her nose. "So even though you cut it off, can it still kill?"

"Yes," Ariel said. "The stinger will remain active for days after the scorpion has died, seeking to inflict one last fatal wound."

Sawyer hopped up and looked at the grotesque stinger twitching about in the vial.

"Ugh," he said. "How big do those things get?"

"The size of a human hand," Ariel said. "Perhaps a little larger."

Ariel opened the vial and turned toward Sawyer.

"Would you care to volunteer?" Ariel asked.

"Hell no," he said, backing away. "You're not stinging me with that thing. No way. Nope."

He returned to his resting spot in the hay pile.

Ariel carefully took the stinger from the vial and turned to Jane, who suddenly realized her peril.

"I don't want to be stung either," she protested as she also backed away. "That is nasty. Ugh."

"You will cure me," Ariel said. "Here." She handed Jane a few hard green berries that looked like miniature green apples.

"Crush these and let their juice drop into the wound," Ariel said, "and speak the words *Nedala'sul rhan.*"

"*Nedala'sul rhan*," Jane said. "That's an easy one."

"Again," Ariel said.

"*Nedala'sul rhan*."

"Ready?" Ariel asked. "The venom is fast. I will be incapacitated soon after the sting. Remember to keep away from the stinger."

Jane nodded.

"Jane, if you fail," Ariel said, "I will die."

Jane's heart began to race. Was Ariel really trusting her this much? Jane took a deep breath and focused.

Ariel held the stinger to her arm and was immediately stung. She collapsed a few seconds later. Her eyes bulged and her breathing became erratic.

Jane knelt and squeezed the green berries as hard as she could, letting the thick juice drip into the wound on Ariel's arm.

"*Nedala'sul rhan*," Jane said, watching the swollen purple bump start to fade. Jane's heart was pounding. What if she had messed up or gotten the words wrong? Ariel would've died in front of her.

"Holy crap," Sawyer said, standing up. "That was scary."

Then they heard the sound of approaching horses.

Chapter Nineteen
The Wizard's Tower

Geoff maintained a tight grip on Ishara's hand as they trotted past the castle gates and entered the city. This is how he'd always imagined that medieval life was like—people scurrying about, selling their goods on the street, small shops with skilled laborers performing their tasks, the smell of cooking meat and fresh-baked bread. Maybe life wasn't that hard, Geoff thought, except in times of war.

"Where're we going?" Geoff asked.

"To the wizard's tower," she said. "Maelord. We should start looking for clues there."

They weaved their way into a crowded square. Geoff was bumped and jostled by the crowd of people.

"What's this place?" he asked. "There's a bunch of people here."

"Trade square," Ishara pointed to a crooked sign that had been haphazardly nailed to a post on a street corner. "People come to sell their wares here," she said. "Since the city has taken in refugees, it's too crowded."

Along the streets and alleys, Geoff saw entire families huddled together or begging for coins and food. He frowned as he watched their struggles.

"Hey," he said. "I thought the refugees would be fine once they got inside the city. Why isn't anyone helping them?"

Ishara stopped and looked at the sad sight. She pulled her hood back just enough for Geoff to see her face.

"Did you think they would be given rooms in the castle as well?" She asked. "No, this is the best they can hope for. They are inside the walls and now they have a chance to survive. That is all. Most humans do not care much for those who are less fortunate."

"But that's wrong," Geoff said. "Someone has to help. People are stepping on them as they walk past."

"What do you want to do?" Ishara asked.

Geoff understood that life could not only be hard, but downright cruel. It wasn't fair. Then again, life wasn't fair back home, either. He wanted to help, but what could he do?

Ishara put a hand on his cheek and smiled.

"I know," she said. "It is difficult, Geoff. They will have to fend for themselves. It would be best if we continue with our task."

Geoff spotted a family sitting on the corner. There appeared to be five of them, and they were all dressed in rags. The youngest child was an adorable little girl no more than five or six, with blue eyes and auburn hair. Her dirty bare feet gripped at the cobblestones and she chewed on something that looked like a shoestring. Her thin, gray-haired mother held her hand and had another arm wrapped around a slightly older daughter. The father and son, who were in similar shape, begged every passerby for help.

"Okay," Geoff said. "But that family there. That one. Can we do something for *them*?"

Ishara regarded at them for a moment. She removed something from her finger and gave it to Geoff.

"Elven-made rings fetch a high price among humans," she said. "Give this to them and tell them it is elven and worth at least one hundred gold coins."

Geoff looked at the beautiful silver ring in his hand. Numerous small inlaid strips were woven together into the slender band. It was a work of art. Geoff shook his head.

"I can't just give this away," he said. "It's yours and it's way too valuable."

"Too valuable?" Ishara raised her eyebrows. "More valuable than their lives?"

"That's not what I meant," Geoff said. "It must be worth a fortune."

"Again, is it more valuable than they are?" Ishara asked. "If you feel so strongly about giving that ring away then I will let you replace it later."

Geoff's jaw dropped. Ishara was smiling at him. Her bright expression warmed his heart.

"Okay," he said. "I will, I promise."

They walked over to the family and Geoff gave the ring to the father while he informed him of its value. The man looked at the ring in his hand and started to cry. He showed it to his wife who yelped with joy.

"Thank ye! Thank ye kindly, young sire!" The man kissed Geoff's hand, which made Geoff blush. "Ye've made us rich! We 'aven't eaten in days."

"No problem," Geoff said, pulling his wet hand away. "You're welcome. Have a good day."

"Aye! We will, young sire!" the man said, bowing. "May the powers bless ye!"

As Geoff and Ishara walked away, Geoff glanced over his shoulder at the little auburn-haired girl. Her head was cocked to one side and she smiled him. He waved good-bye to her and turned his attention to Ishara.

"Thanks," he said. "I'll get you another one."

"I know," Ishara said with a cheerful tone.

Then a thought crept into his head. How was he going to replace a ring like that? The only elves he knew were her and Ariel. What if he couldn't replace it? He had better say something and change the subject.

"So where's the wizard's tower?" he asked.

"There." Ishara pointed down a side street to an octagonal-shaped building three stories high. "That is the home of Maelord."

It was ringed by a small wall with a rusty iron gate. The tower and wall were made of a variety of stones, giving it a quaint, rustic look.

Ishara opened the gate, which made an awful squeak. Geoff winced and looked about to see if the sudden loud noise had attracted attention. To his surprise, everyone continued going about their business and didn't seem to notice them.

They made their way to the front door, which was made of solid oak. Beside the door was a rusty bell with a rope attached to it. Ishara walked around the tower, looking at its walls. Geoff followed her, running his hand over the stones in the tower's wall.

"What're you looking for?" he asked.

"Just curious," Ishara said. "I would not be surprised if the wizard had a secret way of escaping his tower if the need ever arose."

"Do wizards usually have secret escape routes?" Geoff asked.

"I am not sure," Ishara said, "but perhaps the smart ones do."

"Aren't all wizards smart?" Geoff asked.

Ishara turned and looked at him.

"Not all wizards are smart enough to have secret escape routes," she said, "but this wizard was."

"I don't see any door," he said. "How do you know?"

Ishara pointed at a spot on the wall and drew the outline of a door with her finger. "There."

Geoff stepped closer and looked where she had pointed. He only saw stones and mortar.

"I don't see anything," he said.

"It must be a one-way door," Ishara said. "It must open only from the inside."

"Okay, but how do we get inside?"

"The front door, of course," Ishara said, "silly."

Geoff snickered and followed Ishara to the front door. She grasped the handle and tried to open it, but the door was locked.

"I'm confused," he said. "If Lionel and his guards were here and they discovered that Maelord was missing, or worse, who locked the door? Did they lock it behind them after they left?"

"Good question," Ishara said. "I would like to know that myself."

She looked up and down the small street, observing their surroundings.

"Stand there," Ishara said as she took out a small leather pouch and produced two delicate instruments. She gently inserted them into the keyhole and maneuvered the locking mechanism until they heard a tiny click.

"Oh sure," Geoff said. "*I'm* the sneak thief?"

Ishara placed a finger over her lips to quiet him. She quickly pushed the door open and let Geoff go in first. Inside the tower was dark, and a musty smell filled Geoff's nose. There was something familiar about the smell, but he couldn't put his finger on it. He took a deep breath and thought he smelled something metallic, maybe iron.

After Ishara entered she closed the door.

"A good sneak thief," she said, pulling back her hood. "Does not talk so loudly when it is time to be sneaky."

"Sorry," Geoff said, looking around. "I can't see a thing."

"Use your mage stone," Ishara said. "Honestly, Geoff, you must keep up. You will be of no use if I have to think and do everything for you."

"Oh, yeah," he said, reaching into his pocket and pulling out the faceted gem Ariel had given him. He held it in the palm of his hand.

"*Iluminara.*"

The gem glowed white and rose in the air over his head. Ishara was grinning at him.

"See? You are also a wizard." She held up her hands. "Such an impressive combination in one so young. Now please lower the brightness a bit."

Geoff looked at her and then at the floating gem above him.

"Um, how?" he asked.

"How should I know?" Ishara responded. "You are the wizard, not I."

Geoff thought for a second and looked at the glowing

gem. He remembered Ariel had mentioned something about controlling it with his thoughts. He concentrated and the bright gem dimmed, providing enough of a glow so that he could see the interior of the tower.

The octagonal room was a mess. Books and scrolls were strewn all over the floor, and covered tables and chairs and most of the bookcases in the room. It was just as cluttered as his father's study. The smell of musty old parchment lingered in the air. Partially burned candles littered the room, and a few rested on a cobweb-laced wooden chandelier that loomed near the ceiling. In the dim light the horned skulls and jars filled with creepy, gross things on the bookcases sent a small shiver down his back. He noticed there was a spiral staircase in the back of the room.

"Can wizards not straighten up after themselves?" Ishara asked with a hint of indignation. "Is there not a spell to clean this mess?"

Geoff was still taking in the contents of the room when it dawned on him that Ishara was looking in his direction and had narrowed her eyes.

"Oh," he said. "Don't look at me! I didn't do this."

Ishara shook her head and picked up a small stack of scrolls. Dust flew everywhere. Ishara coughed and tossed them away.

"Wizards…," she said.

Geoff smiled. He realized how much he was enjoying himself. Ishara was the only girl to ever pay any attention to him. And she thought he was cute. He felt differently when he was with her. He didn't know what it was, exactly, but she made him feel good. With her, he wasn't a geeky, nerdy guy to pick on. He was someone else. He had value and he mattered. To Geoff, Ishara was kind and beautiful. He'd been teased by girls in school, but he felt – no, he knew Ishara was being genuinely kind to him.

"What're we looking for?" Geoff asked, stepping over a stack of books in the middle of the floor.

"I do not know for certain," Ishara said. "Anything that looks out of place, perhaps."

Geoff rolled his eyes.

"Well," he said as he tapped his chin with a finger. "Hmmm. If I find something out of place, I'll let you know."

Ishara giggled. He bumped into a table and a cloud of dust flew up and made him cough. He waved his hands to clear the air while Ishara laughed at his predicament.

He stopped waving and laughed, too. There was a moment of silence as their eyes met and Geoff grinned at her. Then he noticed a tickle in his throat. He held his breath, but he was unable to prevent another single, loud cough. Ishara laughed so hard she clutched her stomach. Geoff was elated. He had wondered if elves actually laughed, but Ishara found his actions hysterical.

"Geoff," she said between gasps for air and more laughing, "you are adorable."

He wanted to say something cool. Something Sawyer would say so she would like him more, but nothing came to mind. All he could manage in the dusty, dim glow was a smile and a blush. It seemed to be enough for Ishara, because the affectionate look in her eyes was intoxicating. In the dim light, Ishara was more beautiful than ever. And, she was looking at him.

Geoff swallowed. What was he supposed to do? Should he try to kiss her? What if she didn't want to be kissed? His heart was racing as fast as his thoughts, but his feet were glued to the floor. He really wanted to kiss her, but he was too nervous to move.

Ishara smiled and raised her eyebrows a little higher. He was sure she knew what he was thinking. She walked up to Geoff, maintaining eye contact. Geoff's heart was pounding, and a bead of sweat rolled down his temple. He swallowed again. Ishara took his hand in hers, leaned close so her cheek touched his, and whispered in his ear, "*Tel'mor. Nu tel'mor.*" Geoff felt her cheek brush against his as she started to pull back.

"What—" Geoff began, but was interrupted as Ishara kissed him. Her lips were soft and warm. She smelled of honey and wildflowers. This was so cool! *She* kissed *him*! He closed his eyes. Her hand touched his and she kissed him again, this time a short peck on his cheek.

"Shall we begin?" she asked.

Geoff's eyes shot open. Begin what? His knees were shaking and he felt more beads of sweat roll down the back of his neck.

"Begin?" he stammered.

Ishara stepped back and batted her eyelashes at him. Her playful smile was irresistible. Geoff's heart was beating so fast he thought he was going to faint.

"We have work to do," Ishara said. "Ariel gave us a task, remember?"

"Huh?"

"Ariel?" She said.

"What?" He said as he blinked again. Ishara giggled and motioned toward the rest of the dusty room.

"We have something to do," Ishara said. "Are you going to stand there sweating or help?"

Geoff snapped out of his torpor.

"Oh yeah," he said. "We better get to it."

Ishara pointed to the far side of the dusty room.

"You start over there," she said. "I will start here."

Geoff's feet finally responded to his commands and he walked around the cluttered table. He saw an overturned chair and a rumpled rug. Splattered beside the overturned chair and over the rug were dark red stains. The smell of iron was stronger now.

"Blood," Ishara said as she suddenly appeared at Geoff's side. "There is more by the door."

"So much," Geoff said. "Can someone lose that much blood and live?"

"No," Ishara said. "Either the wizard has been slain, or…"

Geoff looked at Ishara.

"All this blood is from more than one person."

"So the wizard put up a fight?" Geoff asked.

Ishara walked around the chair and studied the floor and the rug.

"It certainly seems so," Ishara said as she knelt to examine the stains on the rug. Geoff glanced around the room again.

Geoff motioned to the spiral staircase. "We have a couple more levels to explore. Do you think whoever attacked the wizard could be hiding up there?"

"It is possible," Ishara said. "Let me go first."

Geoff rubbed his arm. It was covered with goosebumps. They could find anything upstairs. He imagined pet monsters and assassins hiding everywhere. They went to the staircase and ascended to the next level with the glowing mage stone in tow. The second level looked like an armory to Geoff. All sorts of armors, weapons, and shields were located here.

"I bet Dad would love to see this," he said. "Dad collects this stuff."

"It cannot be," Ishara said, ignoring Geoff. Her eyes were fixated on something else. Geoff followed her gaze to an exquisite suit of armor that shone brighter than all the other armor around it.

"Elven battle armor," Ishara said.

She rushed to the silver and gold suit of armor and ran her slender fingers over the smooth surface. Geoff had the impression she had found an old friend after years of separation. The armor had a gleam in the dim light. It was much thinner and lighter than any suit of armor he had ever seen.

"Geoff, do you understand what this is?" Ishara asked as she walked around the armor.

"It's a...suit of armor?" he replied.

"This is enchanted armor. There is none better," she said. "There are precious few of these suits in existence. Elven smiths and wizards spend years crafting them."

It dawned on Geoff what he was truly looking at. He touched the armor with the tips of his fingers. It was flawlessly smooth. A sword stroke would probably glance off the surface.

"It's beautiful," he said. "Just beautiful. How old is it?"

"My guess is hundreds of years old," Ishara said. "They are still made, but the materials that go into them are so rare that I do not think any suits of armor like this have been crafted for decades."

"So they're really valuable, then?" Geoff asked.

"They are priceless."

"Okay," Geoff said. "If it is priceless and all, why did the attacker or attackers leave it? Why wouldn't they take it? For that matter, why wouldn't they rob the whole place? Someone tore our room apart to find Sawyer's sword, right?"

Ishara stepped back and looked at Geoff.

"An interesting point," Ishara said. "Why would they leave this treasure?"

"They must've come only for the wizard," Geoff said. "And since his body wasn't found they must've taken him with them."

"Which must mean he is still alive," Ishara said. "Or he was when they took him. Perhaps the struggle attracted attention and they had to leave in a hurry, carrying the wizard."

"Which meant leaving this," Geoff said, tapping on the breastplate. "We don't know if they even came up here."

Ishara smiled. "No, we don't. Perhaps—"

Ishara suddenly stopped, looked at the stairs, and held up a finger for Geoff to be quiet. Geoff held his breath as Ishara placed a hand on her dagger, but he heard nothing. He waited for Ishara to indicate there was no danger. After a few moments, Geoff had to exhale and catch his breath.

"What is it?" he whispered.

"Nothing," Ishara said. "I thought I heard something downstairs."

"Are you sure?"

"As sure as I can be," Ishara said.

Relieved, Geoff took a deep breath.

"I guess we better keep looking," Geoff said. "There may be other clues."

Ishara and Geoff began surveying the contents of the room. Geoff was amazed at the array of weapons hanging on the walls. Some he'd never seen before, not even in drawings.

"Now *this* we take," Ishara said triumphantly as she held up a carved wooden bow. "It will be an excellent replacement for mine."

"Cool," Geoff said. "Is it better than yours was?"

Ishara looked at the bow in her hand. "This is also made by elves," she said, then she winked at him. "But yes, it is better."

Geoff laughed and walked over to examine Ishara's new bow. She was standing beside the suit of elven battle armor.

"Were these made by the same peo…uh, elves?" he asked.

"Yes, they are both of Selra'thel."

"I bet when we find that Maelord guy," Geoff said, "he's gonna want it back."

Ishara grinned. "Perhaps. Until then, I will borrow it."

Geoff nodded toward the shimmering suit of armor. "Maybe we better take that to—"

"Geoff, look out!" Ishara yelled as she grabbed him and spun him around so they were both behind the elven suit of armor. Immediately he heard the impact of six pings against the armor, followed by clattering sounds of objects hitting the floor around them.

The objects had come from the direction of the staircase. Geoff heard something heavier hit the floor with a metallic clunk. The sound of footsteps running away echoed in the tower.

"Stay here!" Ishara ordered.

She leapt from behind their cover and dashed after their assailant.

CHAPTER TWENTY
A CLOSE CALL

"Who the hell's that?" Sawyer asked as he ran to the front wall of the barn and peered through a crack. Jane never took her eyes off Ariel, whose breathing was becoming less labored. Jane took Ariel's hand in hers and squeezed. Was Ariel going to survive? Did she cast the spell correctly? Did she crush the berries enough?

"Uh-oh," Sawyer said. "It's some of those barbarian guys again. They're just outside."

"Ariel," Jane said, placing a hand on her forehead. "Please be okay. Don't die."

"Jane, they're searching around," Sawyer said. "Looks like they're rummaging around or looking for something."

Ariel's eyes closed and her grip on Jane's hand slackened.

"Oh no," Jane said. "No, no, no!"

She placed a finger on Ariel's neck in hopes of finding a pulse and felt only a faint beat. She remembered her CPR training from a class she took last year, and she tilted Ariel's head back as she looked up at Sawyer.

"Sawyer," Jane said, "I think she's dying. Come here and help me! We have to try CPR!"

"Shh. They're coming," Sawyer said in a hushed, alarmed tone. He hurried over and dropped to his knees on the other side of Ariel.

"Jane," Sawyer said. "Three barbarians are coming this way. What're we gonna do?"

"I don't care," Jane snapped. "Keep her head tilted back while I—"

Ariel's eyes suddenly opened and she gasped for air. Jane's heart leapt.

"Ariel!" she said. "Are you okay? Can you speak?"

Ariel blinked several times as she tried to catch her breath. She looked disoriented and her eyes were glazed and watery. Jane felt Ariel's grip on her hand tighten.

"Ariel?" Jane said.

"Jane," Sawyer said looking at the barn doors. "We're gonna have company soon. We gotta do something."

"We can't take on those barbarians," Jane said. "Not without Ariel, anyway."

Ariel rose up and rubbed her neck while she opened her mouth and took in a gulp of air. "Thank you, Jane," she said. "Now both of you should hide."

Jane and Sawyer helped her to her feet. Once she was standing, Ariel's strength seemed to return, and she stood on her own. She slid her scimitars from their scabbards and looked at Jane.

"Hide," she said again. "Now. Go."

"Come on, Jane," Sawyer said, grabbing her by the wrist and pulling her away from Ariel. They hurried to the back of the barn and hid behind the haystack, covering themselves as quickly as they could. Moments later Jane heard heavy footsteps approaching the barn. She raised her head from under the hay so she could see Ariel.

"Better hurry," a gruff voice said. "Don't want to be out here at night. That damned beast is still 'round here."

"Ha!" another voice said. "The wolf had its fill last night."

The barn doors swung open to reveal three large men dressed in black furs and chain mail. They stopped at the sight of Ariel standing alone in front of them. She didn't move, and their mouths fell open as they stared at her for several seconds.

"It's 'er!" the lead barbarian growled. "The elf-witch from last night! Kill 'er!"

All three of the barbarians drew their weapons and charged Ariel. They were loud and frightening and looked like vicious animals. Sawyer wrapped his arm around Jane and pulled her close. Ariel parried and dodged the barbarians' attacks before cutting them down with precise slashes and thrusts with her blades.

The battle was over in seconds.

"Did you see that?" Sawyer asked in awe. "They didn't stand a chance."

Jane and Sawyer crawled out from under the hay and went to Ariel, who was cleaning her blades on the furs of the slain barbarians.

"Those moves you just made," Jane said, brushing hay from her clothes. "They looked like the same moves you were showing Sawyer earlier today."

"They were," Ariel said as she stood up and sheathed her weapons. She looked at Sawyer. "If you apply yourself, you can be one of the few humans ever to master an elven style of combat."

Sawyer glanced at the bodies on the ground. "I don't know

if I can do that," he said. "I don't know if I can kill someone."

"Can you defend your life?" Ariel asked. "Can you defend the lives of your friends?"

Sawyer said nothing.

Jane wondered what kind of person Sawyer would be when he returned home if he killed as easily as Ariel.

"We have laws where we come from," Jane said. "People aren't usually attacked like that. We have violence, of course, but this is different."

"It is different," Ariel said. "This is war. As I said, I hope you never again have to fight for your lives. However, it is best if you are able to defend yourselves."

There was a moment of silence, then Jane spoke.

"When they were approaching," she said. "I thought you were dying. I didn't know what to do. I thought I failed. I thought I messed up the spell."

Ariel placed a hand on Jane's shoulder. "Forgive me," she said. "I should have warned you. The venom is fast and lethal. But I believed in you. I knew you would not let me die."

Jane pointed at Ariel. "You cannot do that to me again," she said. "Okay? That wasn't cool. I was so scared."

"We both were," Sawyer said. "If you hadn't recovered or if Jane had messed up the spell...we would've been killed by those barbarians."

"They were another scouting party," Ariel said. "I am surprised to see them so close to Chalon this soon."

"What did that barbarian mean?" Jane asked, remembering what he'd said before the short skirmish. "He called you an elf-witch from last night."

"Last night," Ariel said, "I attacked the Shadowlord's

eastern army – the one we've seen marching toward Chalon. My plan was to delay them so Lionel would have time to prepare for battle."

"You," Sawyer said, "attacked an *army*? Are you serious?"

Ariel looked at Sawyer and nodded once.

"How…How can you do that?" Jane asked, shaking her head.

"I will tell you later, Jane. You and Sawyer should go and wait for me outside."

Jane and Sawyer stepped around the fallen barbarians. They were rugged and rough looking, Jane thought. There's no way Ariel could expect her or Sawyer, let alone Geoff, to fight these brutes. Yet Ariel slew them with ease. She was the most amazing fighter.

"Jane," Sawyer said as they exited the barn and walked to the three horses tethered nearby. "I can't fight like that. Those three guys would've chopped me to bits. We just saw three people die, doesn't that affect you any?"

"Of course it does, Sawyer," Jane said. "I'm worried too. And if Ariel can take on an army of those barbarians, then what does she need us for?"

Sawyer nodded. "That's my point. Ariel can probably win this war by herself. Maybe we should go home."

"We gave her our word, Sawyer," Jane said. "We have to try. Ariel won't let anything happen to us. I trust her."

Jane looked into Sawyer's eyes. He was searching hers for a sign of doubt.

"Jane," he said as he shook his head and looked down at his feet.

"Trust her, Sawyer. Like I do."

Jane moved closer to him and tilted her chin upward. Sawyer kissed her.

"I cannot force you to stay," Ariel said from behind them. She had finished hiding the bodies and emerged from the barn. She tossed a sword to Sawyer. "Here," she said. "From one of the barbarians. Use this until you find the Stormblade. It is better than nothing."

She walked to the nearest horse and began rubbing its neck. "I cannot win this war by myself," she said. "You should know that I am eternally grateful for what you have done. The truth is you did not have to return; I know this."

Ariel walked to another horse and scratched its nose. "Last night when I attacked the Shadowlord's eastern army, I changed. I became one with nature and I was able to command the elements. My powers have increased."

"If you're that powerful, why didn't you wipe 'em out?" Sawyer asked. "The barbarians didn't stand a chance. Like those three, right?"

Ariel raised her eyebrows and brushed a lock of hair behind her ear. "No," she said. "They did not stand a chance, as you say. They retreated and scattered. There was another foe on the battlefield last night as well."

Jane and Sawyer looked at each other.

"The werewolf," Ariel said. "The same beast that hunted you. It attacked many of the fleeing barbarians. I suspect the Shadowlord was upset with his losses."

"Did you see him?" Jane asked. "The Shadowlord? Did you fight him again?"

"No," Ariel said. "He was not with his army. I do not know where he was, but he has other weapons at his disposal."

"Too bad the werewolf didn't eat him," Sawyer said. "Did the werewolf attack you too?"

"No," Ariel said shaking her head. "It was too far away."

"Hey," Jane said, holding up a finger. "Maybe we can get them to fight each other! The werewolf and the Shadowlord."

"Now that's a good idea," Sawyer said. "Let them kill each other. If the werewolf wins then the war is over. But if the Shadowlord wins, then we won't be hunted anymore. Win-win for us."

Jane looked at Ariel for approval of her idea, but her stoic expression hadn't changed.

"That's a good idea, isn't it?" Jane asked. "Can we get them together?"

"Which one would win?" Sawyer asked. "They're both evil, so who cares, right?"

"No," she said. "They are victims."

Jane and Sawyer fell silent.

"Your idea is not without merit," Ariel said finally, "but for now, we should return to Chalon. Can you ride a horse?"

Jane nodded.

"Yep," Sawyer said. "My uncle had a horse farm. I used to go there in the summer and ride."

"Good," Ariel said. "Choose a horse."

"All right," Sawyer said as he climbed onto the nearest horse. "Let's get outta here before more bad guys show up."

"Ariel," Jane said, "*will* more of them come?"

Ariel looked over her shoulder toward the east. "Yes," she said. "But not for some time, I hope. When this scouting party fails to return perhaps they will be reluctant to come this close to Chalon for a while."

"Will the Shadowlord be leading them?" Jane asked.

Ariel shook her head. "I do not know. His presence would hasten their advance on Chalon; that much is certain."

Ariel and Jane mounted their horses and the three of them rode for Chalon. As Jane's horse galloped along, she had the sinking feeling that something horrible was coming and they would never be the same again. She frowned; she didn't like negative thinking. Such thoughts were self-destructive and not useful for anyone. She shook her head in an effort to get such thoughts out of her mind.

They returned to Chalon, this time entering through the front gates. Jane was surprised they had been kept open. She expected Lionel to close them again as homeless people continued to file in. Their numbers were relatively few compared to the huge crowd that had entered with them yesterday, however. Ariel made sure her hood was pulled up over her head as they entered the city.

The guards watched them closely as they rode by. Some whispered to themselves and pointed at Sawyer. Jane was sure he didn't notice, because he was looking at the crowds of people milling about. A few children with dirty faces and dressed in rags came up to them and begged for food or coins.

"I'm sorry," Sawyer said, holding his hands up. "I don't have anything."

Jane saw the pained look in his eyes. She wanted to help them, too. She wondered how bad things would get when the city came under the Shadowlord's siege. It would get worse. Much worse. People were trying to barter or steal whatever they could to survive and she had read that sieges can last years.

"Ariel," Jane said. "Can't we do anything about this?" Jane motioned to demonstrate the deplorable conditions and treatment of the refugees.

"No," Ariel said, looking over her shoulder at Jane. "This is what humans do to each other every day."

"So we just let it happen?" Jane asked. "Do nothing?"

"This city can only hold so many people within its walls," Ariel said. "At least they have walls to protect them."

"What good is that if they're starved and abused by the townsfolk?" Jane asked. "This is no way to live."

"No," Ariel said. "It is not living. It is surviving. They are doing the best they can."

Ariel stopped her horse and turned in the saddle to face Jane.

"You cannot save everyone, Jane. I know you would try, but they would overwhelm you. Do you remember how you felt when we healed so many people on the way here?"

Jane nodded. "Weak."

"Yes," Ariel said. "Too weak. The others had to help you because you could barely walk."

Ariel nodded and looked around at the hustling throng of corruption and misery. "Perhaps Lionel will come to his senses and help these unfortunate people."

"I doubt it," Jane said flatly.

"We can try to convince him," Ariel said. "If we do not succeed then we will try something else."

"Hey!" Sawyer called above the noisy crowd. "Are you coming or not?"

He had ridden ahead of them and was a good thirty yards away. He rested a hand on his hip as Jane and Ariel nudged their horses toward him. "This is all pretty bad, huh?" he asked.

Jane tightened her lips and nodded. Ariel had been right. What could they do? They continued through the crowded city and entered the castle, where Ariel had to lower her hood and reveal herself if they were to pass through the gates. A large group of displaced farmers had set up camp outside the castle gates, too.

After dismounting and letting a stableboy lead their horses away, Ariel turned to Jane and Sawyer.

"The best we can do for these people," she said, "is to win the war so they may return to their homes. I know that is difficult to understand, but there is no other way."

"How do we do that?" Sawyer asked. "We need help."

"Yes, we do," Ariel said as they started walking toward the castle.

"And help you shall have," said a voice from behind them.

They spun around to see the tall, gallant figure of Trelane approaching. He had also worn a hooded cloak so he could walk among people without being accosted. He walked up to Ariel and bowed his head slightly.

"Lady Ariel," Trelane said, "if I may have a word."

Ariel gave Jane and Sawyer a look that meant every bit of "go away," so they walked to the castle steps and sat on the hard stone. Sawyer put his arm around Jane and blew into her ear, but she ignored him; she was too busy straining to hear Ariel and Trelane.

"Now is the time to attack," she heard Trelane say.

CHAPTER TWENTY-ONE
ROBBERS

Geoff frantically looked about for something he could use to defend himself. He picked up a large, double-bladed battle-axe, but it was too heavy for him to swing. Then something on the floor caught his eye. It was a crossbow bolt. Their attacker had fired five or six of them at him and Ishara. Most of them had broken upon impact, but this one was whole. Geoff grabbed it and ran after Ishara, who had pursued their would-be killer and disappeared down the staircase.

"Ishara!" he called. "Wait! Ishara!"

His mage stone still lit the way for him as he reached the first floor of the wizard's tower. The front door yawned open, and he ran out to look for Ishara, letting out a sigh of relief when he spotted her walking back from the main square at a brisk pace. As he watched her, Ishara looked over her shoulder and pulled her hood over her head.

"Hey, who was that?" Geoff asked. "Did you see who attacked us? Did you get him?"

"No," she said, shaking her head. "I lost our enemy in the crowd."

Ishara pointed above Geoff's head. "Geoff," she said. "Your mage stone."

He glanced upward. Sure enough, he'd forgotten to deactivate his magical glowing gem.

"Oh! Yeah," he said, holding out his hand and letting the gem go dark as it fell into his hand.

"Are you unharmed?" Ishara asked, looking him over.

"I'm fine. Any idea who attacked us?"

"No," she said. "But our attacker was agile and quick."

"At least he was a bad shot," Geoff said, holding up the crossbow bolt.

"Geoff!" Ishara said, grabbing his wrist. "Be careful!"

"What?" Geoff said. He looked at the bolt in his hand. Its tip glistened with a dark brown ichor. Ishara turned his hand over and gently took the bolt from him. She examined his hand, apparently to see if he had accidently gotten any of the brown substance on his skin or cut himself with the sharp tip.

"What's that brown stuff?" Geoff asked, watching Ishara examine the bolt.

"Poison. I do not know what kind, perhaps Ariel will recognize it."

Ishara carefully slid the poisoned crossbow bolt into a leather pouch, looked around, and then ushered Geoff back into the wizard's tower.

"Well," she said, "we are doing something right."

"What do you mean?" Geoff asked. "I don't understand."

"Someone," Ishara said, pulling her hood back and shutting the door behind Geoff, "does not want us here. They are afraid we will discover something important and they are willing to kill in order to prevent us from completing our task."

Geoff activated his mage stone and they walked up the staircase again. Ishara picked up the weapon that had been dropped by their attacker. Geoff thought it looked like an automatic crossbow with a round clip of bolts attached to it. It had an array of intricate levers and various switches, and the workmanship was impressive.

"Dwarven crossbow," Ishara said. "High rate of fire and very accurate."

Geoff scratched his head. He remembered reading about ancient medieval weapons, but this contraption was like the medieval equivalent of a machine gun.

"Hey," he said. "Aren't crossbows able penetrate armor? How're we still here? We should've been pin cushions."

Ishara smiled at Geoff. "Yes," she said. "You are familiar with weapons."

She walked over to the suit of elven battle armor that had shielded them and examined it.

"Look," Ishara said. "Not even a mark or dent. This armor *is* enchanted. Now you know why we are still alive."

"Enchanted?" Geoff asked as he looked the armor over. "Like Sawyer's sword?"

"Not exactly," Ishara said. "But this armor must be imbued with powerful magic. We should take it with us."

"Yeah," Geoff said. "It's really cool."

Geoff touched the armor and ran his finger along the ridges in the helmet. The suits of armor in his house were junk compared this. Ishara rummaged and found a thick burlap sack, then began the process of disassembling the elven battle armor.

"What're you doing?" Geoff asked.

"We are not leaving this armor behind," Ishara said. "It has already saved us. Perhaps it will be useful again."

"Useful to who?" Geoff said as he held the burlap sack open. "Are you going to wear it?"

"Me? No. Even enchanted armor such as this will slow me. This is the armor of a warrior."

"So Ariel, then?"

Ishara shook her head. "Druids do not wear such armor."

"The only other one I can think of is…," Geoff said, his words trailing off.

"Yes, he may be able to wear it," Ishara said. "Besides, our enemy must now realize what this armor is. Do you want them to steal it?

Geoff shook his head. "Heck no. We better steal it first." Ishara loaded the pieces of the armor into the sack. The armor was so light that Geoff was able to lift the sack off the ground and throw it over his shoulder.

"Will it fit Sawyer?" Geoff asked.

"Enchanted armor will fit anyone," Ishara said.

Geoff smiled. The thought of his wearing such a fabulous suit of armor would make him look like a hero, even if he wasn't. Ishara looked around the second floor of the tower one more time before descending the stairs. Geoff followed her. They stopped at the door just long enough for Geoff to deactivate his mage stone and place it back in his pocket.

Ishara opened the door and peeked outside, then she stepped onto the doorstep. Apparently satisfied they were safe, she beckoned to Geoff, and he stepped out into the sunlight. Everything looked normal. Down the small street he saw people in the trade square walk past.

Ishara closed the door and used her tools to lock it.

"Hey," Geoff said. "We never did find that secret door. I would've liked to have seen it."

"Perhaps next time. The others should know about our encounter."

Geoff followed Ishara down the street. She slung her new bow over her shoulder and pulled her hood over her head again.

"I need arrows," Ishara said. "I left my quiver back in our room."

"Ishara," Geoff said. "How did our attacker lose you? Did he outrun you?"

Ishara thought for a moment.

"I do not know, Geoff," she said. "Even in a human city I am not easily eluded."

"They also snuck up on us. Ariel was right. Our attacker has serious skills."

"Indeed," Ishara said. "They do. Remember that, Geoff. Our enemy is deadly. We were fortunate this time."

Geoff stopped. "This time?" he asked. "Will they try to kill us again?"

"Of course," Ishara said, looking curiously at Geoff. "Why would they not attack us again? For that matter, why would the others not be in danger as well?"

"I hope they're okay," Geoff said. "We better warn them."

"Do not worry. Ariel has taken them to a secret place. They will be fine."

Ishara took him by the hand as they approached the crowded trade square. Geoff grinned. He had been kissed by the most beautiful girl he had ever seen and now they were trying to solve the mystery of the wizard's disappearance. Geoff was excited and frightened at the same time.

"Be alert," Ishara said from under her hood. Geoff gripped her hand tighter as they walked into the crowd.

People were still hustling about, and some were still selling their wares. Ishara weaved in and around the people in the square, but Geoff had a bit more difficulty with the burlap sack slung over his shoulder, and his hand began to ache from gripping it so tightly. Ishara looked back at him from time to time as they walked, and he noticed several pairs of eyes on his sack as they passed through the crowd.

Apparently, a kid carrying a sack this size seemed like easy pickings, but one thing bothered Geoff even more than that. It was the absence of the city guard. He'd always thought of them as the local police, but with none around, he and Ishara would have to fend for themselves like everyone else. Plus, if they were caught, how would they explain the suit of armor Geoff carried? Of course they had stolen it, and Geoff wondered if that meant time in the dungeon.

"Shortcut," Ishara said as they turned down a narrow alley.

"Hey," Geoff said. "Where exactly are we going?"

Before Ishara could answer, a gruff, gravelly voice chimed in.

"Yer goin' ta gimme that sack, boy."

Startled, Geoff's mouth fell open as he stopped and turned toward the rough voice. A scruffy, unkempt man stepped out from a doorway just a few feet away. The man sneered, revealing several missing teeth. Those that remained were yellow and brown. He wore a ragged broad-brimmed hat and a vest with black breeches. The man's body odor was so strong that Geoff found it difficult to breathe.

Then he saw another man step from around the corner in front of them. He was large and bald, with a barrel chest and a grossly oversized stomach. His ruddy face twitched and glistened with sweat, and his black beard appeared to have bits of food in it. He was also dressed in rags, and he was scowling at Geoff and Ishara.

"Better do as he says," another voice behind them said. "An' we'll take whatever else you may have."

Geoff spun around and saw a third man, who was brandishing a knife. This man's dark, matted hair was combed over to cover his obvious baldness, and he had a scar across his hooked nose.

Ishara pulled Geoff away and positioned him with his back against a wall. The three robbers closed in on them, looking like a pack of wolves that had cornered their prey.

"I said gimme the sack, boy," growled the first robber. He spat on the ground. "Now!"

The fat robber walked to Ishara and reached for her. As he did, she kicked him between the legs. He let out a sharp yell and fell to his knees. Ishara punched him in the mouth and he fell over. The first robber then produced a large knife and lunged for her. She sidestepped his lunge, unslung her bow, and smacked him on the wrist with a loud *whack*. The force of her blow knocked the knife from his hand.

"Ow! Damn!" He yelled. "She broke mah wrist!"

He grabbed his injured wrist, but as he looked up Ishara brought her bow down on top of his head and he fell forward, crumpling into a heap. His eyes rolled up in his head as he let out a groan.

All of a sudden, a rough hand grasped Geoff by the scruff of the neck and almost lifted him off the ground. He felt a cold blade against his throat.

"Hey, lil missy," hissed the third robber with the scarred nose. "If ye don't stop yer fightin' and resistin', I'll slit this boy's gizzard."

Geoff swallowed. He smelled booze on the robber's breath, and his hands felt greasy. Ishara stood still and met the third robber's gaze.

"Drop that bow and take yer hood down, girl," the third robber ordered. "I wanna see what kind of girl ye are."

Ishara dropped the newly acquired bow and pulled her hood back. Behind her, Geoff saw the fat robber had recovered from Ishara's beating.

"My my," the third robber said. "You're a pretty lil maiden!"

Ishara took a step toward him. "You," she said, "are hideous."

Geoff felt the robber's grip tighten around his neck. "Well, maybe so," he said. "But you're gonna change yer mind 'bout us, right fellas?"

"The little feisty wench owes me," the fat robber said. "I'ma make her pay up real good."

Ishara threw him a look of disgust. Geoff tried to wriggle free so he could help her, but he wasn't strong enough. The robber holding him tightened his grasp and ripped the sack away. He tossed it to the first robber, who had just recovered his knife and was rubbing his head.

"Have a look," he said. "And get that bow away from the elf girl 'fore she beats on ye again."

The first robber kicked the bow away from Ishara while the fat one clamped his meaty hands on Ishara's upper arms, pressing them against her sides. The first robber opened the sack and his eyes bulged with surprise.

"Looky at this!" he said, holding up the ornate breastplate and helmet. "We're rich!"

"Now where would two street rats like you get a fancy suit of armor?" the robber with the scarred nose asked. "Where'd ye steal it from, boy?"

Geoff felt himself being shaken back and forth, and he lost focus for a second or two. His heart was racing and the hair on the back of his neck was standing up.

"Stop!" he said. "You're hurting me."

"Aye," said the robber. "I'll be doing more 'an that real soon. Ye'll see, boy."

The fat robber wrapped his arms around Ishara and lifted her off the ground. Ishara gritted her teeth, swung a leg out in front of her and then it brought down and behind her, crashing her heel into the fat robber's knee.

He grunted and dropped Ishara, then fell against a wall as he gripped his knee. The first robber attacked her with his butcher's knife, slashing at her midsection, but Ishara stepped back and dodged the blow. She followed with a hard punch to his nose. The robber dropped his knife and grabbed his nose, which already had a stream of blood trickling from it. Ishara clasped her fists together, leapt into the air, and brought her hands down on the first robber's head. The blow sent him to the ground.

Geoff screamed as he felt the blade of the robber behind him press deeper against his throat, but then another hand appeared and twisted the robber's wrist, pulling the knife away.

Chapter Twenty-Two
Remembering the Past

Jane and Sawyer followed Ariel and Trelane into the castle. He and Ariel had continued their conversation in the elvish language as they walked side by side. Jane blamed herself for their secrecy, because she had gotten too close as she tried to listen to them.

They made a good couple, she thought with a smile. Their children would probably be superheroes and have an *S* on their chests. Sawyer gave her a nudge with his elbow and nodded forward, keeping his eyes fixed straight ahead. Jane followed his gaze and saw they were approaching the throne room. The large doors were open and half a dozen guards were walking in their direction. The lead guard raised his hand, signaling for them to stop.

"By order of King Lionel the First," he said, "you will come with us. The king wishes to speak with you."

"We wish to speak with him as well," Ariel said.

The guard nodded, and they were escorted to the king. Lionel was brooding over the large table, upon which rested a map of Alluria. He looked up at them as they entered the room, and a scowl etched across his bearded face when he saw Ariel. How sad, Jane thought, that Lionel and Ariel have such a strong mutual dislike that they find it difficult to cooperate with one another.

They were again flanked by guards who scrutinized their every movement.

"Why is there an elven army camped in my kingdom?" Lionel demanded. "Did you think I wouldn't discover this?"

"King Lionel," Trelane said, "we are here to aid Chalon in its time of need. Lady Ariel and I come with news of the Shadowlord's eastern army."

"Oh?" Lionel said, holding a decanter under his nose and sniffing its contents. "What news do you have for me?"

"Last night I attacked the army to the east and drove them back. This has given us time to form a united defense," Ariel said. "If we act together."

"You did this? Alone?" Lionel said, raising an eyebrow. Jane knew from his sarcastic tone that he didn't believe her.

"How can a single druid do this?"

"I surprised them," Ariel said. "They have retreated, but they are regrouping. Today I killed three scouts less than a day's ride east of here."

"Truly?" Lionel asked. "If you are powerful enough to strike an entire army, why didn't you simply destroy them? If you had killed them then we could turn our attention to the Shadowlord's northern army—an army, my scouts say, that is far larger than the one to the east."

"They have been scattered for now," Ariel said. "Is that not enough? Would you have me slay them all?"

"Yes!" Lionel said, slamming his goblet on the table and spilling some wine. "Kill them and we no longer have to worry about being attacked. How simple is that?"

"Very simple," Ariel said with an acidic tone. "I cannot slay an army for you. These barbarians fear magic. That alone is why I was able to scatter them."

Lionel glared at Ariel again, and Ariel met his stern gaze with one of her own.

"I am not your killer," Ariel said, taking a step forward. "With Trelane's forces you are a match for the eastern army. If you act now and attack, we have a good chance of defeating them."

"King Lionel," Trelane said, "Ariel is right. Whether you believe her or not, the elves have come to help you. King Andurys has provided an army five thousand strong to help you defeat the Shadowlord. Will you not accept his aid?"

Lionel turned his gaze from Ariel to Trelane. Lionel's expression softened. Maybe he'll listen to Trelane, Jane thought. At least they don't seem to hate each other.

"Five thousand? That's all? And how can I trust you? Why didn't you tell me yesterday you had invaded my kingdom from the south?" Lionel said. "My father always said elves were not to be trusted."

Jane bit her lip as she watched Trelane. This wasn't going much better.

"Your father," Trelane said, "is not here."

"Do not be a fool. Trelane brings you much needed aid from Selra'thel," Ariel said. "He offers you a chance to save your people and you doubt him. Why?"

Lionel took a long drink from his goblet and laughed. He rubbed his forehead and addressed Ariel.

"Because I tend to become suspicious when an army shows up uninvited in my kingdom," Lionel said, "and an assassin prowls my castle."

"As you wish, King Lionel," Trelane said with a curt bow of his head. "I will not trouble you any further."

He and Ariel turned and walked past Jane and Sawyer. Jane looked at Lionel, who was regarding her and Sawyer with a cool gaze.

"C'mon," Jane said, tugging at Sawyer's hand. As they turned to follow Ariel and Trelane, Lionel called to Sawyer.

"I trust the Stormlord will fight beside us," he said in a mocking tone. "After all, you *are* a hero of the people and they need you now."

Sawyer looked over his shoulder and nodded at Lionel's sarcastic remark.

"I bet he had someone steal my sword," Sawyer whispered. "I wouldn't put it past him, would you?"

"No," Jane whispered back. Sawyer had an interesting thought. To Jane, it totally made sense for Lionel to have Sawyer's sword stolen. Before Count Vilmar was murdered, Seqwil had warned them of Lionel's plot to have that giant warrior at dinner challenge Sawyer for it. How could they trust the king? Jane frowned.

As they caught up with Trelane and Ariel, Jane saw Trelane touch Ariel's elbow and they stopped.

"I did not think him so foolish," Trelane said in a low tone. "I must now consider the possibility that he will attack my army. I may have to withdraw from Chalon."

"I wish I could make him see reason," Ariel said.

"I am sorry," Trelane said. "I cannot force him to accept our aid. Perhaps you will find a way to convince him of our sincerity."

Trelane bowed his head to Ariel, smiled at Jane as he gave Sawyer a pat on the shoulder, and then left.

Jane watched Trelane march out of the castle and a sinking feeling came over her. An opportunity had been missed and now she felt the real danger of being trapped in a besieged city.

"Ariel," Jane said quietly, "what do we do now?"

Her question had apparently given Ariel pause, but Ariel didn't answer as she also watched Trelane leave. Jane looked at Sawyer, who just shrugged. Perhaps Ariel would tell them to go home because there was no hope of winning the war.

"I do not know, Jane," Ariel said at last. "I do not have the answers."

Ariel's words unnerved Jane. If she didn't know what to do, then who did?

"I will try to speak with Lionel again," Ariel said. "Perhaps the two of you would like to spend some time in the palace gardens? I think you will find it quite pleasant."

"Why the gardens?" Sawyer asked. "Why can't we come with you?"

"I want to speak with Lionel alone," Ariel said. "If we are separated, I would feel better if you were somewhere with castle guards nearby."

"Why?" Jane said. "Do you think someone'll try to hurt us?"

Ariel gave Jane a sidelong glance. Jane knew the answer to her question before Ariel spoke.

"Perhaps," she said. "If you prefer, you can stay outside the throne room with the guards."

"Oh, no," Sawyer said, pulling Jane away from Ariel. "Where are the gardens?"

"From here it is best if you leave by the front doors and circle to the back of the castle," Ariel said. "Remember to stay alert."

"Okay," Sawyer said. "Good luck with the king. He's a real pain in the—"

"Sawyer!" Jane said sharply while pulling his hand.

"What?" Sawyer said, looking confused.

"You can't say that. He's just looking for a reason to lock us up."

"Ha!" Sawyer said. "Yeah, that's right. C'mon. Let's go see the gardens and stuff."

"Good luck, Ariel," Jane said. "Don't worry about us. We'll be fine."

Jane and Sawyer raced down the hallway and out the front doors of the castle. She was eager to finally spend some time alone with Sawyer.

—◆◆◆—

Jane and Sawyer held each other's hands while they ran. Ariel smiled. Yes, they would be fine. They had much to learn, but the speed at which they absorbed her teachings was impressive. *Impressive.* Ariel never thought she would use a word like that to describe a human, let alone three human children. Still, an unknown danger *was* near and much depended on them; an assassin within the castle walls was worrying.

She waited for Jane and Sawyer to disappear around the corner, and the smile drained from her face as she turned to reenter the throne room. It was time she and Lionel had a long talk. Lionel threw his hands up when he saw her, and his exasperated expression gave her a small bit of satisfaction.

"I trust you've forgotten something?" Lionel asked in a mocking tone.

"No. I wish to speak privately with you."

Ariel watched Lionel's eyes. Her request had surprised him, and he seemed unsure of his safety. He studied her for several moments, then gave her a quick nod.

"Very well," he said.

Lionel sat on his throne, leaned his head back, and closed his eyes while he pinched the bridge of his nose. Ariel wasn't sure if he was about to have an emotional outburst or if he was considering the alliance proposal Trelane had delivered. If he did not insult and scream at her, then perhaps he would finally act to defend his kingdom.

Lionel stood and walked to a large set of windowed doors behind the throne. He opened them and walked out onto a balcony and looked over the city.

Ariel joined him. A gentle breeze blew through her hair, and she tilted her head back and closed her eyes. The tingling sensation she felt as the cool breeze blew made her feel at ease. After a few moments she looked out over the city below. She thought of the families who had come here seeking refuge. She thought of Willelm and his family. If Lionel's decision was to stay within the walls of Chalon and not ally himself with the elves, then they would all perish.

"My scouts tell me of a monster that stalks the eastern army and attacks at night." Lionel's voice was calm. "It's him, isn't it?"

Ariel nodded.

"Did I ever tell you what happened that night?" Lionel asked quietly. "How Alex saved my life?"

"No," Ariel said in a low tone.

"We...*he* tracked just such a monster to the edge of a ravine on a dreary, rainy night. At the ravine the tracks simply stopped. Rain poured down on us in buckets and there was a chill in the air. The kind of chill that cut through cloaks, armor, and clothes." Lionel took another drink of wine. "I had dismounted and walked along the ravine's edge in an effort to find the beast's tracks. We had Maelord's magic light, so we could see well enough, even though the torches were soaked. Suddenly, from out of the darkness it came. Snarling and gnashing its fangs. I'll never forget those two hate-filled yellow eyes piercing the night as it charged me. I thought I was dead."

Ariel said nothing. This was the first either of them had spoken of that tragic night's events. Clearly, Lionel had been tormented since the encounter. He needed to share his feelings with someone, and this night he chose to reveal everything to her. This surprised Ariel, and in spite of their differences, she was grateful to be with him now.

"I should've been dead," Lionel said. "Ripped to pieces at the edge of that ravine. But Alex pushed me aside at the last minute and bore the brunt of the beast's attack. Hell, I never could hold my footing in the rain and mud—you know that. All I did was flop around in the muck like a damned fish. But I tried to help Alex. Zorn, Shaun, and Maelord fought like heroes."

Lionel's eyes became moist as he continued to speak. "It was a great battle, Ariel. You should've seen us. The kingdom's greatest heroes against a nightmare. Did you know it was Zorn who killed the werewolf?"

Ariel shook her head again. This she hadn't heard.

"An enchanted silver-tipped arrow through the eye," Lionel said. "It was a hell of a shot. We'd always joked and said Zorn was part elf." Lionel laughed a little, but it wasn't a cheery laugh. "At any rate, the beast was dead. We were victorious. But Alex lay there in the mud, bleeding from his wounds. Even at that moment he knew. He knew what was to become of him. There was nothing we could do. Zorn and Alex were great friends. Their sorrowful farewell touched us all."

Lionel wiped the corner of his eye. "That was the last time we were all together," he said. "He bade us leave him. He died that night, or he should've died. If the powers that be had been merciful, he would've died."

Ariel nodded.

"But he lived," Lionel said. "He bears a curse that should never have befallen him. Now I understand what he did. He exiled himself for the good of the kingdom. For the good of the people. After all, what sort of ruler would he be if every night he changed into a werewolf and ate his subjects?"

"He was better than that," Ariel said. "He was a good man."

"Aye," Lionel said. "He was. I miss him. I think even now he fights to protect Chalon. Oh, I know how silly that sounds. But the beast he becomes at night must carry some small sliver, a small spark of the man, right?" Lionel looked at Ariel.

"I do not know," she said, "but I like that thought."

"Aye," Lionel said. "You know, even as a monster he's better than me."

Ariel said nothing. She was content to let him speak.

"As we rode out of the forest that night," Lionel said, "I could've sworn we heard laughter."

"Laughter?"

"Laughter. There was something else in the forest that night. Its laugh was horrible and mocking. Zorn didn't want to leave Alex; none of us did. But he made us obey him. It was what he wanted. We went back to town, but the next morning Zorn had gotten up before any of us and left without a word. I think he was most affected by Alex's fate. We never saw him again."

Lionel turned and faced the north. "Now he leads two armies against us. We were all friends, Ariel. Does he blame me for what happened to Alex?"

"No," she said. "He is no longer Zorn. At least, not the hero you and I knew. He has changed. He is evil now. His heart has gone dark and he cannot be redeemed. I do not know what compels him to wage war on us, but he may yet succeed in destroying us all."

"At least we have the Stormlord with us," Lionel said. "That's something we can rally around."

Ariel remained silent. Lionel apparently expected much from Sawyer, and she didn't yet want to reveal the theft of the Stormblade.

"The children," he said. "Those three human children, why do you care about them? I've never known you to like many humans, much less let them travel with you. What are they to you?"

Ariel thought for a minute. She realized she had asked herself that same question before, but she never truly considered the answer until now.

"I never told you how we came to meet," she said. "It was not long ago. In the Spirewood Forest. I had tracked a goblin raiding party there. Goblins had never dared to travel so deep into the forest, but this group did. I heard their hunting cries in the distance and I knew they were tracking something."

Ariel smiled. "I was enraged. How I imagined what I would do to them once I found them, and I *would* find them. But when I did catch up to the goblins, I saw something else. They had trapped and injured a unicorn, the most precious forest creature of all. They were celebrating their victory when those three human children attacked. They charged a fully armed goblin raiding party with nothing but stones and sticks."

Lionel chuckled and Ariel nodded. "*You* should have seen *them*," she said. "They were magnificent. When I asked them why they chose to save the unicorn at great peril to themselves, their answer was simply that it was the right thing to do."

Lionel laughed and clapped his hands.

"Excellent," he said. "So that's why you help them."

Ariel thought for a moment. "No," she said. "I help them because they are my friends. And they have chosen to risk their lives to help us. I believe they may change our fates, as well as the fate of Alluria. You should be kinder to them."

Lionel slapped the edge of a railing with his hand. "The Prophecy of the Three Travelers? Of course! The Stormlord! The little blond boy," he said. "That one looks familiar to me. He reminds me of—"

At that moment the doors to the throne room burst open and a guard wearing plate mail armor rushed in and bowed.

"Forgive me, my king," he said. "There's a monster inside the castle!"

CHAPTER TWENTY-THREE
SEQWIL FERNCLIFF

The robber's grasp on Geoff loosened, and he squirmed away. Once free, he spun around and saw Seqwil Ferncliff, the elven ambassador from Selra'thel. She was struggling with the robber for control of his knife.

She twisted his arm, and the robber let out a cry of pain and dropped the knife. He threw a punch at Seqwil, but she ducked it and followed with a quick strike to his chin, knocking him backward. The robber growled and sprang forward, swinging wildly at Seqwil. She dodged the first three swings with ease, but the fourth punch struck her on the cheek and she fell to the ground. Geoff punched the robber on the shoulder and tried to push him away, but he shoved Geoff down. Before Geoff could get up, a blur flew past him and attacked the robber.

Ishara kicked the robber in the stomach and then promptly punched his face five or six times. Geoff saw at least one tooth go flying from the robber's mouth before he collapsed, his face smeared with blood as he fell. Ishara quickly retrieved her bow and prepared to use it as a weapon against the other robbers.

The fat robber had gotten to his feet. He was hunched over, grasping his knee and grunting. Ishara moved toward him like a predator, ready to strike. He winced as he watched her, then he looked about and saw his two partners lying unconscious on the ground. Shaking his bald, sweaty head, he turned and lumbered down the alley without looking back.

"You better run!" Ishara yelled. "Coward!"

Geoff went to Seqwil, who was lying face down only a few feet away. His hands shook as he rolled her over. Her cheek was red from the assault, but otherwise she seemed unharmed.

"Lady Seqwil," Geoff said, "are you okay? Can you hear me?"

Ishara appeared at his side. She examined Seqwil's bruise and searched her for any other wounds.

"She will be fine," Ishara said. "Perhaps she will have a headache, but she will recover quickly. How are you?"

"I'm fine. She saved me," Geoff said. "That robber, he was going to kill me. She came out of nowhere and pulled the knife away from my throat."

"Yes," Ishara said. "She saved us both. She was very brave. Stay with her."

Ishara stood and Geoff grabbed her hand.

"Wait," he said. "Where are you going?"

Ishara smiled as she looked down at him.

"I am going to collect our armor," she said. "Keep an eye on Lady Seqwil."

Geoff turned his attention back to the elven ambassador lying next to him, relieved to know she was going to be okay. She was as beautiful as Ariel or Ishara, and she was strong and fast, too. It must be an elf thing. He hadn't seen Ariel or Ishara get punched like Seqwil did, however; maybe she slipped or was surprised by the ferocity of the robber's attack. Behind him, Geoff heard Ishara gathering bits of the suit of armor that had fallen out of the sack.

"Mmm," Seqwil said, rubbing her cheek as she slowly opened her eyes. "What happened?"

"You saved us," Geoff said. "Those robbers were gonna kill us, but you stopped them. Can you stand up?"

"Yes," Seqwil said with a grunt. "I think I can."

Ishara returned with her sack slung over her shoulder. She smiled at Seqwil and placed a hand over her own heart.

"*Hal'inari*," Ishara said. "Thank you for your aid. You fought like a warrior."

"Ha," Seqwil said. "I was never much of a warrior. That is why I became a diplomat."

Geoff and Ishara helped Seqwil to her feet. She wobbled a little at first, but gained her balance after a moment.

"Well," Seqwil said, "I trust neither of you were hurt by those wretched men?"

"No," Ishara said. "However, if you had not come along when you did…"

"Then we shall consider it luck or fate," Seqwil said. "Why were you in this alley?"

Geoff opened his mouth to speak, but before he could, Ishara answered.

"We were exploring the city, and on our way back to the castle when we turned down here."

Seqwil smiled, but quickly winced and touched her bruised cheek.

"It was a good thing I saw you from across the trade

square," Seqwil said. "They must have been interested in the contents of your sack."

Ishara nodded and opened the sack, revealing its contents to Seqwil. Seeing the enchanted armor made Seqwil gasp.

"Elven battle armor," she said. "How did you come by it?"

"We found it," Geoff said, looking at Ishara, who gave him a quick nod. "We're investigating the wizard's disappearance," he continued. "It was in his tower."

Seqwil looked at Geoff and Ishara. "You should keep that information to yourselves," she said. "We'd better leave. Follow me, I know another way."

Ishara pulled her hood over her head and they followed Seqwil out of the alley and into the crowded trade square again. Some people gave Seqwil a wide berth as they walked. It seemed to be a gesture of respect, not fear, Geoff realized.

His heart was still racing after their encounter with the robbers, and he looked about for more potential attackers while they made their way through the crowd. Everyone seemed to be too concerned with their own business of surviving to give two kids much attention, however.

Ishara leaned in close. "We have to teach you how to fight. It will be our secret. I almost lost you and that will not do."

Geoff wasn't sure how to respond, but he knew she was right. If not for Seqwil's timely intervention, he would probably be dead. That realization frightened him, but he kept looking straight ahead. "Okay," he said.

Ishara was a great fighter, almost as great as Ariel. Besides, Geoff wanted to be of more use to her and the others. Sawyer and Jane were learning how to fight and cast spells, so he needed to learn something, too.

They followed Seqwil past the trade square, past the

vendors hawking their wares and people busying themselves with their daily business. It reminded Geoff of the county fair. So many sights, sounds, and smells. He couldn't shake a feeling of impending doom, however. Everyone appeared to be in a hurry to garner as much in both wealth and supplies as possible before the Shadowlord showed up.

The townsfolk looked frightened. At least that's what Geoff thought. He noticed a bearded, middle-aged man with a grim face sitting at a table as they exited the trade square. He was flanked by two muscular, dangerous-looking fellows who were armed with several weapons. Behind them, a few other warriors similarly armed sat on an old rickety wooden bench. The man with the beard watched Seqwil and nodded at her as they passed.

"Who was that?" Geoff asked.

"An acquaintance. His bodyguards can be your bodyguards…for a fee."

"From the looks of it," Ishara said, "he does very well."

"Indeed," Seqwil said, looking over her shoulder. "I have used his rather expensive services in the past. As you know, Ishara, human cities are no place for elven women."

Ishara nodded.

"They are little better than those who attacked you," Seqwil said, "but they do look the part, I suppose."

Seqwil turned down a small side street, which appeared to have expensive, well-built homes. A city guard stood at the street corner and also acknowledged Seqwil with a nod. The various styles of architecture instantly caught Geoff's attention. Some looked like small fortresses or keeps while others looked like simple yet stout stone homes with tiled roofs.

"Pardon me, Lady Seqwil," Ishara said, looking about, "but where are we going?"

"To my house," Seqwil said. "I need to wash and change my clothes after rolling in the muck with those robbers. Keep in mind, this house isn't much, but I call it home while I am in Chalon. Most foreign officials and dignitaries who do not wish to stay in the castle live in this neighborhood."

They walked to a sturdy stone structure with a slanted tiled roof. An undersized stone wall with a gate stood out front. Geoff liked the house immediately. To him, it looked like a cozy country home. It was the type of place where he could curl up on the couch with a good book and lose himself within the pages.

Seqwil went through the gate and held it open for Geoff and Ishara. Geoff noted the gate didn't make a sound. Seqwil produced a brass skeleton key at the solid-looking oaken front door and opened the lock.

They entered the house, which was sparsely decorated. The main room held a wooden table and four chairs. A large earthen-colored rug covered nearly the entire floor. Two comfy-looking cushioned chairs sat before a dark fireplace with an unused cooking kettle in it. The kitchen area consisted of a few cabinets and a table for food preparation. There was a set of stairs at the far end of the room leading to the upper level.

"Lady Seqwil," Ishara said, pulling back her hood and looking about. "Forgive me, but where are your servants?"

"I have none," Seqwil said. "I have no need of them here."

"But your meals," Ishara said, "and the cleaning. Who does that for you?"

Seqwil laughed. "I am capable of cleaning my own home

and preparing my meals. However, I must admit that I tend to favor the feasts in court. It is an excellent opportunity to catch up on the latest goings-on and gossip."

Seqwil gave them a wink and a smile.

"So, please seat yourselves," Seqwil said. "I will change and return shortly."

Geoff watched Seqwil walk up the stairs. When she had disappeared, he turned to Ishara. "I like her," he said. "She's nice."

"Me too. She is from an ancient and noble house in Selra'thel. Her family has done much to further peace between elves and the other races of Alluria."

"I believe it," Geoff said. "I like this house, too. It's like a country cottage. All it needs is a fire and the smell of good food cooking."

"Yes," Ishara said as she looked around the room. "I am surprised by the lack of decorations. Her family home is full of the most amazing art and furnishings. It is breathtaking."

"Oh, that I want to see," Geoff said. "Do you think I could visit your home, Selra'thel, someday?"

Ishara smiled at him. "I will take you there myself. You will be my guest. There is so much to see."

Geoff smiled. He would've never asked a girl if he could visit her home before, but Ishara made him feel comfortable. He could be his nerdy self and she still liked him. How cool was that? But she also inspired him. He didn't know how to explain it, but she made him want to be better. She cared for him—that much was obvious—and he didn't want to let her down.

"I would love that," he said. "I wouldn't want to see Selra'thel with anyone else."

Ishara took his hand in hers and caressed it as she looked into his eyes.

"You say the sweetest things," she said. "Nu tel'mor."

She squeezed his hand. Geoff wanted to kiss her again and ask her what *Nu Tel'mor* meant, but before he could make up his mind which to do first, Seqwil reappeared at the foot of the steps. She looked at Ishara, then at Geoff, and smiled. She seemed to recognize what was happening between them.

"That did not take long, right?" Seqwil said, smoothing the new dress she had just donned. "I did say 'shortly.' Here, perhaps you can make use of these."

She tossed a quiver of arrows to Ishara, whose eyes lit up as she caught it.

"Thank you," Ishara said. "These will do nicely until I can make more."

"Oh," Seqwil said, tapping her forehead. "Please forgive my lack of manners. May I offer you something? Are you hungry?"

Geoff looked at Ishara. Now that he thought about it, he could eat something.

"Thank you," Ishara said. "A nice meal would be welcome after today's events."

"Very good. I so rarely get a chance to cook, much less cook for guests," Seqwil said. "Please make yourselves comfortable while I cook an elven dish for you."

"Shall we help?" Ishara asked.

"Of course not," Seqwil said, waving her off. "I would not think of it. The two of you put your things down and relax. You may not know this, but I am quite a good cook."

They obeyed Seqwil and sat in the soft chairs facing the

fireplace. Seqwil told them amusing stories of humans and elves while she busied herself with cleaning and cutting vegetables. Geoff and Ishara listened and laughed. Seqwil even told Geoff the first time Ishara picked up a bow and tried to use it. It was early in the morning and she had slipped out of her bed and taken a bow from the armory. Not knowing the proper archery technique, Ishara fired the arrow and the bow string had scraped the inside of her arm. She wailed so much and so loudly she awakened everyone in Selra'thel, including the king.

Geoff laughed and looked at Ishara, who closed her eyes and shook her head. He found her embarrassed smile charming.

It wasn't long before they were seated at the table enjoying a wonderful soup, which smelled and tasted of a hint of cinnamon. He couldn't pronounce the name, but it was delicious. Geoff asked for a second bowl, and he would've taken a third if he hadn't been worried he would look like he was making a pig of himself. Geoff shared the tale of the first time he and Ishara met. They had been taken prisoner by brigands and managed to escape. Ishara wakened their leader only to punch him in the nose.

They spent the rest of the afternoon visiting and chatting about whatever amusing events had happened to them. Lady Seqwil wanted to hear about their adventures together, and she seemed to be genuinely charmed by their tales. She asked questions and engaged both Geoff and Ishara with equal enthusiasm. She even served them a rare elven wine she had been saving for a special occasion. Geoff thought it tasted a bit like a grape soft drink with a hint of honey. As evening began to fall and the sun started to set, Geoff realized what an enjoyable day it had been.

"We should return, Lady Seqwil," Ishara said, standing and gathering the sack of armor. "Thank you for your warmth and hospitality. It has been an honor and a pleasure visiting with you today."

"Yes, thanks so much," Geoff said. "I haven't had this much fun in a long time."

"The honor is mine," Seqwil said with a polite bow of her head. "Any friend of Ariel's is always welcome in my house. I shall accompany you to the castle; I have business to discuss with the king."

They left Seqwil's house and walked past the guard into the trade square again. It was not nearly as crowded as it had been earlier. Most shopkeepers had begun to close for the day, bringing their goods inside and sweeping in front of their businesses. Families of refugees and beggars who had nowhere to go were also settling in as best they could, huddled together in doorways or alleys.

Geoff was still bothered by the sight, wishing he could do something for them. At least the family he had given Ishara's ring to was nowhere to be seen. Geoff imagined them staying at an inn and eating a hearty meal. At least they were fine, he thought. It was a reality check for Geoff; he'd forgotten there was a war going on and the city of Chalon was the next target for the Shadowlord. He remembered reading about sieges in his father's books.

It was no fun being trapped behind the walls. Food shortages, potential for diseases, and the danger of boredom led to low morale. Those peasants who had useful skills would have a decent chance of finding employment, but the others were on their own.

As they approached the castle they were stopped by several guards. Geoff noticed more guards roaming about than the day before. He touched Ishara on the shoulder. She threw her hood back and quickly nodded to him. Apparently she had noticed the increased number of guards too.

"What is happening?" Seqwil demanded. "Why do you bar us from entering?"

"Forgive me, Lady Seqwil," a husky guard said. "King's orders. An assassin has found his way into the castle. We are searching for the killer as we speak. King Lionel wishes to have no one enter until the castle is deemed safe."

"I forgive you," Seqwil said dryly. "However, these two are personal guests of King Lionel and I doubt he will be happy or forgiving if they are not allowed to go to their rooms. Now stand aside and let us pass."

The guard's mouth fell open.

"I will vouch for them," Seqwil said. "They are my friends, and as a member of the elven court of Selra'thel I deem it necessary that they should accompany me, as I have business with King Lionel himself. You may now escort us to the king."

The guard blinked a couple of times, then bowed his head and led them into the castle. Geoff had to bite his lower lip to keep from laughing, which became more difficult when Seqwil looked over her shoulder and winked at him and Ishara as they walked.

Geoff was glad to be with Seqwil. He had no idea what he and Ishara would've done had they not been admitted into the castle. They turned the corner and walked down the long hallway to the throne room. As they did, they heard a commotion from an upper level of the castle. Amid yells and screams and sounds of fighting, half a dozen guards emerged from the throne room and raced toward the ruckus. Ariel, Jane, and Sawyer were right behind them.

CHAPTER TWENTY-FOUR
THE MONSTER IN CHALON CASTLE

"Ariel!" Geoff called as he, Ishara, and Seqwil sprang after her and the others.

The sounds of combat grew louder with each step. Was it coming to them? Geoff wasn't sure, but that's what it sounded like. Along with Ariel, the group of guards rounded a corner to the main entry then charged up the grand staircase. The fighting was close. Ishara had unslung her bow and nocked an arrow while she ran. At the top of the staircase, Geoff saw it.

A ghostly spider larger than his father's car back home battled a score of guards. Several bodies littered the stairs, as well as the landing beneath the spider. The creature's loud hissing echoed throughout the entry, sending a shiver down Geoff's back. Ishara let an arrow loose, and it passed through the horrific spider and shattered against the wall behind it. Geoff watched in terror as the weapons of the guards in front likewise passed harmlessly through the vaporous spider.

The creature reared up and struck at the guards with its front legs, sending three of them tumbling down the stairs. Jane and Sawyer jumped aside to avoid being bowled over.

"What manner of monster is that thing?" Seqwil cried, placing a hand on both Geoff and Ishara's shoulders. "How can we possibly kill it?"

The spider was able to attack everyone around it, and their strikes did nothing to it. Behind them, a dozen crossbowmen fired their bolts at the apparition, but they also passed through it.

Ariel leapt onto the stairs in front of the spider, and its long, wispy legs at once began to stab at her. Ariel dodged the attacks and crossed her scimitars in front of her.

"*Tae'nalara!*" she cried. The air rippled as an unseen force propelled the spider back up the steps, and for a second it looked out of focus, like wisps of swirling smoke.

Ariel advanced up the stairs holding her scimitars in front of her. The spider reassumed its ghostly form and hissed.

"*Tae'nalara!*" Ariel repeated, sending the monstrous spider back another thirty feet. Again it hissed, but this time it sounded like rage. Ariel had its full attention, and it charged her with surprising speed. Ariel met the attack head on. She pierced one of its large eyes with a scimitar, which stopped the spider in its tracks. She drove her other scimitar down through its ghostly head. The spider screeched and dissolved into a wispy haze, then faded away.

Everyone stood in place, stunned by what they had witnessed. Geoff couldn't believe Ariel had handled the giant ghost spider so easily; she looked like an action hero from the movies. She sheathed her scimitars and surveyed the room. Her gaze fell upon Geoff, then Ishara, Jane, and Sawyer. Apparently satisfied everyone was safe, she turned her attention to the wounded guards.

"That…was amazing," Seqwil said. "How did she do that?"

"Dunno," Geoff said. "But I'm glad she's on our side."

Jane knelt beside an injured guard, and sprinkled some leaves that Ariel had given her over his wounds. She spoke the druid charm of healing as she placed her hand over the wounds.

"She knows the druid charm of healing," Seqwil said, "but she is human."

"Ariel's been teaching her," Geoff said, watching Jane work. "Jane's pretty good at healing, isn't she?"

"It is not possible. No human has ever...," Seqwil's words trailed off as she focused on Jane. Geoff looked at Seqwil. She was obviously amazed by Jane's ability to heal.

Sawyer walked over to Geoff and Ishara. He slumped against the wall, then slowly shook his head.

"So where did that spider come from?" he asked.

No one answered.

"It looked like a ghost, right?" Sawyer asked.

"Yeah," Geoff said. "How is it Ariel killed the spider when the guard's weapons and Ishara's arrow went through it?"

"Dunno," Sawyer said.

"Magic," Ishara said. "Her scimitars are enchanted."

"It takes magic to fight magic," Seqwil said. "Whoever controls magic controls destiny."

Seqwil never took her eyes off Jane as she helped the injured guards, and Geoff noticed that Ariel was staring intently at Seqwil. That's strange, he thought. Did Seqwil say something wrong? The sound of loud footsteps echoed through the great hall as Lionel entered.

"I demand to know where such a creature came from," Lionel shouted. "Well?"

His gaze lingered on Ariel for a moment, but then he saw Jane healing injured guards, too. Geoff kept an eye on him, watching every move and facial expression he made. Like Seqwil, he watched Jane in disbelief. He walked closer to Jane, not paying any attention to a wounded guard at the foot of the steps.

"How is it you can heal like this, child?" Lionel asked, still looking incredulous. Jane looked up at him.

"Ariel," Jane said. "She taught me how to heal."

Lionel blinked and walked up the steps to Ariel, who had just finished healing an injured guard. She stood as he approached. Geoff walked closer to the bottom of the steps so he could listen.

"Three travelers," Lionel said. "It *is* true, then. How can a human girl cast the druidic charms? I've never seen such a thing before."

"It is her gift," Ariel said, nodding toward Jane. "She is a good student."

A young guard ran up to them and bowed. "My king," he said. "We followed a trail of debris and discovered where the spider came from. It entered the castle through one of the guest rooms."

"Guest rooms?" Lionel said. "Which guest room?"

The guard nodded toward Geoff, Jane, and Sawyer. "Their room, my king."

Geoff looked at Ishara, who was also watching the conversation with increasing concern. Seqwil Ferncliff, however, was nowhere to be found. She must've just slipped away while everyone was recovering from the battle.

"Uh-oh," Sawyer said. "Anyone know what he's talking about?"

"No," Jane said, shaking her head as she walked up the steps.

Geoff, Sawyer, and Ishara followed her. They arrived at the top of the stairs as Lionel let out a long sigh and once again glared at Ariel.

"Is this why you sought an audience with me? To divert my attention so your beastly spider could run amok through my castle?"

Ariel clenched her jaw and raised her chin at the king's accusation.

"I was speaking with you when the spider attacked. It was sorcerous in nature," she said. "I am no sorceress. Therefore, I did not conjure it."

Lionel turned and looked at the others.

"And what about them? Any human sorcerers among them? We have the Stormlord, a human druid, an archer, and…"

Lionel's words trailed off. Geoff now felt the accusing glare of the king. Geoff swallowed and shifted his weight.

"The youngest," Ariel said, "is no sorcerer either. Besides, the ability to conjure a creature like that takes many years of practice."

Geoff squirmed a little and shifted his gaze away as the king scrutinized him. Why was he looking at me? He's nuts! Geoff hadn't conjured that spider, but would the king believe Ariel? To Geoff's relief, Lionel turned back around and faced Ariel.

"Then perhaps you can explain to me how it came from your room?"

"I cannot," Ariel said.

Lionel and Ariel matched gazes. After a few moments

Lionel turned away and walked past Geoff. When he reached the bottom of the steps he called back, "You will be moved to new rooms. I hope you will take better care of these."

Geoff found himself breathing a little easier with the king gone, but Lionel had a good question. How *did* that spider come from their room? Had it been waiting to attack them? How did it get in their room in the first place? Geoff's head swam with questions as he watched several guards thank Jane and Ariel for healing them.

"Perhaps we should gather our belongings," Ariel suggested. "And I too am curious how that spider came to be in our room."

"So a sorcerer conjured that thing?" Sawyer asked. "It was huge!"

"A better question," Jane said, "is *who* conjured the spider?"

"That is the most important question, Jane." Ariel said. "Our enemy has attacked again and revealed more about themselves."

"They did?" Geoff said.

"We must now consider a sorcerer and an assassin to be our enemy," Ariel said. "And perhaps they are one and the same."

"Whoa, whoa, whoa," Sawyer said, holding a hand up. "You mean to say that we have someone trying to kill us who is a sorcerer *and* an assassin?"

"I do not know," Ariel said. "I only said perhaps we may have more than one enemy here, but I cannot be sure."

Ariel turned and walked toward their room.

"Damn," Sawyer muttered.

Geoff and the others followed Ariel to their room. The door was missing, shattered to pieces and strewn all about the hall. Again their room was a mess. Beds were overturned and tables as well as chairs were smashed. Their clothes and packs were scattered all around their quarters.

"Great," Jane said. "Here we go again. I'm glad I didn't bring anything valuable."

Ishara and Ariel remained in the hall, combing through the splintered remains of the door and looking for clues while Geoff and the others began gathering their belongings.

"This is getting old really fast." Jane sighed as she picked up what was left of her dress. "That spider ate my dress, too."

"Okay," Sawyer said. "I'm confused. Did someone sneak in and cast a spell to summon the spider? You mean to say they went through all that trouble just to make us look bad? That doesn't make sense."

"Yeah," Jane said. "We don't need help to look bad."

"That's what I mean. They already stole my sword. Why not summon the spider then? Why do it now?"

"Those are excellent questions, Sawyer," Ariel said. "I wish I had the answers, but I know little about sorcery."

"Is there anyone here who does?" Jane asked.

"Perhaps," Ariel said. "But he has disappeared and may be dead."

Geoff caught a glimpse of Ishara opening her sack and letting Ariel see the contents. Ariel nodded. Suddenly Geoff remembered the events from earlier that day.

"Oh!" he said. "We forgot to tell you guys we went to that wizard's house. Well, it was a tower. But we were attacked by someone. They had this crossbow that fired bolts like a machine gun. We'd be dead if we hadn't hidden behind a suit of armor."

Jane and Sawyer stopped what they were doing and looked at Geoff.

"Why didn't you mention this before?" Jane asked.

"There were a few things going on," Geoff said. "I really didn't have much of a chance until now."

"Did you see who it was?" Jane asked.

"No," Geoff replied. "They ran away."

Jane and Sawyer went back to sifting through debris.

"Oh," Geoff said. "I also forgot to tell you we were also mugged in an alley. Actually, they tried to mug us, but Lady Seqwil showed up and saved us."

"Geoff!" Jane said in exasperation. "What else happened to you today?"

"So Lady Seqwil beat up your muggers," Sawyer said. "She's kinda cool, isn't she?"

"She fought well," Geoff said, "but she got knocked out. Ishara was the one who beat them up, but Lady Seqwil showed up just in time to help."

"I noticed that bruise on her cheek," Jane said. "Muggers did that?"

"Yeah," Geoff answered. "She was great, but she got punched in the face."

Geoff happened to glance toward the hall. Ariel had been looking at him and listening. She turned toward Ishara and tilted her head. Ishara nodded to confirm Geoff's description of the day's occurrences. Geoff looked at the sack Ishara carried. He opened his mouth and was about to tell the others what they had found in the wizard's tower, but Ishara placed a finger over her lips. Geoff shut his mouth and scratched his head. That was strange, but if she didn't want to reveal the suit of armor to the others then she must've had a good reason.

Geoff went back to rummaging for his personal belongings. A pair of guards showed up and waited outside the room with

Ariel and Ishara. After they had gathered their things the guards escorted them to new rooms in another part of the castle. This time Geoff and Sawyer had a room to themselves, while across the hall Jane, Ariel, and Ishara shared a room.

Geoff was pleased to see that these rooms were larger and more lavish than the single room they had shared. The entire floor was covered by a thick decorative rug. The pedestal beds were high, and looked comfortable with a pile of plush pillows on them. The marble fireplace was so big that Geoff could stand inside, and the walls were adorned with various paintings of landscapes. A pair of large windows were set into the far wall. There were solid oak tables and chairs as well. Each table had a bowl of fresh red apples sitting in the middle, as well as filled decorative water basins.

"Now this is what I call an upgrade," Sawyer said. "Maybe the king isn't so bad after all."

"It sure beats being thrown into the dungeon," Geoff said as he sat on one of the beds. "He's been threatening to do that to us since we got here."

"I know, right?" Sawyer said. "And he hates Ariel. I wish she would beat him down."

Geoff snickered. "Me too."

He fell back onto the soft bed and sank into the mattress. Geoff closed his eyes and yawned. He hadn't realized how tired he was; he could fall asleep right then. Sawyer bounced on his bed a few times.

"Geez, what's in these, goose feathers?"

"Probably," Geoff said. "Or maybe wool. As comfy as these are, I doubt they have bedstraw in them."

"Bedstraw?" Sawyer said. "How's that different from regular straw?"

Geoff cleared his throat. "It's a different type of straw," he said. "It's not as prickly as regular straw, so it's more comfortable to sleep on."

"Geoff, you're such a nerd. I think you belong here," Sawyer said. "You know all about castles, armor, swords, and stuff."

Geoff opened his eyes. Sawyer had a point. Reading as much as he did and watching his father work had given Geoff a good education on medieval life. He liked it here. Besides, where else would he find a girl like Ishara? He'd concluded long ago that he wasn't what girls looked for in a boyfriend. He wasn't cute enough or he wasn't tall enough or he wasn't strong enough. Or he was simply a geek. He pretended the hurtful remarks from the girls at school didn't bother him, but they did. They were as mean as Sawyer's jock friends who were always calling him names and pushing him down or punching him.

"Hey, guys," Jane said, suddenly appearing at their door. "Ariel says it's almost time to eat, so you better wash up."

"Is she our mom now?" Sawyer groaned.

Jane giggled. "Don't wash, then," she said. "But you're not sitting beside me smelling like that. Ugh!"

Sawyer laughed and smelled his armpits. "Yeah, okay," he said. "But I don't smell *that* bad, do I?"

Jane walked back to her room shaking her head. Sawyer looked at Geoff.

"Do I?" Sawyer asked again.

"You do," Geoff replied. "I could use a good bath, too."

"We better get to it then," Sawyer said, "so we can get some grub."

Baths had already been drawn for them in the next room.

They washed and met the others in the hall. In light of current events, Ariel thought it might be safer if they stayed together as much as possible. They sat together at dinner, which, as far as Geoff was concerned, was another feast. Geoff especially liked the pheasant, which had been roasted over an open flame.

Geoff looked around. Everyone who was at last night's dinner was here save one.

"Where's Lady Seqwil?" he asked, leaning over to Ishara. "I was hoping she might sit with us."

"I do not know," Ishara said.

After dinner, they retired to their rooms. Sawyer and Jane took some time to kiss at the end of the hall before saying good night. Geoff was already in bed by the time Sawyer returned to their room.

"Sawyer, are you and Jane dating now?"

"Yeah," he said as he climbed into bed. "Sure. I guess so. Why?"

"No reason," Geoff said. "She's really cool, isn't she?"

"Yep. And she's a great kisser, too."

Geoff let the subject drop and yawned. It had been a long day and he needed sleep.

Several hours later he was awakened by Sawyer's heavy breathing. Geoff lifted his head and looked at Sawyer, who was sitting up in bed quivering. His eyes were glazed, and he was sweating.

"Sawyer!" Geoff yelled.

CHAPTER TWENTY-FIVE
INTRIGUE AND CONSPIRACIES

"Help! Help!"

Jane sat up in bed as Geoff's cries pierced her sleepy brain. In the dark, she could just make out Ariel and Ishara hopping out of their beds. Ariel grabbed her scimitars and dashed across the hall to the room occupied by Geoff and Sawyer, with Ishara and Jane close behind. Ariel opened the door to reveal Geoff standing at the far side of Sawyer's bed with a frightened look on his face. Sawyer was sitting up in bed with his eyes rolled up in his head. His breathing was rapid and shallow and he was quivering.

"Ariel!" Geoff said, pointing at Sawyer. "He's in another trance! Just like when the werewolf attacked us!"

Jane watched as Ariel went to Sawyer and examined him. Ishara stood next to Geoff, keeping their distance. Sawyer did indeed look like he was in a trance. Jane looked at the door, expecting to see some horrible beast or a cloaked assassin like the one Geoff and Ishara had encountered at the wizard's tower.

"Ariel," Jane said, "Geoff is right. The last time he acted like this the werewolf was close."

Ariel glanced first at Jane and then at Ishara, who nocked

an arrow and stepped into the doorway. Ishara looked left and right down the hall, then turned to Ariel.

"All clear," she said. "No one in the hall."

"Wait," Jane said. "Where are the guards? We had guards at our door, didn't we?"

"Jane is right," Ariel said, keeping her eyes on Sawyer. "See if you can find where they have gone."

Ishara left the room and disappeared down the hall.

"I better go with her," Geoff said, and he ran out of the room after Ishara.

Jane sat on Sawyer's bed. She wanted to reach out and shake him and jolt him awake. His sheets were moist with sweat, and Jane could feel the heat coming from his body.

"Is it safe to touch him?" Jane asked.

"It is best if we leave him be for the moment. I am not sure if he should be disturbed while he is in this state."

"Ariel," Jane whispered. "The last time this happened to him he was holding his sword. He said it was communicating with him and showing him the coming danger."

Ariel nodded. A moment later they heard the rapid succession of footsteps as Ishara and Geoff returned.

"The guards," Ishara said. "We cannot find them."

"Hey," Jane said, "I think Sawyer's coming around. He's breathing better and his eyes are clearing."

Jane touched his shoulder.

"Sawyer," she said quietly. "Sawyer? Are you okay?"

Ariel sat on the opposite side of the bed and touched Sawyer's cheek. He started, as if someone had put ice down his back. He looked around, but Jane didn't see any hint of his recognizing her or any of the others. He was tense and seemed lost.

"Sawyer," Jane said, "it's me, Jane. We're here. Your friends are here. Are you okay?"

"I…," Sawyer stammered. "Where am I? What happened?"

"You were in another trance," Jane said. "Did you see danger coming again?"

Sawyer shook his head. He winced and rubbed his temples. His eyes had come into focus and he took a deep breath. Jane gently moved her hand up and down his arm. Sawyer struggled to recover his senses, but then his eyes opened wide.

"The sword!" he said. "The Stormblade! It was…I think it was calling to me. It was trying to show me where it was hidden."

"Where is it?" Geoff asked. "Did you see it?"

"Yeah, I think so," Sawyer said. "It's hidden in a dark place, behind a wall or something." He gripped Jane's hand and Ariel's and looked at both of them. "It's here! The sword is still here."

"Where?" Jane said. "Is it in the castle?"

"No," Sawyer said. "It's still in the city. In a barracks or house or something. There were other things hidden, too. Yeah, that's what I saw, the Stormblade was wrapped in a cloth or animal skins and there was a secret compartment. I think it was behind a wall in an alcove or fireplace. I'm not sure."

"There's gotta be hundreds of fireplaces in the city," Geoff said. "We'll never find it."

"Sawyer," Ariel said. "Think. Do you remember the building where the Stormblade is hidden? Can you tell us anything about the surrounding area?"

"No," Sawyer said. "Not much. Two stories, made of stone. Nothing special about it."

"There can't be that many two-story homes here," Geoff said. "We didn't see many today."

"Perhaps he will remember more later," Ariel said, standing. "We should all try and go back to sleep."

"So the sword is trying to show Sawyer where it is," Jane said. "How does that work? And are these fits that Sawyer keeps having dangerous to him?"

"No. The sword calls to its master," Ariel said. "It calls to Sawyer."

The sound of heavy footsteps marching toward the room echoed through the halls. Ishara peeked around the corner of the door, then ducked back inside the room.

"Guards," she said. "Many headed this way."

Several seconds later at least ten guards appeared in the doorway. Their weapons were drawn and they had a grim manner about them, as if they expected a fight. Their leader, the same one who had addressed them when they first entered at the castle, stepped forward. He pointed at Ishara with his sword.

"You, elf girl," he said. "Put down your bow and come with us. By order of King Lionel the First, you're under arrest."

Ariel took a step toward Ishara. Jane wondered if this might be the confrontation that seemed to have been brewing since they arrived.

"What gives you the right to arrest her?" Ariel demanded. "With what crime do you charge her?"

"Murder," he said, producing an arrow exactly like those in Ishara's quiver. "We found this arrow and others just like it in the hearts of the guards posted outside your door."

"Ishara is no murderer," Ariel said. "She is innocent."

"That is up to King Lionel to decide," the guard said. "In

the meantime, she will have to be placed in the dungeons."

"No!" Geoff said, looking to the others for support. "She didn't kill anybody. She's been with us all night."

"Move away, boy," the guard said. "She will not be harmed – if she does as she's told."

Ariel's hands slid a little closer to her scimitars.

"You heard Ariel," Geoff said. "She's innocent. You can't lock her up because you found an arrow like hers."

The guard looked at Ariel, and his features softened a bit. "She will not be harmed. I will look after her myself."

"I will speak with your king," Ariel said. "This—"

"By all means," came a voice from behind the guards at the door. They stepped aside and let Lionel pass. As he entered the room he took the arrow from the guard and held it up. "Speak to me. Tell me of all things regarding treachery and war."

"You are mistaken," Ariel said. "Ishara did not kill your guards."

"She's with us," Sawyer said, stepping out of bed. "Leave her alone."

"Normally, I'd take the word of the Stormlord in such times," Lionel said. "However, these aren't normal times. I assure you we want no trouble. It is because she travels with you and the Stormlord that she will not be mistreated. Take her away."

"I will hold you to your word," Ariel said, glaring into Lionel's eyes. "She is dear to me and my fury will know no bounds if anything happens to her."

Lionel looked at Ariel and nodded before quickly turning away.

"You have your orders," he said as he left the room.

"Ariel, no," Geoff said. "You can't let them take her. She didn't do anything!"

"Do not worry about me," Ishara said. She glanced at Ariel and handed her bow and quiver to Geoff. "I will be fine."

Two guards stepped forward, but before Ishara surrendered herself to their custody she spun around and hugged Geoff.

Geoff's eyes moistened as he gripped her bow and watched Ishara leave with the guards.

"Ariel!" Sawyer said. "We aren't gonna let them take her, are we? She's one of us! You know she didn't kill those guards."

"Yes, I know," Ariel said. "Listen to me, the best way to help Ishara is to find the true enemy or enemies and bring them to light."

"Enemies?" Jane said. "So you *do* think there's more than one now?"

"I suspect," Ariel said, "but I am not sure. We know we face a sorcerer, a skilled archer, and an assassin. If we have a solitary foe who possesses all of those abilities, they would indeed be an opponent to be feared."

"So how do we find them?" Jane asked, feeling a bit frustrated. "Ishara was the only one who even got a glimpse of a hooded figure when she and Geoff were attacked."

Ariel went over to Geoff and placed a hand on his shoulder.

"That may be why she has been made to appear guilty and arrested," Ariel said. "Ishara can fend for herself. She is a fine young warrior."

She paused, and then continued. "Geoff," she said, "where did Ishara acquire that quiver full of arrows?"

"Lady Seqwil gave them to her," he said. "Why?"

Ariel took an arrow from the quiver and examined it. She spun it around and looked down the shaft and inspected the tip. Jane took an arrow from the quiver and looked at it herself. It looked like any other nondescript arrow to her. Sawyer also picked up an arrow and looked it over.

"Arrows tend to be unique," Ariel said. "As unique as their maker. The arrow shown to us earlier by Lionel is identical to these. I am sure of it."

"Wait a second," Geoff said. "You don't think Lady Seqwil had anything to do with Ishara being arrested, do you?"

"I cannot be sure yet," Ariel said, "but after the battle with the spider she said something I had heard before."

"What did Lady Seqwil say?" Jane asked.

Ariel put the arrow down and looked at Jane.

"She said, 'Whoever controls magic controls destiny,' which is exactly what the dark druid said to me before our battle."

Jane remembered Lady Seqwil saying something along those lines, but she was preoccupied with helping the wounded guards.

"I don't believe it," Geoff said. "If she wanted us dead, then why did she help us with the robbers?"

"Geoff's right," Jane said. "It doesn't make sense."

"Unless," Sawyer said, "she wanted to gain our trust for some reason. Maybe throw us off her trail, right? Maybe she wanted to avoid suspicion."

"Why would she do that?" Geoff asked. "Why go through all that trouble when the robbers could've killed us earlier?"

"I agree," Jane said. "Why save him and Ishara if she wanted to kill them? Kill us?"

There was a moment of silence as they thought about Jane's questions. The whole situation was weird. If Lady Seqwil could do all the things Ariel said, then she could probably kill them all in a sneak attack. At that moment something occurred to Jane, something she hadn't considered.

"Maybe," Jane said, "she wants to keep us alive for some reason. But what would that be?"

"That," Ariel said, "I do not know, but if Lady Seqwil is our enemy, then it seems she has been focused on Geoff and Ishara."

Everyone looked at Geoff. His eyes darted from Jane to Ariel to Sawyer.

"Me? Why me?" Geoff asked.

"I do not know," Ariel said.

"How about that prophecy?" Sawyer asked, snapping his fingers. "I don't remember all of it, but there was something in there about three travelers, right? So what if there were only two travelers? Wouldn't that mess up the prophecy?"

"So why save me then?" Geoff asked. He looked at Ariel. "She even cooked for us. She could've poisoned us if she wanted to. I think someone else is doing this."

"These are valid points," Ariel said, "but I am afraid we will not solve this mystery tonight. You three should try to sleep. We have much to do tomorrow."

"Sleep?" Jane asked. "Who can sleep after that?"

"I know," Ariel said, giving Jane a tap on the shoulder. "It will be difficult, but please try."

Jane went back across the hall with Ariel and slipped into her bed. Sawyer and Geoff had climbed back into their beds to try to sleep, so Jane had to give it a go, too. She turned her head and looked at Ariel, who was standing with her arms folded in front of her at the window, her silhouette frozen in place with the moonlight illuminating the room. Ariel appeared to be deep in thought. In fact, Jane thought she looked worried.

"Ariel," Jane said, "is everything going to be all right?"

The silhouette at the window turned toward her.

"Yes, Jane," Ariel said. "Everything will be fine. Now get some rest."

Jane frowned. She wanted to believe Ariel, but she wasn't sure she could. Jane rolled over and fluffed her pillow. It was cool and soft, just the way she liked her pillows and cushions. She closed her eyes.

"Good night," she said.

"Sleep well," Ariel said softly.

Before Jane drifted off to sleep, she thought of Ishara sleeping in a cold dungeon and the hurt look on Geoff's face as she was led away. They really cared for each other, she realized.

An hour or so later she opened her eyes—or maybe she dreamed she opened her eyes—and saw shadows under the door from the hallway. She thought someone had walked past, but they were so quiet she couldn't be sure.

Chapter Twenty-Six
Nighttime Encounters

Geoff wiped his eyes. They burned and they were still a bit blurred from crying. After Ishara was taken away by the guards, he and Sawyer did as Ariel said. They got back in their beds and tried to get some sleep. While Sawyer needed only fifteen minutes before he started snoring, however, Geoff had pulled the covers over his head to muffle himself while he cried.

Geoff was certain he wasn't going to get any sleep while Ishara was a prisoner in a dank, dirty dungeon. He had to do something. He waited until he was sure Sawyer was asleep, then slipped out of bed. He quietly got dressed and crept out of the room and into the hall. His body was shaking with nervous energy and his heart pounded. How could he sneak past the room across the hall occupied by Jane and Ariel?

Geoff swallowed. Ariel can hear anything, he thought, half expecting her to open the door at any moment. He heard himself breathe with each step he took, so he covered his mouth with his hand. He thought his muffled breathing sounded like a train puffing down the hall, however, and hoped he wouldn't hyperventilate and pass out.

Smoldering torches gave the hall a dim, eerie glow. His shadow intermingled with the variety of colors and patterns of the tapestries that hung on the walls. Geoff stopped and turned his head, looking back toward their rooms. Ariel hadn't appeared. Yet. He returned to the mission at hand—to free Ishara.

He stopped at the end of the hall and peeked around the corner. Two armed guards at the end of the next hall were talking in hushed voices. Geoff was too far away to hear what they said to one another, but if their attention remained on their conversation, he might be able to slip across the hallway. It was lined with suits of armor, and if Geoff kept himself hidden behind the armor and didn't make too much noise, he had a chance.

He watched and waited. A few moments later one guard turned his back toward Geoff and the other one yawned deeply. Geoff glided across the hall and slipped behind a suit of armor, then waited and listened. He still heard the low voices of the guards, but no one was coming after him and no alarms sounded. If this castle was similar to the ones he'd read about, most of the dungeons were located below.

Geoff took a deep breath and moved away from the guards to the adjacent suit of armor. He looked back at them, but they were still talking to each other. He continued down the hall to a spiral stone staircase, then stopped at the landing and listened. Other than the faint sounds of the guard's conversation down the hall and the occasional crackle from the torches, he heard nothing. He crept down the circular stairs until he reached the bottom.

A foul, mucky stench greeted him as he moved to a large

opening at the base of the stairs. He covered his nose and placed his back against the cold stone wall. The air was cooler down here and thick with moisture. The stones in the walls were rougher than the stones in the upper levels and scratched his back. Geoff inched to the opening and peered around the corner.

In the flickering torchlight, he saw a guard sleeping at a rickety wooden table. His head rested on the greasy tabletop next to an empty brown goatskin flask and a black leather tankard. A large ring of keys sat beside the tankard. Beyond the guard were cell doors on each side of the long hall. A shiver ran down Geoff's back, because his surroundings reminded him of the catacombs beneath Silverthorne Manor. They were attacked by a swarm of bloated carrion mites and had been lucky to escape with their lives.

Between every other cell was a torch that cast a dim light in the dungeon. Geoff slid around the corner, keeping close to the wall while he approached the guard, and peering into each cell he passed in hopes of finding Ishara. The cells were empty, however, so Geoff continued down the hall until he was no more than twenty feet away from the guard, who had started to snore. The man's black and gray matted hair partially covered his thickly whiskered face, and he was in dire need of a bath. His body odor was overwhelming, causing Geoff to cup both hands over his mouth and nose.

He took a step away from the wall toward the guard and stopped, looking back to the stairs and then down the cell-filled hall. He had to be sure no one else was down here. Satisfied he was alone with the sleeping, smelly guard, Geoff maneuvered closer. The stench was so strong Geoff thought he was going to be sick. He had to hurry.

Keeping his eyes on the guard's face, he reached for the ring of keys. Geoff's hand was shaking, and he made sure to grab the five crude iron keys together so they wouldn't jingle and clink and wake the guard as he slowly picked up the key ring.

He stood and moved back to the wall, keeping one hand over his mouth and nose. Ishara had to be in one of these cells, and now that he had the keys, he was going to rescue her. Geoff slipped further down the hall past the guard, searching in each cell as he passed. When he was far enough away he took his hand from his mouth and sighed.

"Geoff!" said a female voice with a hoarse whisper.

He looked at the cell across the hall. Ishara stood there looking at him with a baffled expression. She glanced down the hall toward the guard and then beckoned to him. Geoff quickly scooted over to her. She grabbed him by the collar and tugged him so hard he hit his head on the cold iron bars.

"Ow," he said.

"What are you doing here?" Ishara asked. "Are you mad?"

"I'm rescuing you," Geoff said, holding up the ring of keys.

Before he knew it she had nearly pulled him through the bars and kissed him. It surprised him, but the kiss alone was worth the trouble of sneaking to the dungeons.

"C'mon," Geoff said. "Let's open this door and get you out of here."

"Geoff," Ishara said, "do the others know where you are?"

"No. I snuck out of my room and came down here. I think we can slip past the guard and—"

"Geoff," Ishara interrupted. "You must return to your room. It is not safe for you to be sneaking about."

Geoff stopped and thought about what Ishara had said.

"What're you talking about?" he asked. "Why don't you want to escape?"

"Because," she said, brushing a strand of hair from her eyes. "If I escape with you that would be the same as admitting I am the assassin. It is best if I stay here, at least for now."

"But you're innocent," Geoff said. "You didn't do anything wrong."

"That does not matter with humans," Ishara said. "And especially not with King Lionel."

Geoff looked at her. "It matters to me," he said.

Ishara caressed his cheek and smiled. "And *that*," she said, "matters to me. Now please go. I will be fine."

Geoff frowned and looked down at his feet.

"Geoff," Ishara said, this time with a sense of urgency. "You must go. If anything happened to you…" Her voice trailed off and Geoff felt her grab his hand and squeeze.

"Besides," she said as she forced a smile, "how can I possibly be imprisoned when I have you to look after me?"

"I think you should come with me," Geoff said, not yet willing to give up. "The guard is drunk. We can sneak past him with no problem."

"I am sure of that," Ishara said, "but I believe Ariel has a plan and for now she needs me here." Ishara squeezed his hand again. "Do as Ariel says," Ishara said. "She will see us through this."

Geoff swallowed and looked away. He wanted to obey her, but found himself rooted where he stood. He opened his mouth to say something, but closed it. Ishara reached through the bars and touched his chest.

"My sneak thief," she said. "You have been so brave…"

Geoff felt his eyes become watery. He bit his lower lip to fight back tears.

"Are you sure this is what you want?" Geoff asked. "You don't deserve to be locked up."

"Yes. Please go back to the others, Geoff," Ishara said. "This castle is too dangerous for you to wander about."

Geoff steeled himself and looked into Ishara's green eyes. She was smiling. Even in this dark, foul-smelling dungeon she was beautiful. Geoff swallowed again and nodded. If he tried to speak he'd more than likely embarrass himself with sobs and unintelligible sounds. He nodded and squeezed Ishara's hand. He turned and started to leave when Ishara whispered to him, "I will see you tomorrow."

Geoff nodded again, which made him feel goofy. He wished he had something cool and heroic to say, but nothing came to mind. He looked over his shoulder to see Ishara gripping the bars of her cell, watching every move he made. He gave her a smile and resumed his sneaking. Having slipped by the slumbering guard before, Geoff was confident he would be able to return the ring of keys with no trouble.

Geoff had forgotten the lingering stench, and as he approached the guard, he breathed in a healthy dose of body odor. He stopped and clapped a hand over his face. Maybe he should keep the keys and leave a bar of soap, he thought, trying not to choke. He quietly set the keys on the table where he'd found them and hurried out of the dungeon, but at the base of the stairs he heard heavy footsteps coming down the stairs toward him.

His heart began to pound as he looked for a place to hide, but he was in the open and had no choice but to duck back around the corner and into the dungeon. He saw Ishara was still looking in his direction, a worried expression on her face. The footsteps clomped down the last of the stairs and approached the dungeon entry. Geoff flattened himself against a tiny recess in the wall between the first two cells opposite the sleeping guard.

A loud belch announced the newcomer as he entered the dungeon, another foul-smelling guard. This one was overweight and nearly bald, and was eating a greasy leg of mutton. He stopped beside the sleeping guard. Geoff shivered with fear, because all the newcomer had to do was look to his right and it was all over. So far, however, he was focused on his late meal.

"Hey, fat human!" Ishara called through the bars of her cell. "I need water! I am thirsty!"

"Shup, ye damn elf!" the guard barked back at her, spewing bits of lamb. He turned and kicked the sleeping guard, who started and almost fell out of his chair.

"Geddup ye sleepin' fool!" the newcomer said. He took a large bite of his mutton and pointed down the hall toward Ishara. "She needs water. Give 'er some."

The guard who had just been roused groaned and stood. Geoff was grateful the fat guard now had his back to him – and also that he was fat, because his girth blocked the other guard's view. As the fat guard continued eating, the other guard rubbed his sleepy eyes and picked up a wooden bucket with a ladle in it. Both of them turned and lumbered down the hall toward Ishara, who was still looking at Geoff. With a quick wave of her hand, she motioned for him to leave, and Geoff wasted no time scooting around the corner and up the steps as quickly and as quietly as he could go. All the while his heart thundered like a jackhammer in his chest.

When he reached the level of the castle where their rooms were located, he took a few deep breaths and looked down the stairs toward the dungeons. He didn't hear anyone coming up, so Ishara's distraction tactic had worked. He glanced up the stairs toward the upper levels. No one was coming down, either. All he had to do was get back to his room and he was safe.

A muffled *thud* came from down the hall. Geoff peeked around the corner and saw the guards who had been conversing earlier lying prone on the floor.

Uh-oh, Geoff thought. This wasn't good at all. As he watched, a figure in a gray cloak slipped from around the corner and pulled the guard's bodies out of the hall. It looked like the figure that had shouted at the castle gates and riled up the crowd against Ariel. It moved like a cat and made no sound. Was it Ariel? It couldn't be, Geoff thought, but the figure was as fluid as Ariel with its movements. Had Lionel been right all along? Then he realized that Ariel was slightly taller than this cloaked figure.

He wasn't able to see the face of the mysterious individual because they had a hood pulled over their head. He did, however, notice that the cloaked figure held an elven dagger in each hand. The blades were slender and slightly curved, and they were longer than most human daggers. Suddenly, the figure stopped and looked in his direction. Geoff ducked back around the corner and clasped both hands over his mouth. He realized too late how loud his breathing had been.

He swallowed hard and forced himself to peek around the corner again. To his horror, the dagger-wielding figure was coming toward him. In fact, it was no more than thirty feet away. Geoff gulped as he slid back from the hallway, his heart pounding again. He looked at the staircase. He could flee up or down, but he wouldn't get far; the assassin would surely hear his running and chase him down. Geoff didn't know what to do. He froze in place, eyes wide and trembling.

Suddenly there was a sound from the hallway, as though someone had opened a door. Geoff heard the rustle and swish of the cloak followed by a rush of air. In another instant the assassin burst past Geoff and dashed up the stairs, turning its head in his direction for a split second as it ran past and then disappeared. Geoff's heart seemed to have skipped a beat and his skin was covered with sweat.

His whole body was shaking, Geoff rushed into the hallway. He didn't care who was there. Anyone would've been better than coming face to face with the cloaked assassin. He was relieved to see Sawyer standing in the middle of the hall wearing only his boxers. His hair was standing up on one side and he was yawning while he scratched his stomach.

"Sawyer!" Geoff called as he ran as fast as he could. "I saw it! I saw the assassin! Just now! It ran past me on the stairs—"

"Whoa, whoa, whoa," Sawyer said, wiping the sleep out of his eyes. "What the hell are you rambling about?"

"You just missed it," Geoff said, looking over his shoulder at the opening that led to the stairs. "The assassin was right here. I think they killed some more guards."

"Really?" Sawyer said. "The assassin was just outside our doors?

The door across the hall opened and Ariel appeared with Jane.

"What is it?" Ariel asked. "Why are you two out of bed in the middle of the night?"

Sawyer pointed at Geoff, but before he could answer Geoff spoke. "I saw the assassin," he said. "It attacked some guards over there and then ran up the stairs when Sawyer opened the door."

Ariel looked at Sawyer.

"I didn't see a thing," he said. "I just stepped out for some air. I had a dream about the Stormblade and couldn't get back to sleep. Then Geoff came running up to me shouting about the assassin. That's all I know."

"Geoff, what're you doing out here all alone?" Jane asked, placing a hand on her hip.

Realizing he had been busted for sneaking around, Geoff decided to come clean and tell the truth. "I went to see Ishara," he said. "I wanted to check on her and…"

His words tapered off when he saw Ariel's stern expression. He looked at Jane and then Sawyer. Neither one appeared willing to come to his defense.

"I wanted to set her free," he said. "We know she's innocent."

"Sawyer, you and Geoff get in the room with Jane," Ariel said, "and stay together. Do not leave the room for any reason. Do you understand?"

Geoff followed Ariel's gaze as she looked first at Sawyer, then at Jane. He swallowed when she zeroed in on him.

"Yeah," Sawyer said. "I got it."

"Take this," Ariel said, handing him one of her scimitars, "just in case."

They stepped inside Jane's room, but before he closed the door, Geoff watched Ariel sprint down the hall and duck into the opening in the stairwell. Geoff strained to listen for any sounds of fighting coming from that direction, but he heard nothing. He worried for Ariel's safety; the assassin was every bit as fast and stealthy as she was, and maybe even more cunning. A familiar feeling of guilt came over him as he listened for any sound. His trip to the dungeons had messed everything up. Ishara was still a prisoner, and now Ariel was hunting a dangerous foe by herself.

"Geoff," Jane said with a hint of urgency in her voice, "close the door. What's wrong with you?"

"Huh?" Geoff replied. Realizing that his mind had wondered again, he closed the door. "Oh, sorry."

"Geoff, you're crazy as hell," Sawyer said as he swung Ariel's scimitar in the air. "Just what did you think was gonna happen after you freed Ishara? Where would the two of you had gone?"

"And," Jane said as she walked to Geoff, "what if Sawyer hadn't gone out into the hall when he did? What do you think the assassin would've done?"

Geoff looked at the closed door. They were right. It was stupid of him to go see Ishara. He had been lucky. Without knowing it, Sawyer had saved Geoff's life.

"They would've killed me," Geoff said quietly.

"It's the key all over again," Sawyer said, pointing the scimitar at Geoff. "Remember? You ran off on your own and activated that archway in your dad's study. That's what got us into all this trouble in the first place. You gotta stop wandering off."

"I just wanted to help Ishara." Geoff blurted this out a little louder than he wanted.

"There's nothing wrong with that," Jane said, "but if you get yourself killed, how do you think that would make her feel? Just do what Ariel says and stay put next time, okay?"

"I will," Geoff said. "Sorry."

"However, I think what you did was brave," Jane said. "And romantic.

"Romantic? He almost died," Sawyer said. "But it worked out, I guess."

Jane and Sawyer turned their attention toward each other, and Geoff stayed by the door and listened. It didn't matter how badly they scolded him, Ishara's kiss was worth it.

"Sawyer," Jane said, sitting on her bed, "I had a dream. Well…I don't know…maybe it was a nightmare. I'm not sure."

"What was it?" Sawyer asked, lowering his weapon.

Jane began wringing her hands. Her eyes became distant and she didn't blink.

"It's hard to describe," she said. "I was flying, I think. Like I was shot out of a cannon or something. I was headed straight for a big, dark hideous castle that was surrounded by wild, desolate mountains. I couldn't stop myself. I was being pulled into the darkness. I…I didn't have a choice."

"Hey, relax," Sawyer said. "It's just a dream, Jane. Look where we are, and look at what's going on. It's enough to scare the crap outta anyone."

Sawyer sat beside Jane and put his arm around her.

"Sawyer," Jane said uneasily as she looked at him, "I have a bad feeling about this. Maybe we should go home."

The room became silent for a moment.

"Are you sure, Jane?" Sawyer asked. "You were the one who insisted we come back. Now you wanna leave because of a bad dream?"

Jane looked at the window in the northern wall.

"I've had the same dream almost every night since we returned."

Chapter Twenty-Seven
The Assassin

The image of a great sinister castle in the mountains flashed before Jane's eyes. Until now, she had dismissed the bad dreams, but the sense of dread and foreboding surrounding the castle had intensified each day. She looked down at her hands, which were trembling, then extended her fingers a few times and shook her hands.

Apparently Sawyer noticed, because he sat beside her and took her hands in his. His hands were warm. They were always warm. Jane liked that about Sawyer.

"Hey, Jane," Sawyer said quietly. "It's just a dream. Seriously, don't worry about it."

Jane shook her head.

"You're right," she said. "I'm just scaring myself. It's just a bad dream, like you said."

Geoff was still standing by the door, but now he was looking at her with a worried expression.

"Don't worry. I'm okay," Jane told him. "Just look at us. Between Sawyer's visions about his sword and my nightmares it's a wonder anyone can get a minute's sleep around here."

"Yep," Sawyer said, standing. "That makes us a perfect match, huh, babe?"

She smiled. She felt like she had distanced herself from the bad dream. She was a little embarrassed that she had revealed it in the first place, but the image had been so real to her.

"Hey, Geoff," Sawyer said. "Why don't you open the door and see if Ariel's out there? Maybe she's on her way back."

Geoff did as he was told, but the instant his back was turned Sawyer grabbed both sides of Jane's head and kissed her.

"I don't see her," Geoff said, closing the door. "I hope she's okay."

"C'mon," Sawyer said, pulling away from Jane and winking at her as she smoothed her hair. "This is Ariel. Trust me, no one's gonna beat her up. No way."

"Yeah, I guess you're right," Geoff said as he stepped away from the door. "Still, you should've seen the assassin. They moved like…well…like Ariel and Ishara."

"Ariel does suspect Lady Seqwil," Jane said, thinking aloud. "And Lady Seqwil *is* also an elf."

"I don't know," Geoff said with a shake of his head. "The cloaked figure I saw tonight would've kicked those robbers' butts easy. But they knocked Lady Seqwil out cold."

The door opened and in stepped Ariel, wearing her usual stoic expression. Everyone fell silent. Jane hoped Ariel was about to say she had killed the assassin. However, she walked to Sawyer and took her scimitar back without a word, then turned to Geoff.

"Tell me what you saw, Geoff," she said. "Leave no detail out, no matter how insignificant it may seem."

"So what happened?" Sawyer asked. "Did you see the assassin?"

"No," Ariel said. "So far only Geoff has gotten a look at our enemy."

She turned to Geoff. "Is there anything you can remember that might be of help?"

"I didn't see their face," Geoff said. "They wore a gray cloak and had a hood pulled over their head."

"Just like you and Ishara." Sawyer said.

Ariel glanced at Sawyer for a second and then turned back to Geoff. She placed a hand on his shoulder.

"Anything else?" She asked.

"Oh yeah!" Geoff's eyes lit up. "Yeah, the assassin carried two long daggers. They looked like they could be short swords, but they were slender and slightly curved."

This new bit of information was apparently the missing piece to a puzzle for Ariel, who stood and walked to the window.

"Ariel," Jane said, "what is it?"

Ariel crossed her arms in front of her and bowed her head as she thought. Jane looked at Sawyer and Geoff, who also had confused looks. Ariel raised her head and turned to Jane.

"What I am unable to understand," Ariel said with a grim expression, "is why an elven assassin from Selra'thel would be here working in league with the Shadowlord."

"So you know the assassin is an elf?" Jane asked. "How can you be sure?"

"Geoff's description of the assassin's weapons," Ariel said. "Only the most highly skilled assassins use such weapons."

"So is it Lady Seqwil then?" Sawyer asked. "She's the only other elf here besides that tall guy, Trelane. Those are the only other elves I saw here."

"No," Geoff said with another shake of his head. "Trelane was a lot taller than the cloaked figure I saw tonight. It couldn't be him."

"That leaves Lady Seqwil," Jane said, "unless we have yet to see every elf in Chalon."

"That's true," Sawyer said, "but whoever it is, they're hanging around the castle a lot and causing all kinds of hell."

"And that," Ariel said, pointing at Sawyer, "is exactly what one would expect in a time of war. An assassin would do their best to create chaos and fear."

"Why not just kill the king?" Sawyer asked. "Take out the leader, divide and conquer — that sort of thing."

"Unless the leader is weak or indecisive," Ariel said. "Then would it not make sense to keep that leader in place?"

"You know," Geoff said, "the cloaked figure I saw was pretty close to Lady Seqwil's height."

Ariel strode around the room thinking. She shook her head. "We need to get into Lady Seqwil's house. Geoff, can you take us there?"

"Yeah, I think so," he said. "It's not far."

"Excellent," Ariel said. "Get dressed and we will pay Lady Seqwil a visit."

Jane looked at the window. It was still dark and her best guess was that daylight was several hours away.

"What, now?" She asked. "How will we get out of the castle?"

"And what about those guards in the hall?" Geoff asked. "The ones the assassin just killed?"

"They are not dead," Ariel said. "Merely unconscious. We were the assassin's targets tonight."

Jane looked at Ariel. "So we were lucky?"

Ariel gave Jane a quick nod. "That is one way to say it. Yes."

Jane walked to the chair on which she had laid her clothes for the next day. Sawyer and Geoff went back to their room to dress as well, but first, Ariel scoured the hallway for any signs of the assassin. She returned to the room she shared with Jane. Jane pulled her breeches on and stopped.

"What is it, Jane?" Ariel asked as she checked the leather pouches on her belt. Apparently she had seen Jane's perplexed expression.

"I was telling Sawyer and Geoff," Jane said, "about a dream I keep having. Has that ever happened to you?"

To Jane's relief Ariel nodded. "It has," she said. "On more than one occasion. Some druids have the gift of premonition. What is your dream?"

Jane frowned. That wasn't exactly the answer she wanted to hear. She sighed and sat in the chair, and Ariel stopped her preparations and walked over to her.

"Jane, tell me," Ariel said, taking Jane's hand. "What haunts your dreams?"

Jane swallowed.

"I've been dreaming of a dark castle in the mountains," she said. "It's like I'm flying and I can't stop myself or turn away. I fly into the cold, dark place and then I wake up. It takes me a while to go back to sleep after that."

Ariel brushed a strand of Jane's dark hair behind her ear and studied Jane's eyes.

"How often do you have these dreams?" Ariel asked.

"Nearly every night," Jane said. "You said premonition just now. Does that mean it will happen soon?"

"No," Ariel said flatly. "Your dreams are only an indication of what may happen, not what *will* happen. Have you seen this dark castle before? Was there anyone else in your dreams?"

"No," Jane said as a shiver ran down her back. "Like I said, it's in the mountains. Somewhere we haven't been to yet. It felt so real and so creepy."

"Do not trouble yourself any further about these dreams," Ariel said. "Try and forget them. Now finish dressing."

Jane did as Ariel said, but she couldn't shake an uneasy feeling that something bad was going to happen. There was a knock at the door. It was Sawyer and Geoff.

"Okay," Sawyer said. "Let's roll!"

"Here, Jane," Ariel said as she tossed a couple of small leather pouches to her. "These components may come in handy. You should have them."

"Yeah," Sawyer said, grinning. "A little weed and herbs never hurt anyone."

Jane rolled her eyes and tucked the pouches away. Ariel opened the door and led them into the hall. They passed the unconscious guards and crept down the main stairs. At the bottom of the stairs they found more guards who had been knocked out.

"Hey, guys," Sawyer whispered as they stepped over the prone bodies, "are we sure we wanna find this assassin? I mean, they leave a trail of bodies wherever they go."

Sawyer had a point, Jane thought. What if the assassin killed Ariel or knocked her out? If that happened they would be in trouble.

"We have no choice," Ariel said. "Our enemy has decided not to leave us be. Stay together."

"Wait!" Geoff stopped and stood still. "Ishara is all alone in the dungeon. What if the assassin wants to kill her? She's locked in a cell and the guards are drunk!"

"Agreed," Ariel said. "We should check on Ishara. I will fetch her bow and quiver. Stay here."

Jane and Sawyer stayed on lookout in the hallway while Ariel went to get Ishara's bow and quiver, but Geoff couldn't wait. He started walking down the hall toward the staircase.

"She's down here," Geoff said, motioning to Jane and Sawyer. "Hurry!"

"Geoff," Jane said as she took a few steps toward him so he wouldn't be overheard, "what're you doing? Wait for Ariel!"

Geoff disappeared around the corner and an instant later they heard him scream. Jane's heart leapt as she and the others ran toward Geoff's cry. Ariel sprinted ahead of them and drew her scimitars as she turned the corner. Immediately Jane heard the rapid ringing of blade on blade. She and Sawyer reached the opening to the staircase and saw Ariel on the steps in a pitched battle with a gray cloaked figure. Geoff was cowering in a corner at the top of the stairs with his legs pulled next to his body.

Ariel and the cloaked assassin matched each other's strikes and blocks. They were so quick in the flickering torchlight that Jane thought they looked like dueling phantoms as their shadows danced across the wall. She knelt beside Geoff, who was shaking.

"Geoff!" Jane exclaimed. "What happened?"

"The assassin," Geoff said. "It sprang at me!"

Sawyer knelt beside Jane, putting his hand on her shoulder while he watched Ariel and the assassin duel. Jane grabbed Geoff by the shoulders and pulled him to his feet. Shouts rang out and an alarm sounded throughout the castle. Sounds of the battle had alerted guards throughout the castle. Jane looked over her shoulder as Ariel and the assassin continued their fight to the lower levels. The assassin's blades matched Ariel's scimitars blow for blow.

Jane felt Geoff grab her arm and squeeze.

"Jane! Ishara is down there!" he yelled. "The assassin was going down the steps!"

Jane spun and grabbed Sawyer's collar.

"Sawyer," Jane said, "we need to get down there!"

Jane, Sawyer, and Geoff looked over the edge of the spiral stairs. Ariel and the assassin had already reached the bottom, and their fighting roused the guards in the dungeons. The guards had drawn their swords, but stayed away from the combatants, apparently not wanting to hazard getting near their flashing, whirling blades. They backed themselves to the wall, swords up and mouths agape.

Jane ran down the steps, followed by Sawyer and Geoff. By the time they reached the bottom, Ariel and the assassin had fought their way into the dungeon hallway.

"Guys," Jane said. "We have to do some—"

Jane never had a chance to finish her sentence, because Ariel landed a disarming stroke and the assassin lost a long dagger. The cloaked figure immediately reached into a pocket and threw a handful of dust in the air. It was no ordinary dust, because as soon as it left the assassin's hand, each speck began to glow a sickly green. The particles seemed to take on a life of their own, and whipped around everyone in the dungeon like angry bees.

Jane waved her hands and ducked her head as the tiny green flecks stung and battered her face. Sawyer and Geoff yelled as they, too, attempted to ward off the green dust.

Ariel also appeared to have been taken off guard and retreated a few steps as she struggled to see. Jane clearly saw the assassin retrieve the long dagger and kick the guard's wooden chair at Ariel. The chair struck Ariel in the chest and knocked her back.

Shouting and the sound of many footsteps thundering down the stairs caught Jane's attention, and out of the corner of her eye, she could see half a dozen guards at the base of the steps with their swords drawn. As soon as they entered the dungeon, they were inundated by the stinging green dust. Only the assassin appeared to be unaffected.

The cloaked figure rushed past Ariel and gave her a strong kick to the side of her head. Ariel slumped against the wall, holding her scimitars up to ward off additional attacks. The assassin ran past the blinded guards and closed in on Sawyer, who was doubled over and rubbing his eyes.

"Look out, Sawyer!" Ishara shouted from her cell.

Suddenly, Jane saw the flash of a long dagger as the assassin prepared for a killing blow to the back of Sawyer's neck. Jane had to do something or Sawyer was dead.

"*Tae'nalara!*" Jane shouted, pointing at the assassin.

A powerful invisible force struck their enemy and Sawyer, sending both flying down the hall. To Jane's horror, Sawyer landed with a loud thud beside the assassin and didn't move. The assassin quickly stood, however, avoiding Ishara's attempt to grab their arm, and charged at Jane. Jane tried to say the repelling charm again, but the green dust flying about stifled her, and all she could do was cough.

As the assassin approached, Jane saw gritted teeth beneath the hood. She had angered their enemy and now she was going to pay. Jane put her hands up to protect herself as the assassin lunged. At that moment Ariel's body slammed into the airborne figure, shoving it aside. As they collided in midair, Ariel's scimitar slashed the thigh of the assassin, who retaliated with a cut across Ariel's back. Both figures fell to the stone floor.

The assassin got up and limped past Geoff and the guards, who were still incapacitated by the green dust. As the assassin staggered to the spiral staircase, Ariel got to her feet and began pursuit. Jane ran out of the cloud of green dust toward Sawyer, who started to move as she got to his side. He groaned and put a hand up to his forehead.

"Sawyer!" Jane cried, wrapping her arms around him. "You're alive! I thought you were dead!"

"Ow," Sawyer moaned. "Yeah I'm alive. What the hell happened? Who hit me?"

"Can you get to your feet?" Jane asked. "Ariel's hurt! There's no time to explain. Hurry!"

"Where is Geoff?" Ishara asked, looking out from her cell. "I do not see him!"

"He's fine," Jane said hastily. "He's just down the corridor."

She pulled Sawyer to his feet and they ran back into the green cloud. Geoff and the guards were still yelling and flailing about trying to keep the green dust from their eyes and mouths. Jane grabbed Geoff's arm and forced him to the steps.

"Come on, Geoff," Jane said. "Let's go!"

They raced up the steps after Ariel and the assassin. The ringing sounds of another pitched battle overhead echoed throughout the stairwell; Ariel and the assassin had resumed their combat several stories up. Even wounded, the two figures moved with uncanny speed and grace, and they continued to move upward as they fought. Because he was taller and athletic, Sawyer moved ahead of Jane and Geoff by ascending the steps two or three at a time.

"Hurry," Sawyer said. "Looks like they're heading toward the top of the tower!"

No sooner had he said that when both Ariel and the assassin disappeared through a door on the top landing.

"Hey," Geoff said between gasps for air. "There's a bunch of guards coming!"

Jane glanced down. At least twenty guards were hurrying up the steps.

Sawyer grabbed her hand and pulled her along. A heavy animal smell greeted them at the top of the stairs, and the air was noticeably cooler. They found themselves on a circular landing atop of one of the castle's highest towers. All around the landing were stalls with bales of hay stacked beside them. Deep and shrill screeches echoed from the stalls. There were large openings in the north and south walls that revealed the night sky.

Ariel and the assassin were circling each other in the center of the landing. Each had minor bruises and cuts, but neither combatant appeared to be willing to surrender. Jane caught a glimpse of the assassin's eyes from under the hood. They looked familiar and now that she had time to focus on the assassin, it was definitely a woman.

Suddenly the assassin held a hand up to her face and appeared to blow them a kiss. A green haze expanded from the assassin's fingers and formed a shape. At first, Jane thought it was a lion, but it soon became clear the form was a massive canine covered with a familiar sickly green fire.

"Hellhound!" Ariel shouted as she stepped in front of the ghostly green creature. "Everyone get back!"

Jane, Sawyer, and Geoff retreated to the steps. The hellhound sprang at Ariel, snarling and snapping its teeth as it barely missed her throat. It followed the attack with a swipe of its massive paw, raking Ariel's arm and forcing her back. Jane looked around for something to throw. She found a wooden bucket nearby and slung it as hard as she could at the hellhound.

The bucket passed through the infernal green hound with no effect, and its attention never wavered from Ariel. Jane saw the assassin glide through the shadows and position herself behind Ariel.

"Ariel! Behind you!" Jane shouted.

The assassin and hellhound lunged at Ariel from opposite directions. Ariel dropped to her back and blocked the assassin's strike while she slashed the hellhound's neck. The beast yelped, dissolved into a green cloud, and blew away. The assassin stabbed at Ariel, but she blocked that attack too, sweeping the assassin's legs out from under her.

The hood fell back as the assassin landed on the stone landing. Geoff gasped and Jane's hand shot to her mouth. She couldn't believe what she saw, either.

It was Lady Seqwil Ferncliff.

Ariel and Seqwil slowly got to their feet, each studying the other. A dozen guards pushed past Jane, shoving her and Sawyer against the wall. Ariel motioned for them to keep their distance.

"Why?" Ariel asked. "Why would you side with the Shadowlord?"

Seqwil looked at the guards. She limped to the northern opening on the landing, then pointed to the north and west with her weapons.

"Your fate is already sealed," she said, turning to face Ariel. "Even with all your power over nature, you are insignificant. You know nothing. An age of darkness and blood comes."

"What do you mean?" Ariel asked, lowering her scimitars. "Why have you have betrayed our people?"

"No," Seqwil said with a shake of her head. "You betray our people by allying yourself with these pitiful humans. If you think those children are the three outlanders from prophecy you are a fool."

"Then I am a fool," Ariel said. "You did not answer my question. Why do you ally yourself with the Shadowlord?"

Seqwil laughed. "Now why would I do such a foolish thing?"

She dropped her daggers and smiled, then stretched her arms out from her sides and let herself fall back off the landing.

CHAPTER TWENTY-EIGHT
REUNIONS

"Nooo!" Geoff shouted from the topmost step. He rushed to Ariel's side. He couldn't believe what he had seen. Did Lady Seqwil just kill herself? Geoff shook his head. Jane and Sawyer joined him next to Ariel, who stared at the spot where Seqwil had been standing. Ariel tilted her head and furrowed her eyebrows. For the first time she appeared confused—and saddened. Her emerald green eyes were moist, but she didn't cry. She took a step and hesitated, then walked to the edge of the landing and looked down.

"We elves can live forever, did you know that?" Ariel asked. "This does not make sense. I have never seen an elf take their own life."

No one answered. Geoff wanted to say something that would console her, but all he could do was stand there. Seqwil had been so nice and pleasant. She had even cooked a nice meal for him and Ishara after she saved their lives.

"I'm so sorry," Jane said. "Is there a chance she survived the fall?"

They stood in silence; any words of consolation seemed inadequate. Ariel's eyes darted left and right, searching the darkness below. A chilly breeze blew through the landing, making Geoff shiver.

"What is it, Ariel?" Geoff asked. "What do you see?"

"I am not sure," Ariel said. "For a brief moment, I thought I saw…"

Her words drifted off as she shook her head. Most of the guards had sheathed their weapons and gone back down the stairs, and the harsh screeching from the stables had subsided. Beside Geoff, a large eagle-like head emerged from the darkness and nudged him.

Geoff looked into the large, pale yellow eyes of the gryphon and rubbed its head. It tilted its head further so Geoff could rub and scratch the back of its neck. The gryphon's behavior reminded him of a playful dog wanting attention.

"Ariel," Jane said, "I don't understand. What was she talking about before she—"

"I do not know," Ariel said. "What would cause her to kill herself? I will go and investigate below. The three of you should return to your rooms."

"The Shadowlord," Sawyer said. "That Lord Zorn guy. She must've been scared he'd kill her if she talked. You know, if she ratted him out and stuff."

"She was frightened," Ariel said, turning around to face them, "but not of him."

"What then? Jane said. "What was she so afraid of that she couldn't let herself be captured?"

"That," Ariel said, "is what concerns me."

"You?" Sawyer said. "No way. Nothing worries you."

Ariel sheathed her weapons, picked up Seqwil's daggers, and walked to the stairs without saying a word.

Geoff looked at Jane and Sawyer. Their frowns told him all he needed to know. He wondered what could possibly be more terrifying than the Shadowlord. Ariel had already faced him and won—at least that's what he thought.

"Come on, guys," Jane said. She took Sawyer's hand, and they followed Ariel. Geoff gave the gryphon a final scratch and pat on the head, then joined them. They walked down the steps, passing several guards who stood aside for them. Ariel's battle with Seqwil had been epic.

Geoff felt sorry for Ariel because this was the third friend she had lost. First there was Eben Silverthorne, then her mentor, Bhael, and now her friend Lady Seqwil was gone. The only good thing to come from this, and it was a good thing, was that Ishara's innocence had been proven and now she would be set free.

When they arrived at their rooms, a robed King Lionel was standing there. His arms were crossed and he was flanked by at least five guards. His frown didn't bode well. Geoff wondered what he had to be upset about.

"Lady Seqwil?" Lionel asked.

Ariel shook her head. Lionel was silent for a moment.

"I'll see to her body," he said quietly. "It'll be returned to her family with full honors."

Lionel sighed and continued, "This sort of incident can lead to war between Chalon and Selra'thel if not handled properly. For what it's worth, I am sorry."

Ariel nodded. Lionel turned around and walked away.

"Hey!" Jane said. "What about Ishara? Now that you know she's innocent, set her free!"

Lionel waved Jane's question off with a flick of his wrist and disappeared around the corner.

"Perhaps tomorrow." Lionel's voice drifted from around the corner.

"What a jerk," Sawyer said. "He's still gonna keep her in the cell? Even after Seqwil was revealed to be the assassin?"

Geoff followed Sawyer's gaze to Ariel, who watched Lionel and his guards walk away.

"Ishara will be released soon," Ariel said. "I need to rest now."

"Why doesn't he let her go now?" Geoff asked. "It's not right to keep her locked up."

"Agreed," Ariel said. "But now is not the time to press the issue with Lionel." She turned to Jane. "I have wounds that need attention. Will you help me?"

It was then that Geoff took a good look at Ariel. She had several cuts on her arms and legs, and a nasty slash on her back. Wow, they hadn't even asked her if she was okay.

"Oh!" Jane said, evidently coming to the same conclusion as Geoff. "Yes, yes. I'm so sorry. Let's get you healed."

"Yeah," Sawyer said. "Sorry, Ariel. We didn't notice how hurt you were."

"It will be morning soon. You two should try to get some rest," Ariel said, nodding at Geoff and Sawyer. "Jane can tend my wounds. We will see Ishara tomorrow."

Geoff followed Sawyer back to their room and closed the door.

"What a night," Sawyer said, taking off his tunic and preparing for bed. "Oh, and you got really lucky tonight. I normally sleep like a rock. I had no idea Lady Seqwil was creeping around in the hallway waiting to kill us."

Geoff nodded at Sawyer's scolding. He was right. Geoff readied himself for bed as well, but he knew he wouldn't get much sleep, because he continued to worry about Ishara. As he hopped into bed and blew out the candle on the nightstand, he thought about her in the cold, dark cell. He remembered how much she hated being a prisoner.

When morning came, there was a knock at the door. Geoff sat up and scanned the room. Sawyer was still asleep, but his snoring had died down to a tolerable noise level. There was another knock at the door, and this time it was a little louder.

"Just a minute," Geoff said as he hurried out of bed and threw some trousers on.

He opened the door and there was Ishara with a huge smile on her face. Before Geoff could do or say anything she bounded into his arms and hugged him so hard he thought she was going to break his ribs.

"Hey! How…how are you?" he asked. "I was worried about you. I—"

Ishara shut him up with a hug. Whatever Geoff had been trying to say and whatever was on his mind was lost forever.

"Good morning," Ishara said, pulling back and looking him in the eyes. "I was concerned about you. The sorcerous assassin…is everyone okay?"

He tried to smooth his pillow hair down. "We're fine. It was Lady Seqwil after all. She and Ariel had a big fight at the top of a tower landing – where those gryphons are, and then the guards came and…"

"Yes?" Ishara prompted him. "Go on."

"And then Lady Seqwil was trapped. She killed herself," Geoff replied. "She just let herself fall out of the tower."

Ishara frowned and looked away. She was saddened to hear that bit of news. Maybe she, too, hoped Lady Seqwil wasn't the assassin.

"I'm sorry," he said. "I liked her. She was nice."

Ishara nodded.

"But what I still don't understand," Geoff said, "is why she saved us from the robbers in the alley."

"Perhaps," Ishara said, "she wished to gain our trust so she could take better advantage of us."

Ishara walked a few steps down the hall then spun around to face Geoff.

"But I think she liked us, too."

Geoff smiled. He realized he usually smiled when he was with Ishara, and he didn't mind that at all. She walked to him, took his hand in hers, and looked into his eyes.

"You are amazing," she said, "and an excellent sneak thief. I am comforted when you are near."

Geoff swallowed. He'd been called nerd, geek, loser, dweeb, goob, and even "Gee-off." But never had someone, especially a beautiful girl, called him amazing.

"Know this, my Geoff," Ishara said. "I wanted to escape that dungeon last night. I wanted to leave with you."

"I know," he said. "I really wanted to get you out of that cell."

The door across the hall opened. Ariel and Jane stepped into the hall and saw Ishara.

"Ishara!" Jane said. "Welcome back. How are you after spending the night in the dungeon?"

Ishara smiled at Jane and nodded. "Thank you. I am fine. I was not harmed."

"I saw you try to grab Lady Seqwil during the fight," Jane said. "You tried to reach her through the bars."

"If only my arms were longer," Ishara said. "You, however, were incredible. You all were."

"*Hal'inari*," Ariel said, placing a hand over her heart. "I am glad to see you again."

Ishara returned Ariel's gesture. "*Hal'inari*."

"What's all the noise out here?" a grouchy-sounding Sawyer asked. He appeared at the door behind Geoff wearing only his trousers and scratching his rear. His thick, dark messy hair stood up on his head.

"Hey, Ishara, good to have you back," he said.

"Get some clothes on, sleepy," Jane said.

Sawyer turned and muttered something under his breath about not getting much sleep. Jane watched him walk back into his room, then was startled as Ariel snapped her fingers near her ear to get her attention.

"Right. What's next? More training?" Jane asked, turning to Ariel.

"Yes," Ariel said. "After we visit Lady Seqwil's home."

"And breakfast," Sawyer added as he reappeared in the doorway with a shirt on and one shoe in his hand.

"He gets grumpy when he's hungry," Jane said.

"I could go for something to eat, too," Geoff said.

"Breakfast first, then," Ariel said. "Go get ready, Geoff."

Geoff gave Ariel a mock salute and went back into his room, leaving Jane in the hall with Ariel and Ishara.

Jane was glad to have everyone back together. As they waited, she watched the morning sun filter through the window at the far end of the hall. Dust particles danced and floated about in the inviting glow of the light, reminding her of tiny birds flitting about.

After Sawyer and Geoff had dressed, they all went

downstairs and had a quick breakfast. There were plenty of guards to keep an eye on them, but the king was nowhere to be found. On their way out of the castle they passed the throne room. The large doors were closed and there were a few guards standing watch.

"Wonder what's going on in there," Sawyer said as they walked by. "Planning our next visit to the dungeons, I bet."

"One visit was enough," Ishara said. "I have no desire to return."

"I'm sure it was," Jane said. "I'm starting to think we were safer in the forests."

Ariel turned to Ishara and Geoff. "Will you show us the way to Lady Seqwil's home?"

They nodded and took the lead as they exited the castle and entered the city of Chalon. As the group made their way through the crowd in the trade square Sawyer felt a tug on his sleeve. He turned to see Derek and Elayne looking up at him with wide grins on their clean faces. They wore new clothes. Elayne looked adorable in her blue dress with white trim.

"Hey there, you two," Sawyer said. "How're you doing?"

"Good," Derek said still smiling.

"There you are!" Josephine called as she appeared in the doorway of a small bakery. "I told you to stay where I can keep an eye on you."

Then her flour-covered hand shot up to her mouth as she recognized who Derek and Elayne had stopped.

"Oh my!" She said. "Wil! It's them!" Josephine hurried over and gave each of them a hug and a kiss.

"Thank you," Josephine said, wiping a few tears away. "Thank you so much for saving us."

"You are most welcome," Ariel said. "How are you?"

"We're fine, just fine," Wilhelm said, appearing in the doorway wiping his hands with a rag. He wore an apron which was nearly covered in flour. He walked to Ariel and smiled. "Thanks to you and your friends, we're fine."

"Do you work here now?" Jane said.

"Oh no, dear," Josephine said. "We own it. We bought this bakery with the money she gave us." Josephine smiled and nodded at Ariel.

"Aye," Wilhelm said. "It's ours now. We spend the day baking bread and sleep upstairs at night. It isn't much, but you'll always be welcome here."

"Thanks," Jane said. "We'll definitely stop by now that we know where you are."

"You have made a wise decision," Ariel said. "I wish you well."

"An' you," Wilhelm said. "Good luck an' be safe – all of you."

After saying good-bye to Wilhelm and his family they continued through the trade square and turned down a street filled with large, stone homes.

"Hey," Sawyer said. "This place looks kinda familiar."

"What're you talking about?" Jane asked. "We've never been here before."

"No, I've seen this place before," Sawyer said, looking around. "I think."

Ishara led them to the large stone house Lady Seqwil had occupied. She stopped and opened the front gate.

"Guys," Sawyer said, standing a few feet back looking up at the stone home. "I *have* been here. That gate; I'm sure of it."

"When did you come here?" Geoff asked. "Ishara and I were here yesterday and Lady Seqwil cooked for us."

Sawyer snapped his fingers and his eyes shot wide open. "This is it! This is the house the sword showed me. I remember now. The sword is here and so is something else."

They looked at Sawyer. Ariel unsheathed her weapons and nodded to Ishara. "Be ready," she said. "We do not know if Lady Seqwil was acting alone."

Ishara opened the front door as before and let it swing ajar. The door made no noise. The inside of the house was dark, with the exception of the sunlight shining through the windows. They stayed behind Ariel and slipped inside. Sawyer closed the door as quietly as he could, but there was a tiny click that seemed to be amplified in the otherwise silent house.

"She doesn't have much furniture," Jane said quietly. "Just a few chairs and tables."

"We noticed that too," Geoff said with a barely audible voice. "Seems like an ambassador would live more lavishly."

"Agreed," Ariel said, scanning the room. "Lady Seqwil's family is among the wealthiest families in Selra'thel."

Jane stayed just inside the door with Sawyer and Geoff, while Ariel and Ishara each took a side and looked over the house as they walked to the kitchen area at the far end. Ariel turned and motioned for them to stay put while she and Ishara went upstairs.

When they had disappeared, Sawyer's gaze fell upon the sooty fireplace. He wandered over to it and knelt. Jane and Geoff walked over to Sawyer and knelt beside him as he stared at the dark fireplace. Jane wasn't sure what to make of his behavior; he was being too quiet.

"Sawyer," Jane said. "What're you doing?"

He didn't answer. Jane frowned. He was acting weird, and she didn't like it. She grabbed his shoulder and squeezed until he looked at her.

"What is it?" she asked.

"You're freaking us out, Sawyer," Geoff said.

Sawyer turned and pointed at the fireplace.

"Something's there," he said. "Behind the wall. I saw it. The sword showed it to me."

Sawyer stood and ran his fingers along the mantle, stopping to examine every groove in the stone. Then he looked inside the fireplace.

"Yeah," he said. "Something hidden…"

Sawyer felt and pushed the stones in the back of the fireplace. There was an audible *click*.

The wall in the back of the fireplace recessed and slid away, revealing a dark nook. He looked at Jane and smiled.

"I found it," he said as he reached inside the secret compartment. He pulled out a long item wrapped in leather, then stood and unwrapped the object. The gleaming blue sapphire in the pommel identified it as the Stormblade.

"Well done," Ariel said. She and Ishara had returned from upstairs in time to see Sawyer recover his sword. "The Stormblade is reunited with its master. The bond between you and the sword continues to grow," Ariel added. "Keep it with you at all times."

"Hey, I see something else in there," Geoff said. He reached into the hidden chamber and pulled out a stack of scrolls. "Here; they look important." Geoff handed the scrolls to Ariel. "I think I felt a lever or handle in there, too."

He reached back inside and tugged at something. A loud

thud followed by a grinding noise echoed in the house. The entire wall with the fireplace slid aside. Behind the false wall was a small cell. A lone candle burned on a wooden table beside a shabby cot. A slim, solitary figure lay on the cot facing the wall. When the prisoner heard the secret door open, he rolled over. His leg was bandaged and his face was bruised. Geoff gasped.

CHAPTER TWENTY-NINE
THE ASSASSIN'S PRISONER

"Dad!" Geoff cried as he rushed to the cell. He thrust his arms through the bars in an effort to reach the man inside. His chest ached from the sudden pounding of his heart.

"Dad, is it really you? How'd you get here?"

His father climbed to his feet and limped to Geoff and embraced him through the bars. His eyes were moist.

"Geoff," he said. "Oh, Geoff. I'm so happy to see you, son."

"I don't understand, Dad," Geoff said, hugging his father around the waist. "What're you doing here? Why are you locked up?"

"Greetings, Maelord," Ariel said with a slight bow of her head. "You have been missed."

"Maelord?" Geoff said as he looked at Ariel.

"Mr. Vincent," Jane said, "how *did* you get here?"

"Seqwil Ferncliff," Mr. Vincent said. "She managed to take me by surprise in my own house. Ariel, she's dangerous. She plans to assassinate you and anyone she considers to be a threat. We have to stop her."

"She's already been stopped, Dad," Geoff said. "We fought her last night in the castle and Ariel cornered her on a tower landing and she jumped off and killed herself."

In his excitement at finding his father, Geoff spoke too fast, but he didn't care. Then he realized what Ariel had said.

"Maelord? Who's Maelord?" Geoff repeated, looking at Ariel again. "This is my dad."

"Then your father is the wizard Maelord," Ariel said. "As I had suspected."

Geoff stood motionless with his mouth agape. What was Ariel talking about?

"What? I don't understand," Geoff said. He felt his father squeeze his shoulder through the bars.

"I'm sorry, son," he said. "I should've told you a long time ago. My real name is Maelord, and I'm a wizard."

Geoff's jaw dropped as he searched his father's eyes for a sign that he was joking. Perhaps this was a big prank at his expense.

"Dad?" Geoff said. "Are you serious?"

Ishara appeared beside him and went to work picking the lock. She said nothing, but she was smiling. Geoff's father bent over so he was eye to eye with Geoff.

"I was going to tell you, son," he said. "I never meant for you to find out like this. Especially like this."

"Maelord," Ariel said, "you should know that your son has the gift of magic as well."

What was she talking about? Him? Oh yeah. She meant that thing with the mites in the Silverthorne catacombs. Maelord beamed with pride and regarded Geoff with a huge grin.

"Of course," Maelord said. "Of course he's a wizard. He's my son; how could he not be?"

Ishara opened the cell door. Geoff dashed inside the cell and wrapped his arms around his father again.

"Mr. Vincent," Jane said, clearing her throat, "it's good to see you again, but this is a real shock."

"I know, Jane," Maelord said. "I'm surprised to see all of you here as well. Thank you for keeping Geoff safe. When Lady Seqwil revealed her plans, I was worried about him. And please, call me Maelord."

Geoff stepped to his father's side and placed an arm around his waist as he helped him from the cell. Geoff strained and staggered when Maelord placed much of his weight on him. He looked down at his father's legs. His left thigh had been bandaged, but a lot of blood had soaked through the wrappings, leaving a dark red stain. Ariel took Maelord's other side and helped Geoff support his father.

"We have much to discuss," Ariel said quietly as they helped Maelord into a chair in front of the fireplace.

"Aye, that we do," Maelord said with a grunt. "That we do."

Ariel removed the bandage and looked at the wound, a deep slice across the front of the thigh. She removed a leather pouch from her belt then sprinkled bits of leaves over the wound and covered it with her hand.

"*Ilinara tae ullnara taethos*," Ariel said as she kept her hand over the wound.

Geoff noticed his father's expression went from grimacing in pain to smiling in relief as he took a deep breath.

"Thank you," he said. "So good to have a druid around."

Ariel smiled and helped him to his feet.

"So what do we do next?" Jane asked. "There's still an army approaching from the east."

"We go to my tower," Maelord said. "I need a bath and a change of clothes. Then we go see King Lionel and try to talk some sense into him."

"Good luck with that," Jane said. "He's been threatening us ever since we arrived."

Maelord's faint smile faded as he regarded Jane.

"He threatened my son?" Maelord asked in disbelief. "My son's friends? Ariel?"

Ariel slowly nodded.

"Jane speaks the truth," she said.

"Of course," Maelord said with a sigh. "Jane has always been honest."

"If you want to cast a spell," Sawyer said, "and put the whammy on him we won't mind."

"I may do that very thing," Maelord said as he looked at Sawyer. "And who might you be?"

"Oh, I'm Sawyer. Sawyer Collins," he said. "Nice to meet you."

Sawyer held out his hand and Maelord shook it. "Likewise," he said. Then he turned to Ishara. "And what is your name?"

"Ishara," she said. "You should know your brave son tried to rescue me from spending a night in the dungeons."

"Really?" Maelord said, looking at Geoff and giving him a pat on the shoulder. "Is that so?"

Geoff nodded absently. He was still thinking about being referred to as brave, and more than that, he was still coming to grips with the fact that his father was here and that he was a wizard.

"We should go," Ariel said. She held up a scroll from the bundle Geoff had given her. "Here is the scroll Count Vilmar carried. This will prove Seqwil had been plotting to undermine Lionel all along."

"I'd never have guessed Lady Seqwil would join with the Shadowlord," Maelord said. "She was cunning and highly intelligent."

"While you were her captive," Ariel said, "did you hear or see anything that may help us? Was she working with anyone else?"

"No," Maelord said. "She prided herself in acting alone."

With that, they set off for Maelord's tower. Along the way, Ariel revealed the close call Geoff and Ishara had with the assassin in his tower. She also revealed they had taken the elven battle armor for safekeeping.

"Bah, it's yours," Maelord said. "It's a hero's armor. You'll look good in it."

"I had planned to give it to someone else," Ariel said. "You are right. It should be worn by a hero."

"It does," Maelord said with a nod.

When they arrived at Maelord's tower, the front door opened as Geoff's father approached, as if it had waited for his return. Inside, Maelord snapped his fingers and a dozen candles were lit and the room shone with a golden glow. Everything was just as Geoff remembered when he and Ishara had last been there.

They filed in, stepping over and around dusty scrolls, books, and scroll-covered furniture. Sawyer disturbed a stack of books that had been resting on a chair, which produced a rather large cloud of dust. Ishara coughed and shot Sawyer an irritated glance.

"I'll be right back," Maelord said. "Make yourselves comfortable."

Ishara frowned as she looked about. Apparently she was simply trying to find a clean place to stand. Ariel sat in the only empty chair and brushed a few pieces of parchment aside before setting the scrolls Geoff had found on the table. Geoff now had a better look at the tower in the candlelight. Yes, this was very much like his dad's study back home, only messier.

"So your dad lives here?" Sawyer asked, looking around. "I like your house a lot better."

"I'm glad you found your dad, Geoff," Jane said, "but didn't you know? I mean, you had no idea he was living here and he was a wizard?"

"No," Geoff said. "He never said a thing. I'm as surprised as you are."

"Okay," Sawyer said. "If Geoff's dad is like a super wizard then he can turn the tide of battle, right? Win the war?"

No one said anything; they just looked at Sawyer.

"C'mon, guys," he said. "You saw what Geoff did to all those carrion mites, and he doesn't have any training. If his dad is a great wizard, then he can blast the Shadowlord's army."

"You're right," Jane said. She turned to Ariel, who was looking up from the scroll she had started to read. "Geoff's dad, Maelord, can win this war, right?"

"I do not know," Ariel said. Then she let the corners of her mouth curve up. "But having another wizard around is certainly a good thing."

Amid another bout of coughing, Ishara opened a window then planted herself beside it. The late morning sun caught her hair and made it sparkle. Geoff watched her close her green eyes and let the sun wash over her pretty face as she raised her chin and breathed in the clean air.

"Hey, Geoff," Sawyer said. "Maybe your dad can bring your maid next time. This place is filthy."

"Sawyer!" Jane said, giving him a disapproving look.

"What?" he asked. "It needs cleaning, that's all."

They heard the voice of Geoff's dad as he moved about upstairs. He was talking, but his voice was muffled. Geoff strained, but he couldn't make out anything his father was saying.

"Who's he talking to?" Sawyer asked, standing. "Is there anyone up there with him?

"No," Ariel said as she picked up another scroll. "He is alone."

Geoff glanced up at the ceiling and then back to Ishara, who was staring at him with one raised eyebrow.

"Does he do that a lot?" Sawyer asked.

"All wizards do," Ishara said, still looking at Geoff. "They mumble to themselves."

Several minutes later Maelord returned. His hair and thin goatee had been combed, and he wore a dark blue robe with gray embroidery on the sleeves and collar. He clapped his hands together loudly, agitating the dust particles floating around him.

"I feel much better," he said, putting an arm across Geoff's shoulders. "Shall we go?"

They left Maelord's tower and went to the castle, with Geoff smiling the whole way. When they arrived at the castle, King Lionel was standing in the courtyard, dressed in lavish red and white robes. An entourage of servants behind him were carrying decanters of wine and trays of food. What caught Geoff's attention, however, was the knight in chain mail sitting atop a gryphon. He was armed with a twelve-foot lance and had a sword at his side.

Lionel nodded and waved the mounted knight away.

When the gryphon flapped his wings, the rush of air felt like a strong wind. Geoff thought they were majestic creatures, with their dark golden fur and wings with brown-tipped feathers. Their claws looked like large curved daggers, and their heads were larger than a horse's head.

"Lionel," Maelord called as they walked to the king.

Lionel spun around at the sound of Maelord's voice.

"Ah, Maelord," he said. "There you are! We'd given you up for dead. Where've you been?"

"Nearly dead," Maelord said. "Lady Seqwil attacked me and held me prisoner in her house. These brave folks rescued me."

He gave Geoff a pat on the back. Lionel regarded Geoff and the others for a moment, then he looked back at Maelord.

"Welcome back, my friend," Lionel said. "Much has happened while you've been away. My sentinels have just informed me that a large force from the Shadowlord's northern army has turned toward Troll Fang Pass."

"And the garrison?" Maelord asked. "How many soldiers do we have there?"

"Two hundred," Lionel said. "Maybe less. If they take the fortress at Troll Fang Pass, the Shadowlord can command all northern trade routes and effectively divide Alluria in half."

"How soon can you get reinforcements to them?" Maelord asked.

Lionel didn't answer. His eyes wandered to Ariel and then back to Maelord.

"Well?" Maelord said, holding his arms out at his sides.

"He will not leave Chalon undefended," Ariel said. "Not for any reason."

Maelord looked at Ariel.

"What? Preposterous," he said. "We can't leave those two hundred soldiers to die."

Geoff let a small grin creep over his face as he watched the back and forth between Lionel and the team of Ariel and Maelord. There was no way the king stood a chance against them.

"Those men will buy us much needed time to prepare," Lionel said. "We can hold Chalon against the Shadowlord."

"No," Ariel said. "You cannot. I have already told you the eastern army has only been slowed. I am sure they are regrouping and intend to burn your city to the ground. Once they link with the northern army, Chalon is doomed."

Maelord squared his shoulders and glowered at Lionel. "Do you mean to tell me that you intend to do nothing but sit here and wait for the enemy to lay siege to Chalon? Those men in the garrison to the north will die in vain."

"They knew the risks," Lionel said coldly as he started to turn away. Maelord's hand shot out, grabbing his shoulder and spun him back around.

"They do," he said. "You, however, do not. You will send help now."

Lionel matched Maelord's stare.

"Even if I wanted to," he said, "it's too late. The Shadowlord will be there long before aid would arrive."

Geoff caught a glimpse of a few nearby guards looking at them.

"However," Lionel continued, "if you wish to save two hundred men and risk the lives of everyone in this city, be my guest. I'm sure you can…what is the term? Ah yes, *port* yourself along with Ariel and the Stormlord to the garrison at Troll Fang Pass."

"Porting doesn't work that way," Maelord said flatly. "You know this. Just as you know it isn't wise to mock a wizard."

Lionel turned and walked away without saying a word. Geoff looked up at his dad and grinned. He was proud of the way he had handled himself with the king, but he wished the king had been punched.

"He will do nothing," Ariel said. "An army from Selra'thel is camped south of here. King Andurys sent them to help defend Chalon. Trelane commands them and he has offered Lionel aid in the battle against the eastern army of the Shadowlord. However, Trelane's forces are outnumbered. Lionel chose not to join that battle either."

Maelord crossed his arms and studied the ground. Geoff thought he was going to come up with a great idea to solve the Lionel dilemma, but Maelord stroked his thin goatee a few times and shook his head.

"Do not worry," Ariel said. "Perhaps if you keep at it, you will change Lionel's mind."

"I'll try," he said. Then he looked at Geoff. "And I think it's time I took on an apprentice."

Geoff's eyes shot wide open.

"What?" he gasped.

"If what Ariel has told me is true," Maelord said, leaning forward, "you have the gift, but you need training. Would you like to learn the ways of a wizard?"

"Heck yeah," Geoff said with a smile. "All I know is how to make a mage stone glow."

"That a boy," Maelord said. "First we need to assess your potential, then I will teach you defensive spells."

"His potential," Ariel said, "appears to be limitless."

"Indeed," Maelord said. "I'm eager to find that out firsthand."

"Then I leave you and Geoff to your training," Ariel said. "We will meet in the castle after dinner this evening."

His father gave him another pat on the shoulder.

"Agreed," Maelord said.

Ariel, Sawyer, and Jane turned and left the castle courtyard. Ishara, however, looked at them for a moment and then turned to Geoff. She seemed to be deciding with whom she was going to spend the day. Geoff waved his hand for her to come with him and his father. Ishara smiled and joined Geoff and Maelord as they headed back to the wizard's tower.

Geoff had so many questions for his father he didn't know where to start. Everything had been such a struggle for him, Jane, and Sawyer since they had arrived in Alluria. It would be a welcomed change if they were finally able to slow down and have fun instead of hurrying about and running for their lives. If the werewolf wasn't chasing them, then it was the Shadowlord or his armies. Geoff looked at Ishara. How cool it would be to see Selra'thel, the kingdom of the elves. By the time they arrived at his father's tower, Geoff was imagining what Selra'thel looked like, with its giant trees and elegant architecture.

As soon as they entered, Geoff noticed the large room looked the same. It was still a mess. The frown on Ishara's face as she surveyed the room, however, tickled Geoff. He did his best to keep from laughing, but when she looked at him, he had to laugh out loud.

"What's so funny?" Maelord asked.

"Oh, nothing, Dad." Geoff said. "It's just that we've never seen such a messy place."

"Mmm," Maelord said, looking about. "It is messy, isn't it? And before you ask, the answer is yes, you must still clean your room."

A bemused Ishara giggled behind Geoff. He glanced over his shoulder at her and she winked at him. Maelord picked up a stack of scrolls from the table and placed them in a nearby chair. He motioned for Geoff and Ishara to sit.

"Now then," Maelord said, "I assume you have a few questions, son."

"Dad, I have a ton of questions," Geoff said. "Like why do you call yourself Maelord? How did you get here?" Why are you here? How—"

"Whoa, Geoff," Maelord said with a chuckle. "Okay, let me try to explain."

Geoff sat quietly and waited for his dad to begin. Maelord sat across from Geoff and Ishara and rubbed his goatee.

"Well now, let's see," he said. "I call myself Maelord because that's my name. And, like you, I was born here in Alluria."

Geoff's mouth fell open. He slowly shook his head as he tried to process what he'd heard.

"I know that's a shock, son," Maelord said, leaning forward and touching Geoff's hand, "and I'm sorry. Like I said, I should've told you much sooner. Believe me, this was not how I wanted things to turn out. We're wizards, Geoff."

"Dad," Geoff said, "this...this is nuts. I was *born* here? Does that make me an alien?"

Maelord laughed and shook his head. "Of course not," he said. "You're as human as the rest of us. If it's any consolation, I was planning to tell you. Especially since I never could keep you from sneaking into my study."

Ishara smiled.

"So you put the archway in the study," Geoff said as he removed the wizard's key from around his neck and handed it to his father. "Then this is your key."

Maelord turned the key over in his hands.

"What archway? Is this the key from my study?" Maelord asked.

"It was in that box on your desk," Geoff said, "the strange one from the Carpathian Mountains, remember?"

"Yes, I do," Maelord said, "but this isn't my key and I didn't place an archway in my study. By the way, it's called a wizard's arch."

"Then how did it get there?" Geoff asked.

"I don't know," Maelord said, "Another question is *why* would someone put it there."

"And yet another question," Ishara added, "would be *who* put the wizard's arch in your study."

"Indeed," Maelord said stroking his goatee again. "It seems we have a mystery on our hands, son."

"So if I was born here," Geoff said, "why are we living on earth?"

Maelord leaned forward.

"Your mother and I wanted you to have a normal life," he said. "We wanted you to grow up away from the distractions of being the son of a wizard. I know you have more questions, and I promise the answers will come, son. Now, let's see what kind of wizard you are."

Maelord motioned for Geoff to stand.

Geoff obeyed and stood in front of his father.

"Now don't be afraid, son," he said. "This is a simple test."

Maelord snapped his fingers. A small flame appeared and danced between his thumb and forefinger. Geoff watched the tiny fire for a moment and then looked at his father. Maelord was smiling. Apparently, Geoff's reaction was what he had expected.

"How'd you do that, Dad?"

"It's easy, Geoff," Maelord said. "Here, hold out your hand."

Geoff looked at the tiny flame and swallowed.

"It's okay," Maelord said. "It won't hurt. Trust me, son."

Geoff held his hand out and his father touched his palm with his forefinger, transferring the small fire to Geoff. It flitted back and forth in Geoff's hand like a tiny dancer without burning him. Geoff laughed with delight.

"It doesn't hurt," he said. "It just tickles a little."

"Very good," Maelord said. "Now transfer it to your other hand."

"How?" Geoff said.

"Hold your other hand up and concentrate," Maelord said. "The magic bends to your will."

Geoff held his free hand up and the tiny flame immediately hopped to it and pirouetted between the palms of his hands.

"Remarkable," Maelord said. "Well done, Geoff."

"Hey, Ishara," Geoff said turning toward her. "Look at this."

"Impressive, Geoff," she said with a small nod.

Geoff turned back toward his father.

"Uh, Dad," he said. "How do I make it stop?"

"Simple," Maelord said. "Just think it away and clap your hands."

Geoff closed his eyes and pictured his hands with no tiny fire in them. Then he clapped his hands as his father said and opened his eyes. The small flame had disappeared.

"Well done," Maelord said. "I'm told you conjured a ball of fire to save your friends. Is this true?"

"I don't know, Dad," he said. "They say I did, but I don't remember. We were in the catacombs when we were attacked by a bunch of carrion mites. One was about to eat me and I…I'm not sure. I panicked."

"Were you there, Ishara?" Maelord asked. "Did you see Geoff cast the spell?"

"No," she said. "However, Ariel reasoned it out and Geoff's friends say there was no one else in the catacombs who could have conjured a spell powerful enough to kill the mites."

"If I did it, then I was lucky," Geoff said. "It was an accident."

"No, son. It wasn't an accident. The magic inside you must've reacted to your situation. Remember, Geoff; magic is yours to control."

"So I was born like this?"

"Of course you were," Maelord said with a laugh. "And don't act like you're abnormal. It's a gift, son. A powerful gift."

Geoff looked over at Ishara, who was still watching them.

"But," Maelord said, "You still need training. There is so much you need to learn. But always remember this; whenever you're in trouble, you can call upon the magic inside you and it will do as you desire."

"Like a ball of fire?" Geoff said.

"Exactly," Maelord said as he held up a finger. "But you must realize, the more powerful the spell the more magic is required, and the toll on you will be greater."

"Ariel said that to Jane," Geoff said. "Jane gets tired after casting a bunch of healing charms."

"Yes," Maelord said. "Same thing. Wait—Jane can cast healing charms?"

Geoff and Ishara nodded.

"Jane is quite remarkable, isn't she? No human has ever been able to do such a thing."

"She will be an exceptional druid," Ishara said, "if she so chooses."

"Knowing Jane," Maelord said, "she will choose to be a druid. Now, before we teach you anything else, you must learn a spell to shield yourself from harm."

Ishara watched as Geoff practiced casting spells. She even took an active role in his training as a volunteer, letting him practice his spells on her-once she had been assured there was no danger.

After Geoff's training, they washed up and went back to the castle, passing the usual crowd of people in the street. Geoff saw more gryphon riders circling overhead, and he looked at Ishara, who had also noticed the increased numbers of sentinels in the evening sky.

Inside the castle, they met the others at dinner in the great hall. Sawyer looked tired, while Jane appeared to be in a good mood.

"Geoff, Ariel taught me three spells today," she said. "One was even an attack spell that I use with acorns. Can you believe that? Just plain old acorns."

"That's cool," Geoff said. "I learned a shield spell."

"Really? I can't wait to see it," Jane said. "Does it keep bad guys away?"

"Yeah," Geoff said. "Sort of, I think."

He glanced at his dad, who was huddled a few seats away speaking with Ariel.

Ishara, who had claimed a seat beside Geoff, mumbled something about messy wizards while casting a playful glance at him. When they had finished their meal, Ariel came over and sat beside them.

"I have been speaking with Maelord," she said. "We have a plan. Get all the rest you can tonight, for tomorrow we go to Troll Fang Pass."

"How?" Sawyer asked. "Isn't that place way to the north? How're we gonna get there?"

"We fly," Ariel said.

CHAPTER THIRTY
THE GARRISON AT TROLL FANG PASS

Jane slept soundly that night and woke refreshed, ready for the new day's adventure. She hopped out of bed and pulled the curtains away from the window. As the golden-red glow of the approaching dawn poured over her, she closed her eyes and tilted her head back, while keeping her arms outstretched.

"It is a glorious morning, is it not?" Ariel asked.

Jane spun around to see Ariel and Ishara, already dressed and ready to travel.

"It is," Jane said. "How long have you two been up?"

"Not long," Ishara said as she picked up her bow. "Sawyer's snoring kept me awake most of the night."

Jane laughed. Of course he was snoring. Poor Geoff, she thought. He must never get any sleep when he shares a room with Sawyer.

A baggy gray tunic and brown breeches hung over a chair beside Jane's bed.

"No dresses today?" Jane asked. "I thought I rocked the last dress I wore."

"Today we may need to move quickly," Ariel said. "I

have no idea what is happening at Troll Fang Pass, but a dress will not allow you to be agile – no matter how much you rock it."

Jane smiled and looked at Ishara, who was also smiling at Ariel's remark.

"You're getting cooler," Jane said. "Just hang around us some more and you'll be totally hot."

Ariel raised an eyebrow.

"That," she said, "makes no sense."

Jane giggled and she slipped on the breeches and tunic, then her traveling boots. She fastened her belt around her waist and spun around as if she were modeling her outfit.

"Well?" she demanded. "How do I look?"

"You look ready," Ariel said. "I will wake Sawyer and Geoff. You should eat something before we go."

Jane had a seat and ate a juicy pear from the fruit bowl in the middle of the table. A few moments later, Ariel returned with Sawyer and Geoff in tow.

"'Morning," Jane said, tossing a pear to Sawyer and then another to Geoff. "Did you guys get any sleep?"

Sawyer had already taken a big bite of his pear and could only reply with a nod and a "mmhmm."

Ariel opened her backpack and removed two long, slightly curved daggers in black leather scabbards. She offered one to Jane and the other to Geoff.

"Troll Fang Pass will be dangerous," she said. "I will feel better if you have these with you."

Jane and Geoff took the daggers. Geoff slid his dagger from its sheath and examined it, and Jane did the same.

"Hey, wait a minute," Geoff said. "These daggers belonged to Lady Seqwil. I recognize them."

"Yes," Ariel said. "Now they are yours. Elven weapons are the finest in the realm."

"Thank you," Jane said, "but wouldn't her family like to have them?"

Ariel shook her head. "No. I doubt Lady Seqwil's family knows of their existence."

"Thanks," Geoff said. "It's so light, like Sawyer's sword."

Ishara took the elven dagger from Geoff and studied it. She turned it over in her hand and tested the weapon's balance.

"Beautiful," Ishara said. "I believe this blade may even harm magical creatures."

"You mean like that green ghost spider?" Sawyer asked, chomping on the last of his pear.

Ishara nodded and handed the dagger back to Geoff.

"Come," Ariel said. "Troll Fang Pass awaits."

"Love the name," Sawyer said. "Sounds like a good place for a fight."

"There aren't really trolls there," Geoff said, "right?"

"The largest and most aggressive mountain trolls live there," Ishara said, "but they will be the least of our worries."

Jane looked at Sawyer, who appeared to be nonchalant about the whole thing. She liked his confidence; it made her feel safe.

They left their rooms and Ariel led them up the stone stairs to the tower landing, where they had cornered Lady Seqwil. On the way up, Jane lagged behind the others with Sawyer. Glancing at Sawyer, Jane noticed his eyes were wide and he kept flexing his fingers. He was nervous, but she had no idea why. She squeezed his hand to get his attention. Sawyer looked at her and grinned.

They arrived on the landing to find three magnificent

gryphons already harnessed and waiting for them. Their handlers were holding their reins. Each gryphon stood over seven feet in height, with muscles rippling under their fur and feathers. Their great claws looked capable of rending steel, and the tips of their wings shone like spun gold in the morning sun.

Ariel went to each gryphon and rubbed its beak while Ishara scratched their necks. The winged beasts enjoyed the touching and rubbing, and screeched, stretched their necks, and playfully shook their heads. Jane went to one of the gryphons and rubbed its side. The fur was warm to the touch, but soft like a puppy's fur. As Jane rubbed and patted the gryphon, she noticed Sawyer was standing several feet away. He looked a little pale. She beckoned him over with a tilt of her head.

"Don't be afraid," Jane said. "They're not wild beasts. They won't hurt you. Touch it, see?"

Sawyer placed his hand on the gryphon's neck and rubbed back and forth.

"Yeah, it's beautiful," he said. "I'm not afraid of it that much."

"What's wrong?" Jane asked. He was clearly bothered by something. He looked around to make sure none of the others were standing too close.

"Jane, you gotta be kidding me," Sawyer whispered in an urgent tone. "I can't ride this thing."

"Why not?"

Sawyer took a deep breath and looked at his feet. He was in near panic mode now. His leg twitched and his eyes darted about. Jane put her hand on his chest. His heart was pounding.

"Sawyer," Jane said in a hushed tone. "What's the matter?"

He leaned over and whispered in her ear, "Heights."

Jane tilted her head and shook it. She was still puzzled. Sawyer rolled his eyes and leaned close to Jane.

"I'm afraid of heights," he said. "I can't ride one of these things."

"How did you think we were going to fly?" Jane asked. "By plane?"

"I don't know," he said. "I didn't think about it much last night when Ariel said we were going to fly."

Jane pointed at the saddle, which was made to accommodate two riders.

"Look," she said, "all you have to do is strap yourself in and hold on."

Sawyer shook his head. "Jane, you don't understand; I'm really afraid of heights."

Jane grabbed his head with both hands and held his gaze with hers.

"I won't let you fall," she said. "Don't worry."

Sawyer sighed and ran his trembling fingers through his hair. Even with her assurances, he appeared terrified.

"I got a bad feeling," he said. "We don't have parachutes or anything. If we fall off that thing then that's it."

"I'll hold onto you," Jane said. "We'll be fine."

Jane kissed him and caressed his cheek.

Ariel appeared and looked over the saddle and straps on the gryphon. Apparently satisfied all was in perfect working order, she nodded to herself and then to Jane.

"Are you ready?" Ariel asked.

Jane looked at Sawyer, who had closed his eyes and was now chewing on his lower lip. Jane took his clammy hand in hers and gave Ariel a thumbs-up.

"We're ready," she said. "But Ariel, we've never ridden one of these before. How do we control it? And how much of a danger is there of us falling off?"

"Once we have you strapped into the saddle," Ariel explained, "there is no danger of falling. And, as far as controlling the gryphon, it is nearly the same as riding a horse."

"See? You can ride a horse, Sawyer," Jane said, giving his hand a squeeze. "And you heard Ariel—you can't fall off."

"Climb on," Ariel said. "I will make sure you are secure."

Jane let go of Sawyer's hand and hopped on the gryphon. She slid to the back of the large saddle to make room for Sawyer. Ariel made sure Jane's feet were in her stirrups and fastened a thick leather strap about her waist. When she was done with Jane she turned and looked at Sawyer.

"C'mon Sawyer," Jane said, extending her hand. "It'll be fun."

As Sawyer cautiously approached the gryphon, his eyes darted from Jane to Ariel, and then to the gryphon. Ariel put a hand on his shoulder and smiled at him.

Sawyer carefully climbed aboard the gryphon. Jane helped him settle into the forward saddle position and immediately wrapped her arms around his waist. She rested her head on his back and felt the tension in his body. She hugged him tighter.

On the gryphon beside them, Geoff and Ishara were already set for takeoff. Ishara was giving him preflight instructions, and Geoff kept asking her if they could start flying. Their laughter made Jane smile. They were good for each other.

"I will take the lead gryphon," Ariel said. "Follow me and do not attempt any tricks while you are in flight."

Ariel peered over at Geoff and Ishara. "That goes for you, too," she said. "No fancy flying, agreed?"

"Okay," Geoff said. "We'll be right behind you."

"How high will we be flying?" Sawyer asked, still tense. "And how long is the flight?"

"We will be at the garrison before you know it," Ariel said. "Enjoy the experience. Jane will not let anything happen to you."

Jane felt Sawyer exhale. He shuddered a little. She snuggled herself as close to him as she could, and her fingers dug into his tunic. Ariel gave Sawyer a pat on the thigh and winked at Jane as she left them to get ready. She must've heard everything they said earlier. Of course she had; Ariel heard everything. Jane's heart started to beat faster.

Flying on the gryphon with Sawyer was going to be awesome. He was afraid of heights, so what? There were much worse things than being afraid of heights. It proved Sawyer was real, and Jane liked that. She let her hands creep up his sides and then she tickled him. Sawyer would've leapt out of the saddle had he not been strapped in.

"Stop that," he said. "Are you crazy? This is serious."

Jane giggled and kissed his neck.

"Crazy for you," she said, giving him another hug. She ran her hands over his chest and shoulders. Sawyer seemed to respond and relax a bit.

"Geoff," called a male voice behind them. Jane looked over her shoulder and saw Geoff's dad, Mr. Vincent, or rather Maelord, approaching from the steps. He smiled at Jane and Sawyer as he passed and went to Geoff.

"Be careful," he said, putting a hand on Geoff's shoulder. "This isn't a game or a joy ride. You're going into a dangerous situation and normally I'd never let you do something like this. But since Ariel is also going, I know she'll look after you."

"As will I," Ishara said.

"Thank you, Ishara," Maelord said, then he turned to Geoff again. "Remember your lessons, son. I wish we had more time to train. Use the knowledge you have and you'll be fine."

"Okay," Geoff said. "Thanks, Dad. Don't worry."

"I always worry about you," Maelord said. "That's what fathers do."

Geoff laughed. Maelord shook Geoff's hand and then Ishara's.

"Good luck, son," he said before stepping away to give them room to fly.

Ariel looked at them one last time and then spurred her gryphon forward. The great beast galloped to the edge of the landing and leapt off, unfurling its fantastic wings and taking flight with a single powerful flap.

"Awesome!" Geoff said. "I've been wanting to do this ever since we first saw gryphons. Let's go."

The gryphon Geoff and Ishara rode immediately sprinted to the edge of the landing, with Geoff cheering at the top of his lungs. It also leapt into the morning air and took flight, following Ariel's gryphon. Sawyer had tensed up again and he was breathing fast. Jane held onto him with all her might.

"You can do this," she said. "It's easy. All you have to do is sit and ride."

As if it heard Jane, their gryphon dashed to the edge of the landing as the others had done. Sawyer screamed as it launched itself into the sky. Jane also screamed; she hadn't expected the ride to start off so bumpy. The immediate rush of cool air against her face was exhilarating, and she couldn't help but laugh as they soared high above the city. She looked down at the people in the streets of Chalon hurrying about their morning business.

Even from high above, the city looked like it was bursting at the seams and on the verge of panic. She saw Geoff and Ishara taking in the views ahead of them, laughing and pointing at different landmarks as they flew. In the distance she saw Ariel and her gryphon flying in an almost casual manner, meandering left then right. More than once Ariel glanced behind her to make sure they were all still following her.

Then Jane caught a glimpse of the awesome mountain range before her, the Dragonscale Mountains. Their white-tipped peaks seemed to go on forever, disappearing into the gray horizon. Dark storm clouds lingered over the mountains, and their rugged beauty made her catch her breath. Suddenly, her feeling of exhilaration gave way to something else. These mountains looked familiar; she had the unmistakable sensation of having made this journey before.

She *had* been here many times before, she realized. In her dreams. She was living the journey she had dreamt about ever since they had returned with Ariel. A feeling of dread rolled over her and she grimaced. Sawyer was right. Something bad was going to happen, and she felt powerless to stop it.

She held Sawyer tighter than ever. His body felt even more rigid than before. He had leaned forward and Jane saw his knuckles were white from the strain of gripping the gryphon's harness so tightly. He continued to look straight ahead.

"Sawyer!" she shouted in his ear. "Something's wrong."

"What?" he said. "I can't hear you."

"I said something's wrong."

"It's a little late now, isn't it?" he shouted over his shoulder. "What do you want me to do? This thing's on autopilot."

Jane laid her head against his back and closed her eyes. They were flying into real danger; she was sure of it. In her dream a sinister presence was waiting. She shivered and squeezed Sawyer so hard that he complained he couldn't breathe. Jane lifted her head and noticed Ariel had pulled further away from them.

"Ariel!" she called.

"Jane, she can't hear you," Sawyer said. "She's too far away."

Jane's heart sank. There was no way to warn Ariel of the impending danger she sensed. The further north they flew, the more helpless she felt.

After several miles, the air took on a chill that cut through Jane like the edge of an elven dagger. The wind began to blow harder, and she started to smell smoke. She lifted her head from Sawyer's back and scanned the landscape below. Why was it so dark? It looked like dusk, but that wasn't right; it must've been lunchtime at the latest. Jane realized they had flown into a large cloud of thick black smoke, and then she saw a rough, gray fortress burning below.

Surrounding the fortress was a sea of figures, some of which were not human. She saw the unmistakable shapes of hunchback trolls, which appeared to be even larger than the troll Sawyer had killed when he found the Stormblade. Catapults from the north and east launched flaming balls of tar and hay at the fortress. The pungent fumes became stifling, and Jane's nostrils burned. The sounds of shouting mixed with explosions and fighting rose to meet them as the gryphons circled the battle. Several arrows flew past them, causing the gryphons to sway and dodge the projectiles.

"Whoa, whoa, whoa!" Sawyer shouted as he ducked his head. "Stop weaving and fly straight."

Jane leaned forward as well, not wanting to make herself an easy target for the archers below. A fiery ball of pitch sailed past them and narrowly missed Geoff and Ishara. Their gryphon swerved rapidly away and disappeared into a column of black smoke.

"We're going down!" Sawyer shouted. "Hang on, Jane."

Jane looked down. The ground was indeed getting closer. Ariel was leading them down into the besieged fortress and into a sea of chaos. Jane was reminded of a painting she had seen once in a museum. It was a painting of hell.

CHAPTER THIRTY-ONE
RETURN OF THE STORMLORD

Sawyer couldn't breathe. He felt like he was free-falling as their gryphon dove toward the ground, and he and Jane screamed all the way down. The rush of smoke-filled air in his face with the swish of arrows sailing past was terrifying. His hands ached from holding the gryphon's reins so tightly, and Jane's fingers digging deep into his sides was squeezing the life out of him.

They landed with a bump as the gryphon trotted and came to a stop. Sawyer's head flew forward and bounced off the gryphon's neck. He touched a cut above his left eye, then looked at his fingers and saw blood.

The others had already landed and dismounted. Ariel rushed over to Sawyer and Jane and immediately unfastened their safety straps.

"Hurry to the keep," Ariel said, pulling them off the gryphon. She pointed at Geoff and Ishara, who were running to a plain, roughhewn house at the back of the garrison. Sawyer heard a *thwack* at his feet and looked down. An arrow had just missed his foot.

"Go!" Ariel shouted.

Sawyer grabbed Jane's wrist and pulled her with him as they sprinted to the keep. All around soldiers were running and yelling as the battle raged. Fires of various sizes burned around them, the smoky air searing Sawyer's nose and lungs. A large rock flew over the wall and smashed through the keep's door, sending bits of wood everywhere. He saw Geoff and Ishara rush into the splintered doorway and turn around. They began to frantically wave their hands.

"Come on, you two!" Geoff shouted. "Get in here!"

Sawyer and Jane dashed inside as an arrow shattered on the stone wall beside the door. Sawyer whirled around and saw Ariel send the three gryphons away. They rose like great winged projectiles from a cannon and disappeared above the blackened sky.

"Man, we're really in it this time," Sawyer said.

Ariel hurried across the courtyard, dodging a few arrows along the way, and joined them inside the keep.

"Is everyone unharmed?" she asked, looking them over.

"Yeah, for now," Sawyer said. "You didn't say we were flying into a pitched battle. We were almost killed."

Ariel unsheathed her scimitars and looked at Sawyer.

"I did not know the attack had already begun," she said. "The Shadowlord has surprised us. Stay inside. They are about to breach the walls. Ishara and I will assist the soldiers."

She looked at Jane. "Your skills will be sorely needed when this is over."

"Those are monsters attacking," Geoff said. "They're huge."

"I know," Ariel said. "They are mountain trolls. Stay here."

Ariel gave Ishara a nod and rushed outside to join the battle on the ramparts. Ishara started after her, but stopped and gave Geoff a quick hug.

"Do not worry. I will return," she said to Geoff. "*Nu Tel'mor.*"

She turned and ran after Ariel, vanishing into the surrounding chaos.

"We better get back," Sawyer said. "Some of those arrows landed a little too close."

Sawyer removed his sword from its scabbard. An immediate feeling of danger swept over him. He spun around and surveyed the messy inside of the keep. Overturned tables and chairs, broken weapons, a smoldering fire in the fireplace, and broken plates and cups lay scattered all about. At least they were alone, however.

"Sawyer," Jane said. "What's wrong?"

"Hmmm?" he said. "I just felt like we were in danger."

"We're in a siege," Jane said. "Of course we're in danger."

"I know that," he said flatly. "It's something else. I think the sword is trying to tell me something again."

"Uh-oh," Geoff said, looking around. "That's never good."

"Sawyer, there's danger all around," Jane said. Then her eyes widened. "Is it the werewolf again?"

"What? No, I don't think so. It's something different."

He stepped forward and peered out the broken door. He looked at the garrison's south wall and saw the unmistakable figure of Ariel spinning and slashing at a mob of barbarians that had just topped the wall. Behind her, Ishara fired arrow after arrow into another bunch of barbarians who had leapt onto the wall from a ladder.

"Get outta the way!" a gruff-voiced wounded soldier shouted as he limped through the door.

Sawyer and the others moved aside. The soldier was

covered in sweat and blood. He pushed past them and settled heavily into a chair, dropping his sword beside him.

"Who're you?" he demanded, grimacing as he held his bleeding left arm. "This is no place for children."

"We came with Ariel," Jane said, pointing toward the door. "We're here to help."

"Help? Don't make me laugh, girl," the soldier said. "Find a place to hide and pray we aren't overrun."

"Really, we wanna help," Sawyer said. "We didn't know you were already fighting. We got here as fast as we could."

"Yeah, I saw you," the soldier said. "So did everything walking or crawling in this battle. What good are children gonna be? I sent for reinforcements days ago."

"They aren't coming," Jane said. "It's just us and Ariel and Ishara."

The soldier looked at Jane and frowned. Sawyer thought he looked like he had just given up.

"I s'pose it's just as well," he said. "The Shadowlord will have his victory. Nothing we can do now to stop him. Only wish I hadn't been the last commander of this garrison."

"It's not over yet," Jane said as she removed her leather pouch and knelt beside the wounded soldier. "Relax; I'll heal you."

Sawyer felt a tingle from his sword, and he looked at the blade. Tiny lightning bolts crawled up and down its length. He stepped outside, and heard a low rumbling sound, accompanied by the ground shaking beneath his feet. An earthquake was his first thought, but then he looked at the north wall of the keep. It was crumbling. The large stones were being pushed up from below the ground and inward.

"Hey, boy," the soldier said. "What do ya have there? That's a magical sword?"

"It's the Stormblade," Geoff said.

The soldier rose to his feet and looked first at Sawyer, then at his arm, and finally at Jane. He seemed confused, as if he wasn't sure if he could believe what he was seeing; a human girl who could cast healing spells and a boy who carried the Stormblade. Sawyer ignored him. Something was tunneling under the wall and working its way to the surface. The Stormblade vibrated in his hand as Sawyer slowly walked toward the weakening northern wall.

"Sawyer!" Jane called from the doorway. "What're you doing? Get back in here!"

As soon as Jane finished speaking, the wall fell with a great crash. The impact tossed Sawyer to the ground and shook the entire keep. A loud roar rang over the battle as a giant creature emerged from under the smashed wall. It was pale and hairless, and its body was ape-like in appearance, with long muscular arms that looked like tree trunks. Its fleshy head rested directly on its wide, gnarled shoulders, and its tusked mouth was large enough to swallow a man. The subterranean monster's eyes, however, were small and squinty.

"Ogre at the northern wall!" Ariel called from the other side of the keep. "The wall has been breached!"

"To the north wall!" the garrison commander shouted. "Fill the breach or we're lost!"

Sawyer barely heard them. He got to his feet and approached the grotesque creature. The blade of his sword glowed with large arcs of lightning. Several options ran through Sawyer's mind. The Stormblade was reaching out to him, communicating and offering help. Sawyer felt like he had found an old friend after a long absence. The power of the Stormblade was now his to command.

Sawyer raised it high above his head and charged the ogre as it lifted its hulk from the ground. Despite its small eyes, it homed in on Sawyer and the glowing sword. It raised a massive fist and brought it down, targeting Sawyer. The ogre's fist struck the ground with a thunderous crash, sending tremors throughout the keep.

"Sawyer!" Jane screamed. "No! Get away!"

She started to run to Sawyer, but was restrained by the garrison commander.

"Let me go!" Jane cried. "I have to help him."

Sawyer heard Jane's shouting, but he focused on the ogre. He leapt into the air holding the Stormblade overhead with both hands. He landed on the ogre's hand and with a single chopping motion, drove the blade deep into the leathery flesh of the monster's hand. Lightning bolts shot from the wound and rolled over the ogre's entire body. It screamed and staggered backward, out of the keep.

Then Sawyer noticed several hundred orcs waving their weapons in the air as they charged the breach. A thought popped into Sawyer's head as the sword vibrated again. He began moving the Stormblade overhead in a circular motion, and as he did, the wind began to blow harder and dark clouds began to form. He brought his sword down in front of him, piercing the ground. Again lightning bolts arced and raced along the ground, this time toward the ogre and the orcs behind it.

They screamed and were thrown back by the violent chains of lightning that raced from one orc to the next.

The ogre recovered and lurched forward, arms extended and ready to tear Sawyer apart. But Sawyer stepped back and slashed the ogre's hand, opening up a dreadful wound that gushed dark purple blood. Again the ogre recoiled in pain. It held its injured hand close to its body and brought its other fist down in a hammering motion. Sawyer dodged the crushing blow, which again sent tremors throughout the keep.

This time, Sawyer maintained his balance and stabbed the ogre's other hand, sending lightning bolts racing up and down its body again. This time lightning from the Stormblade fried the ogre. Its death scream drowned out all other sounds of battle as it shuddered and swayed before falling to the ground in front of Sawyer in a smoldering heap. Sawyer had no time to celebrate, however; movement from the corner of Sawyer's eyes caught his attention. Another large wave of orcs were charging at him.

Sawyer stood atop the rubble that was once the keep's wall and pointed his sword toward the sky, holding it with both hands. A funnel cloud formed in front of him, then another, and another. Each of the whirlwinds moved toward the orcs and rippled with lightning.

The front ranks of the oncoming orcs were tossed about as the whirlwinds attacked and were decimated almost immediately. Sawyer held steady, concentrating on the movements of the whirlwinds. They moved to his mental commands.

"Behold!" shouted the garrison commander, who had stepped into the rainy courtyard and pointed at Sawyer. "The Stormlord has come! He fights with us! Attack! Drive the enemy back!"

There was a great cheer as the keep's defenders fought harder, invigorated by Sawyer's actions. They began to beat the barbarians off the south wall.

Sawyer barely heard them, because he was focused on the battle. He watched the remains of the orc troops scatter back to the north, disappearing into the craggy, gray terrain. Suddenly, something slammed against his right thigh. A sharp, burning pain erupted in his leg and he crumpled onto the broken stone debris. Looking up, he saw an arrow sticking out of his thigh. The pain was horrible, worse than when he had broken his arm during football practice.

He grasped at the arrow, but that only caused him more pain, and he screamed. The shock of seeing an arrow protruding from his thigh had broken his concentration, and the whirlwinds diminished and disappeared. He struggled to one knee, since his wounded leg didn't respond to his commands. In the distance, he saw a contingent of archers form and fire another volley at him. He tried to hold his sword up and conjure more whirlwinds, but he was in too much pain. He slumped over, breathing heavily from the exertion and the shock of being wounded.

He felt a pair of arms wrap around his waist and two hands grab his chest from behind. Then he heard Jane.

"I'm here," she said in his ear. "Don't worry, Sawyer."

He gasped. He thought Ariel had come to his rescue, but there was Jane, lending her strength to his and propping him up.

Ilinara tae ullnara taethos, Jane said over and over again. She had moved a hand down to his wounded thigh and was gently pressing dried leaves against the wound. His wounded leg became numb, and the pain slipped away as Jane chanted. Sawyer lifted his sword overhead and again conjured more whirlwinds. This time he sent them toward the archers. They had already loosed two volleys of arrows, however.

"Jane," Sawyer croaked, "you gotta go. The arrows…"

Suddenly, a glowing translucent disk appeared above them, shimmering with magical energy. Sawyer looked over his shoulder and saw Geoff behind them, arms stretched upward. At least a hundred arrows struck the glowing shield, shattering and bouncing off the magical barrier. Sawyer felt warm, like he was sitting beside a cozy fire. Jane's spell had revived him.

He sent the small cyclones after the archers, who met the same fate as the orcs. Next, he maneuvered his swirling minions to the east and south walls, clearing away the attackers. All the while Jane held him and kept chanting her healing charm and Geoff maintained his shield overhead. A cry arose from the ramparts. Sawyer looked up and saw the jubilant soldiers of Chalon hoisting their weapons high and cheering.

"Is it over?" Geoff asked. "Is the battle over?"

Sawyer grunted. "Let's hope so. Geoff, how'd you do that? You saved us."

"Dad showed me how to do it," Geoff said.

Jane's grip had loosened and her voice was growing softer. She and Geoff had kept Sawyer alive at the expense of their own safety.

"Thanks, guys," Sawyer said, finally allowing himself to relax. "Couldn't have done it without you."

Then a searing pain shot up his leg and through him.

"Ow. Damn, that really hurts," Sawyer said as he looked at Jane. She had lost consciousness and fallen to the ground behind him. Sawyer let the Stormblade fall from his hand as he lay back beside Jane, coughing as he inhaled smoky air.

"Jane," he said. "Jane, are you okay?"

Jane didn't answer, nor did she move. Sawyer shook her shoulder but she didn't respond. With every movement Sawyer made the pain in his leg grew. It was becoming unbearable.

"Geoff," Sawyer said, "go get Ariel."

"There is no need. I am here," Ariel said as she knelt beside him and Jane. She first lifted Jane's head and examined her. She looked at Sawyer and gave him a quick nod. Sawyer sighed in relief. He was glad Jane was going to be all right. He closed his eyes and muttered, "Thank you."

"She needs rest," Ariel said. Then she looked at Geoff. "And you? Are you unharmed?"

Sawyer opened his eyes in time to see Geoff answer.

"Yeah. I'm fine."

Several heavy footsteps approached from the keep. Sawyer tilted his head in time to see the garrison commander with at least five soldiers rushing over to them.

"By the powers," the commander said. "I've never seen the likes of that in all my days. The Stormlord has returned! This is a great day!"

Sawyer pointed at Jane and Geoff. "They helped," he said. "I would've—"

"Help him, help the Stormlord," the commander motioned to a few nearby soldiers. "We're grateful you arrived when you did. We'd all be dead by now if you hadn't joined the battle."

Sawyer felt several hands lift him off the rough stones. Another horrible pain immediately shot through him, making his leg feel like it was on fire. He gritted his teeth as he was jostled and carried to the keep. He raised his head and saw Ariel walking behind him carrying Jane in her arms.

Geoff had picked up his sword and carried it with both hands as he and Ishara walked beside Ariel.

Sawyer looked up. The sky was still dark from the lingering smoke from the burning keep. He heard the sounds of wounded soldiers crying out in pain. Bodies lay everywhere, some beyond help.

A soldier not much older than Sawyer ran up to the commander and saluted him.

"My lord," he said, "the day is ours. The enemy flees back into the mountains."

"Aye," the commander said as he placed a hand under Sawyer's head to provide him with additional support. "They now know the Stormlord stands with us. I doubt they'll be back. See to the wounded."

The young soldier saluted again and hurried away. Sawyer was exhausted. More than once he thought he was going to pass out, but the intense pain in his leg kept him awake. They entered the keep, which was more than likely going to be a triage and hospital for a while.

No one noticed the figure in black armor who sat on a winged beast high above the keep on a rocky outcropping. The runes on his sword began to glow red, matching the red glow of his eyes inside his helm. The dark figure growled from atop his winged mount, never taking his eyes off Jane.

CHAPTER THIRTY-TWO
RELUCTANT HEROES

Jane opened her eyes when something cool and wet brushed across her cheek. Ariel hovered above her, wiping away the dirt and grime from her face. Ariel smiled when she saw Jane waking up.

"You have done well," Ariel said. "Rest for now. You need your strength."

Jane tried to sit up, but her head felt like it was going to explode. Oh great. Another migraine. She hadn't had one since Ariel cured her the last time they were in Alluria.

"Sawyer," Jane said as she winced and closed her eyes tightly. "Is he—"

"He is fine," Ariel said, pointing to the other side of the room. "He is there. Geoff and Ishara are with him. Lie down and rest. You are exhausted from healing too much."

"Yeah, okay," Jane said quietly. "No problem."

Jane lay her head back on the coarse pillow. She could tell by the movement on the bed that Ariel had stood up. Opening an eye, she saw they were in a small chamber. She could hear shouts from somewhere outside through the only window in the room. Someone had opened it, presumably to let in fresh air, but the result was a colder room that smelled like smoke.

Jane pressed the cool, damp cloth to her forehead, letting droplets of water run down her temples and face.

"Here, Jane," Ishara said, taking her hand and placing it on a small mug. "Drink this."

With Ishara's help, Jane lifted her head and sipped the cool water.

"Thanks," Jane said, lying back down.

"You are welcome," she said, adjusting Jane's wool blanket.

As Jane lay there, she heard the others talking. They kept their voices down, probably so she and Sawyer could rest. Sawyer groaned, so she turned her head to see him. He was lying on the other bed, covered by a similar blanket. Ariel sat on the edge of his bed while Geoff and Ishara looked on from the other side.

Jane watched as Ariel stared at him with her usual stoic expression. Sawyer opened his eyes and blinked a few times, but he didn't say anything. Slowly, the corners of Ariel's mouth turned up until she wore a huge grin.

"Hero," she said.

"Who? Me?" Sawyer said with a cough. "Nah. I'd be dead if Jane and Geoff hadn't come along."

"We would *all* be dead if you had not slain the ogre and driven the orcs away," Ariel said, brushing a lock of hair from his eyes. "Rest now, Stormlord."

"Yeah, right," Sawyer said as he winced and rolled over.

Jane exhaled deeply and relaxed. Everyone was alive, and she was grateful for that. Sawyer had been incredibly brave and saved everyone in the garrison when he charged the ogre.

Ariel returned and refreshed Jane's damp cloth in a bowl of water beside her bed. Jane mouthed the words *thank you.*

By the time she woke up, the sun was shining and the smell of bacon frying made her mouth water. She'd slept soundly and didn't dream of the sinister fortress in the mountains. She paused before opening her eyes, waiting for the migraine to return, but to her surprise, it didn't. She sat up and looked around. Everyone was there except Ariel. She yawned and had a good stretch. Ishara and Geoff were preparing breakfast by the small fireplace in the room, while Sawyer remained asleep with his mouth agape.

The door opened and Ariel entered. She smiled at Jane and walked to her bed.

"Good morning, Jane. How are you?"

"Fine," Jane said. "A little hungry, but I feel good."

"You're in luck," Geoff said, holding up a plate of bacon and bread and a hunk of cheese. "They have all kinds of good food here in their stores. Have some."

Geoff gave the plate of tasty-smelling food to Jane, who immediately picked up a thick piece of crispy bacon and ate it. It was hot and a bit greasy, but Jane didn't care. It was delicious. Jane stuffed a piece of coarse wheat bread in her mouth and chewed, savoring the hearty taste as Geoff poured some water into a wooden mug and handed it to her.

"So are we safe now?" Jane asked. "The garrison, I mean. They're out of danger, right?"

"For now," Ariel said. "But I do not believe the Shadowlord will allow his forces to lose two battles when they easily outnumber us."

Jane swallowed and focused on Ariel.

"They will be back," Ariel said. "You can be sure of that."

"Man," Geoff said with a hint of disappointment in his voice. "I was hoping we could fly back to Chalon on those gryphons. That was fun."

"No it wasn't," Sawyer grumbled as he stirred in bed. "It sucked."

Jane went over to Sawyer and sat on his bed, then waved a thick piece of bacon under his nose. Smelling the juicy piece of bacon, Sawyer opened his mouth so Jane could deposit his breakfast. He kept his eyes closed as he chewed the bacon, Jane ruffled his thick dark hair. When she was done she leaned back to study her handiwork. Sawyer looked like he wore a big puffy wig. Jane giggled and patted his head.

"Yeah, yeah, whatever," Sawyer said, keeping his eyes closed and opening his mouth again. "More."

Jane placed another piece of bacon in his mouth and giggled while he chewed.

"How does your leg feel today?" Ariel asked as she looked out the window.

Sawyer held a finger up for a few seconds as he finished chewing and swallowed. Under his bedcovers, he stretched his leg and flexed it. Then he gave Ariel a thumbs up.

"It feels good," he said. "I don't feel any pain at all. It's like I was never hurt."

"You were so brave, Sawyer," Jane said. "You saved the entire garrison from that big ugly thing."

"Hey, what was that monster, anyway?" Geoff asked.

"That," Ariel said, turning back from the window, "was an ogre. Not many can defeat such a creature singlehandedly."

"Sawyer did," Jane said proudly. "He even chased away the attacking army."

"Well," Sawyer said, sitting up, "somebody had to do it, right?"

"You moved well in battle," Ariel said. "You remembered your lessons. Well done."

"Thanks," Sawyer said. "But if it hadn't been for Jane's healing spells I would've been toast."

"And if Geoff didn't shield us," Jane said, "we both would've been toast."

"The three of you work well together," Ishara said. "Thank you for saving us."

"No problem," Sawyer said.

"You're welcome," Geoff and Jane said in unison.

"If you feel up to it," Ariel said, "I think we should continue training."

"Okay, cool," Sawyer said with a yawn. "Can I get five more minutes of sleep?"

Jane gave him a playful punch on the shoulder. "No, get your heroic butt up."

While Sawyer dressed, Jane and the others slipped out the door. The room they had occupied was next to the barracks, which currently doubled as a triage for the wounded. Most of the soldiers stopped their activities and turned to watch them. Jane felt uneasy with so many eyes upon her. She leaned close to Ariel and whispered, "They're all looking at us. I don't like it."

"They mean you no harm," Ariel said.

"If you say so," Jane said, still peering about. "Just makes me nervous with all these men watching me."

"You will get used to it," Ishara said. "Besides, they're waiting to see the Stormlord."

The soldiers greeted them with smiles as they walked

past, while others even saluted them with an arm across the chest. When they reached the front door to the keep, which had been somewhat repaired, a loud chorus of cheers arose behind them. Jane spun around and there was Sawyer. He had just emerged from their room and stood there with an open mouth and wide eyes, staring about the barracks. Chants of *Stormlord!* rang throughout the keep.

"A hero can raise morale," Ariel said, "even rally soldiers and inspire them to fight on against impossible odds."

Jane laughed. Sawyer's confusion tickled her and made him that much more adorable.

"Woo-hoo! Sawyer!" she shouted and clapped. Then she joined in the chants of *Stormlord! Stormlord!*

Geoff, Ishara, and Ariel did the same. Sawyer met Jane's gaze and smiled. He placed a hand over his heart and bowed. The cheers that filled the keep grew louder as Sawyer walked toward Jane and the others. Soldiers slapped him on the shoulders and greeted him as if he were famous. Sawyer looked a bit uncomfortable, Jane thought, but he mostly took their adoration in stride as he passed the soldiers.

"Oh my," Jane said. "There won't be any living with him now."

Sawyer joined them a moment later, rubbing his shoulder.

"Ouch," he said. "They beat the hell outta me."

"Want some more healing, Stormlord?" Jane asked, batting her eyelashes at him.

Sawyer flexed his muscles at her. They left the keep and entered the courtyard. It smelled of manure and smoke, and the chilly air took Jane by surprise as she wrapped her arms around herself. The cheer they felt immediately left them as they saw soldiers placing linen-wrapped bodies in a large grave. Dark red stains spotted the walls and colored the dirt in various places around the courtyard. Jane tried to count the bodies in her head, but stopped after she reached twenty.

"They're going to burn them," Geoff said. "They burn the bodies to prevent the spread of disease."

Then, as if on cue, a few soldiers threw lit torches onto the wrapped bodies.

"I think I'm going to be sick," Jane said, covering her nose and mouth.

"It could've been worse," Geoff said. "Usually the sieging army would send diseased carcasses of animals and bodies over the wall with a trebuchet."

"Geoff," Jane said, "what's wrong with you? We don't need to hear that."

"Oh yeah," Geoff said, apparently realizing he'd supplied too much detail. "Sorry."

Jane's attention was drawn to the northern wall that had been destroyed during the battle. At least ten men worked to repair it. Large chunks of the broken wall had been pieced together in makeshift fashion. The repaired wall wasn't going to withstand another assault, however, especially if another ogre attacked. It was the obvious weak spot in the keep's defenses.

"Stormlord!"

Everyone turned to see the garrison commander approach. His long dark hair blew in the chilly breeze as he walked to Sawyer with a large smile on his weather-beaten face. The wound he had suffered yesterday no longer appeared to bother him. He walked to Sawyer and saluted with an arm across the chest.

"Hail, Stormlord," he said. "I am Renfry, the

commander of this garrison. Thank you for your help in defending this keep."

"You're welcome," Sawyer said with a little hesitation, apparently not knowing how to properly react to Renfry's greeting.

Renfry smiled and looked at the others.

"I've never seen such an arrival on the field of battle. We would've surely fallen yesterday had you not dropped in and saved us."

"We are grateful to have been of help," Ariel said. She nodded toward the broken north wall. "It will not withstand another attack."

"No," Renfry said, turning his head to see the repaired wall. "But it's the best we can do. Besides, they will not attack again; not with the Stormlord counted among the keep's defenders."

"They would be foolish to try," Ariel said, glancing at Sawyer. "But be warned, the Shadowlord also has magic he can bring to bear against us. The darkest of magic."

"Aye," Renfry said. "Dark magic and monsters. At least we now have a fighting chance with the five of you here."

Jane peered about. In the daylight and with no battles raging, the garrison appeared to be small and bleak. Its gray scarred walls matched the rough, craggy terrain that surrounded the keep. The heavy wooden front doors were reinforced with iron bars, which made them an impressive barrier. But they, too, bore signs of battle, having been chopped and burned. Renfry looked up at the sun and squinted.

"It's good to see the sun again," he said. "When the Shadowlord and his army arrived, we were certain our doom was at hand."

"If the Shadowlord was leading the army that attacked," Ariel said, "I am curious as to why he did not join the battle yesterday."

"As am I," Renfry said.

"I would not count on reinforcements," Ariel said. "You and your men are brave, but the Shadowlord has yet to bring the full might of his armies against you and against Chalon."

"I know," Renfry said, looking at the ground. "When he does, we'll be here waiting."

Ariel nodded but didn't say anything. Jane frowned and pursed her lips. She felt sad for Renfry and the warriors who defended the keep. If only Lionel would do something to help them.

"Jane," Ariel said. "Perhaps we can tend the wounded soldiers this morning—heal them and give them hope."

"Aye," Renfry said. "Tell me, how does a human girl come to cast druidic healing charms?"

"I'm not sure," she said. "I just do it."

"It is her gift," Ariel added. "She is remarkable. They all are."

"And the boy wizard," Renfry said, grinning. "The small one. Where did he learn his magic?"

"My dad," Geoff said. "He taught me."

Ariel placed a hand on his shoulder. "He is the son of Maelord."

Renfry raised his eyebrows.

"Indeed?" he said. "I never knew Maelord had a son. That crafty ole wizard."

Geoff smiled.

"And I am Ariel." She motioned to Ishara. "The young archer is Ishara."

Renfry regarded Ariel and Ishara. "I believe the two of you saved the south wall from being breached yesterday," he said. "You fought well. Thank you."

Ariel nodded.

It didn't surprise Jane to hear that Ariel and Ishara had held the south wall and beat back the enemy.

"The ogre shattered the north wall, and the east and south walls had heavy damage from their siege engines," Renfry said. "Our supplies are dwindling. I've begun rationing food, but at most we have perhaps two weeks of food in our stores."

"We will do what we can," Ariel said. "Every man and every sword will be needed when the Shadowlord returns."

A rumble of thunder boomed in the distance. Jane looked to the north and saw dark clouds gathering over the mountains. Something made her shiver and she stepped closer to Sawyer.

"Looks like you're right," Renfry said, as he and Ariel also looked north. "The Shadowlord prepares for another attack."

"When they retreated," Geoff said, "did they leave any of their catapults?"

"Aye, some," Renfry said, squinting at Geoff. "We've begun dismantling them so we can make use of the enemy's weapons."

"Want some help?" Sawyer asked.

Jane shot him a glance.

"What? You're gonna be healing and stuff," he said. "I may as well make myself useful, too."

"Aye," Renfry said. "Your help would be most appreciated, Stormlord."

"Geoff and I can help with the watch," Ishara said. "We will be on the eastern wall."

"Very well," Ariel said. "We all have our tasks for the day. Keep a sharp eye out for our enemies."

Sawyer accompanied Renfry to help with claiming the catapults left behind by the Shadowlord's forces, while Geoff and Ishara dashed off to the steps leading to the top of the eastern wall. Jane and Ariel walked back to the keep. Along the way Ariel stopped and regarded Jane with a grin.

"I am proud of you," she said. "You did well yesterday."

"Thanks," she said. "Without your training, we would've been pretty worthless."

"I do not think any of you are worthless."

They entered the keep and went to work changing bandages and healing the injured soldiers. As the day wore on, Jane would take only small breaks to step outside and stretch or maybe to drink a cup of water. Sawyer and the men and had labored the entire day and managed to break down, move, and reassemble three catapults inside the garrison's walls. Given the amount of rubble strewn about, Jane guessed there would be plenty of ammunition.

She looked up on the eastern wall, where Geoff and Ishara had taken up watch. Ishara appeared to be teaching Geoff how to fight and defend himself. They looked like children playing. Then she noticed Geoff seemed to be catching on. He was throwing punches and dodging Ishara's make-believe attacks. Seeing all was well outside, Jane returned to the keep and resumed her healing duties. She was starting to tire, but she didn't care. She was careful not to show it, however, for if Ariel saw her wearing down, then Jane was sure she would have to stop healing.

By the time they had finished, Jane allowed herself to yawn. She looked out a window and saw that darkness had fallen, and with it came a chill in the air.

Jane shivered and wrapped her arms around herself. A few seconds later she felt someone place a blanket over her shoulders. She looked up. It was one of the soldiers she had healed. He was still weak, but he had gotten out of his cot and given Jane his blanket.

"Thank you," Jane said.

"Can't have our healer shivering, can we? Take care that you don't catch a cold, young lady."

He patted her on the back and returned to his cot. Jane remembered his leg had a terrible gash and he had lost so much blood that she wasn't sure if her spells would help him. Jane pulled her blanket tight and went outside. She stood in the courtyard and looked at the stars.

Even in the broken keep with so much death around, Jane couldn't help but be amazed at their brilliance in the black sky. She closed her eyes and took a deep breath. For a moment she was back home on a chilly autumn day and someone in the neighborhood was burning leaves. Jane had always liked fall; it made her think of Halloween and Thanksgiving and sitting by a cozy fire.

Jane waved to Geoff and Ishara, who were sitting side by side sharing a plate of food. They looked happy. Geoff must be having the time of his life. Good for him; he deserved it. Jane glanced about and saw no one was on the west wall. That was strange; perhaps the soldiers who were supposed to guard it were taking a break. She heard men talking and even laughing a little. She saw the soldiers who had worked on the catapults going inside the keep, along with Sawyer. He appeared to be fitting in with them. He hadn't noticed her standing in the courtyard, but that didn't bother her; she could use some time alone.

She walked to the unmanned western wall and went up the steps. Peering over the edge of the ramparts, she saw why it wasn't manned. A sheer drop of at least several hundred feet greeted her. The cliff seemed to go on forever, disappearing into the cold darkness below. Jane leaned on a rampart and looked out over the mountainous terrain. The moonlight provided some illumination, and in the distance the peaks gave way to rolling hills.

"Beautiful, is it not?"

Jane turned and saw Ariel. She was also wearing a blanket around her shoulders to keep away the cold.

"Mmhmm," Jane mused. "There's so much of your world we haven't seen."

"True," Ariel said. "Alluria is both large and magnificent. Perhaps one day you will have the opportunity to see more."

"I'd like that. Let's hope when this is all over there will be an Alluria to explore."

"Aye," Ariel said. For a couple of minutes, they stood in silence on the wall looking out over a dark landscape encrusted with mountaintops.

"Sawyer seems to have made some new friends," Ariel said. "He is strong, and when he puts his mind to it, a hard worker."

"He doesn't think he's a hero," Jane said with a smile. "He still doubts that he's the Stormlord."

"Reluctant heroes always make the best heroes."

Jane nodded.

"I am tired," Ariel said. "I am going to rest now and I think you should do the same."

"I will," Jane said. "I just want to enjoy this view a little longer."

"Very well. Good night."

Jane watched Ariel turn and leave the wall and walk into the keep. The warm glow shining through the windows looked inviting, but she couldn't tear herself away from the view. Jane yawned again, resting her elbows on the cold, rough stone wall and closing her eyes. How did they come to be here? Jane ran through the list of circumstances that led to this moment. If Geoff hadn't found the wizard's key, they would still be home doing what teenagers usually did. Depending on the day, Jane may have been out with her friends or perhaps sitting in the sunroom doing homework and looking out over her neighborhood. Then a funny thought occurred to her; she couldn't remember what day it was back home.

A gust of cool air brushed by her, giving her goosebumps. She opened her eyes just as she heard a scratching sound right below her on the wall. The hair on the back of her neck stood up, and she felt like she was being watched. Peering over the wall, she saw the distinct shape of a large reptilian head. It looked at her with large, amber, snakelike eyes and hissed.

Jane stepped back from the wall. Her heart began to race as she realized she was in danger. She whirled to run for the keep and stopped as a large, writhing black cloud of smoke formed in front of her. It was even darker than the night. Jane's skin crawled as the smoky blackness churned and roiled. She opened her mouth to scream, but was unable to do so. Then a large man wearing black armor emerged from the smoke and loomed over her. Jane tried to catch her breath. Her heart felt like an icy hand had gripped it.

Jane tried to turn her head, but she was unable to look away from the burning red eyes that held her captive. She wanted to run away, but her feet refused to obey her. All she could do was tremble at the sight of the Shadowlord.

CHAPTER THIRTY-THREE
FOR JANE

The Shadowlord reached out and wrapped an arm around Jane's waist with the suddenness of a coiled snake. Jane felt herself lifted off the wall and carried as if she were a ragdoll. She screamed as she punched and beat on her attacker, but she only succeeded in bruising her knuckles and fingers. She placed her hands on the black armor and pushed with all her might, but she might as well have tried to push a tree down; she had no hope of freeing herself. The reptilian creature that had hissed at Jane now climbed over the ramparts and unfurled its wings.

Jane screamed again, this time as loud as she could. The Shadowlord carried Jane to the winged beast and hefted her over the back of the wyvern as he climbed in the saddle.

"Help! Help me!" Jane shouted. She saw people running from the keep to aid her. Some were carrying torches and others were shouting and pointing. Jane saw Ariel and Sawyer racing to her with their weapons drawn.

"Sawyer! Ariel! Help me!" she screamed. "Help me, please!"

The black wyvern flapped its batlike leathery wings and

Jane found herself airborne with the Shadowlord. She screamed again and squirmed, trying to work herself free from her captor's grasp.

"Jane!" Sawyer called. "We're coming!"

The next instant Jane was propelled upward at extraordinary speed as the wyvern took flight. The Shadowlord kept one hand on Jane's back, holding her in place. The sudden lurch made Jane lightheaded and nauseated, and the rush of cold air made her lungs ache. She turned her head and found herself once again reliving the same dream she'd had over and over again, but this time it was real. Below them, the hilly, rocky landscape gave way to a dark, sinister marsh.

The terrain passed by at incredible speed, and everything became a blur. Jane's heart was pounding in her chest, and the pain made her wince and grit her teeth. A few minutes later she saw the dark castle of her dreams looming in the distance. It was perched on a harsh, rocky mountain, and it was the most evil and inhospitable place Jane had ever seen. The massive walled structure stood alone on the mountain, and was crowned by several towers. It was large, but not as large as Chalon, which was a city of thousands.

The tops of the towers were trimmed with snow, and orange light shone through some of the windows. A feeling of dread washed over Jane as they descended. A terrible fate awaited her in that cold, hard place. The combination of being exhausted and overcome with fear was too much for her. Jane's vision blurred again and then she lost consciousness.

"Jane!" Sawyer shouted as he sprinted up the steps to the western wall behind Ariel. "Hang on, Jane!"

When he reached the wall he found Ariel standing at the ramparts, weapons drawn, with her eyes tracking the fast-shrinking flying object in the night sky, by now only a black speck heading north.

"Is that her?" he asked. "Is that Jane and the Shadowlord?"

"It is," Ariel said flatly. "He has taken her and flies to his fortress, the Iron Citadel."

Sawyer scowled and shook his head as he slumped forward against the wall, hammering a fist on the cold rampart. He couldn't believe what had happened. Jane was gone. Just like that, she had been kidnapped by the Shadowlord. What did he want with her? What was he going to do to her? Horrible thoughts of his dropping Jane from a great height or feeding her to some pet monster filled his mind.

"Sawyer," Geoff said, running up behind them, "what happened?"

Sawyer pressed his head against the stone wall and closed his eyes.

"She's gone, Geoff," he said. "Jane's gone."

"What? How?"

"The damn Shadowlord got her. He grabbed her right off this wall and flew away. She's gone."

Sawyer sheathed his sword. He looked at the northern sky and pointed.

"He took her in that direction. He was riding something…I dunno…a dragon, maybe."

"Where would he get a dragon?"

"Shut up, Geoff!" Sawyer snapped. "Who the hell cares? Wake up! There's all kinds of magic and monsters around.

Jane's been kidnapped and you're asking about a stupid dragon?"

Sawyer glared at Geoff. "Damn! I should've been with her. I knew it was a bad idea to come back."

"Sorry," Geoff said, hanging his head. "What do we do now?"

"How do I know? You and Jane wanted to come back to this crazy world, not me. Now look what happened. Jane might be dead by now and we're probably gonna get killed in a war that means nothing to us. Happy now?"

"Hey, Sawyer, I'm sorr—"

"Yeah, I know. You're sorry. I'm sorry I listened to you and Jane and agreed to go through that damn portal again. Everyone's sorry."

He didn't want to hear anything Geoff had to say. Sawyer glanced around, expecting Ariel to chastise him for berating Geoff, but she had slipped away unnoticed. Ishara was nowhere to be found, either.

"And where's Ariel and Ishara?" Sawyer demanded.

"I don't know," Geoff said as he stepped back and gulped.

That also irritated Sawyer. Geoff was always a weak, goofy kid, which was why he got picked on all the time at school.

"What? Don't you have some super cool spell to bring Jane back? No? I guess your daddy the big bad wizard didn't teach you that spell, huh?"

The anger building inside became a rage and he raised his voice to a near shout.

"Yep, this was a real good idea to come back."

Without saying a word, Sawyer turned and walked down the steps past the gathering of awestruck soldiers, none of whom had apparently ever seen the Shadowlord before. The murmuring and uneasy looks among them indicated a considerable drop in their morale. Their fear also irritated Sawyer. He glanced back over his shoulder and saw Geoff following him at a distance. When Sawyer reached the door to the keep Geoff spoke to him.

"Sawyer, I don't know what we do now. I have no idea how to get Jane back. But we gotta try something."

"Yeah? Where do we start, Geoff?"

"Ariel," Geoff said. "She must know where the Shadowlord took her."

"And where is Ishara? Where was she when Jane was getting kidnapped? She could've put an arrow between the Shadowlord's eyes."

"I don't know," Geoff said, "but it isn't her fault either that Jane was kidnapped. Don't blame your friends. We want Jane back too."

Sawyer threw his arms up.

"Okay Geoff, *buddy*, *pal*," he said. "How do we get Jane back? Use that big nerd brain of yours and figure out what our next move is."

"Hey, c'mon Sawyer," Geoff said. "That's enough."

Sawyer took a breath. Geoff was right. Bullying him wasn't going to help get Jane back.

"Yeah. Sorry," Sawyer grunted. "So how do we get Jane back?"

Geoff turned his head to the north and rubbed his arms while Sawyer folded his arms across his chest and stared at him.

"Like I said; let's ask Ariel for help."

Sawyer pointed at Geoff. "Okay. Now you're thinking."

Without another word, he ran into the keep, with Geoff following close behind. Sawyer went straight to their room. All eyes were on him as he passed the infirmary. He didn't care. As far as he was concerned Jane's kidnapping was their fault, too. This was their war, not his, and certainly not Jane's. He pushed the door open and stepped inside.

Ariel and Ishara had their backs to him and Geoff as they entered.

"Ariel," Sawyer said. "I know how much this war means to your people and all, but Geoff and I need to get Jane back. We're going to rescue her. Can you help us?"

Ariel stopped what she was doing and turned around to face them. It was then that Sawyer noticed her backpack and belongings. She was packing her things. She tilted her head and raised an eyebrow.

"Are you serious?" Ariel said. "After all you have done for us, after everything Jane has done, each of you having risked so much on our behalf. Do you honestly think you need to ask for help?"

Sawyer forced a grin and shook his head.

"But we don't know where she is," Geoff said. "How will we find her?"

"I told you I know where she is," Ariel said, resuming her packing. "She has been taken to the Iron Citadel, to the place where evil dwells."

"But how do we rescue her?" Sawyer asked. "The Shadowlord went toe to toe with you and almost beat you. How do we get her outta there?"

Ariel stopped packing again and looked at Sawyer.

"First we find Jane," she said. "Then we plan her escape. Agreed?"

"Yeah, thanks, Ariel," Sawyer said.

Ariel looked at him for a few seconds, then Ishara handed her a worn burlap sack. Sawyer had seen it before, but he'd assumed it was more druid stuff, so when Ariel pulled out piece after piece of armor and laid them out on the bed, Sawyer's mouth fell open. He couldn't take his eyes off the elven battle armor.

"Wow! I was wondering about that armor," Geoff said. "It saved us from Lady Seqwil at Dad's tower. We hid behind it."

"And now it is yours, Sawyer," Ariel said.

Sawyer marveled at its workmanship, which was far superior to the suits of armor the soldiers of the garrison wore.

"Sawyer."

He snapped out of his mental musings and looked at Ariel.

"It is yours," she said as she gestured at it. "Only a true hero is worthy of such armor. You have earned the right to wear it."

"Me?" he said. "Oh man, this is awesome. Thank you, really. Thank you."

"No, thank *you*," Ariel said.

"It's the coolest looking armor I've ever seen," Sawyer said, running his fingers along the chest piece.

"It's priceless," Geoff said. "The attention to detail is fantastic. What's it made of?"

"Adamantium," Ishara said. "All elven battle armor is made of it. There is no stronger metal."

"Come," Ariel said. "Ishara and I will show you how to wear this armor. You will need it for the task ahead."

"Do we have time? We need to hurry and rescue Jane," Sawyer said.

"This will not take long," Ariel assured him.

For the next several minutes Ariel and Ishara outfitted Sawyer with the armor.

"Hey!" Geoff said, pointing at Sawyer. "The armor! It's changing its size to fit Sawyer. Look at that!"

"Of course," Ishara said as she helped Sawyer with a gauntlet. "It is enchanted, remember?"

"It's so light," Sawyer said, waving his arms around. "It doesn't feel like I'm wearing armor. It feels like clothes."

"As it should," Ariel said. "A foe would be hard-pressed to harm you now."

Sawyer put the helmet on and felt it shrink to fit his head. It was snug like a football helmet, but not nearly as bulky, and his vision wasn't impaired at all.

"Looks like it was made for you," Geoff said. "You look like a comic book hero."

"Perhaps it *was* made for you," Ariel said. "Who knows? Now, if you two heroes would be kind enough to procure some furs from the garrison's storage for us; it will be cold and harsh where we are going, so we must be prepared."

Sawyer nodded.

"Go," Ariel said. "We depart as soon as you are packed. I will not leave Jane to a dark fate."

"Right. We're on it. C'mon, Geoff. Let's get some furs."

Sawyer and Geoff hurried to Renfry, who did a double take when he saw Sawyer's armor. He had the stores opened for them and bade them take whatever they needed. Renfry was, however, concerned to hear they were leaving the garrison. He was counting on their help for the next battle, but Jane came first. For Sawyer, it was an easy choice. The garrison was on its own now.

They gathered the furs Ariel wanted and returned to their room. Ariel and Ishara were done packing and were waiting for Sawyer and Geoff.

"So Ariel," Geoff said as he stuffed his furs and extra clothes into a backpack. "What's going to happen to this place when we leave? Commander Renfry seemed disappointed when we told him we're leaving."

"I am sure he was," Ariel said. "Before we leave I will send a message to your father. Lionel may be afraid to stand against the Shadowlord, but Maelord is not. I have no doubt that he will find a way to send aid."

Geoff smiled. "I'd like to see Dad cast spells in battle."

"A wizard the likes of your father can turn the tide of a battle," Ariel said.

They walked out into the courtyard. The orange glow of torches cast eerie shadows across the battered keep. Ariel stopped and held her arms out from her sides. Next she closed her eyes and swung her head back. After a minute of watching her stand silently with her arms outstretched, Sawyer leaned over to Geoff and Ishara and whispered, "What's she doing?"

"She calls for help," Ishara said. "It is a summons. Soon she will be answered."

"What's she summoning?" Geoff asked. "Is she calling the gryphons back?"

"I hope not," Sawyer said.

He fidgeted and peered into the night sky. This was going to be a long night if he had to fly on the back of another gryphon.

"We shall soon see," Ishara said.

A few minutes later a raven gently landed on her arm. Ariel smiled and greeted the bird with a gentle rub of its chest and back. Sawyer let out a sigh. He felt like a ton of bricks was lifted from his chest.

As they watched, the raven, still perched on Ariel's arm, extended one of its feet and spread its wings for balance while Ariel tied a message around its leg. When she was done she looked the raven in the eyes and said "Maelord."

The raven flapped its wings and flew into the night. Ariel watched after the raven long after it was gone from Sawyer's sight.

"I'd hoped we would have the Stormlord with us a little while longer," Renfry said, walking up to the group, "and a druid's healing charms always come in handy. As would having a wizard and an archer."

"I am sorry," Ariel said, "but we must leave."

"You know what will happen if this garrison falls," Renfry said. "You would sacrifice us all for the sake of one?"

"Of course not," Ariel said. "I have just sent a message to Maelord in Chalon asking him to send as many soldiers as he can muster to help defend your garrison. The war does not hinge on whether we hold this keep or not. Even if we stay, the keep is doomed. Withdraw, leave it for the Shadowlord, and regroup with the army of Chalon."

Renfry searched Ariel's eyes. As he watched, Sawyer thought he had come to the same conclusion as well.

"I'm sorry for Jane," Renfry said with a grim expression. "If you're going where I think you are, then you go to your deaths. The Iron Citadel is impenetrable."

"Perhaps," Ariel said. "No army has ever breached its

walls, but a small band may succeed where an army cannot. We must try."

Renfry looked at the ground and then lifted his gaze. He seemed to survey each of them.

"Every man here wants to join you," he said. "I hope you find your friend. Go and save her if you can, but I don't expect to see any of you again."

"Help will come, but I cannot say when," Ariel said. "Heed my words and withdraw while you can. Save your men and yourself."

"The enemy holds the pass through the mountains," Renfry said. "The only possible route left is through the Shattered Moor. However, there are other dangers within that accursed marshland."

"Agreed," Ariel said. "It is a dangerous path, but we have no choice."

Renfry nodded and looked at them. He seemed to be silently saying good-bye. Sawyer responded with a slight nod to the garrison commander.

"I wish you luck," Renfry said. "May whatever powers for good that remain keep you safe."

Ariel nodded to him and they left the keep. Once outside the walls, Ariel crouched and motioned for them to join her. Ariel looked at each of them.

"Listen well," she said. "Commander Renfry is right. We travel to danger. You should know…we may not succeed. And if we do, perhaps not all of us will return."

Sawyer frowned. He didn't want to hear all the doom and gloom. He studied the faces of his companions. Something was missing, he felt it in his heart. Jane's absence was noticeable. Everything seemed wrong without her in their little group. His gaze settled on Ariel. She was intently observing him. Did she expect a reaction? If so, what sort of reaction? He didn't know how else to prove that he was down for the journey to rescue Jane. It didn't matter to Sawyer where she was or who held her captive. He was going to try and save her even if he had to go to the Iron Citadel alone.

"Are we ready?" Ariel asked.

"Look, I'm going regardless," Sawyer said. "If any of you want to stay, fine. Someone draw me a map and I'll find Jane."

Ariel looked at Sawyer for a minute, then she said, "I once asked Jane why the three of you saved the unicorn from the goblin raiding party in the Spirewood Forest. Without hesitation she simply replied, 'It was the right thing to do'. This journey to save Jane is the right thing to do as well. She also said friends stick together."

Those words sounded like something Jane would say. She was loyal to those she cared for and wouldn't hesitate to offer her help. Sawyer imagined her smile. Then he remembered how she had saved his life the day before in the battle. As she healed him he felt a warmth, or maybe it was part of Jane being transferred to him. At least that's the best way he could describe it.

"She should be here," Sawyer said. "With us. No matter what's waiting for us in the swamps. Like you said Ariel, we have to try. If we don't, then she's as good as dead, right?"

"Spoken like a true hero," Ariel said. "I believe the sword chose well, *Stormlord.*"

Perhaps he could get used to being called 'Stormlord' after all. This time he liked it. Ariel stood and rested her hands on her weapons. She smiled a thin, determined smile and said, "For Jane."

"For Jane," the others said.

Chapter Thirty-Four

Zorn

Smoke. Something was burning. Between sleep and consciousness, Jane's eyes wouldn't open. She was falling, or maybe she thought she was, or maybe she was floating. Why wouldn't her eyes open? She struggled to open them, but she couldn't do the simplest thing. She wanted to wake up. Waves of warmth lapped over her. It was a comforting, relaxing feeling, but there was a sense of danger in the back of her mind. Was she hallucinating? Her head swam with an eerie mindscape, ranging from her running through a maze of dark corridors to cowering in a shadowy corner of a room that watched her.

When Jane did open her eyes, everything was a blur and she doubted if she had really awakened. She was lying in a large, comfortable bed. The smoky smell lingered. It smelled like someone nearby was burning hickory wood. She loved that smell; it reminded her of autumn and how she would help her father rake and burn leaves. She closed her eyes tightly and pressed her knuckles against her eyelids, rubbing them in a semicircular fashion. When she opened them again, her vision had cleared. She lay in a beautiful canopy bed made of dark mahogany with thin, veiled curtains on each side.

Jane raised her head and sat up. Her surroundings were completely unfamiliar. She pulled back a curtain and saw a richly decorated bedroom that took her breath away. The room itself was huge, at least as large as the suites she had stayed in with her entire family when they took what her dad called a luxury vacation. All manner of sumptuous indulgences lay prepared for her. As Jane slid her feet onto the thick, carpeted floor, she saw a white marble fireplace with the remnants of a fire smoldering within. Glowing red embers flickered in the gray ashes. She counted five oversized plush velvet chairs in the room. Each chair burgeoned with plump cushions with various floral patterns.

Along the walls hung paintings of wondrous wild landscapes and lifelike portraits. The portraits gave Jane a small shiver, because they seemed to be watching her. Against the wall, near the oversized bed, was a white marble dressing table with a large round gold-rimmed mirror. Laid out across the smooth surface were brushes, combs, and hand mirrors made of gold and silver. Lying open on the far side of the dressing table was a box made of the same dark wood as the bed. Inside was an assortment of brooches, rings, and necklaces, and the most beautiful piece of jewelry she had ever seen—a tiara made of crystal and gold inlaid with rubies. This was the bedroom of a queen or a princess.

On the other side of the fireplace was an ornately carved wardrobe large enough for Jane to stand in. It was flanked by two large and equally ornate chests. On the other side of the room was a matching wardrobe and chests.

She continued to marvel at her surroundings. The

cathedral ceiling was at least ten feet high, and the large wooden beams overhead looked as if they had just been polished. Then Jane saw a beautiful long-sleeved dress hanging on the other side of the bed. It was an off-white with red and gold lace trim.

"I must be dreaming," she said aloud.

She walked to the dress and felt the fabric with her thumb and index finger. Silk. It was the kind of dress she thought brides in fairy tales wore. It was embroidered with gold thread. Jane shook her head as she admired it. She wouldn't begin to hazard a guess the amount of time required to create such a dress.

Her attention was drawn to two sets of mahogany glass doors on the other side of the room. The curtains that covered the glass were of the same material as those around the bed.

She went to the closest set of doors and opened them. The sun was setting over a gray, craggy landscape. She seemed to be in the tallest tower of a huge, bleak castle. Jane looked down into the courtyard, which was at least a hundred feet below. There was a steep cliff at the far edge of her balcony with jagged rocks at the bottom. Jane leaned on a carved granite rail on which rested two granite gargoyles. She hoped she would see someone below, but the courtyard was empty.

As far as Jane was concerned, it was large enough to hold a football game. How strange it was not to see a single soul milling about. She scanned the courtyard for some grass or a tree or shrub; something green. Anything that indicated there was some life present would've been a welcome sight.

She saw the remnants of a garden toward the far side of

the courtyard. Everything had long since withered and died, leaving only twisted husks of whatever had once grown there. It would've once been a wonderful place, but now all Jane saw was desolation. She closed her eyes and rubbed her temples as she tried to gather her memories. How did she get here?

There had been a battle, maybe the day before. She remembered a giant monster tearing down a castle wall, and rows of bodies burning. Her eyes shot open and her hands trembled at these horrible memories. She had friends too, didn't she? Yes, Ariel, Geoff, and Ishara were her friends, and there was one more. Someone she cared for, but for some reason she only saw his face. His warm smile made Jane think of the dimples in his cheeks. He was funny and charming, too. But what was his name? Her mind was a fog, with images of faces meandering just on the edge of her memory.

Then Jane's eyes widened and she placed her hands over her mouth.

"Sawyer," she said.

Speaking his name brought back everything. She was in Alluria with Sawyer and Geoff to help defeat…oh no! Jane's heart began to pound as she frantically searched for a way out. She had to get out of the castle and back to her friends. She ran back into the bedroom and clutched the door handle. It, too, was made of gold and shaped like a dragon. She pulled and pushed, but the door was locked. She began to beat on the door and shout for help.

After several minutes of pounding and yelling, Jane stopped to catch her breath. The door was solid oak; she would need an axe and a couple of days to hack her way through it. She felt her side for the dagger Ariel had given her. It was missing. She looked around the room for anything else she might use to defend herself. She settled on an iron poker by the fireplace.

A sense of alarm and dread fell over Jane. If they'd taken her knife, what else had they done? She looked at her clothes. They were still in place, and other than her missing dagger, everything was where it should be. She hadn't been harmed.

A jingle of keys from the other side of the door was followed by a sharp click. She raised the poker and took a step back, prepared to defend herself against whoever entered the room. As the door slowly swung open, Jane gritted her teeth and braced for an imminent attack. Her ears throbbed and her chest heaved with every breath she took.

The dark figure of the Shadowlord walked into the room. A multitude of black, smoky tentacles undulated around him, giving him a grotesque, monstrous appearance. The piercing red eyes that looked at Jane from under a spiked silver and black helm chilled her. The Shadowlord stood by the table and seemed to regard Jane for a moment.

"What do you want?" Jane demanded. "Let me go!"

He turned around, removed his helmet with both hands, and faced her. Jane's mouth slowly dropped open. He was striking, with his well-combed dark hair and dark eyes. He looked to be in his mid or late twenties. He smiled thinly at Jane as she raised her weapon higher. It didn't matter how handsome he was; Jane's skin crawled as she looked at him.

"You would have me be a monster, wouldn't you?" he asked.

His voice was deep and commanding, but it was also gentle and flowed like a melody.

"You *are* a monster," Jane said. "Why did you bring me here?"

"What's your name, girl?" Zorn asked, ignoring Jane's question.

"I'm not telling you," Jane said, stepping back.

Zorn lowered his gaze at her, his eyes drilling into her mind. She felt a little queasy, then she became disoriented. She shook her head and blinked her eyes tightly. The feeling of being compelled to answer overtook her.

"J...Jane."

"Well, Jane," he said. "My name is Zorn Malverk. How do you like your accommodations? Are they acceptable?"

Jane didn't answer.

He approached her with his hand out. Jane wanted to hit him over the head with the poker and fend him off, but her arms refused to obey. Instead, he gently took the weapon, looking at her all the while. After he had disarmed Jane he studied her, like he was sizing her up for something. Jane's legs began to shake and her palms were moist with sweat.

"Don't be afraid," he said. "You're an intriguing girl. You have both fire and compassion within you. But there is something else..."

This was weird, Jane thought. He wanted something.

Her cheeks felt warm, as did her hands.

"What do you want with me?" she asked.

Zorn thought for a few seconds as he continued to study her.

"You remind me of something I've lost."

"What's that supposed to mean?"

"To you...nothing," he said, turning back toward the table. "But it's keeping you alive...for now."

Jane winced. It seemed that she was to be an object for his amusement, like a caged animal at a zoo. And when he became bored with her she was as good as dead. Zorn picked up his helmet and looked at Jane again.

"No harm will come to you," he said, "so long as you do as you're told and don't try to escape."

Jane swallowed and nodded haltingly. Despite his threat, she was absolutely going to try an escape when the time was right. Zorn turned and walked toward the door, stopping at the dress Jane had noticed earlier. He held it up for her to see.

"Do you not approve of your dress? It was crafted by the finest makers in Alluria."

"It's gorgeous," Jane said, never taking her eyes off Zorn.

He gently laid the dress across the fluffy bed.

"How splendid you'd look wearing it," he said. "I've been watching you for some time. I'd wager you're the daughter of nobility."

A young servant girl appeared at the door carrying a tray of food. She appeared to be close to Jane's age, but she was slender, almost too slender. Her hair was tucked under a white wimple and she wore a plain gray dress. As soon as she saw Zorn, she cast her gaze to her feet and curtsied. She scurried past him like a mouse and placed the tray on the table, then turned to Jane and curtsied with a smile before hurrying out of the room.

Zorn motioned to the tray of food. "You should eat," he said. "I'll return when you're done."

He turned and left the room. Jane heard him lock the door and then let out a long sigh. In the back of her mind an alarm went off. If that serving girl was any indication of how he treated people, she was in serious trouble.

Jane frowned. She was relieved Zorn was gone, but something about him confused her. He could kill her any time, so why was she still alive?

The aroma of the food made her stomach growl loudly, and Jane realized she hadn't eaten for a long time. She sat at the table and inspected the meal that the servant had delivered. It consisted of roasted pheasant with a variety of vegetables and bread. A tall crystal glass filled with a sparkling wine rested beside her plate.

Wait, what if the food was poisoned? She shook her head. What sense was there in poisoning her? No, he was keeping her alive for some awful reason. She leaned over and smelled the pheasant, which made her mouth water. She pinched off a small piece and placed it in her mouth. It was delicious. Jane sipped the wine, swishing it around in her mouth before swallowing. Nothing wrong with it that she could tell.

She closed her eyes and inhaled deeply. Leaning back in her chair, she let the tension and fear that had gripped her earlier melt away. She relaxed her shoulders and took another drink of wine. Glancing around at all the luxuries in her room, Jane nodded to herself. She could get used to this. It beat running through the woods eating berries and whatever else…wait, who did she do that with? Someone had led her and some friends through the woods, but Jane couldn't remember her name at the moment. Her thoughts had become fuzzy. Oh well, it would come to her later.

Jane savored every bite. It was by far the best meal she had eaten in Alluria. She finished sooner than she had wanted, but she couldn't help it. Pushing herself away from the table, Jane went over to the dress, which still lay on the bed. She picked it up and walked to the mirror on the dressing table. She held it against her body and looked at her reflection. She was surprised to see how well it appeared to fit her.

She looked like a fairy tale princess. She rushed to the bed and gently laid the dress down. She removed her clothes and carefully wriggled her way into the beautiful gown. Looking down, she noticed a pair of matching red embroidered slippers with pointed toes, the perfect footwear for the dress. She slipped them on. To her surprise, they were a perfect fit.

Jane stood in front of the mirror again and twirled around, looking at herself from all angles. Zorn had assumed she was noble, which is exactly how she felt wearing the dress. She pursed her lips and made a pouty face in the mirror, then lifted the back of her hair up and turned her head slightly. There was a clasp on the back of the dress she wasn't able to reach, so she left it unfastened.

Jane caught a glimpse of her eyes in the mirror and stopped. What was she doing? She rubbed her temples with her fingers and tried to concentrate on past events. Her mind was a jumble of images that floated and swirled around in a haze. She felt strange, like she was descending from a cloud of euphoria. A terrible feeling began to creep into her heart. Then Jane remembered everything; she had been kidnapped by the Shadowlord!

Panic gripped her again as she spun about and searched the room for an exit other than the locked door. She didn't have much time; he would return soon and expected to see her in the dress. She had to escape. She rushed to the balcony again. It was cooler now, and she could see her breath in the air. She crossed her arms in front of her and rubbed her shoulders. What did he want with her? Why would he kidnap *her*? A myriad of dreadful things ran through her mind.

Jane went back inside and closed the door to the balcony. Still rubbing her shoulders, she paced about the room looking for a weapon. Wait, she had the poker from the fireplace in her hand earlier, didn't she? Jane glanced toward the fireplace and saw it resting against the stonework, just where the Shadowlord had left it. Why didn't she use it on him? Jane shook her head. Her thoughts were like layers of cobwebs. It was difficult to focus. Something was very wrong with her.

Suddenly she heard a key being inserted in the lock on the door. She quickly grabbed the poker again and dashed to the door. She hid behind it and raised the poker over her head. She kept thinking *knock him out and run, knock him out and run*. The door opened, and Jane gritted her teeth while raising her weapon higher as Zorn entered the room. He had removed his armor and wore a white tunic with black breeches and high black boots.

Zorn closed the door and scanned the room for her. His back was to Jane, making this the perfect time to strike with all her strength. Now, now, now, she thought, but her body simply wouldn't obey. Why couldn't she bring herself to hit Zorn over the head and escape? What was wrong with her? Jane let out a barely audible grunt, but it was loud enough for Zorn to hear. He turned around and saw she was ready to attack him. Zorn lowered his chin and grinned dryly at her.

"Perhaps I should've left my armor on," he said. "I

admire your bravery, but I am not so easily vanquished."

"You kidnapped me," Jane struggled to say. "You're the Shadowlord. You killed—"

"Yes," he said, stepping forward and taking Jane's weapon away again. "I've killed many."

Zorn looked into her eyes and Jane felt herself relax and her breathing become normal. He smelled like roses in a sweet spring rain. He caressed her cheek with his index finger. Jane grimaced, turned her head, and pulled away. His touch made her skin crawl.

"Jane," he said, "do you honestly think this crude piece of iron would harm me?"

He dropped the poker, but kept his eyes on her.

Jane lowered her head. She was so ashamed of herself she wanted to cry. "It's the only thing I could find," she said.

Zorn placed a hand beneath her chin and gently tilted her head up.

"Even if you managed to get past the castle walls, you would perish in the cold."

"I'll take my chances," Jane said.

Zorn opened the door and stepped aside, beckoning for Jane to leave the room.

"Then go. You are free."

Jane looked at the roughhewn hall beyond the door. She took a step toward it. She could go and be with her friends again, maybe even go home. She could be with…another handsome face drifted on the edge of her memory. What was his name? Samuel? Sean? She knew it just a moment ago, but she had forgotten who he was. He was important to her, maybe he still was, but why couldn't she remember his name? She felt Zorn's eyes on her and in her head a command echoed. Jane slowly turned to face him. The smile etched on his face looked more like a sneer.

"You see? I am undeniable, Jane."

Jane felt her dress slip off one of her shoulders. Zorn reached around her. Jane tensed and closed her eyes as she pulled her sleeve up over her shoulder. She felt his hands on the back of her neck. She heard a small snap behind her as Zorn fastened her dress.

"There," he said. "Better now?"

"Yes," Jane said. She was trembling.

Chapter Thirty-Five
The Iron Citadel

Jane tossed and turned that night. Every time she drifted off to sleep, she awoke with a start. The faces of her friends still swirled in and out of her mind. Each one seemed to be calling to her, warning her of something dreadful.

The face she saw more than the others was that of a handsome, tanned teenager. He stood in a sunlit meadow waiting for her to come to him, his smile and friendly face beckoning her. In her dreams Jane tried to go to him, but she was in a shadowy forest, and something prevented her from stepping into the light. She held out her hand and called out.

"Sawyer!"

Jane sat up in bed with a start. She was covered in sweat and she trembled all over. She pulled the covers up around her chin and peered about the room. The fireplace glowed a dim red from the embers of the dying fire, and her room took on a sinister ambiance. A beam of moonlight trickled in through an opening in the curtains covering the doors to the balcony, and one was slightly ajar. Jane caught her breath as she stared at the doors. She was sure she had closed and locked them before she went to bed.

"What's happening to me? I have to get out of here. I'm going crazy."

Jane sighed, "Of course you're going crazy. You're talking to yourself."

Jane lay back down and stared at the canopy above her. A tear rolled from her eye and moistened her ear as she let out a long sigh.

"Sawyer, where are you?"

She turned over and pulled the covers up around her head. She wanted to get out of bed and close the balcony door again, but a chill ran down her back. She sobbed under the covers for a minute, then realized she was acting like a scared mouse. That wasn't like her at all. She gritted her teeth, threw back the covers, and hopped out of bed. She marched to the balcony door and slammed it shut.

Jane turned the lock and stopped. Yes, she had done this just before climbing into bed. How could the doors be unlocked and open? She peeked through the curtains. The haze-covered moon loomed high overhead, its dim light allowing her to scan the balcony. She didn't see anyone or anything out of place; all looked as it did earlier. She pulled the curtain and propped a chair under the door handle for added reinforcement, then went across the room and slid a heavy wooden chest in front of the door leading to the hall.

"No harm will come to you," Jane said in a tone that mocked Zorn's voice. "So long as you do as you're told and don't try to escape. Yeah, right."

Jane jumped back into bed, buried herself under the covers, and curled her knees to her chest, watching the last smoldering embers die.

Morning brought with it a raw chill. Jane opened her

eyes for a moment and then closed them. She was tired from lack of sleep and her head ached. Another migraine. Her ears pounded and there was a stinging pain behind her eyes. Normally she could feel her headaches coming on, but this one surprised her. It must've been triggered from stress and lack of sleep. Jane closed her eyes and rubbed her forehead.

A knock at the door roused her, and Jane winced in pain as she sat up.

"Who is it?"

"Gertrude, my lady. I have your breakfast."

The voice on the other side of the door sounded young and even a little sheepish, or perhaps nervous. Jane carefully rolled out of bed and went over to the barricaded door. She gritted her teeth and pushed the chest back into its original position, noting that it took considerably more effort with a headache. There was another knock at the door.

"My lady, may I come in?"

"Yep, come in," Jane said.

There was a rattle of keys and the door opened. It was the same young girl as before carrying a shiny silver tray of food. She was dressed in the same gray dress, while her head was still covered with a plain white wimple. The servant smiled and curtsied to Jane.

"Your breakfast, Lady Jane," she said as she placed the tray on a nearby table and pulled a chair out for her.

"I'm not a lady," Jane said as she put on a robe. "I'm Jane. Just Jane."

The serving girl curtsied again and lowered her eyes. "As you wish," she said. "May I bring you anything else?"

Jane looked at the food on the table. She wasn't sure if she should even try to eat anything. There was a full platter of fruit, cheese, bread, water, potatoes, and ham. Her stomach growled.

"I assume none of this food is poisoned, because if the Shadowlord wanted me dead he'd have killed me by now."

"Oh no, my lady," Gertrude said. "Lord Zorn has given me strict instructions to see to your comfort. Would you rather have something else to eat?"

"No," Jane said as she sat at the table and poured herself a glass of water from a small silver pitcher on the tray. "What's your name again?"

"Gertrude, my la…"

Jane smiled. Gertrude returned her smile.

"I like your name," Jane said. "You don't hear it every day where I come from. Would you like something to eat?"

"Oh no, please," Gertrude said. "I can't."

"Why not?"

"I'm not supposed to."

Jane studied the serving girl. She looked underfed. She had a friendly face, however, and Jane appreciated that.

"Please," Jane said, pushing an empty chair toward her. "I can't eat all of this food. And since you're here we may as well be friends, right?"

Gertrude wrung her hands and shifted her weight from one foot to the other.

"I'm only supposed to serve your meals and clean your room."

"You can't work and clean on an empty stomach, and we can't let this food spoil, can we? Please have a seat and talk with me."

Gertrude obeyed Jane and sat at the table, but she kept her hands folded in her lap and her head down.

"You don't need to be shy," Jane said as she passed a plate of fruit and cheese to Gertrude. "I have a feeling friends are going to be hard to come by in this place."

Gertrude carefully placed a slice of apple in her mouth and chewed slowly. Jane, however, wasted no time in shoveling a couple of pieces of cheese into her mouth, and she sipped her water as she chewed. She swallowed, and then poured a goblet of water for Gertrude. The serving girl took the goblet and sipped it as well. Jane took a fork and picked a few pieces of hot roasted ham from her plate and placed them on Gertrude's.

The serving girl's eyes widened at the sight. It must've looked like a feast to her. Jane considered how difficult it must be to serve food that she could never eat herself. It would be torture to stand by and watch someone else eat while you were hungry.

"Were you kidnapped too?" Jane asked.

Gertrude looked up from her food and glanced curiously at Jane before shaking her head.

"I guess I'm the lucky one, then," Jane said.

She considered the possibility of asking Gertrude to help her escape. But could Jane trust her? She really didn't have a choice; it was worth a try. For the best chance of success, she and Gertrude had to become friends, which was what Jane had planned to do anyway.

"Where are you from?" Jane asked.

Gertrude swallowed a mouthful of ham before answering. "My family is from a small village in Norland."

"Norland? Where's that?"

"It's the frozen kingdom to the north."

"Really? How is it you're here? You know, serving the Shadowlord and all."

"My family died when I was very young."

Jane realized her question must've brought back terrible memories for the girl and felt ashamed for asking such a personal question.

"I'm sorry," she said. "I didn't mean to—"

"It's okay La-um Jane. I didn't know them well. As I said, I was very young."

"Do you ever want to go home? Back to your village?"

"Oh no," Gertrude said. "It's no longer there. It was burned to the ground."

Jane stopped chewing and looked at Gertrude. She started to put the clues together.

"So your village was attacked by Zorn and you were taken prisoner?"

"Oh no," Gertrude said. "Raiders from Uln attacked my village. I was brought here to serve Lord Zorn. It's the only real home I've ever known."

"Wait, you *were* taken prisoner then? Haven't you ever wanted to escape? Get out of here and start your life over?"

Gertrude sat and thought while she quietly ate another slice of apple. She looked at Jane.

"No. Where would I go? What would I do?"

"Anywhere, anything," Jane said, stunned by Gertrude's answer and her acceptance of a life in servitude. "You can go to Chalon and find work there."

"Chalon? The shining city to the south? Have you been?"

"Oh yes," Jane said. "My friends and I stayed in the castle overlooking the city."

"Is it as beautiful as they say?"

Gertrude's blue eyes were fixed on Jane and she had leaned forward. Jane's first thought was to say that no, it wasn't beautiful, as in a fairy tale, but a crowded, dangerous, and depressing place. She didn't want to crush Gertrude's dreams of a beautiful city to the south, however.

"Yes," she said. "It's a wonderful place."

Gertrude leaned back and took a drink of water.

"Then why do they make war on us?"

"What do you mean?" Jane asked.

"Everyone knows Chalon is led by a bloodthirsty tyrant who will stop at nothing to rule all the lands."

Jane nearly choked on a bit of ham.

"Lionel? Bloodthirsty?"

Jane laughed at the thought of Lionel leading an army anywhere, much less against the Shadowlord.

"You've got it all wrong," she said. "Chalon is under attack. Zorn is the bad guy."

A confused look fell over Gertrude's face as she tore off a piece of bread and placed it in her mouth. Apparently she was having a difficult time believing what she heard, too.

"It's the truth," Jane said. "Armies from here are moving south."

"It doesn't make sense," Gertrude said. "Zorn is a good and just ruler. Why would he wage war on a neighboring kingdom?"

"I think you've been misinformed," Jane said. "I've seen what he's done to villages and farms. It's horrifying. Zorn is *not* a good and just ruler."

They sat in silence for a few minutes, eating their breakfast. Then Gertrude leaned forward again.

"The forests," she said. "Are they as beautiful as the stories say?"

"Oh, yes. The forests are wonderful, magical places.

They're filled with fairies, unicorns, and druids."

"Oh, I so want to see them," Gertrude said, nearly breathless. "To see a unicorn, that would be amazing."

Jane placed a hand over Gertrude's.

"It is," she said with a wide grin. "To see a unicorn is to see love. They're the most beautiful creatures in the world."

Gertrude gasped and covered her mouth.

"You've seen a unicorn?"

Jane nodded.

"Oh, how lucky you are! I wish I could see one someday. Tell me, did it shimmer and glow like in the stories?"

"Oh, yes," Jane said. "They shimmer and their beauty fills your heart. Their fur is so soft and they smell of honeysuckle and wildflowers."

Gertrude nearly jumped out of her seat. She stared at Jane in awe as Jane nodded again. "You *touched* a unicorn?"

"Perhaps we can go to the forest someday," Jane said. "I have a friend who's a druid. I bet she can summon a unicorn for you if you wish."

"A druid?" Gertrude said. "You know a druid?"

"Mmhmm. Ariel. She's the greatest druid ever."

Gertrude's mouth fell open.

"I thought druids only existed in legends and stories. Can they really cast charms of healing? Make things grow? Calm a storm?"

"Oh yes," Jane smiled. "They can do all that and more."

"You are blessed beyond measure," Gertrude said, slumping back in her chair. "Your life is most wondrous."

An idea suddenly popped into Jane's head. She licked her lips and leaned forward to whisper, "Tell you what. If you bring a dead flower or dried plant next time you come to see me, I'll show you something I know you'll like."

"What? What will you show me?"

Jane placed a finger to her lips and winked at Gertrude.

"It's a secret. You can't tell anyone, okay?"

Gertrude looked suspiciously at Jane. She seemed to be considering the possibilities of Jane's secret.

"It's really cool," Jane said, nodding in encouragement. "You'll like it. I promise."

"Cool?" Apparently the term confused Gertrude.

"Oh," Jane said. "Let's just say it's something you won't forget."

Pushing her chair back, Gertrude stood and put her hands together in front of her.

"Very well. If you are done with your breakfast, Jane, may I take your tray?"

"Yes. Thank you, Gertrude."

Jane leaned back in her chair and brushed a lock of hair behind her ear. Her migraine was nearly gone; it seemed a little food and pleasant company helped chase it away. Gertrude took the tray, curtsied, and walked to the door.

"Oh, Gertrude," Jane said, turning her head to see the serving girl. "You don't need to curtsy to me, okay? I'm not a noble."

"As you wish," Gertrude said.

"And...," Jane stood. "May I call you Trudy?"

"I'd like that," Gertrude said with a smile. "I'd like that very much."

She turned and left. Jane noticed she didn't hear the rattle of keys or the door being locked, so she walked to the door and tested the knob. She opened the door just enough to peer outside. Maybe she had a chance of escaping, but she would have to plan well. She had no idea how to leave the castle unnoticed once she left her room, and, she would probably have to survive in cold weather. How far had she been taken when she was kidnapped? How would she get back to the others? Were they coming to rescue her?

Jane went to one of the large wardrobes and opened it. Just as she suspected, nothing but luxurious gowns hung inside. She sighed. They were all awesome. She ran her fingers over the soft fabrics. Velvet and silk. They were hardly the materials needed for a long journey in the cold, however. Jane glanced at the door. Had Trudy left the door unlocked on purpose? If so, she was Jane's new best friend.

Jane went back and opened the door again. Across the hall a torch burned in a sconce. The dark gray stones in the wall appeared to be rough, not like the smooth, fitted stones in Chalon Castle. Jane stuck her head out the door. She didn't see any guards in the hallway. She quickly shut the door and hustled over to her own tunic and breeches, which were draped over a chair by the bed. She got dressed as fast as she could while glancing at the door to make sure no one walked in on her.

Once dressed, Jane opened the trunks next to the wardrobe. The contents of the first one consisted of undergarments, but the second one had a variety of thick furs. Jane picked out the largest, which turned out to be a fur cloak with silver clasps. She threw it over her shoulders and rushed back to the door. Wait, what if Trudy was setting her up? What if this was a trap? No, Trudy genuinely wanted to go to Chalon and see a unicorn. That much was certain. She would find Trudy and together they would escape. Jane opened the door and stopped with a gasp. Standing outside her door was Zorn.

For a brief second Jane saw a seething hatred burning in his dark eyes, then his glare softened and one side of his mouth curled upward.

"Hello, Jane," he said. "You've dressed already. Do you wish to explore the castle?"

Jane wondered if he really wanted to show her around the castle or if he had something else in mind. One thing was certain—Jane wasn't going anywhere without Zorn. At least, not for the moment. Hopefully she would find a way to escape and get back to the others.

As they walked down the torchlit hall, Zorn stared at her. Jane felt his eyes peering at her, or rather *into* her. An urge to look at Zorn overtook her and Jane turned her head and met his gaze. His dark eyes, those eyes that Jane could swim in, captivated her. Her mind became a fog of daydreams and visions of being dressed in fine embroidered gowns being waited on by a host of servants.

Jane forced herself to look away. Something was definitely not right here. She shook her head several times to clear her thoughts. He was doing something to her, messing with her head. But why would he want to do such a thing? Jane bit the inside of her cheek. The pain helped her concentrate. Jane frowned and kept her eyes forward as they walked.

"What're you trying to do to me?" she asked. "Stop it. Now."

Zorn said nothing, but Jane felt his gaze leave her. It was like a great weight had been removed.

"Your will is strong," Zorn told her. I admire that in you."

Jane stopped and whirled on him.

"Leave me alone! Just let me go back to my friends. I don't want to be here. I already told you that. I'm not part of your world and I don't have anything to do with your war."

Zorn glared at her as he also stopped.

"I saw you and the Stormlord at Troll Fang Pass. Do you belong to him? You're his woman?"

"I don't belong to anyone," Jane said through clenched teeth. The question was insulting, and she was beginning to lose her temper. "And besides, that's none of your business."

"Regardless," he said. "You are involved in this war and I intend to make good use of that."

"No. I won't let you. I'll never help you."

"We shall see," Zorn said.

"What do you want with me?" Jane demanded as her face became warm and flushed.

"With you? Nothing."

Jane gasped. An awful realization overcame her.

"You're using me to lure my friends here," she said as her eyes widened. "You're setting a trap!"

Zorn stared at her. He was as stoic as Ariel, but he had a gloomy, sinister countenance about him.

He remained silent and motioned for her to continue their walk.

"Ariel said you were good once. She said you were a hero."

"In war, one side's hero is another side's villain. Would it surprise you to learn that we are defending ourselves and wish to take back our lands that were seized by Chalon and the southern kingdoms?"

"I don't believe you," Jane said. "You've murdered innocent people—farmers and villagers."

"Horrible things happen in war."

"And you chased us. Ariel fought you and sent you flying away."

Zorn nodded. "True. She is powerful."

Jane stopped and faced him. "She should've killed you. You're evil and I won't let you use me to harm my friends."

"And how will you stop me?" Zorn said with a glint in his eye.

Chapter Thirty-Six
The Shattered Moor

Sawyer and the others traveled east for the first two uneventful days of their journey. Ariel had explained this was necessary in order to avoid detection by scouts or agents of the Shadowlord, but Sawyer considered this to be time wasted, regardless of what she said. He'd been in a foul mood ever since Jane was taken from the wall at Troll Fang Pass. No one said much as they trudged along through the rolling hills and green grasslands.

By midmorning of the third day, they turned north toward the kingdom of Gholaran and the Iron Citadel. Ariel constantly scanned the horizon for enemies. They had maintained a good pace, but Sawyer grew more impatient each day. They missed Jane. She had a way of making everyone around her feel at ease, but Sawyer hadn't realized that until they started their quest to find her.

"So what's up with this Gholaran and the Iron Citadel?" Sawyer asked as he walked behind Ariel. "How 'impenetrable' is it?"

Ariel answered without looking back. "Gholaran is the land of the barbarians. Once their territories reached as far south as Chalon and Eastvale. The folk of the southern kingdoms grew weary of their continuous raids and formed an alliance against them."

"I get it," Sawyer said. "The southerners beat them back and took a bunch of land. To the victor go the spoils, that sort of thing."

"How long ago was that war?" Geoff chimed in from behind Sawyer.

"Many years ago," Ariel said. "The struggle was a series of wars known as the Sovereign Wars, which lasted almost fifty years."

"Wow. That's a long time to be at war," Geoff said. "Why did it take fifty years to defeat the barbarians?"

"Barbarians are fierce warriors," Ariel said, "but they hate and fear magic. That is how they were beaten back. It was through the efforts of several wizards acting in concert that the barbarians were defeated."

"Those were dark times," Ishara added. "Most scholars and historians agree the dead outnumbered the living."

"That's it," Sawyer said, snapping his fingers. "Let's get Geoff's dad, Maelord, Geoff and you, Ariel, together. The three of you can nuke the barbarians like before."

Sawyer's suggestion was met with silence for several seconds, then Ariel spoke.

"Nuke? The problem is, this time the barbarians also have magic on their side," Ariel said. "Dark magic and sorcery. They are not so fearful as they have been in the past and a strong leader commands them."

"But didn't you scare them off back when we were at Chalon?" Geoff said. "You used magic then, and they ran for the hills, right?"

"I did use magic," Ariel said, "and they did retreat after they lost many warriors. However, it was not an easy battle to win."

"Still, it sounds like our best chance is to beat 'em with magic," Sawyer said. "Let's get all the good spell chuckers together."

Ariel looked over her shoulder at Sawyer. She appeared to be puzzled by the term *spell chucker*.

Sawyer smirked. "You know, someone who casts spells and stuff."

"They also have the orc tribes as allies," Ishara said, "and orcs do not fear magic like barbarians."

They walked in silence for a few minutes then Sawyer spoke again. "So how much longer till we get to the Iron Citadel?"

"If we make good time in the swamps of the Shattered Moor," Ariel said, "perhaps three days."

"That's a long time," Geoff said. "Will Jane be okay?"

No one answered him. It was a long time to be a prisoner of the Shadowlord. Sawyer hoped Jane would be safe. She had to be safe; he wouldn't let himself think otherwise. She was strong, smart, resourceful, and she'd been learning spells from Ariel. She might even find a way to escape on her own. One thing was for sure—the Shadowlord had his hands full holding her captive.

By late afternoon, they crossed from grasslands and rolling hills to a flatter terrain filled with scrub brush. Sawyer detected a musty odor. It reminded him of a large pile of grass clippings composting in the sun. A thin haze lingered over the ground, which became soggy and uneven. Ariel turned and addressed the group before they entered the marshland ahead.

"Before us lies the Shattered Moor," she said. "There are many dangers within. Stay alert and do not wander."

"If it's such a dangerous place," Geoff said, "then why're we going in?"

"In order to reach the Iron Citadel unnoticed," Ariel replied, "we must travel this route. The Shadowlord and his minions do not often set foot in the Shattered Moor. It is our best chance to avoid being spotted."

"Okay," Sawyer said. "Let me get this straight. The Shattered Moor is too dangerous for the Shadowlord, the guy who's trying to take over the world, but *we're* gonna go there?"

Ariel nodded. "As I said, it is our best chance."

"Okay, you're the boss," Sawyer said, throwing up his hands.

"Everyone stay close," Ariel said. "And keep quiet."

They walked into the mist-shrouded swamp. Ariel led the way, and Sawyer followed close behind her, with Geoff and Ishara bringing up the rear. Sawyer kept one hand on his scabbard in case they were attacked and he needed to draw his sword. The deeper they went into the mist, the more eerie their surroundings became. Sawyer's visibility was limited to no more than twenty feet. He looked over his shoulder and saw Geoff was sticking close. Geoff jumped at nearly every bird call or splash in the dark, murky water.

Sawyer made more noise than anyone as they slogged through the squishy muck. From time to time Ariel would stop and signal for the others to stop as well. Sawyer barely breathed as they waited for Ariel to indicate all was well before they continued their trek. Sawyer's eyes darted about. More than once a dark shape in the gray mist alarmed him, because it looked like it was a creature or a person. As they got closer, however, it was apparent that the shapes were only more moss-covered trees. Soon he realized that unless Ariel, with her keen elven senses, reacted to a sound or shape then there wasn't anything to worry about.

After several hours, the mist began to thin, revealing more of the swamp in which they traveled. Sawyer saw the tops of the crooked and contorted trees. Brown and green vines wound and twisted their way up their trunks, wrapping around the trees like long snakes. Ariel found a place for them to rest on a few fallen trees that provided a fairly dry place to sit. Ishara and Geoff set about making a small campfire, while Ariel and Sawyer gathered more wood.

"Ariel," Sawyer said, "it seems like we're going really slow in this swamp. Is it going to be like this the whole way?"

"No," Ariel said. "At least I hope not. It is best if we are careful as we walk, is it not? Our goal is to arrive safely at the Iron Citadel and rescue Jane."

"Yeah, but it seems like we're taking too long is all."

"I know," Ariel said. "You miss her. As do we all. But we must not become reckless. Our success and perhaps Jane's life depends on our stealth."

Sawyer stopped and looked at Ariel.

"Do you think Jane's okay?"

Ariel seemed to think for a few seconds.

"Yes, I do. Jane is strong. I believe she will do whatever she can to give us time to find her."

"Okay," Sawyer said. "But if or when we find her, how do we get her outta there? That Iron Citadel place."

"We will have the means," Ariel said. "But first, we must find Jane. Perhaps we will be able to signal her."

"Have you ever been there? The Iron Citadel?"

"Once many years ago," Ariel said. "And it was a bastion of evil then as well. I was with a scouting party from Selra'thel. We had heard rumors of strange lights and unnatural creatures there."

"Soooo, how'd it go? What'd you find?"

"We traveled the mountain pass back then," Ariel said. "We penetrated deep into Gholaran. Most of our scouts remained behind while a handful of us went inside under cover of darkness."

"Gholaran," Sawyer said rubbing his chin. "Is the Shadowlord the ruler of that place? It's a kingdom, right?"

"Yes, he is. But Zorn, who was noble born, was not the ruler back then."

"Who was?"

"We never discovered that," Ariel said. "We were sure something evil had taken up residence in the Iron Citadel."

"Well what happened when you went inside?"

"We were ambushed and barely made it out alive."

A sudden screech from behind them in the mist startled Sawyer. He turned his head. Several seconds later, he continued to pick up firewood.

"Who ambushed you?" Sawyer asked. "You don't ever make noise. Did someone else give you away?"

"No. Those of us who ventured into the Iron Citadel were well prepared. An elven scouting party is both capable and formidable. We were attacked by the citadel's guardians, infernal denizens."

"Infernal denizens? What the heck is that?"

"You have seen many terrifying creatures since you have been here," Ariel said. "The creatures we fought that night were undead."

"Undead?"

"Ghouls and wraiths; neither living nor dead," Ariel said. "They feast on the flesh and spirits of the living."

"Ghouls and wraiths?"

"You would know them if you saw them. They are terrifying creatures created from the cursed spirits of men and elves."

"Who created them?"

"I do not know," Ariel said, "Perhaps the dark presence we felt cursed those spirits. Come, we should get back to Geoff and Ishara."

Sawyer grabbed a last piece of firewood and followed Ariel back to camp. They had a small fire burning and Ishara was teaching Geoff how to fight. Geoff seemed awkward and unsure of his movements. Ishara, on the other hand, was as fluid and catlike as Ariel. She easily blocked or dodged Geoff's punches.

"We should continue after an hour's rest," Ariel said. "We must travel as far as we can today."

Geoff and Ishara stopped their training session and sat on a trunk of a fallen tree while Ariel prepared a stew. Sawyer's stomach growled, the aroma made him realize how hungry he was.

"So Geoff," Sawyer said, "have you ever heard of ghouls and wraiths?"

"Yeah," Geoff said. "They're undead monsters, I think. Why?"

"Ariel and some others fought a bunch of 'em the last time they were at the Iron Citadel," Sawyer said. "Just wanted to know if you ever heard of 'em."

Geoff looked at Ariel.

Without looking up from her pot of stew, Ariel added, "It was many years ago. I cannot say for certain if we will encounter such creatures again, but the danger is real."

"What if they're still at the Iron Citadel? How do we fight them?" Geoff asked with a frown.

"With magic," Ishara said, giving Geoff a nudge. "We have a wizard."

Geoff didn't appear to be comforted by Ishara's lighthearted answer.

"And we have Ariel," Sawyer said, "queen of the druids, right?"

"Not a queen," Ariel corrected him. "High Druid. That is all."

"And we have the Stormlord," Ishara added, looking at Sawyer. "You made quick work of that ogre."

Sawyer thought for a minute. None of them realized how he had done such a feat. This was as good a time as any for a confession.

"Hey, guys," he began. "I gotta tell you, all that with the ogre? It wasn't me. It was the sword. It just kinda took over and sorta showed me what to do. I really didn't do all that."

"Of course you did," Ariel said, glancing up at Sawyer. "You command the sword, not the other way around. The sword showed you what to do, but you had the choice. You can choose to ignore the Stormblade, if you wish."

"I dunno," Sawyer said. "It didn't feel like I had a choice."

"Perhaps you simply needed a nudge," Ariel said. "Besides, it would not be a bad thing to do as the Stormblade suggests."

They ate their meal quietly and listened to the sounds of

the swamp. Sawyer found himself keeping an eye on the mist as he ate. He wondered if they would be attacked by the same ghouls and wraiths Ariel had mentioned. They finished their meal and relaxed for a while before continuing their journey.

Evening began to descend as they navigated the swamp. Larger bodies of murky water became more frequent, while the ground became narrow strips of land at times. Their surroundings reminded Sawyer of a maze; one wrong turn and they would hit a dead end and find themselves backtracking and searching for a new route.

Sawyer felt a vibration from the sword he had slung over his back. It was another warning.

"Hey guys," Sawyer said, "something's—"

He was interrupted by an upheaval of mud and water beside him. He whirled and saw a great mound rising from the dark water. It looked like a giant knobby boulder with spikes on its surface. There was a loud sucking sound as the object worked itself free from the mucky bottom.

"Bog drake! Run!" Ariel shouted as she drew her scimitars.

Sawyer pulled his sword as well. Ishara fired two arrows in rapid succession, each penetrating the emerging object. A low growl from beneath the bubbling and churning water reverberated as they turned and ran.

There was a loud *boom* behind them and the ground shook. Sawyer looked over his shoulder and saw a massive, scaled claw had risen from the water and landed where they had been standing. Then a spiked serpentine head appeared. Its snakelike eyes fell on them as the monster climbed out of the water. It opened its toothy maw and let out a deafening roar.

Geoff and Ishara ran just ahead of Sawyer and Ariel. The roar made Geoff put his head down and cover his ears. Ishara grabbed him by the shoulder and pulled him along as Ariel ran beside Sawyer with her weapons drawn. A thunderous crash followed by several smaller crashes continued to make the ground shake as they ran.

"Ishara!" Ariel called.

With a single fluid motion, Ishara released Geoff, nocked an arrow, spun, and let it fly. It flew well over Sawyer's head, and he watched as it struck its mark, piercing the massive swamp beast's right eye. The creature rose up and screeched in pain while it shook its large spiked head. Now that the entire monster was on land, Sawyer could see that it looked like a great wingless dragon.

Ariel stopped, faced the creature, and crossed her scimitars in front of her.

"*Tae'nalara*," Ariel uttered, sending an invisible wave of force at the giant beast. The impact of Ariel's spell knocked it off balance. The creature's body hit the ground with a tremendous crash, causing Sawyer and Geoff to lose their balance. The creature writhed and thrashed about in the mire, sending huge chunks of soggy earth and debris flying. Its long, scaly tail swung back and forth in the air like a great scythe.

Ariel pulled Sawyer to his feet and pushed him toward Geoff and Ishara.

"Go! Run!" she shouted.

Sword in hand, Sawyer ran as fast as he could on the damp, quaking ground as Ishara fired arrow after arrow high over his head. Even though he was desperate to get away, something made Sawyer spin around. Ariel was lying prone on the moist ground.

"The monster's tail got her," Geoff said. He was standing a few feet ahead of Sawyer. "Just after she helped you up."

Sawyer didn't say a word. He sprinted to Ariel as the great form of the swamp creature righted itself and roared again. Sawyer dropped to a knee beside Ariel and shook her. "Ariel! Get up! We gotta move!"

Ariel didn't respond. Sawyer sheathed his sword and picked her up. He looked over his shoulder and saw the monster lunging at him, mouth agape. Sawyer jumped out of the way just as the creature's face plunged into the soil right where he and Ariel had been. Sawyer's heart pounded in his chest as he dashed toward the others with Ariel in his arms.

Ishara had stepped forward and was firing her arrows in rapid succession. The ground shook with each deafening step the creature took, and Geoff wildly motioned for Sawyer to hurry. Suddenly Sawyer was thrown into the air, along with Ariel and Ishara. The creature had spun around and slammed the ground with its tail, sending them flying.

Sawyer struck a tree and became disoriented. He tried to focus, but his vision was blurred from the impact. He did, however, see well enough to make out the figures of Ariel and Ishara getting to their feet. Then he looked up and saw the unmistakable shape of two massive jaws rimmed with long, sharp teeth bearing down on him.

Chapter Thirty-Seven
The Glowing Snapdragon

Jane's stomach churned. She stepped back from Zorn and clenched her fists. Her mind raced with thoughts of her friends falling prey to him, making her head start to throb again.

"I'll find a way to escape," Jane said. "I'll warn them."

"You will fail," Zorn said.

Jane wanted to run away, but his dark, emotionless eyes held her in place. She didn't seem to have any self-control with Zorn. What was wrong?

"Shall we continue our walk?" he asked her.

Jane blinked. She was about to refuse in the harshest, most profanity-laced way, but she lost her train of thought. In her mind, she heard a soft voice reassuring her and telling her everything was okay.

She nodded. Why did she do that? As they continued their walk, she closed her eyes tightly and opened them again. She felt numb, like she was walking in a dream. They strolled down a long, dark corridor, and the statues of gargoyles and other strange horned creatures crouched in the alcoves seemed to scrutinize them. Jane pinched the bridge of her nose and squinted. She was upset at something just a moment ago, but she had forgotten what it was.

"Are you well?" Zorn asked as they descended a grand carpeted staircase that was wide enough for ten people. "You appear to be in pain."

"No, just a little foggy," Jane said as she rubbed the side of her head.

"Shall I have someone fetch you something?"

"I think I'll be fine," Jane said, looking around. "This place is huge."

"It is," Zorn said as they neared the bottom of the dim staircase. "I think you'll like the great hall." He motioned with his hand and Jane gasped at the massive room with its huge fireplace and numerous torchlit columns. Most impressive was the sparkling, golden chandelier hovering over the room. It must've been twenty feet in diameter, and the way the firelight reflected off the large, faceted gems made Jane think they were large diamonds.

"This room has seen its share of important events. It is my favorite room in the whole castle."

"It's beautiful," Jane said, studying the room.

"There're many things for you to see here, Jane. Wonders you can't imagine. You will find the servants most helpful. They will see to your needs."

"Oh yes," Jane said. "Trudy, or Gertrude-has been so kind. I like her a lot."

"Trudy? You've already made a friend, I see. Then she will be your personal servant if you wish; your lady-in-waiting."

"I'd like that a lot," she said.

"So what do you think of Malverk Citadel?"

"Malverk Citadel?" Jane said. "I thought it was the Iron Citadel."

Zorn shook his head. "That's what our enemies have dubbed it. However, as ruler of Gholaran, I named it Malverk Citadel."

"I suppose that sounds better," Jane said. "But I think it's too dark and too lonely. There isn't anything cheerful here. It's so gloomy. There's nothing bright about this place."

"You're bright and strong, Jane. Much stronger than you realize. You have a good heart and that's why you shine."

Jane looked at Zorn. He was admiring the features of her face and neck. It seemed like he was studying her, making mental notes and committing everything about her to memory.

"Ariel said something like that too." Jane held up her hand and turned it over. "But I don't see that I'm glowing or shining. I'm just a girl."

"Ariel is right," Zorn said. "I can assure you of that."

They walked further into the great hall. Jane noticed a portrait hanging over the large fireplace, shrouded in shadows.

"Is that you?" she asked.

"Yes," Zorn said.

Jane stepped closer to the portrait. In the painting, Zorn was wearing a shining suit of armor and giving her the same smile she saw every time he smiled at her now.

"You look…happy," Jane said, standing on the tips of her toes and straining for a closer look in the dim hall. "You're smiling."

Another handsome face surfaced in Jane's mind. He also had dimples. His hair was dark and thick. His broad shoulders and comforting muscular arms used to hold her tightly against his warm chest. Sawyer. That was his name.

A wave of panic arose inside her. She stepped back from the portrait and began to tremble. She wrapped her arms around herself as tears welled up in her eyes.

"Jane," Zorn said, taking a step toward her.

"No!" Jane shouted as she spun away. "Stay back! Keep away from me!"

"You have nothing to fear…"

"You're the Shadowlord! You're evil and disgusting."

Jane ran out of the great hall. She wound her way through corridors lit by torches and populated with statues of tall warriors, submissive maidens, and menacing gargoyles. Where was everyone? Jane searched as much for another living soul as she did for an exit. She couldn't believe it; in this expansive castle she had only seen a few people. Where had the servants gone? Where was Trudy?

Jane's heart drummed in her chest as she ran. She had to find a way out of the castle. Her friends would be looking for her; she knew that. She turned a corner and saw a set of wooden double doors at the end of the hall. An overwhelming feeling of excitement came over her as she raced to the doors, encouraged by the daylight that filtered through the slim space at the bottom. That was her way out.

Jane grasped the ornate iron handles and pulled, but the doors were locked. She pushed and pulled several times, hoping they were only stuck. What was she going to do?

"Allow me."

The sound of another voice just behind Jane startled her and she leapt back against the wall, clutching her arms. Zorn regarded her with a curious look. He held a large skeleton key in his hand. He opened the doors with the key, letting in the cold sunlight.

"You're free to roam, but you cannot escape. Gholaran is a harsh land. If you leave this place, you will die."

Zorn stepped back and gave her room to go outside. Jane looked at him. His gaze was cold and emotionless. It didn't seem to matter to him if she lived or died. Jane exhaled and stepped outside. She wasn't ready to give up yet. Hopefully, she could make use of her newfound freedom and discover a way out.

There was a chill in the air as she surveyed the courtyard. Once again, she had a feeling that they were the only ones in the castle. It was odd; a castle of this size must need an army of servants to maintain it. Jane didn't see any guards patrolling along the walls or the grounds either.

She pulled her fur cloak around her as a far-off rumble of thunder caught her attention. Dark gray clouds gathered in the distance.

"It rains often here," Zorn said, "and the snows can be deep."

Zorn extended his hand. Jane looked at it for a moment and shook her head. His gaze had become pleasant, but she had no intention of trusting him. Several wrinkled brown leaves swirled past as they strolled.

"Why is everything withered and dead?" she asked. "You don't have any trees or flowers here. Look around. It's as gloomy as your castle. Everything is dead. Nothing is growing."

"Most plants don't survive here," Zorn said. "As I said, the climate is too harsh."

"It can't be that bad, can it?"

"I'm afraid so. For years my people have tried to eke out a living by farming rocky fields."

Jane looked at her feet as they walked. She stepped on a brown leaf and heard it crunch. In this high, desolate place she felt like they were the only two people in the world. It would've been a nice stroll had their surroundings not been bleak and gray. A thought occurred to Jane as she crunched another dry leaf beneath her foot.

"Do you have a garden? I have something to show you," she said with a hint of excitement in her voice.

Zorn gave her a puzzled look, then he motioned with his head.

"To the back of the castle, just around the corner. Why?"

"C'mon," Jane said, nearly sprinting. "You might like this."

Passing through an old arch, Jane saw the remnants of a wonderful garden. Rows and rows of withered shrubs and plants must once have formed a maze of colors and fragrances. Jane found a withered flower, which stood by itself.

"Do you know what the name of this flower is?" Jane asked.

"Glowing snapdragon. Jane, what're you doing?"

"Just watch," she said.

She knelt on the hard soil and ran her fingers along the dried stalk of the lone flower. A few brown wrinkled petals fell to the ground.

"I bet it was beautiful, wasn't it?" Jane asked.

"Yes. Glowing Snapdragons are rare and they are among the most beautiful of flowers."

Jane closed her eyes and exhaled. She recalled a druidic charm that Ariel had taught her. It was her favorite.

"*Ehlia talo*," Jane said as she touched the flower.

Jane felt warmth and energy leave her body and flow into the flower.

"Astounding. Simply...astounding."

Jane didn't have to look at Zorn; she knew he was both surprised and impressed. She opened her eyes and saw a wondrous, flourishing flower of purple, white, and yellow at her fingertips. She looked up at Zorn, beaming with pride.

"Do you like it?" she asked.

"Of course," Zorn said. "You are amazing. How is it you can cast such spells?"

"Ariel taught me," Jane said, turning her attention back to the flower. "*She's* the one who is amazing. She taught me other cool spells and charms, too."

Zorn knelt beside Jane.

"Aye, she is amazing. Jane, do you mean to tell me the high druid herself is teaching these spells to you?"

"Mmhmm," Jane said without looking up.

Jane felt his fingers brush her hair over her ear and then he placed his hand under her chin and gently turned her head so she faced him.

"There has never been a human druid before," he said. "And Ariel is not known for her love of humans. Why does she tutor you in the druidic arts?"

"She's my friend," Jane said. "You remember what it was to have friends, don't you?"

"That was a long time ago," Zorn said quietly. "I had forgotten what it meant to be truly good."

As Jane looked at him, she thought she saw a hint of sadness in his eyes, but only for a moment. She turned back to the snapdragon.

"It won't survive in the cold," she said. "Do you have a

pot or something we can use to bring it inside?"

"Perhaps," he said motioning to a small, dilapidated wooden shed. "Shall we go look?"

They found a brown clay pot and shovel in the shed. After they had dug up the snapdragon they stood and Zorn offered it to Jane, but she pushed it toward him.

"No. It's yours. My gift to you."

Zorn stared at the snapdragon for a few moments, and Jane saw pain and sadness in his expression. He looked at her, but didn't smile.

"Thank you, Jane," he said. "No one has ever given me such a beautiful gift. This is your garden now. Do with it as you please."

That night Jane was awakened by the deafening boom of thunder and bright flashes of lightning. She groaned and rolled over in bed, pulling the covers over her head. The constant heavy pounding of rain on the glass in the balcony doors sounded like drums to Jane, but as she listened to the storm outside, she thought she heard something else.

She raised her head off the pillow and slid the cover away from her ears. Between the sounds of the storm she heard the unmistakable sound of an animal wailing. Something was in pain. Jane slipped out of bed and went to the balcony doors. Pulling the curtains aside, she found herself looking into the pitch-black night.

A moment later there was another flash of lightning, and through the pouring rain Jane saw a solitary figure in black armor in the courtyard below. Jane concentrated to get a better look during the flashes of lightning. It couldn't be Zorn, could it? He was screaming, but the storm masked most of his wails.

Then she saw the man in black punch the head of a statue in the courtyard. She opened the door and stepped out onto the balcony. The frigid rain poured over her as though in buckets, giving her a jolt. Her breath drifted away and disappeared into the night. She wiped her eyes, then wrapped her arms around herself and leaned over the balcony for a better look.

The black-armored man ripped the headless statue from its worn pedestal and lifted it over his head. He slammed it into the rain-drenched ground with such force it shattered into small pieces. Again the figure screamed, and this time she realized it really was Zorn. Already shivering from the cold, Jane dashed back inside and quickly dried off. Again and again Zorn screamed. Jane thought he should suffer. In fact, he deserved it.

This may be a chance to help him, however. Talk to him. What if she could convince him to stop the war? That was worth getting chilled in the rain. Jane dressed in the clothes she wore when she had arrived and wrapped a fur cloak around herself. She pulled a cover from the bed and put it over her head to help shield herself from the rain, but she knew it wouldn't last long in the downpour.

Jane hurried downstairs. Opening the door, which nearly blew from her hand as the wind gusted, Jane went outside. In the cold of the night she clearly heard Zorn. His screams sounded as if he were in pain. Pain mixed with rage. Jane hurried to the courtyard and peeked around the corner of the castle. Zorn had drawn his runed sword and sliced through several statues.

Jane took a step forward and Zorn turned to look at her. She gasped. His face was twisted by so much anger he looked more like an animal – or something worse. His eyes flashed in the night and he stomped toward her, sword still in hand. Realizing she shouldn't be there, Jane screamed and turned. She ran back toward the door, but stumbled over a broken stone in the path.

Before she could get up, she felt him standing over her. She rolled over, and held up a hand to shield herself from the rain striking her face and eyes. Another flash of lightning revealed Zorn glaring at her with blood-red eyes. His face was contorted into a frightening sneer. Rain dripped from his armor as he fell to his knees beside Jane and dropped his sword.

She trembled at the sight of the Shadowlord. As she lay in the rain she kept her eyes on him while she managed to find and grasp a loose stone, which she kept hidden behind her back. Zorn's chest heaved and he looked up. In the rain, it was impossible to determine if he was crying, but Jane thought maybe he was.

"You would be doing me a favor," Zorn said, his voice almost quivering as he nodded to the stone in her hand. "I've done horrible, unspeakable things in service of a queen I never wanted. I see the faces of the slain every night. They haunt me."

He looked at her. "I hate what I've become, Jane."

"You can stop this," Jane yelled as another crack of thunder rumbled overhead. "We can help you."

Zorn shook his head, "You don't understand. It's too late. You've no idea what it's like to have your soul torn apart. There are no words to describe the agony…"

Zorn stood and walked away, leaving Jane shivering in the cold rain.

Chapter Thirty-Eight

Creatures of the Night

Geoff landed in the tall, wet weeds after being tossed into the air by the thunderous bog drake. There was a sharp pain in his leg, and he glanced down. He had landed on a large slime-covered rock. Geoff looked at the behemoth and shuddered. It was the most terrifying thing he had ever seen and it was about to devour Sawyer. Sawyer screamed and raise his sword, which looked pitifully small compared to the bulk of the creature.

The next instant Geoff saw a bright blue and white flash as lightning erupted from Sawyer's sword. The bog drake's body rippled with arcs of lightning. It roared in pain and recoiled from Sawyer, but only for a moment. Geoff suddenly remembered what his father had said: *Use your imagination and your magic will take whatever shape you desire.* Geoff held his hands out in front of him in the direction of the bog drake. He felt a familiar surge of energy from deep within.

A blinding light appeared in Geoff's hands, and then a crooked bolt of lightning lanced through the air and struck the bog drake as it again lunged at Sawyer. This time the creature let out a high-pitched screech as the lightning from Geoff's hands engulfed it. It backed away from Sawyer and turned its attention to Geoff. His heart sank and his stomach churned as he stood frozen in place. He had angered the bog drake, which now charged at him.

It tore up huge chunks of earth and debris as it launched itself toward him. It had opened its mouth and was making ready to swallow him when three arrows struck the creature's head and body. Ishara was shooting arrow after arrow as fast as she could while running toward him. He saw the look of panic in her eyes and her mouth was moving. She shouted something to him, but he didn't hear it over the sounds of the bog drake's charge.

His entire body trembled at the sight of approaching death. On the other side of the creature, he saw Ariel running beside it and slashing at its legs with her scimitars, but nothing slowed the enraged bog drake as it came closer.

Geoff staggered backward, screamed, and extended his hands again. He felt a sharp pain in his chest and was blinded by another flash of light as a second bolt of lightning erupted from him. The smell of something burning filled his nostrils. The bog drake let out an ear-piercing screech and rose on its hind legs while it flailed about with its front claws. Its entire body was covered with white arcs of lightning.

A light-headed feeling came over Geoff, then he felt a twinge of pain in his chest. His vision began to dim, but he maintained the bolt of lightning for as long as possible. Everything began to spin, but the monster suddenly stopped screeching and its massive scaled body went limp. Geoff dropped to his knees in the mud, and before he collapsed, he watched the bog drake fall with a booming crash. The world faded, and everything went black.

When he awoke, he was lying by a small campfire. It was nighttime, and the evening had brought a bitter chill to the Shattered Moor. Geoff's thick hair was wet and he shivered slightly. Even though he was wrapped in a couple of blankets, he felt cold and drained inside. He lifted his head. Sawyer sat beside him with a blanket draped over his shoulders, but there was no sign of Ariel and Ishara as Geoff looked around the camp.

"They went out scouting for enemies," Sawyer said without taking his eyes off the fire in front of him. "How're you doing?"

Geoff groaned as he struggled to sit up. He had become entangled in the blankets and flopped around. Sawyer reached over and pulled Geoff to a sitting position.

"I'm okay, I think." Geoff said. "Did we kill that dragon?"

"No," Sawyer said. "You did."

Geoff looked into the fire and tried to remember what had happened. It had charged him, and he knew he was going to die, but then he did something. He released the magic inside as a last ditch effort. His ears still throbbed and hurt from the creature's screeches and roars.

"I killed it?"

"Yep. Just like you fried all those carrion mites when we were in the catacombs."

"Oh," Geoff said. He looked at Sawyer. "Did anyone get hurt?"

Sawyer shook his head. Geoff extended his cold hands toward the fire. The warmth of the flames provided a cozy feeling and helped him relax. He looked into the darkness that surrounded him and Sawyer. Hopefully Ariel and Ishara would return soon. He felt more comfortable when they were near.

"That's twice you saved my life, Geoff," Sawyer said, looking at him. "Thanks."

Geoff nodded and once again turned his gaze to the hypnotic dance of the flames of the campfire.

"Hey," Sawyer said. "I mean it, Geoff. I knew I was a goner. Thanks for saving me. You're all right."

Geoff met Sawyer's gaze and for the first time he realized Sawyer was being gracious toward him. Sawyer hadn't normally been one to thank anyone for anything, but this experience was different. Sawyer seemed different.

"You're welcome," Geoff said. "You would've done the same for me."

Geoff kept his eyes on Sawyer, who thought about what he had just said. Sawyer nodded.

"Yeah. I suppose I would."

"I hope we don't run into any more of those…what did Ariel call it?"

"A bog drake," Sawyer said. "While you were sleeping she told us it was the biggest she had ever seen. How did you cast that lightning bolt at it?"

"I'm not sure. Dad said to use my imagination as I cast my spells and the magic will take whatever shape I desire."

"That's really cool. Way to go, Geoff. I owe you big time."

"No you don't," Geoff said, rubbing his shoulders. "Friends help each other; it's what they do. Jane said that and now we're going to rescue her. It's the same thing."

"You're right," Sawyer said. "We're gonna get her back."

Sawyer's voice became hard and he frowned as he stared

grimly into the fire. After a minute or two he touched Geoff's arm and spoke. "Listen to me, if something should happen—if we can't save Jane or if I get killed—you go back home right away, got it?"

The stern look in Sawyer's eyes took Geoff off guard. Things had taken a turn for the worse and Sawyer seemed to doubt if they would succeed.

"Yeah, I understand," Geoff said, "but we're going to rescue Jane. I know we will."

"I hope so, Geoff. I hope so."

"And nothing's gonna happen to anyone. We'll be okay. All of us."

"Cool," Sawyer said. "If the Shadowlord shows himself again you blast him like you did that dragon."

Geoff and Sawyer chuckled.

"Count on it," Geoff said.

They sat for several minutes staring into the fire, neither saying anything. Geoff wondered if Jane was still alive. Until that moment, he hadn't given much thought to what he and Sawyer would tell her parents if she were dead. He frowned as he considered the consequences of any of them dying.

"Why did he kidnap Jane?" Geoff asked.

"Dunno," Sawyer replied. "But whatever the reason, it ain't good."

Geoff continued gazing into the fire while he thought. In spite of his assurances to Sawyer, deep down he also felt like something bad was going to happen. With Jane's fate being uncertain, he wondered if even Ariel could pull them through this mess.

"I hope she's okay," Geoff said, "being locked away in a big castle with ghouls and wraiths and who knows what else."

"So they're like zombies? They eat people?"

"No…well I'm not sure. I guess they're like zombies."

Sawyer rubbed his forehead and sighed.

"Do you know any spells that'll kill them?"

"Not really. I could try another lightning bolt or a fireball, maybe."

"Yeah," Sawyer said. "That fireball should do it. Just make sure I'm not anywhere near you when you break off another one of those spells."

"Okay." Geoff smiled and yawned. He rested his head in his palm and closed his eyes. He could fall asleep so easily. The crackling campfire had warmed him enough, and its warm glow reminded Geoff of the fireplace in his house. He used to lie in front of it and read his books while his dad sat in his favorite recliner preparing the next day's lecture.

After several more minutes, Ariel and Ishara came into view. Each had a full armload of firewood, which they deposited quietly by the fire. Ishara grinned at Geoff.

"I am afraid our quest to save Jane will take a little longer than I had originally planned," Ariel said. "The battle with the bog drake did not go unnoticed by agents of the Shadowlord."

"You're kidding," Sawyer said. "What sort of agents? Let's take 'em out and get to Jane."

"That would not be wise," Ariel said. "The bright flashes from Geoff's lighting strikes were seen for leagues. As I said when we began this journey, our best chance to save Jane is to remain undetected. So we must veer west for the next few days and circle back to the Iron Citadel. It will not be easy, and the path will take us dangerously close to the Shadowlord's army."

"So Geoff's light show was seen by the bad guys," Sawyer said. "He didn't have a choice."

"Indeed," Ariel said turning to Geoff. "Bog drakes are particularly vicious hunters. There are very few in the realm who can singlehandedly slay a dragon, and none are so young as you, Geoff. Thank you."

Ariel bowed her head slightly to Geoff.

"So that's what wizards do, I guess," Sawyer said. "They blow up things and kill dragons."

"And now he has earned the title of Dragonslayer," Ariel said. "Well done."

"Thanks," Geoff said. "So can I have some cool armor like Sawyer's now?"

Ariel and Ishara laughed.

"You are silly. Wizards don't wear armor," Ishara said. "It can interfere with their spell casting."

"Really? I didn't know that," Geoff said. "Dad didn't tell me."

"And," Ishara added as she tapped Geoff's shoulder, "a good sneak thief would never wear armor because they would make too much noise and it slows their movement."

"Oh," Geoff said.

"There ya go, Geoff," Sawyer said. "No armor for you."

"However," Ishara said as she held out her hand toward Geoff, "a dragonslayer deserves a trophy."

Geoff looked at her hand and saw she held a long fang, which had come from the bog drake.

"I took this for you," Ishara said. "It will make a lovely handle for your dagger once it is polished and fitted."

"Wow! Thanks," Geoff said as he took the fang from Ishara. It was nearly as long as Geoff's dagger, but he didn't care. It would make for a spectacular-looking weapon. It wasn't one of the longer fangs from the bog drake; those were almost two feet in length. This one was about eight inches long, but looked every bit as wicked as the other fangs.

"You should get one too," Geoff said, looking at Ishara. "Then we can have a matching pair."

She smiled and took a second dragon fang from a leather pouch at her side and held it up. Geoff grinned from ear to ear.

"She's one step ahead of you, Geoff," Sawyer said.

Geoff handed the fang back to Ishara.

"We need to make good time tomorrow," Ariel said. "Geoff, you and Sawyer need rest. Ishara and I will keep watch tonight."

"By the way," Geoff said. "Where are we? Are we near that bog drake?"

"Nope," Sawyer said. "After you killed it and made so much racket, we had to pick you up and put some distance between it and us in case the Shadowlord's scouts saw it."

"Oh," Geoff said. "Are we safe?"

"For now," Ariel said.

Geoff lay down by the campfire and curled up to keep warm. The sounds of various crickets chirping and frogs croaking mixed with the occasional crackle and hiss of the campfire. Sawyer stretched out nearby, keeping one hand on his sword. Geoff yawned and closed his eyes.

By the time morning arrived, Geoff felt refreshed. He was no longer tired, and since he hadn't eaten last evening, he was hungry. He sat up and looked around their camp. Sitting by the fire was a small wooden plate with bread, cheese, and apples. Behind him, the sound of movement and voices drew his attention.

He turned and saw Ariel was training Sawyer how to fight with a sword again. This time, Ariel was also in the process of showing Sawyer how to sweep an opponent's legs out from under them. Sawyer was getting much better at fighting with a sword, Geoff thought. Ariel had taught him a couple of elegant attacks that Geoff had only seen Ariel use in battle. One move in particular was a spinning, slashing strike, first to the torso and then to the legs. Ariel said it was a difficult move for any opponent to defend against.

"Good morning, Dragonslayer," Ishara said.

Geoff spun around and saw Ishara sitting on the ground several feet away. She was polishing and smoothing the dragon fang she had shown Geoff.

"Hey," Geoff said. "Thanks for breakfast."

"You are welcome. Hurry and eat. We need to continue to the Iron Citadel when you are done."

"You sound like Ariel," Geoff said as he took a bite of cheese. Ishara raised an eyebrow like Ariel.

After Geoff had eaten, they resumed their trek through the Shattered Moor. They trudged through the mire, with Ariel and Sawyer in the front rank and Ishara with Geoff close behind. Geoff wondered if Sawyer meant what he said when he thanked him for saving his life. He seemed to be genuine, but would he revert to bullying him again when this was all over? If for some reason they were unable to rescue Jane, Geoff had no idea how Sawyer would react.

That evening they made camp. Ariel seemed to be somewhat tense and kept looking around.

"What're you looking for?" Geoff asked as he helped Ishara with the cooking.

"I am remaining vigilant," Ariel said.

"Yeah," Geoff said. "It's just that you seem a little worried."

"I am fine," Ariel said. "There are more bog drakes in this mire, along with a host of other dangers."

"So far, with the exception of the bog drake," Ishara said. "We have been fortunate."

"Yep," Sawyer said. "Everything's going real good."

That night Geoff and Sawyer rolled themselves in their blankets and went to sleep while Ishara and Ariel took turns standing watch. The boys had offered to help with the watch, but Ariel refused. Before Geoff fell asleep he made a mental note to ask Ishara if elves ever slept.

Sometime later, in the middle of the night, Geoff and Sawyer were awakened by a spine-chilling howl in the distance.

"What the…" Sawyer said as he reached for his sword and got to his feet.

Geoff also climbed to his feet. Ariel and Ishara were standing at the edge of camp peering into the night.

"Is it…," Geoff swallowed. "Is it the same werewolf that's been hunting us?"

Ariel answered without looking at him.

"Yes."

Chapter Thirty-Nine
The Shadowlord's Chambers

The next morning, Zorn sat across from Jane as she nibbled at the breakfast Trudy had brought. After what she had seen the night before, Zorn's presence made Jane nervous, and she avoided making eye contact with him. Her hands shook and she fidgeted in her chair, but after several minutes she finally spoke. "What happened to you? Last night you said things…"

Zorn shook his head.

"Someone as young as you shouldn't ask such questions. The answers would frighten you."

"Like last night?"

Zorn turned his head and looked at the gray sky through a window.

"I tried to help a friend," he said, "but I failed. My arrogance has cost me much."

"Isn't it a good thing to help a friend?"

"Yes."

"Who was your friend?"

"His name was Alex," Zorn said, turning his gaze to Jane. "And he was the bravest man I've ever known."

Jane stopped chewing. Zorn tilted his head as he studied her.

"You know this name, don't you?"

Jane looked down and didn't answer. She felt a haze drifting over her under Zorn's penetrating glare.

"What're you doing?" Jane demanded. "Get out of my head."

"Tell me about your friends," Zorn said evenly. "I wish to know everything."

Jane resisted for another few minutes, then she began to speak of Sawyer, Geoff, Ishara, and Ariel. Zorn appeared to listen intently while Jane spoke of her friends. She spoke of Sawyer and how he battled a river troll to win the Stormblade. Under Zorn's determined gaze, however, she added that Sawyer was lucky and that he had admitted to slaying the troll by accident. Jane also shared her experiences with Ariel and mentioned that she had learned numerous druidic spells and charms from her.

Zorn seemed particularly interested in Geoff, especially after Jane mentioned his father was a wizard named Maelord. It was obvious that Zorn recognized that name. He quizzed Jane about Geoff so much that she felt like she was on a witness stand undergoing thorough cross-examination. Some part of Jane kept telling her she was saying too much, but she couldn't help it. When Zorn looked at her she just kept talking. She told Zorn about everything, including the archway in Geoff's house and the key to activate it, which hung around Geoff's neck.

There was one other thing that interested Zorn almost as much as Geoff and his father—the werewolf. Jane noticed he knew something about that, too. He certainly knew that

Alex was the werewolf. Zorn's face twisted with a frown when she spoke of Alex, but there was also a little respect.

On the matter of Chalon, Jane found herself to be a little jabber jaws, revealing Lionel's indecision and lack of leadership. She didn't like him from their first meeting, she said; he was insulting and arrogant. She wished Ariel had slapped some sense into his thick skull. A thin smile etched across Zorn's face when he heard that.

"They were never fond of each other," he said. "Some things never change."

Jane's head began to clear, she was able to form her own thoughts again and she realized she had given him everything he wanted. She glared at Zorn and gritted her teeth.

"Ugh! I hate it when you do that," she said, pushing herself away from the table. "I told you to stay out of my head."

"You have a strong will," Zorn said. "Stronger than most."

"Not strong enough, evidently," Jane said. "How do you make others do things they don't want to do?"

"It's a gift."

"A gift? It's more like an irritant. Did your queen give it to you?"

"Yes, one of many gifts from her. I'm also strong and fast."

"Yeah, I saw what you did to those statues last night."

"Power such as mine comes at a price, Jane. A high price."

"So if you win this war, what will you do to those who fought against you?"

"I haven't given that any consideration. Should they be executed?"

"No. Enough people have died already."

"Jane, you must know that many more people will die. This war is a long way from being decided. If we're to throw off the chains placed around our necks by Lionel, we must be prepared for a difficult struggle."

"Just don't hurt my friends, okay? Promise me that."

Jane searched his eyes for the answer she wanted to hear. Several seconds later he nodded to her.

"So long as your friends do not take up arms and fight against me, they will not be harmed."

Jane pointed her finger at Zorn. "That includes Ariel and Ishara."

Zorn leaned back and glanced out the window again; apparently he had grown tired of this conversation.

"Promise me."

"Jane…they are elves and they hate humankind. They—"

"No," Jane insisted. "They don't hate humans and they're my friends, too."

She met his gaze yet again. This time his reluctance to agree to Jane's request for a promise was obvious.

"I mean it," she said.

"Jane, as I've already said—if they do not stand against me then they will not be harmed."

"Including Ariel and Ishara?"

Zorn nodded. "Including the elves."

Jane smiled.

"But Jane, I will defend myself if they attack me. I hope you've exacted similar promises from your friends."

She hoped another confrontation with her friends would never happen. As their faces drifted into her thoughts, she remembered Sawyer giving her his cocky smile and playfully flexing his muscles, Geoff and his very first girlfriend, Ishara, and Ariel, who had become so important to her.

"I must go, Jane. I will return later."

She watched as Zorn got up and left the room. It seemed to her that once he left she was able to think clearly again. She growled and stamped her foot. He did that mind control thing again. She went to the door to her room and opened it. Peering outside, she saw no one.

Jane stepped into the hall and closed the door. As she approached the wide staircase, Trudy appeared with a wide grin on her face.

"Hi," Jane said. "You're happy. What's the occasion?"

Trudy curtsied and bowed her head. "I have something for you, Lady Jane."

Trudy motioned for Jane to join her by an alcove.

"I thought you were just going to call me Jane?"

"I've been instructed to respect you as highborn, a queen even."

Jane laughed.

"Me? Highborn? I don't think so."

At the alcove, which was inhabited by a statue of a warrior holding his sword overhead with both hands, Jane looked at Trudy.

"Did you bring a dead flower?" Jane asked.

Trudy's eyes lit up and she pulled a shriveled brown stem from her pocket.

"Perfect," Jane said as she took the stem and winked at Trudy. She held it close to her lips and smiled.

"*Ehlia talo*," Jane whispered.

Before their eyes, the brown stem elongated and flourished until it became a vibrant red rose.

"Oh my! It's so beautiful."

"Here," Jane said, handing it to Trudy. "It's yours."

Trudy curtsied and stared at the rose. "Thank you, Lady...I mean Jane."

"You're welcome," Jane said. "Now, I want to see Zorn's room. Will you take me there?"

Trudy turned pale and stopped. Her lower lip quivered. This was strange. Why would her request to go to Zorn's room elicit such a response?

"What is it, Trudy? What's wrong?"

"Why do you want to see his chamber? No one is allowed there," Trudy said, glancing toward the stairs. "Lord Zorn will be very angry. We shouldn't disobey him."

"Oh Trudy," Jane said. "We'll be fine. He won't know we were ever there. I want to see if I can find out more about him."

Trudy swallowed and continued to fidget on the steps as she turned the rose around in her hands.

"Relax," Jane said. "It'll be all right."

"But Jane, he will know."

"Trudy," Jane said in a hushed tone as she looked around. "Do you want to leave?"

Trudy smiled and nodded.

"Me too," Jane said. "If I stay here, he will use me to kill my friends. I can't let him do that. I need your help. If you can gather supplies, I have furs in my room that will keep us warm. Oh, and we need weapons."

"Weapons?"

"Yes," Jane said. "Anything you can find will do. As soon as you've gotten food and weapons we can leave."

"As you wish, my lady," Trudy said. She gave Jane another quick curtsey and turned toward the steps.

"And please don't curtsy or bow or call me 'lady'; Jane will do."

Jane stopped on the same step as Trudy and looked at her. Trudy seemed unsure of how to react or what to say. Her eyes darted around and her lower lip quivered.

"Don't worry. We're friends, remember?"

Trudy smiled and led the way down the wide staircase to a dark hall that was one floor beneath Jane's room.

"Why is it so dark? I can't see a thing," Jane said.

"Lord Zorn wishes to keep the hall unlit," Trudy said. "He's fond of the dark."

"We need some light. Do we have any?"

"Yes," Trudy said, pulling a torch from the wall. "Wait here and I'll go light it."

Jane watched as Trudy trotted back to the staircase and lit her torch with one that was already burning on the wall. She returned and guided Jane down a long, dark corridor. Jane immediately noticed a layer of dust everywhere and cobwebs hanging from paintings, sconces, and even the ceiling.

"Are you sure we have the right hall?" Jane asked.

"Yes," Trudy whispered. "He wishes to be left alone so he can attend to his business."

"But it's filthy," Jane said, dodging a cobweb hanging from the ceiling. "No one cleans here?"

"No."

They arrived at two large double doors. They were dark, like they had been painted black, or maybe the wood itself was black.

"This is Lord Zorn's chamber."

Jane opened a door and saw nothing but a small beam of

sunlight filtering in through the large window on the far side of the chamber.

"C'mon," Jane said. "It's pitch black in there."

"No. Please, Jane," Trudy's near hysterical whisper was unnerving. She offered the torch to Jane. "We can't go in there. Please don't. It isn't allowed."

"Fraidycat," Jane said as she took the torch and entered the dark chamber.

In the light of her torch, Jane saw what had been a most luxurious room, but now dust layered much of the chamber. Plush cushioned chairs and beautiful carved tables filled the large chamber, and a carved marble fireplace rested on the east wall. In the far corner stood a broken mahogany mirror. Directly across from the fireplace was a king-sized four-post bed made from the same wood as the doors. Jane walked to the bed. There was no layer of dust there.

"Jane," Trudy said. "Please hurry. We can't linger here."

Trudy sounded as if she was beginning to panic, and Jane turned and looked at her. Trudy was still in the hallway and her eyes had started to glisten.

"We must go. If Lord Zorn ever found out," Trudy looked down the hall again, "we would be killed."

"Trudy, it's okay," Jane said in a calm voice. "I'll just be a min—"

Jane gasped and dropped her torch. Trudy reacted to Jane and brought her hands up to her face and gasped too. Jane sat on the edge of the bed staring at a swirling column of black smoke in the corner behind the door.

"Jane!" Trudy cried. "Please, please! We must leave!"

Jane didn't answer. She was staring at the black smoke. There wasn't a fire, so where did the smoke come from? Despite

Trudy's pleas, Jane found herself drawn to the shadowy corner. She stood up, picked up her torch, and took a few steps in that direction. She held the torch out in front of her, but the closer to the smoke-filled corner she held the torch, the dimmer it got; it was as though the torch refused to illuminate it.

Jane tried to tear herself away and join Trudy in the hall, but something moved within the smoke and held her attention. In her mind she heard a malevolent voice say her name. Terror gripped her and she began to tremble.

"Jane, we must go now!"

Jane nodded but kept her eyes on the dark corner.

"I'm coming."

Then the smoke separated, revealing the hideous black armor of the Shadowlord. Jane thought she heard someone whisper her name. She stepped back and screamed. In the hall, Trudy screamed as well and dashed back toward the stairs. Jane ran after her, torch and flower in hand. They rushed up the stairs to Jane's room and slammed the door behind them. Jane hugged the potted flower and Trudy sat in a chair crying and shivering uncontrollably.

"We're doomed, we're doomed," Trudy said over and over while she rocked her body back and forth.

"The Shadowlord...Zorn, will he...what will he do?"

Trudy shook her head vigorously.

"You don't understand, Jane," she said as tears rolled down her cheeks. "No one is allowed in his chambers. He has killed for less."

Jane closed her eyes and took a deep breath. She looked down at her hands. They were shaking.

"Jane, please listen to me," Trudy said. "We must leave here now. We're in such danger."

"Can you get us past the castle walls?"

"I think so," Trudy said with a nod. "I'll get us some food and knives. If you can bring furs for the cold, we can leave now."

"Okay. Be careful, Trudy."

"Jane, he isn't who he says he is. He's tricking you."

"I know. He has some kind of way of controlling my thoughts."

"Yes," Trudy said, standing up and casting a nervous glance at the door. "He's not what he seems. Don't trust him."

Jane nodded.

"All right. Trudy, get the supplies and come back. I'll pack some clothes and furs and we'll escape now. Right now."

Trudy wiped her face, then went to the door and opened it. She stuck her head out and looked up and down the hall.

"I'll be back as soon as I can," she said, still clutching her rose. "You've been kind to me, Jane. I'm grateful for your friendship."

"Me too," Jane said. "Friends stick together; it's what they do."

Trudy smiled and closed the door behind her. Jane tried to undo the buttons of her dress, but her hands shook too much. She tore at the dress and ripped her way out of it. She hurried and put on her tunic and breeches and scanned the room for a weapon. Her eyes passed over the poker by the fireplace, but she decided against it. She went to her dressing table and grabbed a small pearl-handled knife. She remembered everything now. The Shadowlord had kidnapped her and flown her to this dreadful castle.

Jane pulled the cover from her bed and threw it on the floor. She searched the wardrobes and trunks for anything that might prove useful during their escape. She piled a few thick tunics and fur cloaks on the cover and tied it into a big bundle.

A few moments later Jane heard a knock at the door, and she rushed across the room and opened it. Her hand flew to her mouth and she nearly fainted. Zorn stood in the doorway. Jane dropped her bundle and backed away.

"You really are amazing, Jane," he said as he entered the room. "I believe you're the bravest girl I've ever met."

Jane ran to the other side of the table and brandished her knife.

"Get away from me!" she yelled. "Stay back or—"

"Or what?" Zorn asked. "You'll kill me? You're far too good a person to do that."

"Let me go," Jane said. "You've no right to keep me here."

"I'll keep you here until you bore me," Zorn said. "Then I'll decide what to do with you."

Jane met his gaze and lowered her knife, feeling herself drawn into those dark eyes again. A silent command told Jane to lay the knife on the table, which she did. A split second later Zorn flicked his wrist and sent the table flying through the air. It crashed against the wall and splintered to bits.

Jane screamed and ran toward the bed. She tried to scoot across it as quickly as she could and run for the door. Zorn was much faster, however, and he pinned her against the wall. His tight vise-like grip around her arms immobilized her. He lifted her from the ground with the same ease he threw the table against the wall as she screamed again.

"Scream all you want," Zorn said. "Did you think I would not know you invaded my chamber? What did you hope to find there? I should break you in half for that!"

"No! Let me go!" Jane yelled as she kicked him, but she may as well have been kicking the wall. He pulled her closer. Jane saw his handsome face had become a twisted, rage-filled scowl. She tried to turn and wriggle out of his grasp, but it was no use. She was trapped. Jane closed her eyes and screamed again as loudly as she could. Then Zorn lowered her and let her go.

"Forgive me, Jane," he said. "I did not mean to hurt you. I cannot help myself. I'm drawn to you like a moth to a flame."

Jane's eyes lingered on his. She tried to look away, but she couldn't. Wait, she had plans to go somewhere. She was going to leave, wasn't she?

"It's been a long day. Perhaps you should get some sleep."

He picked her up and placed her on the bed. Jane suddenly found it difficult to keep her eyes open. As Zorn left the room, she drifted off to a peaceful slumber.

Hours later, something awakened Jane in the night. Her mind was foggy, so she wasn't sure what she had heard. Perhaps it was a door slamming or a scream, but whatever it was, it brought her out of the best sleep she'd had in days. She rolled out of bed and opened the doors to the balcony. The moon hung high overhead.

Jane watched her breath as she blew into the air. She walked to the far edge and looked out over a rough marshland way to the south. A chilly breeze blew and made her shudder. She stepped back into her bedroom and closed the door.

Far below, on the jagged rocks lay the broken figure of a young servant. Her white wimple stained red. A rose lay beside her, its petals breaking off and blowing away.

CHAPTER FORTY
AN OLD ENEMY, A NEW ENEMY

The morning sun fell across Jane's face and awakened her. She lay in bed, looking out the windows of the balcony doors. She stretched and let out a little squeak as she yawned, then closed her eyes and sighed. She felt like she was floating on a cloud, drifting in a mild breeze. She shook her head and blinked. Didn't she have plans? She stared at the ceiling, trying to remember what she was going to do. It didn't matter. She made up her mind that today was going to be a beautiful day. She was eager to get back to the garden. She was curious if she would come across any new plants or flowers she hadn't seen before.

She stepped out of bed and saw the shattered table. Bits and pieces were strewn about that side of the room. How did that happen? She seemed to remember something about the table yesterday. She and Zorn were standing over it, but then her memory faded.

A knock at the door interrupted Jane's thoughts.

"Come in," she said.

The door opened and an elderly servant entered. Like Trudy, she also wore a white wimple, and her wrinkled face reminded Jane of a badger. She curtsied to Jane and looked for a safe place to lay the breakfast tray.

"Where's Trudy?" Jane asked her.

The old woman stopped and looked at Jane. She apparently no idea to whom Jane was referring.

"Oh, sorry. I meant Gertrude. Where is she?"

"She has gone, my lady. Lord Zorn sent her away."

Jane jumped to her feet. She was shocked by the news.

"When? Where did Zorn send her?"

The old servant shook her head and continued to look about the room for a suitable spot for the tray.

"I asked you a question," Jane said. "Where is my friend Trudy?"

"Oh, I beg your pardon, my lady. But you'll have to ask Lord Zorn. I don't know."

Her answer irked Jane. Normally, she was pleasant to her elders, but Jane thought the old woman had tried to ignore her on purpose and Jane hated to be ignored. She didn't think much of this new servant, so she let her lay the breakfast tray on the bed and hurry out of the room. Jane was going to have a word with Zorn about the change in servants. She liked Trudy. Jane glanced at the broken table and admonished herself for not telling the old woman to get some help and clean it up.

She hurried and ate her breakfast. Ignoring the finery in her wardrobes, she dressed in her tunic and breeches. She grabbed a warm throw and wrapped it around her shoulders as she left the room. She also grabbed the small brown leather pouch full of acorns that Ariel had given her. She bounded down the stairs, through the great hall, and out into the courtyard. The bleak surroundings didn't bother

her, because the sun was shining overhead.

Jane walked around the castle to the garden. She stopped and looked at the castle walls. While predominantly constructed of massive gray stones, they had large iron buttresses reinforcing them. Half a dozen spires extended upward from the dark gray castle, giving it a menacing appearance. Jane hadn't noticed that detail before, but it seemed obvious to her now.

She stopped and surveyed the courtyard and garden. Still not a single person around. Jane decided not to worry herself with that. She had plans to make the dead garden a colorful oasis. One thing bothered her, though. How was she going to keep the flowers and plants alive in this chilly weather?

She took a deep breath. It was a problem she would have to figure out later. She walked around the garden and found some crumpled brown stalks bunched together.

Jane knelt and examined them. She wasn't sure if they were flowers or weeds.

"Oh well," she said with a sigh. "Let's see what you are, shall we?"

She placed a finger on the dried stalk.

"*Ehlia talo.*"

Jane opened her eyes and saw a beautiful vibrant red and white tulip.

"Beautiful," said a voice from behind her.

She turned around and saw Zorn. He was staring at her.

"I envy you," he said. "Your gift is miraculous, Jane."

She stood and looked down at the newly reinvigorated tulip.

"Thanks," Jane said. "I wasn't sure how that one would turn out."

Zorn looked over the rest of the garden.

"Do you plan to revive the entire garden?"

"Yep."

"Do you have enough magic inside you to do this?"

"Yep."

Zorn looked at Jane.

"I believe you do," he said. "I just realized there has never been a druid here. I look forward to seeing your garden."

"Me too," Jane said, "but there is the same problem we had with the snapdragon. How will we keep the flowers alive in the cold?"

Zorn looked over the garden again.

"Torches," he said finally. "We'll light large torches in the evenings. I'll have servants place them every ten feet. That should keep them warm."

"Good idea," Jane said. "Oh! And where's my friend Trudy?"

Zorn looked at her. "Trudy?"

"The young serving girl from Norland," Jane said.

Zorn shook his head. The name appeared to be unfamiliar to him.

"You know," she said. "Trudy? Gertrude? The girl who brought my breakfast yesterday?"

A spark of recognition crept across Zorn's face.

"Oh, yes. I sent her away."

"Why? Jane said. "And where did you send her?"

"We need supplies," Zorn said. "She and several others went for supplies."

"I like her. I wish you'd asked me before you sent her away."

"I didn't take that into consideration," Zorn said. "I must go. An emissary is expected to arrive soon and I must prepare."

"Really? A visitor? Who?"

"You are such a curious young lady, Jane," Zorn said. "You shouldn't concern yourself with such matters. However, let's call her a potential ally."

Jane narrowed her eyes and gave Zorn a suspicious look. Now she was really curious. Who was the mystery guest?

Zorn turned and left, walking to the castle with a quickened pace. For an hour afterward, Jane used her druidic charm to revive and rejuvenate flowers and plants, but she only succeeded in restoring a fraction of the dead garden. She was, however, satisfied with the results; the variety of colors reminded her of the wildflowers of the Spirewood Forest, the place where they had met Ariel.

Although it was a challenge to get them out of the hard ground, Jane managed to dig up a few tulips, roses, and lilies, and then she arranged them into a nice bouquet. At that moment, several horns sounded from the front of the castle. She stood and looked toward the front gate. Who was blowing the horns?

Two burly barbarians in leather armor rushed to the large ironbound gate and worked the loud opening mechanism. On the castle wall, four other barbarians faced outward from the castle, their gazes transfixed on something or someone. Where did they come from? They seemed to appear from nowhere. However, thought Jane, it might be an excellent welcome for the emissary if she presented the visitor with the bouquet of flowers. She rushed toward the gate as it opened to reveal a single rider on horseback.

Jane took up position inside the gate and watched the rider approach. The armor worn by the visitor reminded Jane of Sawyer's. Was it him? Her heart leapt and ached in her chest. She stepped forward and held the flowers out in front of her as she smiled. Sawyer would take the flowers and like them; he had no choice. Then she remembered Zorn had said the emissary was a female, so she lowered her hands.

The rider's white horse high-stepped and pranced into the courtyard. The rider wore decorative silver elven battle armor that had a blue sheen, and an ornate gold and silver spear hung across her back. Beneath her elaborate helm, the rider had long hair as black as a raven. But it was the emissary's eyes that captured Jane's attention. They were a light steel blue; the color of a cloudless sky. Jane smiled and performed a small curtsey while she offered her newly created bouquet to the visitor.

"Greetings," Jane said in a bright and cheerful tone. "You're most welcome…"

The rider only glared at Jane as she rode by, and the piercing gaze from those bright blue eyes sent a shiver down Jane's back, for there was a burning hatred in them. It was as if Jane had offended the visitor in some unforgivable way simply by speaking to her. The rider never said a word, but kept her eyes on Jane, even looking over her shoulder after she had passed.

The emissary rode to the front doors of the castle and dismounted her horse in a single motion. The doors to the castle opened and a large barbarian stepped out. The emissary removed her helm, revealing a stunningly beautiful elven female. Her features were every bit as lovely as Ariel's. Her lean, muscular frame exhibited both power and grace.

The elven warrior entered the castle with the barbarian. Why would Zorn want to speak with such a dreadful person? This didn't make sense. Jane ran to the large double doors and peeked inside. The barbarian led the visitor to the great hall, their footsteps echoing as they walked. They went to a side chamber and closed the door. Jane stepped inside the doors and looked around. She appeared to be alone. Laying the flowers down in a corner behind the double doors, she moved to the door of the side chamber as quietly as she could.

She was thankful she had worn her traveling clothes with her soft leather boots, because they allowed her to be quieter. Once at the door to the chamber, she noticed it wasn't completely closed, so she leaned closer to hear the voices from within.

"Save your ramblings for your mindless servants," said the elven warrior. "What do you want, Zorn?"

"Very well," Zorn said. His voice sounded like it was deeper and hollower than earlier. "Your hatred of humans is well known, Talia Spearslayer. My forces are ready to lay siege to Chalon. I offer you command of my armies. They're strong and fearless—"

"They are worthless," the elven warrior snapped. "Is this a joke?"

"My barbarians have swept across Alluria," Zorn said. "They are no joke."

"And this one? The one who led me to this room? Do you think he is a warrior? I see a bag of muck, nothing more."

Jane peeked through a small crack between the door and the wall. She saw the large barbarian growl and take a step toward the elven warrior. In a split second she had unsheathed a long dagger and thrust it through his heart. The barbarian had a surprised look on his face as he looked down at the dagger protruding from his chest then crumpled to the floor. Jane covered her mouth to muffle her gasp.

"As I said, muck. I have no interest in your war, but if you dare attack Selra'thel again I will kill you myself and feed your carcass to the crows."

"My queen indicated you would be interested in joining the war against humans," Zorn said.

"Queen Lysis has given you false hope," the elven warrior said. "I hate her orc hordes as much as your barbarian rabble."

Queen Lysis? Jane had never heard of her before.

"Very well," Zorn said. "If I pledge not to attack your elven lands, what will you offer in return?"

"Nothing. I do not care for you or Lysis," the warrior said. "Kill every human you see; butcher them all. This is not my war."

Zorn and the one he had referred to as Talia Spearslayer stood in the center of the room, staring at each other. Jane held her breath as she looked on. It seemed like a small flinch from either one would start a pitched battle. Zorn had fought Ariel and nearly killed her, yet he hesitated when confronted by this elven warrior.

"You should know," Zorn said, finally breaking the silence, "that Ariel Windsong has become the high druid and she fights *with* the humans."

The elven warrior clenched her fists.

"She befriends them," Zorn continued, "and teaches them the ways of the druid."

"You lie," the warrior snarled. "Ariel would never teach a human the druidic ways. Humans are dull, wretched creatures."

"It's rumored she travels with three human children—outlanders. Does that interest you?"

"Outlanders…the prophecy…" Her words trailed off as she walked about the room and appeared to consider Zorn's words. She spun and looked at him.

"That plain human girl with the flowers at the gate, she is one of the travelers?"

"She is," Zorn said.

"Why is she still alive?"

"Information," Zorn said. "And bait. We may be able to lure Ariel and the others into a trap."

"I wonder if it is something else," the warrior said. "What will Queen Lysis say when she finds out you harbor the enemy within your walls? She will tear your little flower girl to bits as you watch."

"Let me worry about her," Zorn said. "I seek an alliance with you. Join me as I take Chalon and burn it to the ground."

"No, I will not associate myself with you. Conquer Chalon and raze it yourself. Divide Alluria with your Scarlet Queen as you choose. I do not care. However, I will do something you cannot."

Another moment of silence fell over the room and then she said, "I will kill Ariel and the outlanders. But I expect to be paid handsomely. Five times your weight in gold."

"Done," Zorn said. "Ariel was last seen at Troll Fang Pass. You can start searching for her there. But be warned, Ariel is not to be trifled with."

"I have faced her before," the warrior said. "In fact, I welcome another battle with Ariel."

"So be it," Zorn said. "She travels with two human boys

and an elven archer. One of the boys carries the Stormblade and the other is a fledgling wizard."

"They are nothing," the warrior said. "When I am done with Ariel, I will kill them, too. First, that ridiculous girl with the flowers must die. I do not require her as bait."

Horrified, Jane stepped back from the door. Her heart pounded as panic set in. What was Zorn doing? She had been fooled into thinking he simply wanted to know more about her and her friends, but he had just given information to the elven warrior so she could kill them. Jane furrowed her eyebrows as she stepped away from the door. She was furious she had been brainwashed by Zorn into thinking everything was fine. Once she felt like she had a good enough distance from the door she ran outside.

She had to warn the others that Zorn was sending another assassin after them. This one seemed to be as dangerous as Lady Seqwil, perhaps more so. The front gates were still open and the guards on the wall were gone. This was her chance to escape while the late afternoon sun still shone overhead.

Jane pulled her throw around her shoulders tightly and hurried to the front gates. She continually glanced over her shoulder looking for any pursuit, but there was none. Once she was beyond the massive walls, the dangerous reality of her situation suddenly became apparent to her. A small band of barbarians warming themselves by a small fire just outside the walls watched her. Jane felt their eyes on her, but she ignored their looks and tried to walk nonchalantly down a rocky trail that led into the Dragonscale Mountains.

Once she found herself beyond the sight of the barbarians, she ran. The chilly air made her lungs ache, but she wasn't about to slow down. She turned a corner in the road and stopped. She looked down at a valley that was almost a mile away. It was dotted with campfires and populated with thousands of barbarians. The first thing that went through Jane's mind was that Chalon was doomed.

To her right, Jane caught a glimpse of movement among the rugged and harsh terrain. A small group of four barbarians kept watch by a corral of horses. Jane ducked behind a boulder. If she could get close enough and steal a horse, she might be able to get back to her friends before Zorn's newest assassin found them. She glanced back over her shoulder again to make sure she wasn't being followed.

She noticed a small goat trail leading away from the main path. It looked rough, but it was passable. The sun was beginning to set and the gloominess of dusk started to cover everything. Jane inched closer to the penned horses, all the while keeping an eye on the barbarians. They were talking among themselves in crude, profanity-laced speech.

After a few minutes, three of them sauntered away toward the far side of the corral. The fourth sat with his back against a boulder, and soon dipped his head and closed his eyes. Jane didn't dare wait any longer. She picked up a rock the size of a baseball and crept to the lone barbarian. She smelled his rank body odor before she was ten feet away.

The sound of his snoring made it easier for her to slip up close. Jane raised the rock high and brought it crashing down on the barbarian's head, and he slumped to his side, unconscious. Dropping her rock, Jane hurried to the corral and opened the gate. She grabbed a bridle and picked out a sturdy-looking brown stallion. She hurried with the riding gear and quietly led the horse out of the corral.

She hopped on the stallion and rode down the goat trail. It was getting dark now, and she was sure Zorn was looking for her, since she had been away for some time. She rode for the better part of an hour until darkness and the rough terrain forced her to dismount and walk; she was fearful of the horse stumbling over the loose, jagged rocks on the uneven trail.

Even though the temperature had fallen, the back of Jane's neck was moist with sweat. She was tired and hungry, but she hadn't had time to plan or pack food for her escape. Although the moon lit her way, the trail she followed ran perilously close to a cliff. More than once she staggered, kicking a loose stone or two over the edge.

She was determined to get back to her friends and to Sawyer, however. Now that she was free of the Iron Citadel, her head cleared and she became angry with herself for telling Zorn so much about them. She had placed them in terrible danger. How could she be so foolish?

A mile or so further to the south, the trail curved far enough away from the cliff that Jane felt better about her chances of avoiding a fall. She found a small area level enough to stop for a rest, and sat on a large rock. She patted the stallion's neck. It was starting to shiver, so Jane placed her shoulder wrap over the horse's back and rubbed its nose.

"I wish I had an apple for you," she said, "or at least some oats."

"You're a resourceful girl, Jane."

The deep voice came from just ahead of her on the trail. She looked in that direction and saw Zorn standing before her, fully armored with the exception of his helm.

"I never thought you'd make it this far," Zorn said,

taking a step toward her. "But now you must return. It isn't safe here at night."

"No!" Jane yelled picking up a rock and throwing it at him. "Stay away! You're a liar! You sent another assassin to kill my friends and you're going to kill me!"

"I still have use of you," Zorn said in an even voice. "I do not intend to harm you."

"Shut up! I don't believe you," Jane said, scanning the ground for another rock. "I don't know how you did it, but you charmed me somehow and I hate you for it."

Jane's horse jerked and rose up on its hind legs, pulling the reins from her hands and causing her to fall. It dashed back up the trail before she could recover. She felt Zorn's firm grip around her shoulders as he hoisted her to her feet. Jane slapped his face and pulled away from him. Whatever happened from this moment on, she was going to fight. Behind her, a low growl rose from a small overhang twenty feet away.

"Jane," Zorn said, drawing his sword. His voice sounded strained. "Listen carefully. Get behind me and stay there."

Jane spun around as Zorn positioned himself between her and a large, black, fur-covered figure with glowing yellow eyes crouching at the edge of the craggy overhang.

CHAPTER FORTY-ONE
THE SHADOWLORD'S SECRET

Jane screamed as the werewolf leapt from the overhang, snarling and with claws outstretched. Zorn pushed Jane to the ground as he extended his sword to meet the beast's lunge. The werewolf slammed into Zorn, and they landed twenty feet away, perilously close to the edge of the cliff. Zorn managed to drive his blade into the beast's upper arm, however. As he scrambled to his feet, the werewolf stopped and sniffed the wound in its arm, which was smoking. The runes in Zorn's sword glowed a vivid red and hissed. Jane smelled burned hair.

For a moment the werewolf turned its malicious gaze on Jane, and its burning yellow eyes held her in place. Jane trembled at the sight of the monster, but she dared not move or incite the beast. She was closer to it than she had ever been, and it was even more terrifying than she'd remembered. Saliva dripped from its fangs and it flexed its claws, which were designed to rip and tear.

"Don't move, Jane," Zorn said. He swung his sword back and forth in front of him, and the hissing of the burning runes drew the werewolf's attention away from Jane.

"Over here!" Zorn called.

The werewolf snarled and snapped in Zorn's direction. It hunched its back and moved to its left, apparently in an attempt to gain a better attacking position. Zorn also moved to his left, matching the werewolf's moves and maintaining a distance of at least fifteen feet.

"Jane," Zorn said over the loud growls and snarls of the werewolf, "move back to the outcropping to your left, but don't make any sudden moves."

Jane tried to swallow, but was unable to get anything past the lump in her throat. She kept her eyes on the large black werewolf and stepped backward. It immediately turned its head and snapped in her direction. The creature's gaze kept Jane in place, and the hate in its eyes made her blood run cold. Her right leg began shuddering uncontrollably. Zorn again stepped between the werewolf and Jane, drawing the beast's attention once more.

"Jane, move back," Zorn said as he pointed his sword at the werewolf. "This is my fight."

Jane backed up to the rocky overhang from which the werewolf had launched its attack. Zorn's black cloak began to writhe and move of its own accord. It expanded to three times its size, and a dozen smoky black tentacles whipped about in the chilly night air. The two dark figures faced each other, apparently searching for an opportunity to strike.

The tentacles would lash out at the beast every now and then, but the werewolf would bite or slash through them. When a tentacle was severed, it simply evaporated and another emerged from the cloak. The werewolf's hind legs coiled. It was ready to strike at any moment.

This was her chance to escape, Jane realized. While those

two villains battled she could slip away. She was about to turn and dash down the path when she realized the werewolf would come after her after it killed Zorn. She knew she wouldn't get far. Zorn was evil, but he had saved her from the werewolf. Perhaps a spark of humanity still resided beneath the darkness of his soul.

Jane searched the ground, but there wasn't enough plant life to cast the entangling spell that Ariel had taught her. Then she remembered the pouch of acorns Ariel had given her. She felt the outside of her breeches for the pouch, which she found tucked in a front pocket.

Jane frantically reached for the pouch. At the same time, the werewolf attacked Zorn, pinning him to the ground. Zorn punched the werewolf in the snout and slashed its arm with his sword. The punch landed with such power that Jane thought he may have broken the werewolf's nose, but it seemed to have no effect. The runed sword, however, did cut into the beast's arm, causing it to yelp. Then the werewolf began to savage Zorn, picking him up and slamming him to the ground with bone-crunching force. Zorn cried out as the fangs from the beast ripped through his armor and into his flesh. Jane nearly ripped her breeches as she pulled the pouch of acorns free.

Jane had to do something to help him; he was being torn apart before her eyes. She emptied the pouch of acorns in her hand and took one to throw. A piece of Zorn's armor flew past her and struck the rocky overhang behind her. Turning back, she could see that Zorn's writhing black cape had wrapped its tentacles around the werewolf in an attempt to immobilize it. Zorn had dropped his sword, and his now bare arm looked dreadful.

She raised her hand over her head and whispered, "*Ana'thel.*"

She threw the acorn at the werewolf. As her projectile flew through the air, it glowed with a green hue. The acorn struck the werewolf's chest and exploded, engulfing it and Zorn in a green flash. The beast yelped and was thrown ten feet away, but it landed on its back and rolled to its feet. This time its hateful glare was directed at Jane, and it snarled and lunged at her. Horrified, Jane trembled as she threw another acorn. She again uttered "*Ana'thel*", but as the acorn flew toward the werewolf, Zorn reached up from the ground and grasped the beast's hind leg, stopping its charge.

The second green explosion sent both Zorn and the werewolf flying in different directions. Zorn landed hard on the rocky ground, flipped over twice, and lay motionless. The werewolf was thrown to the edge of the cliff, but its momentum carried it over the edge. It clawed the ground in an effort to prevent itself from falling, tearing away huge chunks of earth and leaving deep claw marks in stone. It fell over the cliff despite its attempts, however. Jane heard its panicked growls and watched the malevolent yellow eyes disappear as the beast slipped away, still clawing at the walls of the cliff. She fell to her knees, shivering and exhausted.

She clutched the two acorns she had left and stared at the spot where the werewolf fell, remaining rooted where she was, dreading the thought of seeing those hateful yellow eyes again. She plucked an acorn from her hand and cocked her arm, ready to throw it the moment she saw any sign of the beast.

"Jane," Zorn said weakly.

He was lying on his back holding out his left hand to her.

The entire right side of his body was in horrible shape. Jane rushed to his side and knelt beside him. She placed her hands over the wounds to stop his bleeding, but there was too much damage. Jane shook her head.

"So much blood," she said. "I don't know if my healing charms will help."

"Jane," Zorn said. "Are you okay?"

"Yes, I'm fine," Jane said trying hard not to cry. "But you're not."

Jane searched her pockets for the leather pouch of healing components Ariel had given her, but then she remembered she had left it back in her room at the Iron Citadel. She was so stupid. Zorn had followed her and saved her life. If anything happened to him she wouldn't be able to forgive herself. She looked at her hands, which were covered in blood, as were her tunic and breeches. She looked back at Zorn. He appeared to be losing consciousness and he didn't seem to be breathing.

Jane placed her hands on what appeared to be the most grievous wounds.

"I'll try," she said. "I'll do my best."

She took a deep breath and closed her eyes. The words came to her.

"*Ilinara tae ullnara taethos,*" she said, but she felt nothing—no sensation of energy from inside or any tingling. Nothing happened. Did she mess up the words? No, she got the words right. Maybe the bits of dried leaves were a critical part of the spell. She had to try something to save him. Maybe a different spell would work. Again Jane closed her eyes and concentrated.

"*Ehlia sa maros,*" she said. This time she felt a wave of

energy well up from deep inside and pass through her fingers to Zorn. But then she felt something else. A sinister black mass prevented Jane's healing magic from entering him. It was the same feeling Jane had when she tried to heal Ariel after her battle with him. A thick darkness not only stopped Jane's spell, but in her mind, she saw Zorn was shrouded in a black cloud. Jane tried again, but her spell was rejected once more.

The strain of trying to force her spell into his body caused Jane's head to hurt. It was a sharp pain, like someone had stuck a needle in her temple. She wasn't going to give up, however.

"My spells aren't working," she said. "I'll keep trying."

"No," Zorn said. "Jane, get me to my wyvern. It will carry us home."

"Your…wyvern?" she repeated. "What is it and where is it?"

With his uninjured hand, Zorn pointed to his sword. Jane reached over and picked up the heavy sword. Immediately the sword burned her hand, and she felt a terrifying and evil presence.

"Ow!" she cried, dropping the weapon. "What was that? Your sword burned me. It *meant* to hurt me."

"Give it…to me," Zorn said.

Jane pulled the sleeves of her tunic over her hands and again picked up the sword, which immediately seared her sleeves. The smell of burning cloth filled Jane's nostrils as she dropped the sword within Zorn's reach. She waved her burned, blood-soaked hands in the cool night air and blew on them. Zorn grasped the handle of the sword and looked up into the night.

"What do you want me to do?" Jane asked.

She desperately wanted to revive him, but nothing worked. Then a troubling thought popped into her head. What if she had *lost* her ability to heal others? Ariel would never forgive her. Jane ripped her sleeves from her tunic, placed them over Zorn's wounds as well as she could, and maintained pressure.

Seconds later, she heard the flapping of large wings as something descended from the sky and landed beside them. It was the same winged creature that brought her to the Iron Citadel. Its leathery black wings ended with hooked claws, and its barbed tail whipped about. It looked at Jane and hissed, revealing several rows of needle-like teeth.

She fell backward at the sight of the black wyvern.

"It won't harm you," Zorn said. "Don't be afraid. Get me to my mount."

Jane looked at the wyvern. It wore a large leather saddle on its back.

"Jane. Hurry…"

Jane got to her feet and helped Zorn up. He leaned against her so much that his weight almost made her tumble over, but she recovered and propped him up as he sheathed his sword. They staggered to the wyvern, and Jane helped him climb into the saddle. After he had gotten himself situated, Zorn reached down and offered Jane his hand.

"Come."

Jane looked at his hand. Something inside told her to refuse. It was a mistake to return to the Iron Citadel. She should try and run away, to take her chances and try to find her friends.

"Jane," he said.

Jane looked up at Zorn. She blamed herself for his

injuries. Her hand shook as she resisted, but something made her take his hand, and she climbed into the saddle behind him. She held onto Zorn as they flew north, back to the Iron Citadel. She quickly released a hand and wiped tears from her moist face. She had lost her best chance of escaping Zorn and the Iron Citadel.

They landed in the courtyard by the front doors. The entire castle was dark, and it looked deserted. Jane climbed down. Her legs were unsteady at first, but she managed to keep her balance. The wyvern let out an ear-piercing screech that startled her.

"Don't worry," Zorn said. "It announced our return… that's all."

A moment later the front doors opened and four large barbarians clad in brown and black furs hurried out to meet them. Jane was pushed aside as they helped Zorn from his saddle and carried him inside. They never said a word, which struck her as being strange as she hurried after them. It was as though they were following silent orders. They took Zorn to the great hall and placed him on the couch by the fireplace.

One barbarian attempted to start a fire, but he was too clumsy with his handling of the flint and tinder, and barely produced a single spark with each strike. Jane walked over to the fireplace and held a cold, trembling hand over the wood in the fireplace.

"*Ignara.*"

A small fire erupted beneath her hand. The barbarian shouted and jumped back. His face was twisted in both shock and rage as he drew his sword. Jane thought he was going to kill her where she stood.

"No," Zorn said.

The other barbarians looked at her and then Zorn, but did nothing. The one who had drawn his sword stood still and glared at Jane. She wasn't sure what caused her to shiver more, the near-death experience with the werewolf, the crazed-looking barbarian waving his sword at her, or the cold from their flight. One thing was sure, she was exhausted.

"Leave us," Zorn told the barbarians.

They obeyed with only a grunt or two of protest. Jane turned back to the fire that had grown and drenched her in a warm glow. In the light of the fire Jane saw that she was covered in blood. With everything that had happened, she'd forgotten about that. Her hands were a dark red, as was everything she wore.

"Now what?" she said. "Do you have a doctor or someone who can help? You've lost so much blood, see?"

Jane held her bright red arms out to demonstrate her point. Zorn looked at her, but didn't say anything, which made her uneasy.

She looked around the dim chamber and saw another couch sitting against the wall at the edge of the firelight. A light gray blanket had been thrown over it. She hurried over and grabbed the blanket.

She returned and slipped off her blood-soaked boots. The floor was cold. Staying on the balls of her feet, she dashed back to the fireplace and wrapped the blanket around her so she was completely covered. She noticed that Zorn looked pale, but his eyes never seemed to leave her. She bit her lip and stepped closer to the fireplace.

"Are you going to die?"

"No."

"I've always tried to see the good in people and every situation," Jane said with a sniffle. "You saved me from the werewolf."

"I think you can handle yourself well, Jane. Perhaps I saved the werewolf from you."

Jane let out a small laugh as a tear ran down her face again. She wiped it away.

"Why did you save me, Jane?"

Jane took a deep breath and exhaled.

"Because I'm not a monster. I'm not like you."

She heard Zorn struggle to his feet, but Jane kept her gaze on the fire. The flames swayed and swirled about like small ballet dancers. She trembled as she felt his presence behind her. Zorn wrapped his left arm around her shoulders. Her heart pounded in her chest and her breathing quickened.

"You really are amazing," he said. "But now I'm going to show you not everyone can be saved."

"I know what you are now," Jane said between breaths. "I figured it out."

He turned her around. Jane tried to keep from looking into Zorn's deep, dark eyes. He wiped a tear from her cheek.

"Will it hurt? Dying, I mean?"

"You may not realize this yet," he said as he lifted her chin. "But in a way, I'm going to save you."

Zorn pulled her closer. She crossed her arms in front of her. She wished she could see her parents again. She had wanted to do so much with her life, but time had run out. A sharp pain surprised her as his fangs penetrated her neck.

Jane opened her mouth to scream and tried to push away, but he was too strong. She began to feel drowsy and a wave of darkness washed over her as the room started to spin. A moment later Jane's eyes closed and her blanket fell to the floor.

CHAPTER FORTY-TWO
THE TRUE ENEMY

Geoff had grown tired of slogging through the mud of the Shattered Moor. He was glad to be on dry land again, but the desolate, rocky ground beyond the swampland proved to be difficult, and their rate of travel hadn't increased. His feet and ankles hurt from numerous small cuts from the jagged rocks. Ishara kept looking over her shoulder at him, since he had fallen behind the others, but he managed to catch up at the top of a craggy hill.

Sawyer, Ariel, and Ishara were standing in place, looking up at something. No one said anything. Geoff followed their gazes up to a dark, imposing castle in the distance that rested on a high cliff, and he shuddered. Even from a league away, he thought it was a horrid, creepy-looking place.

"The Iron Citadel," Ariel said. "The fortress of the Shadowlord."

"So Jane's in *there*?" Sawyer asked, taking a step forward.

"Yes," Ariel replied. "This is where he would have taken her. Here is where he launched his attack upon Alluria."

"It's ugly," Geoff said. "Who would want to live there?"

"Not Jane, that's for sure," Sawyer said. He turned to

Ariel. "Do you think she's okay?"

"I hope so," Ariel said. "Jane is both strong and brave. She will find a way to escape."

"Look there," Ishara said, pointing down and to their left. "The Shadowlord's northern army."

Geoff and the others turned and looked in the same direction. In the distance, beyond the rolling mists, was a great black movement toward the south. It looked like a giant black snake slithering through the trails and ravines of the Dragonscale Mountains.

"Tens of thousands," Ishara said. "A force of that number has never been seen before. They march to Chalon."

"What about the garrison?" Geoff asked.

No one answered. He knew what that meant. Commander Renfry and his soldiers at Troll Fang Pass were doomed. Geoff glanced back at the dark castle that loomed above them. The trek there would take most of a day.

"Wait a minute," Sawyer said. "If the Shadowlord sent his army south, now would be the time to sneak in and rescue Jane, right?"

"Our chances to avoid being seen are better, yes," Ariel said.

"Would he be leading his army?" Geoff asked.

"I do not know," Ariel said.

"There's one way to find out," Sawyer said. "Let's go get Jane."

"Wait," Ariel said. "Now that we are this close we must plan. We cannot simply walk into the Iron Citadel and expect to survive, much less find Jane."

"So what do we do?" Sawyer asked as he threw his arms up. "I thought we were going to sneak in."

"Not us, them," Ariel said as she pointed at Geoff and Ishara.

Geoff felt everyone's eyes on him.

"What?" Geoff said.

"The two of you are best suited to enter the Iron Citadel and find Jane," Ariel said. "Sawyer and I will remain outside."

"Aren't you and Ishara the best at being quiet?" Sawyer asked. "I never hear either of you make any noise when you walk."

Geoff nodded emphatically and gulped.

Ariel walked to Geoff and placed a hand on his shoulder.

"In this case," she said, "the two smallest members of our company are best suited to sneak into the Shadowlord's castle."

Geoff looked down. Ariel placed her hand on his shoulder.

"You will do fine, Geoff," Ariel said. "Ishara and I have spoken and she has assured me that your sneaking skills will serve us well."

Geoff gave her a nod. "I understand," he said, "but I'm scared. What if we run into ghouls and wraiths?"

"Then a wizard will be needed," Ariel said. "Your spells will be more useful than mine."

"I don't understand." Geoff said.

"My magic," Ariel said, "powerful as it is, is woodland based. That means I must be around living, growing things in order to be most effective."

Geoff glanced at the brownish-gray and black terrain. He didn't see so much as a single blade of grass.

"I have a question," Sawyer said. "Actually, I have two questions. What am I going to do while they go look for Jane and what if they're attacked? You've seen what Geoff can do. He'll blow up half the castle."

"You will be with me to help make ready our escape when we have Jane," Ariel said. Then she turned back to Geoff. "And as to Geoff blowing up half the castle, make sure it is the half with the Shadowlord in it."

"Okay, looks like we have a plan," Sawyer said, clapping his hands. "But how do we escape when we have Jane? That's a lot of troops down there. We can't take 'em all on."

"We fly," Ariel said. "As before."

Sawyer looked at Ariel for a moment and then rolled his eyes.

"Gryphons. Damn, isn't there any other way?" Sawyer asked.

"I cannot think of any," Ariel said. "We will need to fly fast and far."

"Aw hell," Sawyer grumbled.

"Why didn't we just fly up here?" Geoff asked. "That would've saved us days of walking in the swamp."

"True," Ishara said. "Gryphons would have gotten us here sooner, but our chances of being noticed would have increased as well."

"Oh," Geoff said. "But what if we flew at night?"

"It was possible," Ariel said. "But I was unwilling to take that chance with Jane's life in the balance. If the Shadowlord were to become alerted to our presence, then we would never see her again."

A gloomy silence fell over the group as they sat and rested. Geoff munched on an apple from his rations and watched the others. Even Ishara was silent as she checked her bow and inventoried the arrows in her quiver. Geoff looked at his apple. If they failed and were captured, it wasn't much of a last meal. After an hour, Ariel stood.

"It is time," she said.

They climbed higher and higher over the rocky terrain in the cold mountain air. Ishara had found a small trail running along a cliff that led to the castle. She also found evidence of the werewolf, and signs of a battle. Ariel bent closer to have a closer look at several dark stains on the ground.

"Is that blood?" Sawyer asked. "It's really dark."

"Did someone kill the werewolf?" Geoff asked.

"No," Ishara said as she walked to the cliff's edge. "But it did fall...some."

"What does that mean?" Sawyer asked. "It fell *some*?"

"I can see many places where it could have broken its fall," Ishara said. "There was a battle here, but I am not sure who the werewolf fought."

"Jane?" Geoff asked. "Maybe Jane escaped and it attacked her."

"I do not believe this is Jane's blood," Ariel said. "But this does look like a piece of her tunic."

Ariel held up a torn and ragged blood-stained sleeve. Geoff and the others gathered around for a closer look.

"If that isn't Jane's blood," Sawyer said, "whose is it?"

Ishara picked up a twisted piece of black metal. Geoff recognized it as a partial shoulder piece for a set of plate mail.

"The Shadowlord?" Geoff blurted out. "Maybe the werewolf killed him."

"Do not be so sure," Ariel said. "But it appears the Shadowlord may have been injured."

"Good," Sawyer said. "Let's get Jane while we can. If he's hurt, he won't be much trouble."

"Whatever happened here happened a day ago, two at most," Ariel said. "He may have healed by now."

"No way," Sawyer said shaking his head. "Look at all this blood. He's gotta be dead…" Then Sawyer realized something. "Jane. What if she healed him?"

"Why would she do that?" Geoff asked.

"There are too many questions for us to answer," Ariel said. "We will rest here for the night and tomorrow we rescue Jane."

Geoff got little sleep that night, and it wasn't because of the cold or the chill in the wind. He imagined all sorts of evil creatures in the dark fortress above them. He had no idea how he and Ishara would find Jane in that huge castle, sneak her out, and get away without being seen. Sawyer tossed and turned beside him. He wasn't snoring, which meant he couldn't sleep either.

As Geoff lay there looking at the dark structure against the night sky, he saw an orange and yellow light flickering in the uppermost tower. He sat up. More than likely, someone had started a fire in a fireplace. He looked at Ariel and Ishara, who were sitting together on the rocky overhang above him. They had also seen the light in the tower.

"Ariel," Geoff said.

"Yes," Ariel said without taking her eyes away from the castle. "You and Ishara should begin your search for Jane in that chamber."

Sawyer sat up and yawned. He also noticed the light in the tower.

"So Jane's in that room?" Sawyer asked. "That's a tall tower."

"I hope she is there," Ariel said, pulling her fur cloak tighter around her. "And yes, that is a very tall tower. Get some rest."

"I've been wondering," Sawyer said as he lay back down. "How're we gonna fly outta here? I haven't seen any gryphons since you sent them away at the garrison…what was it? Troll Fang Pass?"

"I will summon them," Ariel said. "They will come, but I need to concentrate while I am summoning. You must protect me during that time."

Sawyer seemed to consider Ariel's words before he scratched his nose and rolled over. Geoff realized Sawyer was probably thinking exactly what he was and there were a lot of things that could go wrong with their plan to rescue Jane. Geoff bundled himself up under the fur cloak he used as a blanket as he thought of Jane. Was she okay, or was she wounded and dying? Geoff closed his eyes as he lay back down. They would find out tomorrow.

It wasn't until nearly midday that Ariel let them begin their final approach. Gray clouds had formed and a light drizzle began to fall. Geoff thought the Iron Citadel looked even eerier in the rain. Ishara had scouted a path that would keep them hidden while they crept up to the castle walls, and Ariel found a suitable spot under a jagged outcropping to position herself for summoning her gryphons.

"Are we ready?" Ariel asked.

Everyone nodded.

"Go find our Jane," Ariel said to Ishara. "We will await your signal."

With that, Ariel turned and sat on the ground with her legs crossed. She closed her eyes and rested her hands on her knees. Sawyer unsheathed his sword and held out his hand to Geoff.

"Good luck," he said as Geoff shook it. "Bring her back."

Geoff swallowed and nodded. He wasn't sure how to react to Sawyer's well wishes. Ishara pulled Geoff away, and as they ran, he heard Sawyer call out behind them.

"And if you see the blackhearted bastard that kidnapped Jane, fry his ass."

Geoff and Ishara made their way toward the castle wall, stopping often to hide behind large boulders and craggy sections.

"Geoff," Ishara said, "there are guards on the wall. You must stay close."

He peeked out from behind their current position and surveyed the top of the wall, but saw nothing.

"Where? I don't see any—"

Ishara pointed to a spot above the castle gates. Geoff squinted. Sure enough, after a minute he saw movement. One, maybe two guards were there.

"We will enter there," Ishara said, pointing to a small ironbound door in a far tower near the edge of the cliff. "I see no guards in that tower."

Geoff kept his head down and stayed behind Ishara as they dashed from hiding place to hiding place. He worried if he would slip on a wet rock and give them away. That would ruin everything. No, he had to stop thinking like that. They were going to get inside and they were going to rescue Jane. Geoff shook his head to rid himself of his negative thoughts.

After several minutes of rock hopping, they arrived at the small door. Its iron edges were rusty, but it looked solid.

"Keep watch, Geoff," Ishara said as she knelt and pulled a few small tools from a pouch on her belt. Geoff looked left, right, and up while Ishara picked the lock in a couple of minutes. She pushed the door open a little, but it squeaked loudly. Geoff held his breath and again swiveled his head about, looking for guards. Ishara took a small vial of thick brown liquid from her pouch and poured its contents on the hinges.

She slowly opened and closed the door until it no longer squeaked. They ducked inside the dark tower and hid behind the columns of an open arch that led to an empty courtyard.

"Geoff," Ishara said as she pointed to a spot in the courtyard. "Look."

Geoff peered around the corner and immediately saw a vibrant array of colors in the far corner of a dead, brown garden. His heart leapt.

"That's gotta be Jane's work," he said excitedly. "I know it."

"Agreed," Ishara said as she surveyed the rest of the courtyard. "She is alive…but where?"

Laughter came from a rickety shed at the far edge of the garden. Geoff strained to hear. He heard two voices, but he wasn't sure what they were saying.

"Who is it?" Geoff asked. He looked at Ishara, whose elven hearing was far better than his. Her lips were tight.

"This is not good," she said, crouching and readying her bow.

Geoff turned his attention back to the shed as more laughter erupted from within. Then two figures appeared. One was a tall, well-built man with dark hair. He wore a beige tunic and black breeches and had a sheathed longsword by his side. The other figure was a teenager with brown hair pulled back into a ponytail. She wore a baggy blue tunic and tan breeches.

"That's Jane! She's still alive," Geoff said in a hushed tone. "We can get her and be out of here before anyone notices."

There was no reply from Ishara. Geoff looked over at her and saw she had an arrow nocked and had drawn her bow. Geoff held his breath and waited for her to fire. Jane screamed, and Geoff looked back to the garden. Jane and the dark man were throwing clods of dirt at each other. Then the dark man grabbed Jane and hoisted her over his shoulder. Jane playfully beat on his backside as he trotted around the garden with Jane draped over him. Jane was laughing and carrying on so much that Geoff had to blink and look again.

She seemed to be having fun.

"Ishara," Geoff said. "What's happening? She's happy. And who's that guy?"

Ishara lowered her bow and placed a finger to her lips for Geoff to be quiet. What was Jane doing? The dark man placed Jane back on the ground and watched as she went back to work in the garden. Geoff leaned further out to get a better look, but as he did his foot slid across the stone walkway and dislodged a small rock.

He and Ishara ducked back around the corner as the dark-haired man whipped around and looked in their direction. Geoff grimaced. Ishara wore a grim expression on her face, but she didn't move. A few seconds later he heard footsteps approaching.

"Hey, where do you think you're going, Zorn?" Jane asked.

The footsteps stopped for a minute, then Geoff heard them grow fainter as the dark-haired man walked back to Jane. Ishara looked at Geoff and let out a sigh. Geoff realized his knees were shaking and his heart was racing.

"That was close," Ishara whispered. "Too close."

They observed Jane and the stranger for a few minutes longer. He jammed long metal sconces into the ground and placed torches in them while Jane cast several rejuvenating spells on dried brown flowers. The burst of color each time she finished her spell was captivating. Geoff notice that they didn't seem to mind the chilly drizzle.

"Why is she working on that garden?" Geoff asked. "I don't understand."

Another figure emerged from around the corner of the courtyard. He had come from the front gates. He was a big man and wore black furs, and he carried a battle-axe that Geoff thought might be as large as he was. The man's face was thickly bearded, and his large arms exhibited scars from many battles. He walked to the dark-haired man and bowed his head. Geoff was too far away to hear what they said. He glanced at Ishara, who held up a finger again as she listened intently to their conversation.

Then Zorn and Jane followed the barbarian to a castle door and went inside.

"Now, Geoff," Ishara said as she jumped to her feet and dashed for the same door. Geoff also sprang to his feet and followed Ishara across the courtyard. Ishara tried the handle of the door and it opened slightly. She slipped inside and held the door for Geoff.

It took a little time for his eyes to adjust to the dark, but Geoff saw a corridor ahead of them that opened into a large room. Ishara closed the door behind him and motioned for him to follow her. They crept down the corridor. Geoff heard Jane's voice before they got to the large room.

"I'm going to change this wet shirt while you're in your meeting," she said. "I'll be in the garden when you're done."

"Very well," the dark-haired man said.

Jane turned and skipped up a wide staircase while Zorn went into a room on the other side of a large fireplace. The barbarian left the great hall and disappeared into the darkness. They heard a door open and close at the far end of the hall.

"That room is huge," Geoff said. "And look at the fireplace."

Ishara shot him a stern glare, indicating he was too chatty. She and Geoff waited for a minute and then ventured out into the great hall and over to the room the dark-haired man had entered. The door was closed, but Geoff heard voices. Ishara looked up at the second floor, then touched Geoff on the shoulder.

"I will go up a level and try to observe from there," she said. "You stay here and *do not move*."

"Wait," Geoff said. "Do you think it's a good idea to split up?"

Ishara pointed with an arrow to a location above him. "I will be there," she said. "We are not splitting up, but you must not make a sound."

"Okay," Geoff said, and with that Ishara dashed up to the second-floor landing and crossed over to an open arch with a pulled curtain. She looked down at him and nodded. Geoff tried to look through the keyhole. He could only see the dark-haired man. He was kneeling on one knee. Geoff concentrated and listened to the conversation inside the room.

"My queen, I assure you all goes as planned. We—"

"Silence! I should tear you apart and dine on your heart for your failures."

The terse voice was a woman's voice. There was something strangely familiar about it. Geoff wasn't sure what it was; maybe there was an echo in the room. The woman's voice made Geoff shiver, and goosebumps ran down his arms.

"You fail me at every turn. Why are your armies not at Chalon?"

"Please, my queen. The High Druid, Ariel, attacked my eastern army before they reached Chalon and drove them back."

"I gave you the power to defeat her. I gave you armor, a sword, and a cloak of shadows. And still that is not enough."

"She's become a force of nature. Ariel is not easily defeated."

"Perhaps I should turn her? A dark druid as powerful as Ariel will be most useful."

"There's something else, my queen. Last night I fought the werewolf and—"

"And lost! The beast prowls just beyond the walls of your castle each night. How is it you cannot find the man and kill him? And what of the garrison at Troll Fang Pass? Why have you not crushed its defenders?"

"Ariel and her friends intervened."

Geoff saw quick movement as someone wearing deep red robes flashed before his eyes. He heard a loud *smack* and Zorn fell backward. Geoff looked up at Ishara. She had an excellent spot and saw everything. The horrified look on her face made Geoff's heart sink, however.

"I know about her friends," the woman said. "The young Stormlord, the boy wizard, and the girl druid. Kill them. Kill the outlanders."

CHAPTER FORTY-THREE
SAVING JANE

Geoff peeked through the keyhole again and saw Zorn return to his kneeling position with his head bowed low.

"My queen, the girl druid; there has never been a human druid. I'm sure Ariel and the others will come for her soon. I intend to trap them. I have begun to turn her. She may be of use—"

"Do as I say," the woman hissed. "The pieces are in place. I have already unleashed my orc hordes. The battle for Chalon approaches. I will not risk her reuniting with her friends."

"As you wish, my queen. What of the knights of Caladar?" he said. "My spies have reported they approach from the west."

"They are no longer a factor in this war. My orcs ambushed them and decimated their ranks."

Geoff looked at Ishara again. She was preparing to fire an arrow when the sound of Jane's singing echoed in the great hall. Ishara backed away from the curtain and moved toward the staircase. She motioned for Geoff to retreat back to the corridor from which they had entered. He obeyed and left the great hall as quietly and as fast as he could, then watched as Jane descended the stairs.

When Jane reached the second floor, Ishara showed herself. Jane was surprised and enthusiastically hugged her.

"Ishara, it's so good to see you again! How are you? Where're the others?"

"Shh," Ishara said. "They are waiting for you outside. We must hurry."

"Okay," Jane whispered. "How is everyone?"

"They are all fine, Jane. Please hurry."

They came down the last flight of stairs and hurried across the floor of the great hall toward Geoff. He glanced back at the door he had been listening at, and was relieved to see it was still closed and none of those inside had apparently heard them.

"Hi, Geoff," Jane said, giving him a hug. "It's great to see you again. How did you find this place?"

Something was different about Jane; she was acting weird. Ishara gave Geoff a warning look and shook her head. Geoff understood that to mean he should reveal as little as possible to Jane.

"We...um..." Geoff began. "We just kind of got here and were looking for you."

"Where's Sawyer and Ariel?" Jane asked.

"They are outside," Ishara said quickly. "Come, they want to see you."

She took Jane by the hand and led her down the dark corridor to the courtyard, with Geoff close behind. Once outside, Ishara removed a small clay jar from one of her pockets and opened it.

"What're you guys doing?" Jane asked. "Where's Sawyer and Ariel?"

"They're coming," Geoff said, watching Ishara dip an

arrow tip into the jar that contained what looked like tar. "They'll be here soon."

"Wait a minute," Jane said, narrowing her eyes and looking at them. "You're both acting bizarre."

"Jane, who was that guy you were with earlier in the garden?" Geoff asked.

"Oh, that's Zorn," she said with a smile. "I'll introduce you. This is his castle. You know, we have the whole war all mixed up. He isn't the bad guy we thought."

"Of course," Ishara said, handing Jane the arrow with the tar-covered tip. "Please light this for me. I will return in a moment."

Ishara took out another arrow and nocked it. She looked at Geoff with a grim expression on her face and then disappeared around the corner to the front of the castle.

"Geoff," Jane said, "I don't get what's going on here. Why does she need this arrow lit?"

From around the corner, Geoff heard Ishara's arrow shots followed by two sudden, short cries of pain, and then nothing.

"Jane," Geoff said licking his lips, "please light the arrow for Ishara. We'll tell you later."

Jane studied him for a moment, shook her head, and dropped the arrow.

"No," she said. I'm not doing anything until you answer my questions, Geoff."

"Please, Jane," he said, picking up the arrow. "I promise I'll tell you everything."

"No," Jane said. "I thought you'd be happy to see me again and I at least thought Sawyer and Ariel would drop by, too."

"They are coming, Jane," Ishara said as she reappeared. "We need to send them a signal so they know where to find us."

She took the arrow from Geoff and held it up to Jane.

"Please," Ishara said.

Jane sighed. "Okay, but only because I trust you guys."

She pointed a finger at the tar on the tip of the arrow.

"*Ignara.*"

The tar burst into a small flame. Ishara immediately launched the arrow over the castle wall.

"Since when does Ariel need a signal to find someone?" Jane asked.

"Well, it's more for Sawyer," Geoff said. "You know how he is."

Ishara nocked another arrow and glanced back at the dark castle and courtyard.

"Yes, I know how he is," Jane said, watching Ishara. "What're you doing, Ishara?"

Ishara didn't answer. She seemed to be intent on watching for more guards. Geoff stepped in between Jane and Ishara, hoping to draw Jane's attention back to him.

"Jane, are you feeling okay?" he asked. "We thought you'd be happier to see us."

"I am happy to see you, Geoff," Jane said. "But something isn't right."

"Jane, do you remember that Zorn is the Shadowlord?" Geoff asked in an even tone.

"Of course I do," Jane snapped. "I'm not stupid, Geoff."

She put her hands on her hips and frowned as she looked at him and Ishara. Jane's suspicions had been roused, and there wasn't much he could do about that. He had to think fast and try to change the subject.

"We thought the werewolf got you, Jane," he said. "We found blood and a piece of your tunic and some mangled armor."

Jane looked at him. She appeared to have trouble remembering, then her face lit up.

"That's right!" she said. "I was on a small trail to the south and it attacked me. Zorn saved my life, but he was hurt. We barely survived."

"It was lucky for him you were there to heal him," Ishara said. "The amount of blood he lost would have killed any other man."

"Well, I didn't heal him," Jane said. "My spells were useless. I'm not sure why."

"Like when you tried to heal Ariel after her battle with the Shadowlord," Ishara said. "The evil inside him would not allow it."

"No, no," Jane said. "You got it wrong. He's not evil. Just talk to him and you'll see. He's—"

"There they are," Geoff said, pointing to the three gryphons that had appeared in the gray sky. They were flying low, with Ariel on the lead gryphon followed by Sawyer on the second. The last gryphon had an empty saddle. They glided over the wall, made a sharp turn, and landed. Ariel and Sawyer hopped off their gryphons and rushed to Jane.

"Jane," Sawyer said as he ran to her and wrapped his arms around her. "You're alive! Are you okay?"

Jane barely returned his hug.

"What's the matter, Jane?" Sawyer asked.

Geoff and Ishara ran to their gryphon and climbed aboard. Ishara scanned the castle walls while the others talked.

"Nothing. I'm fine," Jane said. "You guys look great, even in the rain."

"Jane, we must go now," Ariel said. "The danger is too—"

"Go? What're you talking about? There isn't any danger here."

One of the gryphons screeched and started. The noise it made was loud enough that Ariel went back to calm it.

Sawyer grabbed Jane's shoulders and looked into her eyes. "Jane, do you know where you are? You were kidnapped by the Shadowlord. We're here to save you. Let's go."

Jane pushed his hands off her shoulders and her face became flushed.

"No! I'm not going anywhere!" Jane shouted. "You're all acting crazy!"

Sawyer placed a hand on her arm. "Jane, listen to me. We gotta go. We're in danger. Now get on that gry—"

Sawyer never had a chance to finish his sentence because Jane slapped him across the face. He was stunned, and blinked as a trickle of blood ran from his lower lip.

"Jane, listen to him," Ariel said. "Come with us. There is no time."

"No!" Jane shouted. She turned to push past Sawyer, but he caught her in his arms. She struggled and tried to wriggle free, but Sawyer kept his hold on her. Jane screamed and hit Sawyer with her fists several times about the face and chest.

"What the hell's wrong with you?" Sawyer asked, trying to grab Jane's arms to stop the beating. "We're here to save you!"

Jane screamed for help and landed a solid right cross to his chin. Sawyer kept hold of her with both hands, but Jane continued to hit him. Suddenly Ariel appeared beside Sawyer. Jane was still screaming when Ariel pulled her from Sawyer's grasp and slapped her. Jane immediately went unconscious and Ariel caught her. Sawyer ran a finger under his nose. He looked at the blood and frowned.

"Sawyer," Ariel said as she turned and threw Jane over her shoulder. "We must go!"

Ariel draped Jane over the saddle of her gryphon, then Sawyer turned to get on his mount when the door to the corridor swung open. Geoff gasped. It was the dark-haired man, Zorn.

Sawyer turned and faced him. Zorn was taller than he was and a little older. Zorn regarded Sawyer for only a second, then he saw Jane lying across the gryphon's saddle.

"You've arrived much earlier than expected," Zorn said. "But no matter. You're here now. You've come to die."

He took a couple of quick steps toward the gryphons, but stopped when Sawyer drew the Stormblade from its scabbard.

"What'd you do to her?" Sawyer shouted. "Tell me!"

Zorn lowered his gaze at Sawyer and sneered.

"She's mine, boy."

Apparently that was more than Sawyer could stomach. He charged Zorn. As he did, the Stormblade began to spark with tiny arcs of lightning that roamed up and down the blade.

"Sawyer!" Ariel called as she slid off the gryphon and pulled her scimitars.

Zorn drew his black blade and easily dodged Sawyer's headlong attack. The next instant he turned and parried several attacks from Ariel. The runes on the Shadowlord's black sword began to glow red.

"Ishara, can you shoot him?" Geoff asked.

"As soon as I have a clear shot," she said as she aimed at the Shadowlord.

Ariel spun and slashed high and low with her weapons with blinding speed. The Shadowlord was forced back while he tried to fend off Ariel and an occasional attack from Sawyer. Their movements were so fast, Geoff thought the fight resembled a fast-forwarded combat scene on television. Only Sawyer moved at normal speed; however, it was Sawyer who landed a blow to Zorn's left side.

The Shadowlord yelled and writhed in pain as he was covered with small arcs of electricity. Ariel took advantage of the situation and slashed him twice across the chest and then kicked him in the abdomen. The Shadowlord tumbled backward in the rain, landing a few feet from the open door. Sawyer raised his sword over his head and lunged at him, but the Shadowlord got to one knee and parried Sawyer's swing.

In one motion the Shadowlord rose to his feet and backhanded Sawyer with a fist. This time Sawyer fell backward. As he tried to recover, Ariel spun and landed a back kick to the Shadowlord's head. He landed face down. Ariel immediately swung a scimitar at his neck.

Before her blow could sever the Shadowlord's head, he rolled to his side and parried her attack. Then he swept her legs with a powerful kick. Ariel fell backward and the back of her head hit the ground.

"Ariel!" Geoff cried.

She lay on the ground and shook her head in an effort to recover her senses. Ishara shot the Shadowlord with three arrows as he got to his feet, each one a direct hit to his chest. He looked down at the arrows. Geoff's mouth dropped as he pulled them out one at a time.

"That's not possible," Geoff uttered.

"Tell him that," Ishara said through clenched teeth as she nocked another arrow and took aim. Before she could get her shot off, however, Sawyer sprang at the Shadowlord. Their blades clashed, and sparks flew everywhere. Sawyer pressed the attack, angrily hacking and thrusting at the Shadowlord. One side of his face was red and had begun to swell. Ariel got to her feet and rejoined the battle. Between her and Sawyer, they forced the Shadowlord back toward the castle door.

The gryphon Geoff and Ishara was on screeched and flapped its wings, and the other gryphons became anxious and screeched too. Geoff saw movement from the front of the castle. Seven fur-clad barbarians had emerged and were rushing toward them, yelling and waving their swords and axes in the air. Ishara turned her bow on them, picking them off as they ran.

"Ariel," Ishara called, "we are outnumbered!"

"Sawyer, get on your gryphon and go," Ariel said. "We'll be right behind you."

"I'm not leaving you," Sawyer said as he blocked an overhead attack from the Shadowlord. "We can take him."

Ariel landed a slash on the Shadowlord's arm, causing him to stumble backward. She immediately grabbed Sawyer and pushed him toward the gryphons.

"Listen to me," she said. "Go!"

Sawyer growled as he obeyed Ariel and hurried to the gryphons. Ishara finished off the last of the charging barbarians and turned her bow on the Shadowlord. The gryphon on which Geoff and Ishara sat bucked like a wild bronco. Ishara dropped the arrow she had aimed at the

Shadowlord and grasped the reins to regain control of their mount.

Sawyer ran to his gryphon and turned around. Lightning ran up and down the length of his sword. A low rumble of thunder overhead caught his attention. He raised his sword with both hands, pointing the blade toward the roiling clouds.

Ariel and the Shadowlord continued their battle, with Ariel landing a few more slashes across his arms and leg, which caused the Shadowlord to drop to a knee.

"Ariel," Sawyer shouted, "move back!"

She looked over her shoulder at Sawyer then up at the brewing, dark swirls and sprinted toward the gryphons. The Shadowlord recovered and stood up. His rage-filled face looked as dark as the clouds overhead. Geoff squinted. Did he see fangs, too? In the rain and bouncing around on a bucking gryphon it was hard to tell.

There was a blinding flash as a large bolt of lightning struck the ground in front of the Shadowlord. The explosion sent water, stone, earth, and the Shadowlord tumbling. He struck the wall of the castle and crumpled to the ground. It was a collision that would've killed anyone, but the Shadowlord began to stir.

"He's still alive," Geoff said. "How?"

Ariel grabbed Sawyer by the shoulder and shoved him to his gryphon.

"Go," she said. "There will be another time for this."

Sawyer did as he was told, but he still looked uneasy in the saddle. Ariel hopped on her mount, quickly made sure Jane was secured in the saddle, and urged her gryphon airborne. The gryphon Geoff and Ishara rode also sprang into the air with a sudden jump. It snapped Geoff's head back, and he grabbed Ishara's waist to steady himself. The wind whipping about made the rain sting his face and eyes. In the courtyard below, the Shadowlord roared in rage as he watched them fly away.

Geoff looked far ahead, and could just make out Ariel on her gryphon with Jane lying across the saddle. He looked over his shoulder. There was Sawyer, teeth clenched and hanging onto his gryphon's neck with both hands, his dark hair blowing in the wind and rain. Geoff let out a long sigh of relief. They made it. They had gone into the Shadowlord's castle and rescued Jane.

He happened to glance down while they flew. From the high altitude he clearly saw a dark mass moving south through the Dragonscale Mountains. It was the Shadowlord's army and they were marching toward Chalon.

CHAPTER FORTY-FOUR
GATHERING CLOUDS

The gryphons flew south as evening fell. It wasn't long before they had flown out of the rain and outdistanced the Shadowlord's army. Ariel's gryphon veered to the west and began to descend. Ishara pointed to the ground. "Look, Geoff," she said. "The Troll Fang Pass garrison."

Geoff leaned over enough to see. There appeared to be much more movement about the garrison. In fact, there seemed to be more figures manning it. There was a large contingent of soldiers camped outside as well. Apparently, Ariel's message had been received and help had arrived for the beleaguered defenders of the garrison.

"Not enough," Geoff said. "Not nearly enough."

"I know," Ishara said. "But they are elves. They have not forsaken humans. This is a good sign."

They landed in the garrison's torchlit courtyard. Ariel dismounted and examined Jane to make sure she was not harmed. The door to the garrison keep opened and the unmistakable figures of Trelane and Renfry emerged. They appeared to be in good spirits. Geoff slid off the gryphon and Ishara did the same. Sawyer tried to dismount his gryphon, but lost his balance and landed hard on the ground.

"Geoff," Ishara said. "It was brave of you to go into the Shadowlord's castle and find Jane."

"You're the brave one," he said. "I almost gave us away. I was terrified."

Ishara leaned close and whispered in his ear. "Me too."

Geoff smiled.

"Ariel," Renfry said. "By the powers, I never thought I'd see you or your friends again. Welcome back."

"Thank you," Ariel said. She turned to Trelane. "*Hal'inari.*"

"*Hal'inari,*" Trelane said, bowing his head slightly. "Maelord sent word when he received your message. We came as soon as we could."

"Thank you," Ariel said. "We must talk. There is much to discuss."

Sawyer had carefully slid Jane off the saddle and cradled her in his arms. Geoff noticed his lower lip was swollen and had a small cut, and his jaw was puffy and had turned a bluish-black. Jane was still unconscious, but she appeared to be okay.

"What's wrong with her?" Sawyer asked.

"I don't know," Geoff said. "Maybe Ariel does. Are you okay? Your jaw…"

Sawyer didn't answer. Ariel motioned for them to follow her. She led them to the back of the keep and up a rough wooden staircase. On the second level, they entered a larger room with a simple wooden bed, a table, and three chairs. There was a green and brown painted trunk at the foot of the bed and a stone fireplace with a small fire burning in it.

"My quarters," Renfry said. "Use them for as long as she needs."

Sawyer placed Jane on the bed and brushed several strands of hair from her face, then sat on the bed beside her.

Ariel sat on the opposite side of the bed from Sawyer.

"Ariel, I don't get it," Sawyer said. "She recognized us, but she didn't want to be rescued. What's wrong with her?"

Ariel placed her hand on Jane's forehead and felt her cheeks. She shook her head and frowned.

"I am not sure," she said. "This is odd."

"Can you help her? Heal her or something?" Sawyer asked. "You gotta have a spell that will—"

"Sawyer," Ariel interrupted him, "to help her we must first discover what has happened to her."

"Chalon also sent reinforcements," Renfry said. "And we have several midwives who can nurse her back to health."

"I do not know that there is time for that," Ariel said as she stood. "The Shadowlord's army approaches from the north and I assure you he is determined to crush this garrison."

"Can we not make a stand?" Trelane said. "We have repaired the outer walls."

"No," Ariel said. "We will be overrun."

Renfry and Trelane looked at each other.

"Surely we can defeat them," Renfry said. "We now have the elves under Trelane's leadership, the high druid, and the Stormlord."

"The Shadowlord's northern army numbers in the tens of thousands," Ishara said. "If we stay here, we die."

"It's true," Geoff said. "There's too many to fight."

"We have seen the northern army," Ariel said. "We were

fortunate to find Jane and rescue her."

"There's something else," Geoff said. "The Shadowlord...I don't think he's the one we need to worry about."

All eyes in the room turned to Geoff. He swallowed and looked at Ishara before continuing.

"When we were in the Iron Citadel, we heard him and someone else talking. It was a tall woman in red. She gave him orders to kill us."

"It was Queen Lysis," Ishara said. "The Scarlet Queen is the true enemy. The Shadowlord is only her minion."

"You are sure of this?" Trelane asked. "Queen Lysis has always been one to protect the borders of Uln with great zeal, but she does not have the army to wage war upon us."

"And Caladar," Renfry said. "They will—"

"The knights of Caladar were attacked by the Scarlet Queen's orcs and defeated," Ishara said. "Queen Lysis boasted as much when we eavesdropped on their conversation. I saw her. It *was* Queen Lysis."

"The Caladarian knights defeated?" Renfry asked. "I don't believe it."

"I heard that too," Geoff said. "They were ambushed. Ishara isn't lying."

"I have heard rumors of Queen Lysis," Ariel said. "She is said to be an immortal sorceress of tremendous power. She rules Uln with absolute authority."

"Hey Ariel," Sawyer said. "What's this?"

Sawyer was pointing at Jane's neck. Ariel sat back on the bed and examined her. On the right side of her neck, directly on the carotid artery, were two small reddish punctures. The wounds were slightly raised and appeared to be partially healed. Ariel frowned.

"Well?" Sawyer demanded. "What is it?"

"Those look like teeth marks," Geoff said. "Like a vampire bit her or something like that."

"Geoff," Sawyer said, rubbing the back of his neck. "That's not helping."

"No," Ariel said. "He is right. She has indeed been bitten by a vampire."

The room was quiet for several moments.

"Oh, c'mon," Sawyer said. "Are you serious? So now Jane's gonna turn into a bat and fly around biting people on the neck?"

Ariel tilted her head and looked at Sawyer.

"Of course not," she said. "Why would you say such a thing?"

"Because that's what vampires do," Sawyer said. "They suck the blood from their victims and explode into flames if sunlight hits them."

Ariel looked over her shoulder at Geoff with a raised eyebrow. Geoff shrugged and gave her a nod.

"Yeah," he said. "Sawyer's pretty much got it right. That's the way it is in the monster movies back home."

Ariel blinked. Obviously Geoff's explanation didn't make sense to her either.

"Nonsense," Ariel said. "The lore of vampires in your world is silly."

"So who bit her?" Sawyer asked. "Who's the vampire?"

He looked at Geoff, Ishara, and then Ariel before rolling his eyes.

"Oooh, the Shadowlord," he said. "We should've killed him when we had the chance."

"Jane fought us," Geoff said. "She didn't want to leave.

She seemed to be obsessed with the Shadowlord."

"So?" Sawyer said with a hint of agitation. "What the hell do we do? How do we help Jane?"

"Now that we have her back," Ariel said, "we must try to help her remember who she was. It will be difficult for Jane because she is under the Shadowlord's influence. Keep in mind she will always seek to return to him. Stay vigilant and do not leave her alone for an instant."

Ariel looked at Sawyer. "So long as the Shadowlord lives Jane will never fully recover."

Sawyer stood and slammed his fist into his hand. His eyes flashed and he made a sweeping gesture with his arms. "We had him, Ariel! You and I, we could've killed him and helped Jane while ending this war at the same time!"

"Even with Zorn dead," Ishara said, "Queen Lysis will never stop. Sooner or later we must face her, too."

Sawyer looked down at his feet, then threw his hands up and muttered, "Whatever," and stormed out of the room.

Geoff had only glimpsed Queen Lysis, but he'd been terrified. He remembered how frightened Ishara had looked as they listened to the queen and Zorn. Anyone the Shadowlord bowed to had to be dangerous. A small shiver ran down Geoff's back. He remembered her voice. There was something about it that froze him to his core. As far as he was concerned, she exuded evil, and he dreaded the thought of facing the Scarlet Queen.

Three midwives entered the room and with hot water, fresh sheets, and extra blankets. Ariel stood and left the room, but not before she told the midwives that Jane was not to leave the room under any circumstances. Renfry placed a guard outside her door, too.

Geoff and Ishara followed Ariel as she left the chamber, then walked down the steps and out of the keep.

"Ariel," Geoff said, "Sawyer and Jane, they—"

"I know," Ariel said. "I know, Geoff."

They walked to the wall where Jane had been kidnapped by the Shadowlord. A solitary figure leaned on a rampart gazing to the north. Ariel took a place beside Sawyer and also looked north.

"You must believe we can save Jane," Ariel said. "She would never give up on you and she will need you now more than ever. I know you are angry, but do not let that anger consume you and cause you to make rash decisions."

"Yeah," Sawyer said. "It's just that we were so close to killing him."

"No. We were not," Ariel said. "We wounded Zorn and we angered him. His wrath will be terrible when he comes for her."

"When he does, I'll be waiting," Sawyer said bitterly.

"We will all be waiting," Ishara said. "We have Jane back and she needs our help."

"And," Ariel said as she gently turned Sawyer's head so he faced her, "our love."

She caressed his swollen, discolored jaw.

"*N'tara*," Ariel said.

Sawyer's jaw returned to its original size and color, and he rubbed his chin.

"Thanks," he said.

They turned to the north, feeling the chill in the air and looking at the night sky. Geoff took a deep breath.

"Guys, I think we can do this," he said. "We can win."

Two hooded figures stood motionless at the edge of a craggy cliff overlooking the garrison. Their elven eyes scanned the keep and the troops surrounding it.

"I am surprised King Andurys sent Trelane," the slightly smaller figure said. "He is a most capable leader."

"Yes, he is a brave and cunning warrior, but it will not be enough to save the humans."

"And you, Talia? Have you agreed to do the Shadowlord's bidding? My guess is you would rather have skewered him."

"I considered it," the taller figure said.

"Do you believe the three human children who journey with Ariel are the travelers of prophecy?"

"It matters not. I do not concern myself with such gibberish."

"They are not normal dull-witted humans," the smaller figure said as she pulled her hood back. "They have abilities which set them apart. Do not underestimate them."

"I never underestimate my opponent," Talia said as her sky-blue eyes flashed. She took a deep breath and leaned against her spear. "At last I will have a chance to face Ariel again."

"Ariel," the smaller figure nodded. "She has grown in power and is supremely skilled in combat. Without her, the others are nothing."

"Agreed, Seqwil," Talia said. "I should have killed her a long time ago."

THE END

Books by Mitch Reinhardt

Wizard's Key
Book One of the Darkwolf Saga
Winner: 2017 Young Adult Book of the Year – NYC
Big Book Awards
2017 Finalist: The Wishing Shelf Awards

The Iron Citadel
Book Two of the Darkwolf Saga

Coming soon by Mitch Reinhardt:

The Scarlet Queen
Book Three of the Darkwolf Saga

Bloodmoon
Book Four of the Darkwolf Saga